THE GWYTHIENIAN

Odan Terridor Trilogy: Book One

Savannah J. Goins

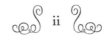

This book contains brief, vague flashbacks of sexual abuse. Many people who have experienced this in their past have found this story to be cathartic and helpful in their growth and healing, but discretion is advised for readers sensitive to this theme.

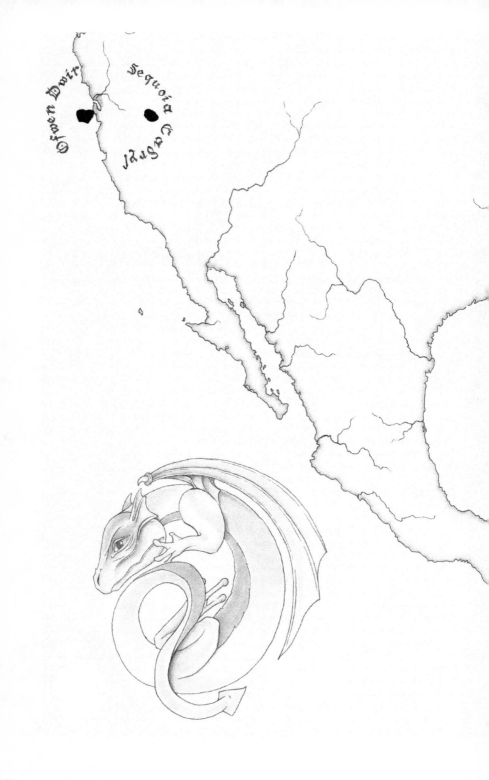

Ofwen Dwír

Sequoia Casper

See page 348 for glossary and pronunciations of places and names

Branches brushed against each other behind me, but there was no wind. My eyes locked on his as he mouthed, "Get down!" I crouched back to the ground just as he leaped up into the air above me. His body winked out of existence mid jump.

Wow, he is good.

Dry twigs crunched as he landed, speeding into the trees. There was a roar, then a crash. Trees fell. A loud, wet *thunk* and a muted yelp-growl.

Seconds passed, then a minute. My heart pounded. Why wasn't he coming back?

THE GWYTHIENIAN

CHAPTER ONE

*C*old sweat dripped down my forehead. I shivered, trying to forget what I just saw.

It never worked.

Sitting up from my mattress on the floor, I rubbed some warmth into the goosebumps on my arms. A thin, shiny layer of frost coated the bottom of the window. I reached for it and my fingers came away wet, leaving smears in their wake.

Crap. The heat's out again.

I scribbled away a small section of condensation from the windowpane, peering through the bars. Sure enough, a fresh layer of sparkling white blanketed the concrete. I barely saw it in the early morning dimness.

Strange marks disturbed the new snow—like giant footprints. But they couldn't be animal tracks. Not even the local zoo could have anything with feet that big...

A flash of brown pulled my eyes from the snowy ground. Something disappeared behind a dumpster. Or had I imagined it? I rubbed my eyes. Mornings were never my strong point. The nightmares were still too fresh on my mind. Caleb, the barn, the blood...always the same and never less paralyzing. Most details would fade away, but I always remembered the gist of what happened.

Fighting to escape the tangled mess of quilt and sheets, I rose from the floor, longing for the comfort of music to distract me. But we couldn't even afford cellphones, much less an iPod or an MP3 player. I'd stumbled across an old cassette player once at a garage sale, but I used it to death in no time, along with the thirty-some-year-old eighties mixtapes it came with. Since then, it was back to nothing but the car radio. So I would have to bear the pounding silence for a little while longer.

I shrugged off my ratty sweats and exchanged them for a pair of loose jeans. Pulling a giant sweater over a loose long-sleeve t-shirt, I fished around in the top plastic drawer for the fuzziest pair of socks. My hand came back with my warmest, longest pair, but they'd been too small to reach around my chubby legs for several years. With a wistful sigh, I stuffed them back in and settled for a pair of thick ankle socks. Reminding myself that it was better this way, I walked out of my room toward the kitchen.

I opened the fridge to scrounge for lunches and found it mostly empty. Making a mental note to go to the grocery store as soon as possible, I pulled out last night's leftovers—spaghetti and meatballs. If I'd had access to quality ingredients, I would've made something fancier—or at least made my own sauce and meatballs. But meals that called for so many ingredients were too expensive—no matter how much I enjoyed cooking them.

"Mom! I'm heading out, okay?" She always took more time rustling around in the bathroom than I did.

Backpack and lunches in hand, I hurried outside to the car to get it warming, regretting once again that we hadn't had enough money after the week's necessities to buy coffee. It'd been several weeks since we'd had that luxury, and we both felt it.

Some steaming hot caffeine would be really nice on this freezing, January morning.

Moments after the squeaky door slammed shut behind me, my ancient tennis shoes were quick to remind me how *not* waterproof they were. As I rushed out to our battered Oldsmobile, the fresh slush on the ground seeped through the worn fabric. I rolled my eyes. It was going to be one of those days, was it? This was only Tennessee! It wasn't like we lived in Iceland or something. Fortunately, our car was only a few steps away.

The poor old hunk of metal Mom and I shared really should have gone to car heaven many years ago. Bits of faded grayish paint stubbornly held their places against the encroaching rust that had mostly taken over. Except, of course, for the one garish orange fender—the only replacement we'd been able to afford.

I yanked on the driver's side door, but the lock had slipped into place without permission. I struggled with the key for a few seconds before it popped back up. Maybe the car liked to think it was worth being broken into.

Shortly after I plopped into the driver's seat, Mom opened the passenger door and lightly slid in. "Happy birthday, Enzi!" she beamed at me.

I stared blankly at her as she settled into our ancient chariot—affectionately dubbed the *Tin Can*.

It's already the sixth? Must have lost track of time.

Mom grinned enthusiastically, trying to hide the exhaustion in her smile. But I saw the regret behind her eyes. Birthdays had always been like this. She was ashamed that once again we couldn't afford to stray from the budget for her to buy me so much as a dollar coffee for a birthday present.

"Uh, thanks, Mom!" I tried not to show that I completely spaced the date.

"Oh my gosh! I can't believe you're *seventeen!* How old does that make me? Ugh, I don't even want to think about it."

No matter how much older than me she may have been, she was still prettier—petite with a clear complexion and slender features. I was almost twice her size, though not much taller.

"Come on, Mom." I threw the car into drive and hit the gas, pleased that the pedal decided not to stick this morning. "You're only eighteen years older than me. After next year, I'll be closer to your age than not." I watched from the corner of my eye as she tucked a cluster of grays behind one ear. The many years of single-mothering and juggling multiple jobs had aged her beautiful face prematurely.

"That's true! Wow, you've grown up so fast. You'll be an award-winning chef, cooking full-time in a penthouse one day. Just you wait."

Did a job like that even exist? Where someone could do nothing but cook and jam out to music all day? And get *paid* for it? That would be the life! But we could never afford the kind of education it would take to get somewhere like that.

"Hey, have you noticed the weird marks in the snow out behind the complex? It looks like some giant animal or something has been walking around out there."

She rolled her eyes, smiling ruefully. "A giant animal, huh? Alright, fine. I'll stop talking about how you keep growing up whenever I'm not looking."

"Uh...sure." That wasn't what I was going for, but it answered my question.

We wobbled across the cracked parking lot—careful to avoid the now hidden potholes—and onto the dingy road, bouncing and rattling at a steady pace. The carpet on the ceiling dropped down, blocking my view. Glaring at it, I shoved the pushpin back into the ceiling, wishing it would quit flopping around. The other twenty-something pins held up their bit of ceiling lining just fine. Why couldn't this one do the same?

It was still dim enough outside for me to tell the difference in the headlights' abilities to illuminate the road. One was smashed, but the bulb still worked enough to outshine the faded glow of its twin. The old *Tin Can* was a sorry sight for sure, but she got us where we needed to go.

And she had a functioning radio, which was all I cared about.

My fingers twitched toward the dials, desperate for the sweet distraction of musical sounds, but I gripped the steering wheel instead. Mom didn't feel the same way I did about music. Sure, she would want me to turn it on if she knew I wanted to listen to it, but I wouldn't do that to her. I'd seen how much it hurt her. So it would just have to wait.

"What do you think about taking the shortcut to work?" I ventured, already knowing the answer. But it was my birthday. Maybe she'd—

"You know I don't like that bridge."

I sighed. "I know you don't like *heights*. That bridge is perfectly safe." But I steered us down the long route anyway.

We bounced and trundled over the back roads, making our way to Main Street. Passing many snow-dusted skeleton trees, I admired the untainted snow on the side of the road, not yet marred by morning traffic.

My mind wandered as I drove on autopilot. Another birthday. Funny how some people claimed to actually *feel* a year older on their birthdays. I'd experienced several others so far and never felt any different afterward. That always puzzled me. Seemed like a person should feel different somehow...triumphant, for making it through another whole year alive and sane... for reaching that milestone. Maybe some people did.

But not me.

As we neared the location of Mom's twelve-hour shift, the tall streetlamps flickered off with the growing natural light. The blanket of snow was utterly mutilated here, morphed by the busier traffic of town into gray slush lines.

We approached a sheer mountainside covered in beautiful, glistening icicles. I let myself stare—as best I could while driving. Their shimmering glory captivated me, but something about them seemed to bother Mom. I never quite figured out why.

She always glanced away from the frozen rock wall. And if I caught a glimpse of her face, I'd swear she looked… embarrassed. Why a stunning, jagged mountainside covered in giant, shining icicles should make a person feel *embarrassed*, I couldn't imagine. Maybe she was embarrassed about being so afraid of heights?

Even before I was old enough to sit in the front seat, I remember calling her attention to them in a moment of childish excitement. She always agreed they were very beautiful, but she did so without turning her eyes to them. She'd said once that it was because of her fear of heights, but the thing was, we weren't ever *on top* of the mountain. We drove past the *bottom* of it. I'd heard of people getting queasy from looking up at something very high. Maybe that was it.

She sometimes hitched a ride home with a friend after work, and I wondered if it was because she didn't like driving by the mountain in daylight. Whenever she caught a ride with someone else, she wouldn't be home until well after dark. If it somehow was the icicles that bothered her, maybe knowing they were there wasn't a problem as long as she didn't have to see them.

At the same time, finding another way home could be a ploy to try to get me to spend time with friends after work. But if that was the reason, it was wasted effort, because I'd been running low in that department for years.

In any case, I was glad I hadn't inherited that particular fear. I loved looking at the icicles.

We arrived at Mom's windowless warehouse of a work building and I stopped the car in front of the door. She grabbed her lunch and slid out, waving goodbye through the window. "Have a great birthday!"

"I will!" I promised, not sure how I'd manage it. She walked around a puddle in the parking lot, giving it a wider berth than was really necessary. She claimed not to be superstitious, but avoiding puddles—and swimming pools and aquariums and the ocean exhibit at the zoo—was another one of her quirks.

The moment I was out of the parking lot, I turned on the radio, breathing for the first time that morning as the music poured itself into my soul, relieving the ache.

Music was the best part of my world. It was my freedom. When I listened to music, I escaped *everything* else. I could escape the pain of never knowing my father and of seeing how much my mother still grieved for him, and the guilt of knowing how hard she worked for our survival. I could escape the pain of betrayal thrown back in my face every day from the girl who'd been my childhood best friend, and from everyone at school who believed the lies she told about me.

Music was like a drug. If I went too long without having at least a few minutes to float on the serenity of the sounds, the hopelessness came back, sinking its dagger-claws into my chest and paralyzing me. But when I felt the music all around me— loud enough that I could sing at the top of my lungs without hearing the racket of my own voice—I almost believed I could fly away and be eternally safe and free. It was moments like those that I lived for.

Best of all, I escaped the horror of Caleb and all the shame and powerlessness I couldn't escape otherwise. When I turned the music up loud enough, it surrounded me, like a soft blanket, covering my body and protecting my mind from all the pain.

As one station switched to commercials, I turned the dial to another. That new Vince Macklan song was playing, the one that I only knew a few words to. I tapped my thumbs on the steering wheel as I went, enjoying my birthday for the first time so far.

While tapping the wheel to the beat with one hand, I touched the purple stone suspended from a chain around my neck with the other. Crappy as the cheap, silver-colored chain might have been, I'd barely ever taken it off since mom gave it

to me years ago. It was the only pretty thing I owned, the only pretty thing about me.

If rocks could be wild, this one would be. Its many natural facets and imperfect edges caught the light and made it dance like magic. The color of amethyst, it glistened like a diamond just pulled from a fresh water stream. It was about the size of a quarter—maybe a bit bigger—and much more spherical.

The familiar ache of loss clawed at my heart again. The stone had arrived with my father's belongings after he'd died in combat. Mom had it made into a necklace for me. It was the only thing of his that was mine, besides the picture of him surrounded by other young men in camo uniforms. That crinkled image lived on, folded safely between the pages of *The Horse and His Boy*. I thought he might like that one better than my Jane Austin titles, since it was about a guy.

It was strange to think that I was nearly the same age as those men in that picture, who once seemed so ancient to me.

I wished I could've known him. I wished I could've heard him sing "Happy Birthday" to me. I wished I could've felt him carry me up to my crib when I was little. Would he have sung lullabies? Whispered good night? Called me silly nicknames?

Thanks to some military mishap that killed him and his whole troop, I would never know what kind of dad he would've been. They'd never told us what really happened, of course. You could trust the government to keep everything a secret from us civilians. All *classified* and stuff. Oh well. Would I really want to know?

My hand squeezed the stone tighter. I liked having something of his near my heart, as cliché as that sounded.

I checked the mirror just in case, but I was still visible. I sighed. It wasn't working today. It'd been a while. I couldn't figure out how to make it happen. But if only I could learn how to control it! Then I wouldn't need to be fat anymore. I wouldn't need to hide.

Glaring at the reflection of my double chin, I tucked the stone beneath the roomy fabric of my sweatshirt.

When I reached the crowded parking lot of my high school, I wished again for some earbuds and a nice phone so I didn't have to stop infusing my soul with musical goodness. But no such thing for me. So I had to amble on inside and endure the presence of a bunch of unpleasant people and the droning on of a bunch of uncaring teachers about a bunch of uninteresting things.

Yay for birthdays.

CHAPTER TWO

I sat in the parking lot long enough to hear the end of the song, dreading the impending silence.

"Ugh." Taking the keys from the ignition, I stepped out and headed away from the sanctuary of my trusty *Tin Can* and toward the miserable school building.

The main section was an ugly old concrete monstrosity. A newer mismatched brick addition stood forlornly on the left side, but even that one was faded and covered in lichen.

As usual, my loose hoodie over an even looser tee shirt with a baggy pair of non-descript jeans attracted no attention. It was like I was invisible to everyone, which was exactly what I wanted.

I made it to my first classroom unnoticed and slid into a backrow corner desk, still longing for some tunes to fill the time between now and when the teacher decided to show up. I craved distraction.

As my eyes skipped around the room, I caught a glimpse of Jillian Richmond. The neckline of her bright-green skintight sweater plunged profoundly, showing off the depths of flawless, tan cleavage. Her blonde, beach-curly hair was done up in a perfect messy bun, revealing a pair of silver earrings dangling from shapely ears. She laughed with the boy whose desk she sat on.

She was unbearably beautiful.

Her best friend, Carlie Jacobs—also known as my upgraded-bestie replacement—sat on Jillian's other side. Carlie was equally as gorgeous, but opposite of Jillian, in a way. She sported dark brown hair—so dark that in some lighting it looked black, and set off her pure, porcelain skin with a vampire-like regality. She tended a little more toward the gothic side, but with excellent taste, and her dark clothes always contrasted with her practically iridescent skin to her advantage.

Several students surrounded her, cheerfully wowing at something on her desk. Probably some amazing drawing she'd penciled in an uncannily short amount of time.

That was the thing about the two of them. While they were miserably gorgeous, they weren't the typical dazzling, yet empty-headed dumb blonde types. They were beautiful *and* talented.

Horribly talented.

Carlie, with her artistic skills as if she'd already graduated art school twice, doodled masterpieces on her notebook pages and had even sold a few paintings for a lot of money. I'd seen things that she'd scribbled and then thrown away, maybe because she didn't think they were good enough. They made my best attempt at sketching look like toddler scribbles. Not that I compared myself to her, of course.

And Jillian played the violin with breathtaking precision. She was brilliant in an orchestra and fabulous on her own. And her style consisted of sexy, revealing clothes that bordered on the verge of lingerie. Naturally, every guy in the whole school drooled after her everywhere she went. I didn't get it. How could that not scare her? But she seemed to revel in it.

I was a balloon compared to their hourglasses, shorter and plumper than the two of them put together. My skin was closer to the color of Carlie's, but with a yellower hue and acne. While

I didn't want the attention that they always got, I did wish I could be as beautiful as they were, just so I wouldn't have to be embarrassed of my dumpiness.

But it was better that way. I was safer.

In addition to my physical shortcomings, I had *no* talent. While I loved music, I couldn't make it to save my life. And I couldn't draw or paint or anything either, as much as I wished I could. So, they had me beat in every way. There was no sticking my nose up at their lack of intelligence as I pranced off to advanced classes. It was they who were in the advanced classes, not me. I had nothing on them.

Nothing, except one seriously crazy piece of jewelry.

But I never showed that off. That was my secret. Of course, Jillian had seen it when Mom first gave it to me years ago, back when she and I were the closest of friends. But a lot changed since then. Did she even remember I owned something like that?

Next thing I knew, class had ended and the bell was ringing. I sped off to hit the bathrooms before next period.

I reached the bathroom and closed myself in a stall. A few moments later I'd flushed the toilet and was at the sink, turning on the hot water. I tried not to look in any of the mirrors, but the whole wall was lined with them, so they were hard to avoid. That one scar sneaking up the side of my neck was hard to miss. Not to mention, I was twice as heavy as most girls my age. I frowned at my chubby reflection, pulling the necklace from inside my sweatshirt to look at it instead. That was all the beauty I had going for me.

It shimmered, even in the dim light. Its purple surface somehow always glistened beautifully. My eyes fell away from the reflection of the stone as I scrubbed and rinsed my hands. Two toilets flushed behind me. I turned off the hot water and reached for a paper towel.

"Well if it isn't Morbidly Obese Mackenzi."

My eyes closed. *Not now, Jillian.*

"Gross," Carlie scoffed.

Ugh. Both of them.

Raising my eyes back to the mirror, I saw them there, right behind me.

"Whoa, Scar-face, what are you *wearing?*" Jillian stared at my reflection.

I rolled my eyes, hate for their stupid nicknames simmering in the pit of my stomach. Yes, the one scar refused to be hidden by clothes like the others could be, but it still wasn't on my *face*.

I whirled on them. "My clothes, genius." I tried to pour all my contempt into a glower. I hoped it was fierce enough to make up for my fail at words. Brilliant comebacks were not my area of expertise, even though my clothes were a frequent subject of their snide comments.

"Where'd you get that necklace?" Jillian pointed to the stone I hadn't had a chance to shove back into my sweatshirt.

Shoot! My heart raced. That was none of their business. Why'd I have to be so careless today?

"Give it to me." She held out her hand, smiling venomously.

I bolted for the door, but their lighter, more athletic frames beat me to it and blocked my way. I could charge through them, but what if they grabbed the necklace as I passed? Or what if they pulled me back by my clothes and snatched it then?

"What?" Carlie smirked. "Did you steal it or something?" She made a grab for it.

I covered it with both hands and turned sharply, knocking her slim, porcelain arm away with my shapeless one. "No! I did *not* steal it."

They looked me up and down and shared a knowing glance between them. When their eyes returned to me, I was really sweating. They were taller and probably stronger than me. And they were used to getting their way.

"Well it's not like you could afford something like that. And it's *definitely* not like any guy would look at you twice, much less give you any jewelry. That leaves stealing it to make yourself feel better about how much you suck. Am I right?" Jillian glared down her perfect, tan nose at me.

No, you're not right. "Look, either way, it's none of your—"

"Stop lying!" Carlie smacked me so hard across the face that I reeled into the first stall. I caught my balance, then slammed and locked the door. My heavy breathing echoed through the empty stall, my face burning where she hit me.

The girls laughed and two pairs of shoes approached, echoing off the tiled floor as I frantically searched for an escape route.

"Come on, just give it up. It's not like it's actually *yours*. And there are two of us and only one of you. You know there's no other way out of this!"

As their shadows grew under the door, I kicked myself for ending up even farther from the way out of the bathroom. I braced myself against the wall. *I could hide the stone, or... or... swallow it or something. Or maybe....*

Closing my eyes, I directed all my focus to the back of my mind, the place where I could just barely be aware of the ability. It was like a smooth concrete wall covered in soapy water—and I had to get to the other side. But it was too slippery to climb and too thick to break through. Like an impossible math problem. There *was* an answer. It was just really hard reach.

I need to be invisible. I need to be invisible.

I mentally hurled the words at the wall, but I couldn't break through. I knew a way existed somewhere, but there were no handholds. It was so hard to focus.

Jillian pounded on the stall door. "Get out here, Scar-face! I *am* taking that necklace whether you like it or not, and I'm getting *really* tired of waiting!"

They couldn't take it. It was all I had left of my dad! But why wasn't it working? What was I doing wrong?

A soft, metallic noise came from the door. I opened my eyes to see the little circle over the locking mechanism jiggling. Their shadows overlapped as they tried to get the lock undone from the outside. *Too fancy for crawling under the door.*

I closed my eyes and focused again, reaching up to tuck the necklace back into my shirt in preparation for their break in.

Then *crack!* There it was! The moment my fingers touched the stone, a fissure appeared on the slippery surface of the barrier in my mind. I tried to reach for it, to think toward it. I could almost get ahold of it… and then I had it. Something was there and I mentally held on for dear life.

When I opened my eyes and looked down at myself, I was no longer there.

CHAPTER THREE

*A*ngry fist falls replaced the jiggling of the lock. "Get *out* already! Come on! This is ridiculous!" The room echoed with Jillian's shouts and bangs.

"Stop pounding on the door, Jillian," Carlie spat. "Just crawl under and unlock it from the inside. Then we'll have her backed into a corner!"

"Me?" Jillian shouted. "Why should *I* crawl all over this nasty floor? *You* do it!"

"No! You're the one who wants the necklace!"

"What*ever*! If *you* want it, *you* go get it!"

Carlie scoffed. "Just come out already. You know we'll win this one way or another. We always do."

I backed as far from the door as I could. If they got in and happened to reach out and feel me there, invisible, well...I had to admit, it would be kinda interesting to see. But it probably wouldn't save the necklace.

When I didn't answer, both girls put their eyes up to the crack between the door and the wall of the stall.

"What the...how is she not there?" Jillian shrieked as Carlie burst into the next stall looking for me.

I grinned, allowing a little glimmer of hope to sprout in my chest. *This just might work.*

The other stall doors clanged and echoed as they searched, followed by a colorful smattering of cuss words.

"She must've gotten out of the bathroom somehow!" Carlie ran to the main door and pulled it open, probably checking the hallway.

"But how?"

Carlie darted back to my stall and peered through the crack again. "Maybe she crawled over to the next stall and snuck out behind us while you beat the crap out of the door. Nice job making enough noise for her to sneak past us!" She sprinted back to the main door and yanked it open. "Come on, Jillian, let's go find her!"

Their running footsteps faded as they bolted down the hall. Smiling wryly, heart still pounding, I was flattered that they thought me slim and coordinated enough to not only fit between the stall partition and the ceiling, but also hoist myself over without making any noise.

I let out an exalted laugh. "Ha!" Maybe this birthday wouldn't be so bad after all.

The room echoed again as I opened the creaky stall door. Still wearing a huge invisible smile, I stepped out, checking the mirror in spite of myself. To my delight, I couldn't see my reflection.

I squeezed the stone again and then released my hold on it to see what would happen. The moment I let go, I felt the mental fissure in the wall closing up. Despite my concentration, my mind slipped and I lost my grip on the ability. My reflection appeared in the mirror.

I grimaced.

My eyes were drawn to that tendril of scar. It climbed high enough up the side of my neck that not even a collared shirt could hide it. I glared at the stubborn flesh, loathing it with every fiber of my being. Not only had I been through all that, but I couldn't even hide the evidence! Would I have to carry it with me forever?

Just then the bell rang. I pulled off the necklace and tucked it into my pants pocket. My jeans were baggy enough that the stone would be well hidden there. I didn't want it around my neck where Carlie or Jillian could snatch it later.

As I hurried to English, memories of how I got the scars crept to the forefront of my thoughts. To distract myself, I mulled over the few other times I'd managed to conquer that slippery wall—those times I'd turned invisible.

The first time I disappeared I couldn't believe it actually happened. Who would? It was on the day that I returned from the hospital after the last of many rechecks. I'd been looking forward to my first real shower since the incident. With all the stitches, I'd had to wash my long hair in our tiny sink—the kind where the faucet was idiotically set right up against the back wall of the bowl—and bathe myself with a warm wet cloth, which didn't actually stay warm for long and didn't make me feel clean at all. But the stitches were finally removed and I was done with hospital visits.

I took the longest shower of my life. So refreshing.

Wrapped in a towel afterwards, I left the bathroom and went into my room for clean clothes. As I rummaged through my plastic dresser drawers for something to wear, I lost my grip on the towel and it dropped to the floor. Being alone in my room with the door closed, it didn't matter that I wore nothing besides the necklace. But when I straightened with clean clothes in hand, I was face to face with myself in the full-length mirror hanging on the back of my bedroom door.

I barely recognized myself. The dark circles under my eyes and something else about my face made me look too old to be ten. And from my torso to my neck…there were so many scars. All that horror was supposed to be over, but it was still strikingly present.

I couldn't bear the hideousness of my reflection. I looked like Frankenstein's monster. Grotesque. It was then that I'd first wished myself invisible.

And my reflection vanished.

I was so stunned that I grabbed the mirror and ripped it off the wall. It flew across the room and shattered into thousands of pieces.

My reaction to the mirror surprised me. It wasn't like me to be violent, but I'd faced too many shocks too close together. Mom ran in to comfort me—I must have been visible again by then. I lay in her lap in the towel, sobs wracking my overwhelmed little body as she stroked my hair and whispered motherly reassurances.

Up until that first time, I was very boy-crazy and I wore bright and fashionable clothes, even though they all came from secondhand stores. Colorful tank tops and miniskirts were my favorite. I spent the majority of my time with Jillian talking about which boys were the cutest, while comparing outfits, nail polish, and hair styles. We both knew that all her stuff was nicer than mine, but that was back before it mattered.

Now I was afraid to face my friends at school, even Jillian. And especially my crush. Would he still like me back once he saw my scars? I wouldn't be able to hide them all.

When I returned to school, it was already too late for me. They all thought I was ugly, especially Jillian. And she'd already spread the rumor to the whole school about what a psychopath I was.

It wasn't until later that I started to fear I would end up alone—like Mom. Only she'd had someone who loved her once. I would never even have that.

The next time I turned invisible, I started putting two and two together. The old *Tin Can* had broken down a couple miles from home and I didn't have a phone to call Mom or a tow truck. Even if there'd been a way to get in touch with Mom, she didn't have another car to pick me up in, and we couldn't afford a tow. But being out in the open like that terrified me. It made me feel exposed. As scared as I was, I hated my cowardice, so I forced myself to abandon the safety of the blessed old *Tin Can* and make the trek home, necklace tucked safely in my shirt.

The streets were quiet at that time of night, only a few cars passed by. But then a dark-haired, light-skinned man zoomed toward me on a shiny red motorcycle. He looked so much like Caleb that it froze me in place and set my heart pounding with terror. I desperately needed him to *not* see me. I wished again that I was invisible.

Then I felt a barrier in my mind—like an important thought I'd just forgotten that was barely out of reach of being remembered. The motorcyclist was almost upon me.

Somehow, I managed to charge through the mental barrier with ease. Maybe it was the level of fear, the adrenaline. I looked down at myself and saw the ground beneath me, the crumpled grass of my footprints under my see-through feet. It was a very strange experience, being invisible.

I'd realized after he passed me that it wasn't Caleb, but my whole body had shaken with fear all the way home.

CHAPTER FOUR

*A*t last, the bell rang. I darted to the parking lot, anxious to avoid another encounter with Jillian and Carlie. I backed out of my parking spot and headed to work, trying to be grateful for the end of the longest part of the day instead of dreading what came next: four hours in a hot, smelly, sorry-excuse-for-a-kitchen.

I was a classic burger flipper in a greasy fast food joint, where the customers were about as pleasant as the microwaved plastic-wrapped burgers they ate.

My uniform consisted of baggy khakis and a stained off-white polo made of odd fabric and several sizes too big. While I did prefer my clothes to be a size or two up rather than skin tight for the sake of blending in, the bagginess of this getup was something else entirely. I always waited until I got there to change.

The money helped Mom with the bills, so I sucked it up and started the four-hour countdown. My manager—who'd hated my guts since my first day—practically met me at the door.

"Enzi Montgomery! I sent out the change in schedule days ago. You aren't on this afternoon. Beat it and start checking your email!"

Change in schedule? That's ridiculous! I had the same hours for two years because of school and picking up mom, and she *knew* I had limited access to a computer. We sure didn't have one at home, and there was always a line for the ones at school. The public library had computers, sure, but I never had spare time to go there. Why bother if my schedule had been unchanged for so long? I'd be late to work if I sat around waiting for an available computer to check my email only to find out I was supposed to be at work ten minutes ago.

But I kept all that to myself. She didn't give a crap, and I couldn't risk getting fired. It would be easier to find a way to scrape by with four hours less pay than with losing the job. It took every ounce of self-control though.

So I wouldn't have to flip burgers or get burned with frying oil on my birthday? What a bummer! I guess if it had to happen, today was the day for it.

I moseyed outside and sank into the old *Tin Can*, pleased at the unexpected free time. Mom wouldn't need a ride for another few hours. I could get a jumpstart on homework, and without Mom there, I could blare music from the car all afternoon—key turned backwards, of course, to conserve gas.

Turning on the radio, I flipped past two stations playing commercials before coming across *Fly Away* by Alice Amaranth—one of my favorites. I turned it up and sang along.

Fly-y-y away, wild and free, over the sea. Fly-y-y away, I'll never go back, I'm stronger than that...

As my thumbs drummed on the steering wheel, I passed my shimmering wall of frozen mountain. The sun glimmered off the icicles like expensive crystal glasses. The way the colors raced through them as I drove by made it look like they each lived a thousand lives in an instant. They were like magic windows, only allowing onlookers to glimpse the shadows of the colors of the magic stored within.

Why couldn't Narnia be real? There was something delicious about the idea of other worlds, hidden just beyond my reach. I longed to escape, to have all my problems magically vanish and to be the queen of a bright and beautiful Other Place. To not be poor anymore, to have everything anyone could ever want. Maybe a silly thought, but it sure would beat living in *this* world every day.

Glancing in the rearview mirror, I pulled out the necklace and tried to disappear again. No luck.

I eased my foot off the gas, glancing in my rearview to make sure I wasn't brake-checking anyone. I had the road to myself, so I slowed even more and gazed at the shiny works of art. So many bright colors sparkled through them. Bits of blue from wherever the sky wasn't obscured by winter clouds, and from the distant sunset, tomato-red, curry-orange and eggplant-purple. And there was a dark smudge—maybe from the *Tin Can's* reflection—that moved along the mountainside with me. It seemed too big to be a reflection of the *Tin Can*, but there was nothing else on the road.

Then it was gone. I passed the ice-clad cliff and all its tiny, tantalizing shimmers and colors. Somehow, the limited time I had to stare at them made the moments more magical.

Speaking of magic, how was I able to disappear? It obviously had something to do with the necklace—and it seemed easier if I touched it—but how was that even possible? Did my dad know there was something special about this stone when he found it? Did he hope that one day it would be mine and I would discover its power?

What if he hadn't picked it up randomly, what if he'd had it for longer, and been using its abilities? What if he died because he turned invisible and someone saw it happen and got scared and shot him? Or what if he was killed because someone else learned about it and wanted it for themselves?

Nah. That last theory was garbage. If someone had killed him for it, they would have taken it from his corpse and I wouldn't know it existed. But still, it could have something to do with his death, couldn't it?

I pulled into the spot in front of our place. The fine snow from this morning had melted into slush, making it impossible to see where the parking lines used to be. So I parked as well as I could in front of number seven. I exited my regal carriage, the last song I heard repeating in my head.

I really need you now. I really just don't know how I've gone on alone for so long all this time....

It was so full of emotion and so beautiful that I listened to it even though I couldn't relate to losing a lover. I'd lost people that I cared about—my dad, Jillian—and I missed them, but I didn't *need* them. I survived this long without them, I would keep on surviving. I wasn't bitter about it. It just was what it was.

I retrieved the stack of bills from our little compartment in the post box and headed in the direction of our ramshackle front door. It squeaked obnoxiously as I opened it. Walking through, I tossed the mail onto the counter along with the car keys. A bright blue envelope caught my attention. After locking the door behind me, I investigated.

It was an advertisement for a Caribbean cruise. I snorted. What a waste of resources to send such a thing to *our* address! No *limited time* or *amazing discount* would make that a possibility in our future.

I flung that one into the can, picking up the rest of the pile and sorting them into categories: junk mail for the garbage, and bills for Mom. She insisted on handling all the finances herself. I usually did the grocery shopping and most of the driving around, but bills and insurance and all that was her job.

It was because she felt guilty that I had to grow up so fast and help so much with everything else. She told me she wanted to take this one burden fully on herself. I guess it was better for her to have the job, because math was clearly not one of my strong points. The one time I'd tried to help to surprise her, I hadn't been able to get the numbers to add up right.

The bill from the water company. The bill from the trash company. The bill from the electric company. The bill for rent being due on the apartment. The bill from my lengthy hospital visit seven years ago that we were *still* paying for—why hadn't insurance helped more with that? I never understood why, but Mom had dealt with them as much as they could be dealt with.

I neared the end of the pile. The car payment was overdue. Again. And there was a letter from the Green Hills Specialty Hospital.

I glanced back at that one. Had I misread something?

No, that's what it said. Who would be writing to my mom from a specialty hospital? She didn't have any family that I knew of. Everyone had died or been estranged when she was young, and the bills for my extended hospital stay were from Martin Regional, not this Green Hills Specialty place.

Pushing my pointer finger under the sticky tab, I ripped the envelope open and unfolded the letter.

Dear Mrs. Montgomery, we regret to inform you that the mental state of your husband—

"Your husband?" I spewed.

They must've meant late husband. Or that could be the wrong Mrs. Montgomery. Mom and my dad had been married, but he was gone. They must have the wrong person.

His mental state?

I read on, though I must have been reading someone else's mail.

We regret to inform you that the mental state of your husband, Mack Montgomery—

I reread the name. That was my father's name. My *deceased* father's name. What was this?

We regret to inform you that the mental state of your husband, Mack Montgomery, has not improved with the use of the new pharmaceuticals previously discussed. At this time, we have no other options for attempts at improving his state of mind, nor can we confirm that his condition can be kept from deteriorating. But there are two new drugs coming on the market in the next six months that do have potential in your husband's case. We are cautiously optimistic that one of these new medicines will be able to help him. You will soon be receiving consent papers that you will need to return to the hospital fully read and signed, if you wish to give your husband this chance at improving his mental capacities.

Sincerely, Dr. Jennings, Physician Director GHSH PhD Cognitive and Behavioral Neuroscience

There must've been a mistake. They had the wrong Montgomery's address. That was probably what happened. Besides, the Mrs. Montgomery in the letter knew her husband was alive and had medical conversations with a doctor about him. Mom wouldn't be able to handle all of that medical stuff. All the decisions and crap they made her sign when I was in the hospital had overwhelmed her. And it wasn't like her at all to lie.

We loved and trusted each other.

More than anyone.

She was my closest friend. She never lied, especially not to me.

I reread the letter. My thoughts swirled as my heart beat faster. There were plenty of Montgomerys in the world, and the woman's first name wasn't listed, just her last name. So her name could be anything—Betty, Susan, Lorie—there was no reason it would have to be *Lisa* Montgomery. And so what if it was *Mack* Montgomery, of all the male first names out there? There were plenty of Mack Montgomerys in the world, right?

Yes, that was it.

My dad wasn't in a mental hospital. He was dead and buried, years ago.

What was wrong with this man? Had he lost his ability to speak? Or was he paralyzed, confined to a wheelchair because of brain damage, maybe?

I wiped my sweaty palms on my jeans.

Retrieving the envelope, I flipped it over to inspect the address. Maybe there was another Mr. and Mrs. Mack Montgomery living somewhere nearby with a similar one.

Nope. The letter was addressed to a Mrs. Lisa Montgomery, number seven, Old Wood Drive.

I grabbed the counter with my free hand. Could it be possible? Could the person I'd so longed to know and missed my whole life actually be alive, but not really himself? Could the person I've always trusted with my life have been lying to me all along?

I must be missing something.

It wasn't possible. Mom wouldn't do that to me. We hadn't talked about him that much, but she'd always seemed sincere. We were always honest with each other. That was our policy. We'd been through hell and back together, and that made two people closer than an easy life could.

I looked at the microwave clock. Three hours until Mom would be waiting outside the warehouse for me. But I had to talk to her *now*. I couldn't have these questions hanging over my head all afternoon!

Surely she would have an answer for all this.

I knew they wouldn't let me into her building—only employees allowed. And there were no phones around. But the library had a public phone!

Snatching up the keys, I stuffed the letter in my sweatshirt pocket and raced back out the door.

I sped as fast as the old junk pile would allow, swerving and wobbling around curves and skidding to a stop in front of the library with a screech of protest from the sorry old brakes. Jumping out with the letter in hand, I ran inside.

I dialed Mom's work and waited, tapping one foot impatiently.

"Tennessee's best logistics company, Jer'my speakin'." This guy had the twangiest southern accent I'd ever heard and spoke about as fast as a slug runs. "How can—"

"I need to talk to Lisa Montgomery as fast as possible. It's an emergency!"

"Just a sec."

Staticky on-hold music trickled through the speaker. Several long moments went by, and then finally, "Enzi? Enzi, are you okay? Are you hurt?"

"No, Mom. Calm down. It's okay. I just found something in the mail that I need to ask you about."

"... okay."

Was it just me, or was that a really long pause?

"So I found this letter," I pulled it from my pocket to look at it again, "from Green Hills Specialty Hospital." Was that a gasp? "It says some crazy stuff. Mom, it says something about meds for Mack Montgomery. Who is dead. Do you have any idea why this letter came to our house?"

No mistaking it, this was *definitely* a long pause.

Oh my gosh. Could it be true? Was he alive? And she knew? For how long? "Mom?"

Nothing.

"Mom? What's this all about?"

"That, uh...that's him...your father...yes."

Her words rang in my ears. Had I misunderstood her? My head felt woozy. I leaned against the wall and slowly slid to the floor.

"He's alive?"

"Yes."

"And you didn't tell me?"

"No, I didn't."

Roiling anger competed with confusion. How could she? "How long have you known?" I barely squeaked the words out.

"A while." Her voice was a whisper now too.

Reeling, I dropped the phone. It swung away from me, dangling from the stand.

He was alive. I had to find him. I needed to know who this person was. But where was he?

There was a line of computer stations in front of me. I had the name of the place and his doctor. Internet search. Address. Map. Directions.

Shakily, I got to my feet.

I was going to find my father.

CHAPTER FIVE

The *Tin Can* and I hit the interstate in a matter of moments. The old hunk of metal was a blur of mismatched rusty colors as she sped down the highway. She'd probably never run that fast in her long, long life.

As I followed the directions on the paper from the library, questions crept back into my mind. What was wrong with him? Something psychological, apparently. How long had Mom known that he was alive? Why hadn't she told me?

I needed to pay attention, I couldn't afford to get lost. There wasn't any time. But keeping the questions down was a struggle. How had he lost regular brain function, and how much of it was still there? Would I even be able to talk to him? Did he even know he had a daughter?

Oh! That's my turn…almost missed it. My two left tires may have lifted into the air a smidge as I veered off at unadvisable speeds.

Why would Mom hide this from me? Was I born out of wedlock or something? No, I'd seen their marriage license and my dad's dog tags. We all had the same last name.

Shoot! Ninety-five is too fast. I'll get pulled over and lose more time. Plus I'm spending unbudgeted gas after missing work hours. We can't afford a speeding ticket!

I eased my foot off the pedal and tried to take a calming breath.

It wasn't effective.

What could she want to hide from me? Maybe she'd left him because he was abusive. He could have been slowly losing his mind for a long time. Or maybe he left her because she was such a giant liar.

For being a specialty hospital, it was surprisingly close to our apartment. Was that why she'd been so against moving after what happened with Caleb? She wanted to stay close to this hospital? I mean, I hadn't told her who it was, so she didn't know I had to face him again and again. He'd graduated a few years ago, but attended college somewhere nearby, and there was no telling when he'd just show up in town. But she'd always said it was because we couldn't afford to move. Maybe she meant something other than money? My fingers gripped the steering wheel with knuckle-whitening fury. It made sense. There was nothing else important enough to keep us here.

And insurance being so weird…I didn't know how all that worked, but it should have helped us more than it did. Maybe all that money was being diverted to bills for my dad?

An angry *honk!* made me slam on brakes. I'd drifted into the next lane right in front of a semi. "Crushed by transportation vehicle" was not how I wanted to die. I had to pull it together.

I couldn't risk getting in a wreck and dying or getting amnesia and forgetting about the living father I needed to meet.

That would make things easy for Mom, though. If I wrecked and forgot everything that'd happened in the last few hours, she would go on letting me believe a lie. I could never trust her again.

Tears welled in my eyes, blurring my vision. I could barely see. I needed to wipe the tears away so I could drive safely. Speeding around a turn, I didn't expect the red light. I slammed on brakes again, swerving on black ice this time.

"Ah!" I pumped the breaks, but they didn't cooperate. I skidded through the red light into oncoming traffic.

More horns blared furiously. Cars and trucks swerved to miss me. I headed right for a shiny black sedan, and it didn't change direction. The *Tin Can* slid alongside it, scratching the doors and bending the rear bumper. There was a snap and a reverberation, and we finally came to a halt.

I gripped the wheel, hyperventilating. Did that just happen? A glance in the rearview mirror proved it did.

Numerous vehicles stood still, pointing in all different directions. The expensive-looking sedan was only a few feet away with a hideous scar across the side where the *Tin Can* took some black paint and left bluish rust in its place. The driver threw open the door, jumped out, and marched toward me, looking murderous.

Oh crap!

He whipped out a phone and aimed it at my license plate, still marching.

I needed to get out of this, now. I couldn't pay to fix his car, and I couldn't afford to stand around. It was already six thirty-five and the website said visiting hours ended at seven!

My foot bore down on the gas, but nothing happened. The pedal was stuck.

The big man grew closer in the side view mirror. Another coaxing… zilch.

I pressed down the lock on the driver's door, quickly eyeing each of the others to make sure they were in place as well.

Shoving my toes under the pedal, I wrenched my foot up to pull it free. My shoelaces caught on something. I slammed my hand against the steering wheel. "Ugh!"

The guy was only a few feet away. I jiggled my shoe and it finally came loose. I pressed the pedal again...

"Come on, you can do it, you can do it..."

Knock, knock. Knuckles against my window.

With a pitiful sputter, the engine revved and the car lurched forward.

Yes! Time to go!

Without a glance at the man, I pressed the pedal all the way down, hoping I wasn't overdoing it again with the black ice. The *Tin Can* obeyed and moments later I saw the man in my rearview, running fruitlessly after me, shaking his fist and probably shouting all kinds of profanities.

I'd gone too far on this one. I couldn't go around wrecking people's cars and not making up for it.

Breathe.

When I arrived in the parking lot of the hospital, heart still racing, it was six fifty-two. I claimed a parking place and left the *Tin Can* to fend for herself as I rushed into the building. My heart still pounded in my ears. I was sweaty, too. Still wearing my baggy jeans and sweatshirt from this morning. What would he think of me? If he could even think at all? This was not exactly the impression I wanted to make.

"Hello," I called to the receptionist, sprinting to her desk. "Can you please tell me where I can find Mack Montgomery's room?" It felt so weird to say his name out loud, knowing he was alive now.

The woman lifted a finger to her glasses and slid them down her nose, giving me a good once-over from above the rims. Then she met my eyes, with a look of deepest indifference. "Who are you to the patient?"

"His daughter." My voice shook. Now *that* was really weird to say.

The receptionist typed away on her computer for a moment, her crazy-long manicured nails clicking. "He's in room three-twenty-seven." She squinted at the screen. "Now hold on a minute. I don't have a daughter listed. Only a wife."

My fingers twisted themselves into fists. *Only a wife listed, huh? Thanks, Mom.*

She looked up at me with an explain-your-self sort of face. "I can't let you in if you're not on the list."

"Why?" I had to see him!

She tilted her head scornfully at me as if the answer to my question was common enough knowledge that a stray dog would know better than to ask. "Because it's *illegal* for me to let anyone see him if he or his nearest of kin have not given permission."

"But I *am* his nearest of kin! I'm his *daughter*!"

She glanced away from me with a "you're-*such*-an-idiot" expression and scrolled down her computer screen. "I am not *allowed* to disclose personal information about our patients here. If you really *are* his daughter, come back tomorrow with your mom and your ID and we might be able to get somewhere." And then she turned back to her computer and started typing, totally ignoring me, as if I'd already left.

My clinched fists tightened, fingernails biting my palms. "Excuse me!" I struggled to control my voice, "I *have* to see him today! I am his daughter, but I don't have time to go get my mom and come back before you close. Can't you make an exception? If not, I will demand to speak to your manager." Was that overdoing it? It didn't matter. I needed to see him.

She looked back up with that infuriating indifference and exaggerated the movement of her arm and hand to pinch the edge of her desk. I thought that was an odd way to show your irritation with someone, until two armed officers appeared from the door to the right of her desk.

Ah, hidden security button. Of course.

The two hulking figures approached me. One was dark-skinned and had the most grossly enormous muscles I'd ever

seen. The other one—whose blond head was a good foot closer to the ground than his fellow officer's—was also muscular. But his brawn paled in comparison.

"What's the problem?" Muscles crossed his arms and looked down his large nose at me.

"This young lady marched in here demanding to visit someone in the hospital. But her name is not on his list of family members or approved visitors. And she refuses to leave."

I glared at them.

Mr. Blond stepped around the desk and grabbed one of my arms, turning me toward the door.

"But he's *my dad!* I need to see him!"

Muscles firmly gripped my other arm and they walked me out.

Why? I'm so close! And now I'm being escorted out of the building?

Once we were outside, Muscles said, "Please find your car and leave the premises."

"But I'm his *daughter!* Why am I not on the list? I've got my ID in the car, wouldn't that be enough for today? I can bring my mom back tomorrow!" But would she even help me with this? Why had she made sure to keep me off the list?

"No, what you need to do is leave."

"But I *am* related to him! Couldn't I get a blood test or something done for proof? I could—"

"No, kid. You need to leave, or you will be detained for causing a disturbance."

A light bulb flickered in my head. If they detained me, I would still be in the same building as my dad, right? So maybe there was still a chance… "I wouldn't be held in this dump, would I?"

"Yes, yes you would. For at least 24 hours."

Ding! Ding! Ding!

I jumped forward and jerked my arms away from them, even managing to shake off Mr. Blond's grip. Muscles's fingernails dug painfully into my upper arm as he fought to keep ahold of me.

"But I want to be on the list!" I shrieked like a child throwing a fit.

Mr. Blond had both hands on me again an instant later. "Stop this behavior or you will be forcibly detained!"

"But I don't want to be detained!" I wailed, trying to pull off some forced tears. "I want my name to be on the list! I want to see my fatheeerrrr!" I did my best impression of bursting into sobs and continued to fight against their grasps, knowing that *not* escaping them was the key.

They turned me around toward the building again, but instead of walking me back through the main doors, they dragged me around a corner. Then the real adrenaline kicked in. I second-guessed this idea. Here I was with two men on the backside of a building. But I shoved those fears aside, that wasn't what was happening here. This was what I'd aimed for, and there was no getting out of it now. I did continue to pitch a ridiculous fit though. That part was kinda fun.

Mr. Blond yanked roughly on my arm as he swiped an ID badge by the sensor next to the door.

"Please let me see him for a couple of minutes!"

"Your name is never going on the list, sweetheart, I guarantee," Muscles mumbled.

They hauled me through the door, and it shut itself hard without either of them touching it.

We were in an office. A few crappy wooden desks were placed at random around the room, each strewn with papers. I wondered if any of them contained information on my dad. Maybe a picture of what he looked like now?

But they shoved me through the room too quickly. After the next door, the scene was totally different. It looked like an old jail. Metal bars everywhere. Holding cells?

Crap. Why had I expected something less sophisticated? How was I going to get out of *this?*

My fit-pitching waned a bit as the scenery distracted me, so when Muscles's walky-talky sputtered, I jumped. They both snorted and Muscles let go of me to answer.

"Jankowsky here, over." Some static.

This was my chance. There was no way I could manage to break away with both of them holding onto me. But with just one… the smaller one….

Composing a tired and defeated look on my face, I fought the resistance in the back of my mind for a finger hold on that slippery surface. But I couldn't find the crack this time. I tried to focus harder, but nothing. With my free hand, I very slowly pressed the stone against my chest.

Wham! There it was—the slippery surface in the back of my consciousness. I dug at it with my mind, wrenching it apart. Mr. Blond's grip relaxed as he took in my expression—carefully schooled disappointment and exhaustion.

I was almost there. But I would need a distraction for the best chance of success. Without changing my focus, I tried to pay attention to when it was Muscles's turn to talk again. The next time he let out a word, I ripped my arm from Mr. Blond's grip with all my strength, and ran for it.

"Hey! Stop!"

I took off, losing all the headway I'd made at the wall and knowing they could still see me.

Heavy boots pounded behind me. I had only seconds to make this work, and then I would be out of options. I ran through the closest door, deeper into the building.

The next room was storage, full of high shelves bursting with boxes. *Yes! Things to hide behind! If I can get out of their sight for a second, I might be able to gather my thoughts well enough to disappear.*

I darted past the first couple of rows and slid into the next one. Searching for the mental crack in the slippery wall was not easily done while running. I'd have to find a safe place to stop for a few moments if I was going to have any chance.

I reached the other side of the room and turned to jog down that line of shelves.

"Hey!" Mr. Blond saw me as he ran past my row and in a flash he'd turned back after me. I spun and high-tailed it in the other direction.

More boots stomped closer and closer, and then *crash!*— the high pitch tones of glass shattering were followed by a heavy, echoing *boom*. I dared a backward glance. Muscles had apparently come from somewhere Mr. Blond wasn't expecting, and they'd collided, knocking down an entire shelf of glass containers.

Swerving around the next shelf, I crouched behind a large metal machine.

Two deep breaths to slow myself down were all I could spare. A moment later and my eyes were closed, concentrating on the wall. I gripped the stone tightly in my hand and the crack appeared. I tugged at it, trying to focus my way through it.

A heavy scraping sound… metal against concrete. One of them lifted the fallen shelf out of the way. Two pairs of boots pounded toward me.

It had to be now. I held my breath, trying to avoid the distractions.

One of them turned my corner. Two more heartbeats and he'd see me, unless…*Crack!*

The boots ran past, the glass in the treads scraping the concrete floor with each step.

I opened my eyes and looked down at myself.

Nothing.

Yes!

Standing, I listened for where the officers were headed. They ran in the wrong direction. I crept to the end of the row, looking for a way out. A glowing red exit sign hung above a door on the opposite wall. I avoided the broken glass mess and reached the door a moment later. Panting, I reached out to turn the knob with anxious fingers. I grasped it, slowly turned it, and… it didn't open.

Oh crap.

CHAPTER SIX

*J*ust my luck! But I wrenched the knob one more time and...*score!*

The door opened outward and I peeped around the corner, heart racing, hoping no one would be there to see it opening on its own. The bleach-white hallway was deserted.

Clack, clack, clack. There were the boots again, stomping their shattered-glass treads my way. I stepped across the threshold and closed the door quietly behind me. Shouting came through the door, getting closer. My focus on staying invisible wavered. I didn't have time to run to one of the open doorways.

The knob turned.

I pressed against the wall with the door hinges, sucking in my stomach to get as flat as I could. If they opened the door too wide, it would bump into me and give me away.

The door opened, swinging toward me, and I flickered back into view.

Crap!

I held my breath.

"She's not back here." Muscles glanced into the hall and then dropped the door handle. "She's gotta be hiding behind something in the storage room. Let's check—" the door slammed, cutting him off.

Whew! I'd managed to get away from them, but now anyone else could see me. I grabbed the stone again, trying to focus. But the crack didn't appear. Just thinking about it gave me a headache.

Maybe I needed to give my mind a break. I tried again, but got nowhere. I needed another plan.

Everything was incredibly white. White walls, white floors, white signs labeling the white doorways into the various rooms on each side of the long, white hallway. It felt very... *sterile.*

There were white carts with medical equipment and medication bottles on them. I considered nabbing a pair of glasses and a clipboard off one of the carts to help me blend in. Could I pass for someone old enough to be an employee here? It might be possible. But my clothes! I still had on the jeans and baggy sweatshirt. Hardly professional attire.

It was the click-clack of high heels that I heard this time. Multiple sets, coming from around the corner ahead. I darted into the closest room and hoped they weren't heading for it.

The click-clacking passed me and I caught a glimpse of four women in business clothes entering a room on the other side of the hall. The walls echoed as their door slammed shut. The coast was clear.

I found the stairs and hurried up the first flight, anxious to meet this person who should've been in my life well before now. Was it possible for my heart to beat any faster?

Huffing and puffing, I reached the third floor. *That was a lot of stairs.* As I searched for the correct room number, I tried to dry my sweaty palms on my jeans.

Room three-twenty-seven, *finally.* I was both eager and terrified to knock on the pale, windowless door. What would he look like? I didn't even know how he'd been hurt. What had caused the brain damage? Was it a car accident? Would his hair

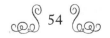

still be the color it was in his army picture? Would he know who I was? Would he be happy to see me? Did he even *know* about me? Maybe he didn't, or maybe he did and he thought that I knew about him all this time, too, and didn't want to see him.

Bracing myself, I knocked. At first the sound was so light that I barely heard it myself, so I struck with more confidence and force. Still receiving no reply, I dared to open the door a crack, in case he was asleep or not even in the room—like out for physical therapy or something.

On the far wall was a queen-size bed sprawled with pillows and a humongous comforter. The room was bigger than I expected. Fancy rugs accented hardwood floors in a few places. The largest rug had three easy chairs perched on it with a mahogany coffee table situated between them.

Ritzy. Huh. How in the world are we affording this? Maybe this is what happened to the insurance.

The walls were covered in gaudy wallpaper that seemed a little too cluttered for the rest of the room. I couldn't tell what the pattern was trying to be. There was a window on the left wall—were those *bars* on the outside? It seemed weird to have bars on the windows at a hospital that was high-end enough to provide this level of accommodations for its patients.

I half expected to see my mysterious father seated in one of the chairs, enjoying some coffee or reading a newspaper, but he wasn't. I stepped into the room and threw another glance around, locating a human-sized lump under the bedspread.

My heart sped up even more. *That must be him! My actual, biological father!* But he was asleep. Should I wake him up? Or did he need his rest? It would be so disappointing to come all this way and not at least see his face, and if I went back out, or even waited in here for too long, I was bound to be discovered eventually and I would never get back in after that.

I stood frozen on the threshold. Indecisive. It'd barely been two hours since I discovered his existence. Had I come so far only to give into fear now? If I didn't at least try to get a better look at him—to see his face and confirm that it really was the man in the photo wedged between the pages of *The Horse and His Boy*—I'd regret it forever.

So I took another leap of faith—how many had I taken just today?—and stepped all the way into the room. The door slammed shut behind me and I jumped out of my skin. I'd expected it to stay open, but it must have been the same kind as the one outside the security area downstairs. When I turned away from the door and back to the hospital bed, the man was moving under the covers. I winced. *Great.* Waking him up by slamming a door was hardly the best way to meet your father for the first time.

Fumbling with the tangled sheets, he asked eagerly, "Have you found it yet?" He had a gentle voice—a little hoarse with sleep.

"Did I find what?" I found myself replying. Going along with whoever he assumed me to be was less intimidating than marching in and claiming to be his surprise daughter. Maybe that would be too much of a shock for him. How sick was he, anyway?

"The rock." He finally got untangled from the sheets and peered at me. "Oh, you must be a new nurse. Sorry, I thought you were someone I already knew."

His face was haggard and wrinkly—too old for his age. He was eighteen, like Mom, when they got married. How could this be him? He looked so different from the photo, with his now scraggly gray hair.

"No, sorry," I stuttered, not sure what I was apologizing for. "I'm…new. You said you want a rock?" Did he mean my purple one? Did he know what it could do?

"Yes, but not just any old dirty brown rock. I need a *particular* rock." He looked conspiratorially around the room, as if to make sure we weren't being overheard by the walls. Something was wrong with his arm, but it was too dim to see. "You see, a long time ago, I found a certain purple rock in a place far away from here, and there was something very special about it."

Oh my gosh! He *did* know! Could he be from another world? Could he use *magic?*

"I found it and knew that it mattered, so I kept it. But then…" His eyes grew wider and his voice became more strained. "Well, you won't believe me. They never do." He looked down at his lap like a dejected child.

"I will believe you." I found myself promising. He was my father! I wanted to know what he had to say. He must've used the rock to turn invisible, too! *I knew it!*

He looked at me doubtfully. "Right after I picked it up, monsters attacked me."

I stared back blankly. *Monsters?*

"They wanted the stone, so they picked me up and flew around, fighting over me in midair! They ripped at me and roared at each other and there was blood everywhere. They tore me apart. And then they dropped me from the sky, and it was a long time before I woke up again."

Flying monsters? Was he talking in his sleep? What kind of medication did they have him on? There was something…*off* about the way he moved.

"Please, you have to find it for me! They want it back, and if I don't give it to them, they'll come after me! They will *kill* me for it!"

Yes, definitely insane. "Who wants it?" I humored him. "Who's going to try to kill you? The monsters?"

"Yes! The dragons!" He threw his pajama pant-covered legs over the side of the bed and tossed the sheets away.

Then I realized what was wrong with how he moved. One of his legs was a prosthetic. He was trying to get out of bed with limited success because one was not real. Had he lost it in a battle? Where'd he get the monster story from?

Was it the drugs?

He stumbled and fell to the ground. I crossed the room instinctively to help him up, but when I reached for where his arm should be, I found only air. He really was missing an arm, too! So he'd literally lost an arm and a leg? What'd happened to him? Were stories about dragons his way of coping with PTSD or something?

Before I recovered from the shock enough to help him, he'd already managed to pull himself up with his only arm and steady himself. I got my first close-up look at his face. His eyes were haunted, full of gripping terror and desperation. The emotions there were so strong that I couldn't tell whether there was any resemblance between us.

"The dragons are coming for it! I have to give it back. Please, help me!"

I backed away, bumping into what I expected to be the window, but it poked my back. I turned to see what it was. Metal bars on the *inside* of the window, as if to protect what was *outside* from what was *inside*, instead of vice-versa. The wallpaper fluttered as I scrambled around the bars, but it wasn't wallpaper at all.

Hundreds of loose sheets of paper taped to the wall and to each other were so plentiful that I couldn't find the original paint color beneath them. Each page was covered with symbols of some kind—no, the same symbol, drawn in different sizes and at different angles, sometimes multiples overlapping. It was a collection of lines and curves that I'd never seen before. There was a circle in the middle, divided into fourths by two intersecting lines. On the outside of the circle, to the left and above, rays like sunshine sprouted and expanded. On the right side there was a single star, and beneath that was a straight line over a squiggle. What could that mean?

I turned back to the man who was supposed to be my father, looking into his eyes again as he repeated the fearful warning, more intensely this time. "They are coming! Please, help me find it so I can give it back and live! The other nurses, they don't listen to me anymore. They think I'm crazy. Please, will *you* help me? I don't want to die!"

What could've happened to make him think that?

He gripped the bedside table and hobbled toward my place by the window.

"You must find it!" he begged fervently.

I altered my course for the door.

"Okay, I'll go look now," I lied, voice shaking as I fumbled for the knob. My fingers finally landed on it.

But the knob refused to turn.

It was locked. From the outside.

CHAPTER SEVEN

I risked turning away from him to face the door and give it a harder tug.

No luck.

On a hunch, I checked above the doorframe for a key, but that also turned up nothing.

I was locked in a room by a door that was made to be impenetrable for people who had as much motivation to leave as me and a whole lot more time to find a way. I wasn't escaping without someone opening the door from the other side, and when they did, they wouldn't be pleased to find me here. If there was even any of me left to find by the time someone arrived… What did angry people who were out of their minds do with people who got locked in with them? There was no good end to this situation.

"They carried me up into the sky to take it from me. I didn't know! I would never have touched it if I'd known. It's only a matter of time before they come for me…to *kill* me." His eyes gleamed. "Unless you find the rock. You must! *Please!*" The agonizing wails were terrifying. "Please. Help me. Or I'll die!"

The door whooshed open. A middle-aged woman dressed in slacks and a neat sweater marched in and glared ferociously at me. "*Miss* Pratenger! If you will be so kind as to leave the room!" Gesturing out the door with her other arm, she scowled with an air of such authority that no one would have considered refusing her.

I was relieved—and disappointed. And a little terrified of this person.

I hurried through the door without sparing him another look. What a disaster this had turned out to be. Who was Miss Pratenger?

"Calm down, Mr. Montgomery. No one is coming to kill you." The door slammed shut on his pleas.

My rescuer's enraged eyes fixed on me again, and I remembered just how much I was *not* supposed to be exactly where I was. Before I could open my mouth to explain or apologize, she was shouting.

"What were you doing?" Exasperation bled through every syllable. "Going into a restricted room *without* clearance and *without* assistance! What kind of idiot did the university send me? You risked your *life*, Miss Pratenger, and the life of the human being on the other side of that door!" She jabbed a finger toward it. A name badge was pinned to her sweater. It read "Dr. Jennings."

Fancy meeting you here.

"This is absolutely unacceptable behavior, Miss Pratenger." She straightened herself and hardened her face as if to declare a death sentence. "We have a zero-tolerance policy for such conduct in this hospital. Therefore, I'm afraid I'll have to end your internship before it has even begun. You are entirely expelled from gaining any experience here, Miss Pratenger. I will escort you out."

"But I'm not—"

"What you are, is *leaving*."

She grabbed my arm in much the same way as one of the guards from earlier, except she was scarier. She pushed me through the hallway, down two flights of stairs, and out a side

door into the parking lot. I was too afraid to tell her that I wasn't whoever she thought I was. I felt sorry for this Miss Pratenger person. Who knew what would happen when she showed up?

"I will be in touch with your instructors, Miss Pratenger." She shoved me away. Disapproval dripped from every syllable. "You can be assured they will hear of this." She slammed the door in my face.

I stood for a moment, frozen. How could that crazy guy be my father? What could've happened? There was no way that his dragon-monster story could be true. Dragons weren't real. Neither were monsters. Well, at least not the kind he was talking about. Maybe some big piece of machinery hit him in the head and he had a distorted memory of it.

But it *was* him. He knew there was something important about my stone, even if he thought dragons wanted it. And if magic was real, maybe monsters weren't that impossible either.

I half expected the guards to have impounded my car or something. When I found the *Tin Can* unchanged, I wondered if they were still looking or if they'd given up. They'd probably get into a lot of trouble for losing me. Then again, no one knew that they'd tried to detain me, only that they'd escorted me out. Maybe they decided to let me slip through the cracks.

As I stepped into the car, my hand went to the stone, and I was so glad I'd left it tucked under my sweatshirt. If he'd seen it and recognized it…well who knew what he would've done.

When I got home, I collapsed onto my mattress. *What a day.* Realizing I'd forgotten to pick Mom up, I groaned. But not feeling particularly charitable toward her at the moment, I decided to stay where I was. She could get a ride with someone else. I knew there would be a fight when she got home, and I wasn't eager to rush it. The later she arrived, the longer I could avoid the inevitable. Besides, it was so late now that she was probably already on her way.

How could she do this to me?

Did she think I couldn't handle it or something? Well it *had* been a shock today, of course, but I hadn't been prepared at all and I'd been raised to think he'd always been perfectly ordinary and that he was currently a very normal dead guy. If she'd been honest with me, I could've grown up knowing—and accepting—the truth.

And to think that we'd always been so close! We always told each other everything, every secret. We laughed together and cried together, talking about how our days went and sharing our dreams for the future someday when we'd have more money...

Had all that been lies? What did I even know about her that was true? Anything? Was she really the person I'd always thought?

As if on cue, the front door creaked, and her soft footsteps crossed the linoleum. Any moment she would knock on my bedroom door, and I hadn't decided yet if I was ready to see her.

But I didn't have the choice. She pushed the door right open after two knocks, though I gave no invitation. A moment later she sat next to me. I avoided her eyes, disgusted with myself for being fooled by her and hating the thought of losing the person in whom so much of my security rested.

I decided to take the lead of the conversation. "So, *Mom*, why have you been lying to me my whole life? Why did you want me to grow up thinking that my father was dead? How could you lie to me, about this?"

"Enzi, I—"

"What?" I couldn't unclench my teeth. "Thought I couldn't take it? Thought I couldn't handle the fact my father is out of his mind? Well maybe if I'd been raised with the truth, instead of a bunch of lies, I would've accepted the idea by now, instead of having to deal with the shock of finding everything out *today!*"

"Trust me, Enzi, I wanted to tell you, but—"

"And maybe," I was shouting now, "you shouldn't *lie* to someone for her *whole life* and then expect her to *trust* you about anything!"

I couldn't take her anymore. I was too pissed. I leaped off the mattress and stormed out of the room, slamming the door behind me. I was going to get in the car and drive around to cool off. It didn't matter how much gas I wasted.

But more questions pounded through my head, demanding answers. They forced me back into my room to face her.

"Why the heck does he think he's going to be attacked by flying monsters? And why does he think they'd want this rock?" She didn't know about the rock's abilities, did she? Surely she would've told me. Well, that was hardly a sure thing anymore. "It *is* this rock, isn't it?" I pulled my stone out from the collar of my tee shirt, dangling it in front of her accusingly.

She looked at it and then back to me with a stricken face.

"So it does have to do with this? What else aren't you telling me?" I was almost whispering now, suspicious. Surely, she couldn't know about its ability.

I was struck by how small she looked. Teary, red-faced, slumped. The type of posture that always pulled me with magnetic force to her side to comfort her. I'd always assured her we would find a way to manage. I'd always been there for her.

Maybe I shouldn't have been.

She lifted her wet eyes to my face, whispering in a broken voice, "You know the story. When they told me he was dead, they shipped me his possessions. There was the uniform he'd worn on the day that he died—er—supposedly. I went through the pockets and that stone was in it. I didn't know why he had it. He wasn't into geology. But for some reason he'd liked it enough to keep it, so I kept it too. It's my favorite color. Eventually I had it made into a necklace for you, thinking you might like to have something of his to carry with you."

I stormed out again, this time determined to take a drive. This was the same story she'd always told me, only now it sounded rehearsed. When I was little, it sounded very important and valuable, every time she told it. But now, I questioned the validity of every detail, and that was exhausting.

I snatched the keys off the counter and barged through the front door, wishing the *Tin Can* had the kind of key fob that started the engine from a distance. I dove into the car and turned the key, fighting tears. Backing up, I pulled out onto the main road, plowing over the curb and then barely dodging a lightless lamppost. I didn't know where I was going. I just needed to go.

Eventually I found myself at the icy mountain—my mountain. I parked next to it and got out with the foggy notion that a walk through the woods might do me some good. I was too heavy to find extended running or walking refreshing, but I was restless and needed to do something.

The sheer mountain face was only a few steps away. By the time I reached it, the moon and stars were brilliantly reflected in each of the glassy icicles. I touched one, but the heat from my finger melted it, marring the reflection. Pulling my hand away, I took a step back to admire the height of the cliff. Slowly, I walked along the base of it. Its hugeness and solidity brought me comfort and security—it wasn't going anywhere.

If only an escape existed behind this mountain and I could break it open with a thought, like I could break through the wall in my mind to disappear. An escape into another world would be pretty nice right about now.

Maybe my dad didn't know what the stone could do— maybe he really did just pick it up by mistake. But if I could get back to him somehow, and he could do something with it that would make him think he was turning it over to the monsters, maybe he would think that they would leave him alone and he would feel safe again and would maybe go back to being himself. Maybe I could dress up like a dragon and recruit one of the nurses to get him to me and make him think he was giving the rock back. But I didn't know anything about psychology. Could something like that help? Or would he wake up with the same issue again the next day?

Had Mom tried anything like that? What had their relationship been like?

Why did people lie to each other so much? Didn't anyone realize how painful it was? So much worse than physical pain. How could people do that to each other? I'd lived the past seven years without friends because of Jillian's lies. Now as if that wasn't enough, I discovered that I had not only been lied about, but exceptionally lied *to*.

What a lousy birthday. I'd had some cruddy birthdays before—not getting the gift I wanted because it was too expensive, not having a birthday party because it was too expensive, not having a birthday party because I didn't have any friends, etc.—but this had them all beat exponentially. It was laughable. How did someone end up unlucky enough to get all this dished out on them in one day, and on their *birthday* of all days? What a joke.

Something dark reflected in the icicles. I whirled, heartbeat accelerating, terrified that it might be Caleb. But of course, no one was there. Just the *Tin Can* parked a few yards away on the shoulder. I'd reached the edge of this mountain—a little farther than I thought.

I let out a sigh. But when I looked back at the icicles, the dark spot was still there. What was it?

Peering closer, I saw shapes that my mind wanted to piece into something, but it wasn't quite clear enough. Something was there, but it was...blurry, almost. Not actually blurry though. It was like my mind was really tired in the area that was trying to process what it saw.

Was I about to pass out? No, the moon glinted off the other icicles clearly, nothing blurry about that.

I tried once more to focus on the shape. Were those...eyes? And...and a *snout?* No, I just had dragons on my mind. And insanity running in my family, apparently.

I leaned against the rock face and slid down, not caring if the icicles melted a little into my sweatshirt.

A twig snapped. My head flashed around to see what was there, but still, no one. I was ridiculously paranoid.

I stood and took a step back toward the *Tin Can,* and then *snap!* Another twig? I hurried, speed walking now, and glanced back. I made out the light of two eyes level with mine, peering right at me. I shot off at the speed of a terrified rabbit to close the distance between me and my car. There was no time to focus on turning invisible.

It hadn't been here, in these woods. It'd been miles from here, in the old barn behind Jillian's house. And it'd been in the daylight, not at night. But that didn't make the dark any less terrifying.

If someone was over there right now, that was too close. Slamming against the car, I took hold of the handle and yanked with all my might, but my fingers slipped off without affecting the door. I peered through the frost that had formed on the corner of the window and saw the problem. *Drat that lock!*

In what felt like the clumsy slow motion of a nightmare, I groped around in my pocket for the keys, found them, and then failed to enter the correct key into the lock twice before succeeding. Finally, I heard the click of victory as the lock jumped back up into view. I glared at it fiercely for all the trouble it'd caused as I ripped open the door and leaped inside.

Slamming the lock back down, I started the car and sped away. In the rearview mirror, I thought I saw something—someone. But I wasn't sure.

I quickly put distance between me and the woods, but I still didn't feel safe. What if that really had been Caleb out there? He could've been following me the whole time, and I would never have noticed with how quietly he moved and how lost in thought I was.

The memories of his weight on me, the horrible stench of his sweat, threatened to throw me into a panic attack. I breathed deeply, gripping the steering wheel for dear life.

By the time I pulled up at home, the adrenaline rush had evaporated, leaving me exhausted again. I wanted my comfy mattress on the floor, but I didn't want to get out of the car.

He couldn't have followed me on foot, and there hadn't been any cars behind me on the road the whole way home. But here I was, safe with the doors locked. I *wasn't* safe out on the pavement between the safe car and the safe house. I was probably being a little ridiculous. He couldn't be there. That probably hadn't even been him out there in the woods.

But still.

So I stared out into the darkness, keys neatly arranged, sticking out from between my fisted fingers in case I needed to power punch anyone.

CHAPTER EIGHT

He loomed over me, approaching in slow motion. I needed to run, to get far away from him. But I couldn't make my legs work. It was like being suspended in molasses.

The cats yowled, annoying him with their cries. There was blood, and then he was closer. Too close. I wanted to die.

"*E*nzi, I just want—"

"I'm hardly in the mood to talk about things *you* want right now, Mom." I had a lot more to say on exactly how I felt about her at the moment, but I couldn't find the words. I didn't think there was any collection of syllables in existence that could have described my feelings toward her.

She'd waited for me on the couch. I hadn't come inside until the sun was up. The heat was back on and it was a welcome relief after my freezing night in the car.

I walked to my room and picked out some fresh clothes and a towel. After starting the shower, turning off the light, and stripping out of my dirty clothes, I waited the customary several moments for the water to get warm. I felt for the necklace. My fingers found nothing but skin.

My heart skipped a beat. I fished through the pile of dirties on the floor—nothing. Had I lost it in the woods last night? I couldn't go back there, not after I'd seen those eyes.

I must have left it in the car—Maybe it fell off and is hanging out on the floorboard.

I threw on the clean clothes and rushed outside to inspect the *Tin Can.* The necklace was nowhere to be found. It wasn't in the car, front or back seats. I even looked in the trunk, though I hadn't opened it in ages. It wasn't in the parking lot or on the walkway between the car and the door. It wasn't on the counter where I put the keys. I checked the dirties again, just in case. But it wasn't there or anywhere else in the apartment.

It must have flown off when I mad-dashed to the car last night.

It was Saturday now. How likely was it that Caleb might be out for a drive? If he was even in town. He wasn't around that often but whenever he was, he showed up without warning.

But I had to get that necklace back! It was too important. It could be the only chance I had of saving my dad! I had to risk it.

I could at least inspect the side of the road from the safety of the car.

Grabbing the keys off the counter I bolted back outside.

"Enzi, where are you going?"

The door slammed. I didn't have time to answer.

On the way back to my mountain, I tried to distract myself with music, but there wasn't anything good on. Morning talk shows—which I passionately despised—had commandeered most of the stations. Only one played music, and the words *They're always watching me, watching me, I can't escap*e… in the creepy voice of Paul Malborne, were hardly helpful. I punched the knob and listened to silence instead.

I felt in the pocket of my sweatshirt, even though I hadn't worn it yesterday, hoping the necklace might somehow be in there. But I only found the debit card.

I reached the place where I'd parked the previous night and slowed to scan the shoulder. Every few minutes, my gaze checked the woods for unwanted company. So far, all clear.

A glimmer on the faded pavement caught my eye, and I pressed harder on the pedal. But it was only a shiny fleck in the asphalt where some slush had melted away. Where was my stone?

Another shimmer reflected the sun's rays, and this time it looked purplish. I rolled closer.

Yes! There it lay, peeking out from the snow slush on the edge of the pavement. Its brilliance contrasted starkly with its surroundings.

I pulled off and threw the car in park, taking the keys from the ignition in case the lock slipped again.

I ran to the stone and picked it up. Once fastened around my neck, its slight weight against my chest felt familiar and comforting. I looked down to see it there, where it belonged. Its beauty was enhanced against my faded black sweatshirt. It glimmered proudly, shiny as if I'd just taken it from a stream instead of the nasty greyish sludge.

The road rumbled under my feet as a flash of red approached. I looked up to see a familiar car. My relieved smile wilted at the edges. *His* car.

The windows were too tinted for me to see who drove. Maybe, by some miracle, it was a stranger's car just passing through.

But a beat later, the piece of living horsepower screeched to a stop and zoomed backward to park between me and the dear old *Tin Can* before I could even take a step toward my refuge.

Oh. No.

Fear tore at my gut. Paralyzing terror. My muscles shook. I reached to cover the stone with one hand, searching for the crack in the slippery, smooth wall. I saw the fissure in my

mind's eye, but I couldn't touch it. It was as if it were coated in unbreakable glass. I clawed at it, but got nowhere.

The driver's side door opened. The bare shred of focus I'd managed to spend on the crack leaped away to join the rest of my mind in waiting to see who would emerge.

Carlie stepped from the driver's seat.

I breathed. I'd take her over him any day. *Please be just her.*

And then the passenger door opened.

No...No...

Jillian stepped out. They closed their doors in unison.

Caleb wouldn't be in the backseat, would he? He'd probably throw Carlie over a cliff before he'd let her take the wheel. And he and Jillian had broken up ages ago. It wasn't like he'd do her any favors.

No matter, it was once again two of them versus one me, and the necklace was present. And this time, I had no place to hide to gather enough concentration to disappear. They were between me and my car. They would catch me in a moment if I ran for the woods, and I could hardly scale the mountain. I'd only managed to get away from them in the bathroom because the open stall had been right next to me.

"Thought we'd forget about it, did you?" Jillian laughed and rounded the car.

"No bathroom stalls to lock yourself in this time." Carlie swished her long dark locks over one shoulder. "How *did* you escape last time?"

I opened my mouth, but no words came out.

"Where *did* you get that necklace, anyway? I seem to remember you were being really selfish with information last time." Jillian eyed the fist I'd closed around the stone.

I backed up several steps. "Knock it off, guys. You can't have this." My witty comebacks were in full swing, naturally.

"I bet you really did steal it." Carlie paused in her approach to inspect her perfectly manicured nails.

That seriously pissed me off. But like the brilliant orator I was, I had absolutely no smart lines to whip out and spit back at her. I would think of an incredibly witty reply sometime three hours or so later, when they were long gone and I'd already embarrassed myself beyond redemption. Certainly not in time for it to be useful.

"Come on, Mackenzi. What even is it? Stop covering it up—I want to see it again." Jillian's lip-glossed grin reminded me of a scheming crocodile. "You've never worn anything pretty before. I'm just curious."

"Amethyst?" Carlie closed in.

"Look, guys, it's just a rock. It's not a precious stone or anything." Well, not the type *they* thought it was anyway. "And it's my dad's, so I really need to hang onto it." Was there any chance Jillian would remember how much I'd grieved for him, how much I'd wanted to know him? Any chance she would pity me and convince Carlie to leave me alone?

Jillian narrowed her eyes. "No, it's not. Your dad's dead. You're just saying that to be difficult. Come on. Where'd this thing come from?"

Her words hurt, though I wasn't surprised. Of course she wouldn't remember. Or at least wouldn't care anymore.

Leaves crunched behind me. *Caleb?* I whirled. Had they planned to pin me in like this? Was he going to help them steal my necklace, or was he planning to do worse?

My heart pounded in my ears as a silhouette took form within the trees. Tall, definitely a man. He emerged from the shadows.

Not Caleb.

This man had dark skin and longish shaggy hair. Wearing jeans and a light brown jacket, he stood several inches taller than Caleb would have and looked like he could be in his late teens, maybe early twenties. He was not the man who inhabited my nightmares, but he was a guy, and guys tended to be very susceptible to Jillian and Carlie. I may not have to worry about living my nightmare again in real life—which was certainly a relief—but I could kiss this necklace goodbye.

Out of the corner of my eye, I saw them adjust their postures to better display their feminine charms.

Yep. I was out of luck.

"Hey!" Jillian called in a sexily distressed tone of voice. "That bitch stole my necklace! Could you get it back for me? Please?" She batted her eyelashes at him, and Carlie stepped forward, displaying a gorgeous smile.

"Actually," he said in too deep a voice for someone my age, "I was under the impression that *she* is the one who needs assistance in the area of bitches stealing necklaces."

I did a double take. *Did he just say what I think he said?*

I was so shocked that I almost burst out laughing. No one had ever said anything like that to Jillian Richmond or Carlie Jacobs, or probably anyone in their families or extended families in the history of the world, and I had the pleasure of being present for the one time someone actually had the guts to do it. And in *my* defense, too!

Their eyes narrowed. Jillian's jaw dropped and Carlie leaned forward as if she couldn't believe her ears. But he wasn't looking at them.

He stared strangely at me, almost as if he recognized me as some long lost best friend. But we'd never met, I would've remembered his face. Calling him *attractive* would be the understatement of the year, and I would remember someone who could dish it back out to Jillian like that. If he'd been from around here, he would've known that I was the least popular of the unpopular kids. What could he be thinking?

The eye-catching stone was at my chest, but he was definitely staring at my face, searching my eyes for something. As if I actually *was* someone he'd never expected to be so lucky as to see again.

He strode right past the two most popular and gorgeous girls in town, toward *me*. Again, my heart pounded, but this time with confusion.

"Are you alright?" That deep voice again...

Wow. He was even more good-looking this close up. His chocolate-brown eyes never left mine as I stuttered a reply. "Yeah, thanks." Pitiful. Why were words so hard?

"Can I walk you back to your car?"

Whoa. No one had ever asked me that before. "Sure."

He placed himself between me and the girls, and though his legs were much longer than mine, he shortened his strides to keep pace with me.

We reached the *Tin Can* and I wished he didn't have to know that was the kind of car I drove. Of course, there must be some kind of misunderstanding. Why was he paying me any attention when those two were right over there?

I stole a glance at them and their open-mouthed outrage lifted my spirits. Even if there was some kind of misunderstanding and I would never see this guy again, the looks on their faces were beyond priceless.

His eyes were on me again. What did he see?

"Well, uh, thanks for...you know." What had I just said?

"No problem."

His smile...generous lips, teeth not perfectly straight...but somehow, I knew they couldn't be improved upon.

My stomach jumped.

Wait, what was that? There was something *nice* about the startling feeling.

I reached behind me for the handle and tugged on it, hoping to smoothly slip into my car and drive away. Whatever he thought he saw, I was sure to disappoint him in the end. I didn't know him. I wanted to leave before he realized he had the wrong girl. I wanted to remember the exquisite look on his face as he smiled down on me.

The handle resisted.

Oh no! I yanked again. *You stupid, lazy lock! How could you do this to me? I left you alone for all of five minutes!* I reached in my sweatshirt pocket for the keys, but they weren't there.

"Oh, here. I think these must have fallen from your pocket." He dropped the keys into my hand.

"Uh, thanks." How'd I manage to lose them so quickly?

"Sure thing." He stepped back so I could open the door, reaching one big, brown hand my way. "Shaun, by the way."

"Oh, hi. I'm Enzi." His hand was so warm, that for a moment, I forgot it was winter. That weird feeling came again and I jumped back, breaking the connection and slamming against the *Tin Can.*

Carlie shouted, "She stole that thing, you know! You're helping a thief!"

"They seem like really great friends," he laughed, never taking his eyes from mine.

I snorted and his grin widened.

"And that rock really is beautiful. Does it always look like that?"

"Like, uh, what?" I was distracted by his smile. Despite his deep voice, he really looked about my age.

"Like it has just been pulled from a stream."

"Oh. Yeah, it does," I said lamely. "It was my dad's. He found it a long time ago, and then my mom gave it to me." Why was I rambling? He didn't want my life story!

"That is very interesting. Do you know where he found it?"

That thrilling feeling in my stomach hardened and dropped into my toes. *Oh my gosh, not you too!* He wanted one—probably for his gorgeous girlfriend or something. *That* was why he chose me over them for the moment. What was I thinking? "Look, I've gotta go." I fell back into the car with all the grace of a drunk elephant.

He leaned in close to me and I flinched back, still in the habit of preserving personal space.

"Keep it safe," he whispered, closing the door for me. With a wave, he stepped back and stood as if to watch me go.

Keep it safe? Did he know something about it? No, of course he couldn't. He must've meant that I needed to keep it hidden from Jillian and Carlie better. Yes, that was it. So maybe he was still a decent-ish guy.

I dared to look in the rearview mirror once and was stupidly flattered and a little creeped out to see that he watched me drive away. Then he turned and headed back to the woods, pulling off his jacket. How could he be warm in weather like this? Whatever. Guys were always trying to pretend crap like that— that it wasn't freezing cold when it really was and that injuries didn't hurt when they actually did. He was probably going to go introduce himself to Carlie and Jillian—probably took off the jacket to display his muscles or something.

With the stone safely around my neck and music blaring in my ears, I drove toward home. Then my stomach rumbled, and I remembered the current lack of groceries in the house. With a slight groan, I diverted my homeward path to the grocery store.

CHAPTER NINE

*A*fter grocery shopping, filling up on gas—ouch, I'd really blown it with my expeditions the past two days—and cooking dinner, I went to eat in my room. Dinner was usually something we enjoyed together those rare occasions we were both at home, but not tonight.

Dipping the grilled cheese in the tomato soup, I hesitated, knowing it wouldn't be the flood of flavors I craved. The white bread and yellow cheese slice should be rye with some expensive, unpronounceable cheese, and if it had to be tomato soup it could use a little milk and garlic. I sighed and bit into it. *Maybe one day...*

I tried to catch up on homework, but I couldn't focus. I was usually pretty proficient at getting homework done quickly, but there were too many distracting thoughts tonight.

I wouldn't be able to risk wearing my necklace to school for a while. Even if the nice stranger—Shaun, was it?—was suddenly a member of my high school. It wasn't like I'd be around him much. No matter how nice he may be, we wouldn't be moving in the same circles. Especially since I didn't have any circles in the first place.

But I couldn't leave it somewhere obvious around our apartment either. Nobody had broken in before—we obviously didn't have anything worth stealing—but now someone thought I did, and they were more right about that than they knew.

I stood up from the desk and removed the necklace. We didn't have a safe or anything, and my room wasn't cool enough to provide a loose floorboard with a hidden compartment. Valuables always seemed to go in the sock or underwear drawer, so maybe I should be more original and go for a drawer containing a different genre of clothing. The shirts drawer it was! *Such brilliance.*

Back to homework.

I couldn't stop thinking about what Shaun had said. *Keep it safe.* Why? Did he know something? If I ever saw him again, could I ask him? Or would it be risky to reveal I knew there was something to know about it? Or was I making everything too complicated while he was just a nice guy advising me not to wear it around Jillian and Carlie for a while? Plus, I could've dreamed up everything about the ability it gave me. At least one of my relatives suffered from a mental health problem.

I gave up on homework and cradled my head on my desk, wishing I could escape from all this. Wishing I could fly away from everything and live alone in the wild, with no one to ruin things for me and no homework to do and no responsibilities. If only there was a way to get through the icicles and enter some beautiful world on the other side. If only there was such a world on the other side of anything.

The next thing I knew I was awakened from sleep by a bird tapping insistently on my window. They did that from time to time—perch on the bars and tap away. Super annoying. I lifted my head and read the alarm clock. Wow, I'd been out for two hours! Kind of late for a bird to be out, tapping on the window.

A man's face appeared on the other side of the windowpane.

I gripped my desk with white-knuckled terror. Caleb? But then I saw the longish shaggy hair and dark skin. Shaun? His eyes were wide and beads of sweat rolled down his face. What was wrong? Why was he here? How'd he find me?

I was too curious about the stranger who'd stood up to Jillian and Carlie to resist finding out what was up. So I pushed on the window, but it was stuck.

Oh, right. I'd totally caulked all the way around it for better insulation last winter…shoot. We'd have to talk through it.

"Hey, sorry to barge in on you like this, but I need to talk to you. That necklace you had—you still have it right?" His voice was muffled through the thin glass.

So it *was* about the necklace. There was no way he could know what it was. "What's it to you?" I hoped Mom wouldn't overhear and come investigating.

"Very important. Can you prove that you have it?" He gripped the bars.

Proving that I had it wouldn't hurt anything. And his voice was so nice, I kinda wanted to keep him talking.

I crossed the room to my plastic dresser, opened my shirt drawer and took out the necklace. I went back to the window, holding it up for him.

"There. See?" *You made me ruin my brilliant hiding place.*

"Can I hold it, please, to authenticate it?"

Not a chance. "Sorry, window won't open. Plus, I have no way of knowing that you wouldn't steal it. It used to belong to my dad, so I can't give it up. This is personal—"

"Yes actually, it *is* personal, for me too. There are a lot of things about that rock that you are not aware of. It is very important. It has been lost for a very long time. The Gwyth—" He snapped his mouth shut. "My, uh, *friends* need it."

"Sure they do." Maybe he wanted to steal it and pawn it off. Just some kid, looking to make some fast cash. Well not with this he wasn't. Unless… "What do you mean, 'authenticate it'?" Could he know about what it could do?

"I mean examine it to see if it is the rock that I think it is. Look, it is really important—a matter of life and death for some of us, maybe even all of us."

I was still very suspicious of him, but the possibility did nag at me. What if that were true? I mean, his suspicions were right. This was a very special rock. What if it was a matter of life and death for my dad, somehow. At least a matter of freedom from fear or eternal captivity by it. Would Shaun understand him?

My curiosity was piqued. "What do you know about my dad?"

"What makes you think I know anything about your dad?"

Narrowing my eyes, I tried another approach. "So if this were to be the right rock, how would it be a matter of life and death to someone? Does it have…like, powers or something?" *Ugh! Way too obvious!*

He cocked his head. "What do *you* think?"

I pursed my lips. What should I do? It was too valuable a thing to lose, but if it was really a matter of life or death…but how likely was it that his whole story was true? What reason did I have to trust this guy at all?

"If you can prove to me that the rock in this necklace is a matter of life and death, and give me some logical form of assurance that I'll get it back, then I might consider thinking about the possibility of potentially letting you borrow it."

"There is proof that I know you will accept. But you have to come outside, or let me come in—"

"Absolutely not! That's not a fair chance. You'd take it from me and leave me knocked out or dead while you ran off with what might be my dad's only chance at recovery!"

"Okay, okay." He patted the air in front of him in a downward motion with both hands. "I can prove it. But I cannot do that yelling through a window. I need to whisper it in your ear. The consequences of the wrong people overhearing would be dire."

Telling me that there was someone more dangerous than the guy creeping outside my window was hardly a selling point for me joining him outside with the rock. But dang, what if this was the answer to what happened to my dad? I wanted to know what this guy knew. Maybe he knew why my dad thought he saw dragons when he picked it up. Maybe he would know how to heal him.

Going outside with him, necklace in hand, was a terrible risk. It would take no effort for him to incapacitate me and steal my most valuable possession.

But the need to know was too strong.

I walked out and stalked across the living room, glad to see a line of light under the bathroom door. I wouldn't have to walk past Mom. Pausing in the kitchen, I stuffed my feet into my ratty old tennis shoes and threw the sweatshirt from earlier over my head. I left through the creaking front door and walked around the apartment complex, winding the necklace around my wrist so I could hold onto it.

"So?" I asked when I found him staring impatiently into my window.

He jumped at my voice.

"What, surprised a little? Well not nearly as surprised as me! So you better get to inspecting the rock and explaining yourself."

"Let me see it." He held out one large, brown hand.

I placed the stone in it, with the chain still twisted around my wrist so that he couldn't snatch and run. He was so close. This was a horrible idea. What was I thinking? I was too vulnerable out here alone with a guy I didn't know. My heart hammered as I tensed to make a run for it.

He held it with the tips of his fingers, caressing the surface with a large, brown thumb. "This is it," he whispered.

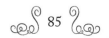

"What is *it*, exactly?"

He was so engrossed in his examination that he didn't seem to hear me.

"Come on, man, you promised to explain if I came outside, and here I am and you haven't explained a thing! What's going on?"

"Yes, I will. But it would be best if you came with me to the place where the rock is from. I need help, and you are the only living being in the world who can help me."

"Come with you? I don't even *know* you! I'm not leaving with you to go anywhere, and you promised to explain!"

"Alright, alright. Calm down. What if I told you about something that only you should know? And what if that something was a mystery to you, something difficult for you to believe and understand? What if I was able to explain *that* to you?"

"Alright. Go on. I'm listening."

"You were near some form of a water-covered surface last night. When you looked into the water at the same time that you touched the rock, you saw something."

My eyes widened and I barely restrained the gasp. I couldn't show my true feelings. Had I really seen something in the icicles?

"And when you let go of the stone in the necklace, the image disappeared. And then you touched it again, and the image was back. It was something dark, and it was difficult to focus on. You probably never determined what it was. Am I right?"

I stared at him. How could he have known that? "Yes."

"And that was not the only time it has happened, was it? I can explain all that to you." He searched my eyes for something.

"Well go on and explain then."

"You were looking into another world."

Another world? No way. What could that have to do with Dad? Was that where he'd found it? Maybe I could learn what really happened if I went. And I've always wished I could get out of this place.

But how could that be? If I dared to believe it, I was asking to have my hopes crushed. I wanted more than anything for it to be true, but how?

"What kind of place is it?" I squeaked.

"If you want me to explain further, you will have to come there with me. There are things I cannot talk about here. It is not safe. Please, you must come. This rock is desperately important, but it will only work if you are with it. I cannot fix anything without you."

What needed to be fixed? Did I dare go with him? Of course not! Believing in other worlds was crazy. It was illogical, impossible. A battle warred within me, the incredulous adult fighting with my inner child—the part that still really wanted to believe in magic and possibilities. The adult was winning, a better debater with legitimate arguments. But in the end, the temptation was too great. I needed to know what was going on, to learn more about what happened to my dad. It was crazy, but I desperately wanted to try. Another world.

An escape. A place with no Caleb and no lying Mom. A place with answers.

I had to give it a chance. I had to. For Dad. "Alright. I'll come. How do we get there?"

He brightened. "Here, let me show you."

I took a step closer to him. The next thing I knew, the most delicious smell hit me—peppermint Christmas candles and warm chocolate chip cookies. It came from him. A cloth in his hand was on my face. That was kind of weird, but I didn't mind. I breathed deeply. Then there was nothing.

CHAPTER TEN

*S*omething poked my shoulder. I tried to move away from it and felt similar blunt jabs on my back and the backs of my legs.

Where am I?

When I finally wrenched my stubborn eyelids apart, blackness was all I saw. The warm, moist air smelled like damp earth, but the ground wasn't soft like soil. It was rough and bumpy, like a pile of potatoes. As my eyes focused, the blackness took on a blueish tinge, and there was a soft ray of light falling from the ceiling on one side.

But home is gray and cold. Where's this place?

My pulse skyrocketed as I bolted upright, everything flashing back to me. That guy, Shaun, the other world talk, the necklace…I rubbed my eyes, trying in vain to get them to focus better.

Something cold brushed my cheek. I flinched back, grabbing at it with my other hand. The stone! The necklace was still tied around my wrist like it'd been when I'd gone outside to talk to Shaun, like a total idiot. Why hadn't he taken it? That was what he wanted, wasn't it?

I fumbled to unwind it from my wrist and yank it over my head, shivering involuntarily as the cold stone slid against the skin under my shirt. Relief calmed the fear for a moment, but only a moment.

"Ah! You are finally awake."

I jumped and scurried backward, landing hard on the bumpy floor. "What? Who are you? Where am I?"

"You are in a different realm." The voice was big, deep, and distinctly male. "You are in Odan Terridor."

Had Shaun actually taken me somewhere outside our world? He'd claimed he could, but...was I supposed to be scared to death or thrilled?

A large something shifted behind the ray of light, and then stepped into it.

He was huge, definitely not human. A red newt-like face with huge, dark eyes stared down at me. Sea monster-like earflaps popped out from either side of his head. A short neck led to reddish-brown forelegs with giant, tree frog feet and toes. The rest of him was still hidden in the darkness, but from what I could tell, it was the creature I'd seen in the icicles. And it was a kind of dragonish-looking monster, just like what my dad thought had attacked him. *Have I gone as insane as him, or was he right all along?*

"What *are* you?" Trembling, I hoped that wasn't a rude question to ask. "Why am I here?"

"I am a Gwythienian. We Gwythienians are the race that inhabits Odan Terridor. You are here because of the rock. Something has happened—"

"Shaun kept saying something about needing me to use it or something. What does that mean? Why me?"

"*You* are needed."

"Needed for what? What are you going to do to me?" I hoped the quiver in my voice wasn't too noticeable.

"Rest assured, you were not brought here for harm to be done to you. But the rock had to come, and it could not come without you. It will not work for anyone else." His deep voice was grave.

"But why? What do you need me to do with it? And where's Shaun?" I glanced around hoping for some human company, even if he had just knocked me out and kidnapped me.

"He is not here. You will not be seeing him ever again."

"Why not?" Was I going to be a prisoner here forever? Had something happened to Shaun? I wanted to give him a swift kick in the pants for convincing me to come out and listen to him in the first place, and then knocking me out and hauling me off when I'd already said I'd come. The jerk.

"That is not important."

Why couldn't he tell me? What secrets was he keeping?

"Okay, so what's going to happen to me while I'm here? What do you need me to do? I would like to go home as soon as possible. Please? Is that a possibility?"

A little while ago I may have been all Neverland and Narnia and escaping from my boring world where I couldn't afford anything, but my piece-of-crap old mattress on the floor of a familiar, monster-less bedroom was sounding *pretty* nice right now, in the face of this creature.

"You will be allowed to go home once we have accomplished what we need to accomplish."

"Wait, so I'm working *with you* on something that has to do with the rock?"

"Listen, human. If you would shut up I could explain it all too you."

Oh. Okay then. I wasn't sure if I was supposed to apologize or take the hint and say nothing. Silence seemed like the safer choice.

His eyes shone bright in his reptilian face as he regarded me. How dangerous was this thing? Was I really even seeing it, or was I becoming as insane as my dad?

Suddenly, the sea monster-like earflaps flicked back and forth and he turned his head to one side, as if listening for something.

I tried to listen too, but I couldn't hear anything.

He turned back to me—eyes wide, earflaps still flicking. "That is better. You *must* take care to be quiet. I will not hurt you or come any closer to you. I will stay here where you can see me, alright? It is of utmost importance that you remain silent. We do not want the others to hear your human voice. Nod if you understand."

I nodded vigorously. Who else was here? What about my explanation?

"Good," he whispered. "I do not ask you to trust me yet. You would of course be very foolish to trust someone you have only just met. But I do remind you that I have lived here my whole life, and because of that I know much more than you about what is safe and what is not. And since I need you to help me use the rock, I have every motivation to keep you alive and safe. Your best interests are mine as well, so *please* remain calm and quiet."

Who was he worried might hear me? What did he think I could help him do? I couldn't really know that he told me the truth, but how likely was I to escape from him if I did refuse? And I was curious, if a bit terrified. So I nodded again.

"Then sit still and pay attention while I explain some necessary details. We need to move quickly. It will not go well for us if they find you."

CHAPTER ELEVEN

"The rock you wear around your neck is one of four," the creature began. "Each one corresponds to one of the realms. They were made to unite the realms in a time when there was much turmoil, and no leaders.

"You see, each realm has unique gifts among its members, but each member is only able to use the gift to a certain degree. Some are strong in their abilities—those are called the Cadoumai—while some are weak or have no ability at all. Whoever had the strongest form of their realm's gift would rule because of power alone, not because they were respected by the people. Each rock enhances the abilities of the one who possesses it to the level of the strongest Cadoumai. Possession of a rock meant authority, and this way the people could choose whom to give it to.

"There was peace for many generations, until a few years ago when all four of the stones went missing. My realm is blamed. They were stolen by…some of my own kind, I regret to say. 'Betrayers of the Realms,' they are now called. They were stolen just before the time when Possession was to be transferred from one generation to the next. As a result, all the Possessors are old now. Without the rocks, they cannot be relieved of their burden, nor can the next generation choose their leaders, as is their right.

"A certain Gwythienian, Tukailaan by name, left Odan Terridor many years before the rocks were stolen—long before I hatched. He was not the one who stole them, but there is a chance he could have gotten ahold of them. He is very dangerous, very strong. He has done some horrible things. If he were to gain Possession of our rock, he would be more than unbeatable, and his reign would be one of tyranny.

"It is common knowledge that a person can only become the Possessor of the rock of their realm. No one should be able to possess the rock of another realm, and so no one should be able to possess multiple rocks at once. But if someone did, especially Tukailaan, we would be doomed. Though this should not be possible, we still fear it.

"Everyone's deepest fear is that he found them. Perhaps he is biding his time, awaiting the opportune moment—the deaths of the current Possessors, or an opportunity to kill them himself. We have spent years searching for them, dreading that we have been too late, yet here is one of them now, dangling on a chain around your human neck, of all things."

"So this really is one of *those* missing magic rocks?" I thought sheepishly how funny and horrible it was that it'd spent the better part of the last several years tucked into my oversized tee shirts. A valuable object that belonged to another world, unknown to human kind.

"Yes. You see now why the human you accuse of kidnapping you was so anxious about it."

Okay, so unknown to *most* of human kind anyway. Had Shaun grown up here or something? How'd he get involved?

"Now listen closely, this is more important than you could ever imagine. Do you know where the other rocks could be? Please tell me you do, but please answer quietly."

"I'm sorry. I don't," I whispered, truly wishing I did. "My mom always told me that she found it in the pocket of my father's uniform when it was sent back with his belongings after he, um, passed away." Perhaps my cherished story of how the rock came to me was all made up. "But she is the most profound liar I know, so that may not be true." Bitterness seeped into my bones as I wondered yet again how much of the foundation of my identity was phony, thanks to her.

The creature deflated at my words, as if I'd crushed all his hopes. "Of course not. I knew you would not…I just hoped. Do you know where your father acquired it?"

"Sorry, I don't really know that either. I do know he never went to another country—he was always stationed in the States. But I have no idea where he was when he supposedly found it. I'm sorry."

"Very well. At least Tukailaan does not have *our* rock. That is something." He stood on all fours and shook himself like a wet dog. "There has been virtually no communication between Odan Terridor and the other realms since we informed them of the loss of the rocks. They are beyond furious with us and we are not well thought of outside of our own realm. But the time has come for contact to be made again.

"One of the rocks has been found, and it gives me hope that one of the other realms could have uncovered something about another rock. The Keeper would forbid any such expedition, but he is old and does not understand, nor does he know that you exist. But regrettably, his prejudices prevent me from informing him of your existence."

He didn't sound like he regretted it all that much. Instead, he appeared pleased, as if he couldn't imagine anything more convenient.

He mumbled, "I could be expelled from my realm for this. But what sort of life is mine here anyway?" He stared into my eyes. "It will be dangerous, but it is the only way. So I am taking you and the rock with me to travel to the other realms—to tell them of the good news and find out if they have any of their own. We will start with—"

"Wait just a second! You haven't asked me if I want to come. What if I don't?"

"But you have to," he said unapologetically. "Do you not understand? We need to prove to the other realms that this is one of *the rocks*. But I cannot do that without you present. *You* are its Possessor."

CHAPTER TWELVE

"*I* would have to kill you to gain Possession myself, and I do not wish to do either."

"What!? But I didn't kill anyone!"

"I did not say you did."

"Well how'd I…"

"Gain Possession?"

"Yeah."

"The first person to touch the rock after the death of the previous Possessor becomes the next."

"So it's last Possessor is dead?"

"That is the most confusing part in this situation, because he's not. But we will get to that later."

Wow. *If* all that was true, there was a lot at stake. It was hard to believe, but there actually was one incredibly good reason to believe him.

I turned invisible when I touched the rock. If that unbelievable fact was true, then an unbelievable story about why it worked could also be true.

So I had *Possession*—whatever that was—of this power rock thingy, did I? What interesting abilities besides invisibility could that give me? "So what does possessing the rock mean, exactly?"

"It means that an impossible thing has happened. Until a few days ago, I had always thought it was not possible for anyone to gain Possession of a rock from any realm besides their own. I certainly never would have guessed a *human* could gain Possession of any rock at all, since humans were excluded from the realms before the involvement with the rocks in the first place. But somehow, you did. It is a miracle, but also a terrifying thing. If a human can gain Possession of our rock, Tukailaan could gain Possession of any of the other realms' rocks. And perhaps more than one."

"But how did you know I have Possession of the rock?"

"Because I saw you see me in the Vorbiaquam."

"The what-what?"

"The Vorbiaquam. One of the gifts of the Gwythienians is the ability to see through water—"

"But anyone can see through water, can't they?" I interrupted, thinking I'd found a hole in his bizarre story. "I mean, if it isn't muddy. Water—where I'm from anyway—is usually clear." Maybe the water in this world was colored or something.

He frowned. "Yes, thank you for that helpful disruption to inform me that clean water is transparent." He didn't have eyebrows, but he raised the place where an eyebrow would be above one eye.

Narrowing my eyes, I crossed my arms. *The sarcastic little pinhead.*

"The Vorbiaquam is like a human device for talking from long distances and being able to see each other's faces on a screen, except that it cannot be transported. It is a great cavern in the heart of our realm, with constant walls of waterfalls all around. The ceiling is stone, but pure, clear water cascades down from its edges. If you have the gift of the Gwythienians and can see through water, you can look for other beings and places in it. For example, if a Gwythienian wished to see her mate in a time of war, she could go to the Vorbiaquam and seek him out. The next time he bent over a brook for a drink, he would see her in the water, looking for him. They could know that each other was alive and well. It is a central part of our culture here, though at this time few of my people value it as they should."

"So it *was* you that I saw in the icicles?"

"Yes. More than once. The first time that I looked into it and saw not another Gwythienian, but you, a *human*, I couldn't believe it. And though you were moving at a great speed, I saw the rock around your neck, and I knew it was the missing rock of my people because it enabled you to see me. Though you could not see me well—as it is a skill that must be developed— your eyes moved with me as I moved. If you could see me too, then you must somehow have the gift, and that would only be possible if you somehow managed to gain Possession of our rock."

So *he* was the dark image I saw in the mountain when I drove past. I'd thought it looked not quite right to be the reflection of the *Tin Can.*

"I was amazed. But I could see the evidence of it. I also knew that you did not know of your Possession. It was your ignorance that allowed me to seek you out myself, instead of having to report the issue to the Keeper, Padraig."

"Why did that make a difference in your decision? I mean, whether or not I knew that I 'had Possession'." I made air quotes over the strange concept.

"Because if you had known about your Possessorship, I would have perceived you as a threat, wondering what else you may know and what you planned to do with your abilities. But since it was clear that you were not aware, I was not obligated to report you to Padraig, who would most certainly have killed you at the first opportunity."

My eyes widened. "Why would he have killed me? Is he in league with Tukailaan?" It wasn't like I'd intentionally picked this rock out of all the rocks in the world to cause trouble for someone, especially not these creatures that I didn't know existed until today.

"Padraig and Tukailaan are twin brothers. But while Padraig does bear a grudge against humans, they are certainly not in league. I do not know what all Tukailaan did in the past, but Padraig was there for it, so he is most strongly averted to him of all."

"How did you know that I didn't know?"

"I knew you were oblivious because your ability only worked when you touched the rock. Someone who unknowingly has Possession of a rock cannot use the abilities unless his or her skin is in direct physical contact with it. What person would ever think of trying out an ability they did not know they had? Thus, it only worked for you by accident.

"The last time I saw you in the Vorbiaquam, it was dark outside. So I was able to find your general location by the stars I could see in the sky above you and the constellations they made. Once I was as sure as I could be, I sent Shaun to collect you. I doubted you would come with me."

"You're probably right about that," I mumbled. "No offense."

"In any case, since we have settled on the fact that you *are* the Possessor beyond the shadow of a doubt, we should now find out what it will allow you to do, besides somewhat being able to see through water."

"Okay." I stood slowly. "But wait, I don't even know your name. Who are you?"

"Oh, of course. I am Gaedyen. I will spare you my lineage, as I believe that is not part of the traditional human greeting."

"Okay, thanks, I guess." What was the polite response to that? "I'm Enzi, and I'll spare you my lineage, too."

"Excellent. Now, it is my suspicion that this rock, as it belongs to my realm, has provided you with versions of the gifts of the Gwythienians. Besides seeing through the water, we can turn invisible. So we will start with invisibility."

"Start! What do you mean 'start'?"

"Try to be invisible."

The crazy thing was, of course, that I *had* done that before, and as demanding as this creature was, I wanted to impress him, or at least surprise him. So I closed my eyes and found the wall, but it was perfectly smooth—no crack. When I touched the stone, the fissure appeared. I tugged at it, pushed on it, but I couldn't get through. "Well I was able to make it happen twice yesterday, but for some reason I'm struggling right now. Any tips?"

"You should not need to be touching it now that you know of your Possessorship, but your being a human could be getting in the way of the laws of nature, I suppose. Try again."

I tried and failed. Maybe because I was human I lost the ability to turn invisible once I knew of my Possessorship. This was getting too complicated. "Why does it even matter if I can turn invisible on demand or not?"

"Because you may need the ability while we are traveling. We are going to visit the other realms, remember? And vast as Odan Terridor is, it does not stretch all the way to Maisius Arborii, which is located in your South America, of course. And even if it did, your scent would give us away if we journeyed through my realm the whole way. So we must instead travel through your world, the above ground, and we will likely both need to be invisible at some point."

"So you can turn invisible too? And wait, South America? Like the continent?"

"Yes, I hatched with the gift. And yes, the continent."

Well it would be interesting to see whose was stronger in the end. I hoped it would be mine. Was that even possible? "But if we're going to another world, why do we need to go that far? Can't we get into the next world straight from here? Would the rock help?"

"No, the rock does not work that way. The entrance into Maisius Arborii is located near Venezuela, so that is where we must go. Now, show me how you turn invisible."

I was too caught off guard to just make it work with him watching. "Can't you give me any hints?" I hedged. "How do *you* turn invisible?"

"Among the Gwythienians, it is not something that can be taught to the young ones, it is something they must figure out. And once they do figure it out, they are equally incapable of describing it other than saying they wanted to be invisible and then they were."

"Okay." Didn't they have a slippery mental wall they had to push through to get to the ability? Or was that just a wonky *me* thing? I closed my eyes. Trying again, I thought, *I want to be invisible. I want to be invisible. I need to be invisible.* I strained toward the rift in the wall, but I barely reached it, much less tore through it. "Can you still see me?" I was pretty certain of the answer.

His whole body sagged. "Absolutely."

"Well it would be nice if you had some tips. I'd like to know how the creatures who are supposed to do it are able to."

His brow furrowed. "Sometimes when the young ones finally figure it out, it is as a result of being frightened and inadvertently using invisibility as a defense mechanism. They wish they were invisible because they need to disappear to be safe. And then they are. Maybe it is because you do not really feel like you need to be invisible."

"Well maybe—"

"Shh! Someone is coming!" he whispered harshly. "Be quiet and stay here. And whatever you do, *do not make any noise.*" He slunk away into deeper darkness, dragging a long tail behind him. The tip of it flicked into the light for an instant, revealing an almost diamond-like shape on the end.

Well, that was reassuring. I sat back down and tried to listen for whatever it was that he'd heard. Several silent moments passed.

A huge hand covered my mouth—my whole face—as a strong arm wrapped around my waist and dragged me backward. My mind flashed back to Caleb grabbing me before I could escape. I felt the panic attack coming on...

I struggled—the self-defense instructors had told me not to give up so easily—trying to shout for help as loud as I could, but my pleas were muffled. I bit down hard on the hand, and when it jerked away, I tried to scream. The scream was always hard to get out. It was more like a gurgle.

"Quiet, human, be quiet!" Gaedyen's voice was there again, urgently shushing me. "It is only me! Calm down! I can still see you."

I tore away from him and breathed heavily, heart thundering and eyes brimming. "What the heck were you thinking! Why'd you grab me? You expect me not to scream when I'm attacked and dragged off? What the heck, man?" I shook with the memories his actions conjured, dragging my hands over my face to remove the tears.

"We needed to see if feeling endangered would make invisibility come to you. I was trying to help," he replied, completely unabashed.

What an idiot. My rage bubbled over. "Help? You scared me to death!" I took a long, deep breath. "Well, how'd that work for you?"

"Not at all." He frowned, sounding as pissed as I was. "You are still completely visible. And did I not expressly tell you not to scream? You had one job! Now others are going to come to investigate what made that non-Gwythienian noise!"

As if on cue, I heard a faint shout come from somewhere in the dark.

"Listen!" He cocked his head in the direction of the noise. "Did you hear that? They are already on their way!"

"And whose fault is that?" I glared up at him. "So what if they do? Maybe they won't appreciate you bringing me to this place that's supposed to be a secret from humans and all that, but won't they be glad to find out that one of the rocks has been found?"

"You are missing the point!"

He grabbed me around the middle with one long forearm and hoisted me against his side. In less than a second, he was bounding on his other three legs toward a light in the distance.

"I just told you our Keeper has a grudge against humans! And you are in Possession of our rock! You are not a Gwythienian or even a member of any of the other realms! You are a human, a human! If they find you, you are dead!"

CHAPTER THIRTEEN

"Well thanks for dragging me into this nice little death trap! What the heck were you thinking, having Shaun bring me to some place where everyone wants to kill me? So much for needing me alive." *Was I going to die here?* I trembled.

He raced ahead tripod-style without answering my question. I slammed uncomfortably against his side with every stride.

As soon as we reached the opening in the floor, he dove through it and we dropped straight down. My stomach thrilled at the fall. I would've screamed, but the terror stuck in my throat. There was a whoosh, like wind against thick fabric, as he unfurled a pair of mighty wings and we abruptly slowed.

My eyes hurt from the sudden bright light and the wind of our movement. Everything was a blur. When my vision cleared, the view was disorienting. We'd exited through the floor, and yet—instead of caves or tunnels—we were gliding over a vibrant scene.

It looked like we fell out of the sky over a vivacious spread of nature. The lush green foliage and trickling stream several dozen feet beneath us didn't belong underground. The exotic plants looked like they should be in a jungle, or some other unusual place. Their leaves, stems, and flowers were all different from the ones I was used to from home.

I looked down at the massive arms—if you could call them that—that kept me airborne. Smooth, reddish-brown scales covered their bulging muscles. He had long, flat fingers and wide toes. He held me straight against him, one long arm around my shoulders and another reaching down over my legs. Could I trust this thing not to let me fall? I gripped his arms tighter with my own, just in case. The scales were blunt and cool under my fingers.

We dropped close to the ground and banked left, my body swinging out against the turn. The ground rushed up as he let go and I flopped unceremoniously onto the hard dirt floor. My velocity rolled me forward for a couple seconds before I finally skidded to a halt. A sharp rock cut my face and a larger one bruised my shin as I crash-landed. He met the ground gracefully a small distance away and then turned to cross the distance between us.

For the first time, I saw his whole body. He did look a lot like a dragon, except for the newt-like shape of his head. He was reddish-brown all over, redder in some places and more brown in others. He was about twenty feet long. Nearly half of his body was the powerful, lizard-like tail.

I couldn't read his facial expression, but everything about him glowed with regality. He didn't slither like a lizard. He approached like a king: quick but smooth, bearing himself well and never stumbling.

"Ouch," I emphasized, scowling at him as I brushed myself off.

"I am sorry. But you did not give me much of a choice. I had no chance to prepare to carry you in flight and thus no chance to consider how I would land without the use of either my fore or hind legs and without crushing you. We Gwythienians do not usually carry fragile, living things or have to land without legs," he scoffed, as if this was the most obvious thing in the world.

"Well then, how did I get into Odan Terridor?"

"Shaun brought you down." He glanced behind him.

I followed his gaze but didn't see anything. "And he carried me the whole way? Come on, dude. The kid has some biceps going for him, sure, but I'm no ballerina."

"Shaun brought you down," he repeated more forcefully, avoiding my eyes.

"Okay." I stood and continued to brush dirt out of my clothes. Why so touchy? I was the one who'd been dropped out of the sky. He had nothing to be pissy about. "So, now what? Aren't we on the run from someone trying to kill me? Why'd we stop here?"

"There has been a change of plan. We *were* going to travel through the root tunnels up high to get to the Vorbiaquam, and then go back into the root tunnels to get into the above ground…"

So the floor had been made of *roots*! That's why it felt like a pile of potatoes. Where did they come from?

"…but they heard you scream, so we had to abandon that plan. They may have already found your scent there. We will have to go through Odan Terridor itself to get to the Vorbiaquam and then take stone tunnels back out. Now listen closely. You absolutely must not wander away from me and you must do what I say while we are here."

I scoffed. "You want me to do whatever you say after you had me brought to a place where everyone wants to kill me?"

His frown deepened. "If you had listened in the first place and had not screamed, we would still be safely discussing our plan of action in peace where no one would have thought to interrupt. Now, because you did not heed my words, you are scratched and bruised and my whole plan is compromised. I am having to alter it on the fly, which is never a good idea.

"But the core of the matter is that this is not your world, and if you want to survive you are going to have to take my advice. I know things about this place that you do not. Once again, I am not asking you to trust a total stranger whose species you did not even know existed an hour ago, I am asking you to take the advice of someone who wants you to stay alive and who knows every aspect of Odan Terridor better than you. Will you please respect my decisions while we are down here? That is your best chance for survival."

As much as it hurt my pride, I had to admit he made an excellent point. I knew nothing about this world. Exciting as that was, it was also serious enough that my life was in danger. But I still didn't appreciate all his crap about me screaming. He was totally asking for that, grabbing me from behind like a creep. And while the running and flying and crash-landing had distracted me, they hadn't purged the freshly-stirred up memories from my mind.

But I didn't want to think about that.

Dad had been right about the monsters. Maybe he wasn't that crazy after all. If I stuck with this creature, maybe I could find a way to help him. I had to try.

"Alright, fine. I'll follow your lead." I flicked my hand at the air, rolling my eyes. "But why do we have to go to the Vorbiaquam thingy first? Why can't we just leave?"

"Because there is information that we need to have in order to enter the first realm."

"What kind of information?"

"I will show you when we get there. I flew us over the shallower shrubbery, from now on there will be high enough brush for you to walk under, though you may have to duck occasionally."

"Why didn't you turn invisible when you were flying just now?"

"Because you were unable to call upon the rock's power to turn invisible yourself, I had to remain visible to shield you from sight. We were fortunate no one was on the ground beneath us. That was a poor method of escape.

"Until we reach the road, it would be more noticeable to any other Gwythienian who might happen upon us if I were to go invisible, because I would still be moving plants and leaving foot prints. They would wonder why I was trying to hide. So while I choose to remain visible now to be less conspicuous, I urge you to continue to try to turn yourself invisible as we run. And avoid touching anything as much as possible. The air smells of human enough without your scent being on every object you cross, and it would seem very conspicuous for there to be moving shrubs a few feet *away* from me. Alright? Now we move."

He took off before me and I jogged after him, hating once again how out of shape I was. It was hard to keep up. I focused on the arrow-like tip of his giant lizard's tail and tried to stay within a few feet of it while dodging thick, green stalks and giant leaves as much as possible.

I sought out the crack in the wall many times. I tried it with the rock tucked into my shirt, bouncing against my skin. He'd said that once you knew you had Possession, it should work without being in contact with your skin, but maybe my being human screwed that up. So I pulled the necklace off and held the stone tightly in my fist, fighting the mental blockades again, without success. I put it back on, but the way it bounced as I ran worried me that the clasp might break and I might lose it, so I tucked it back in for safekeeping.

We ran around rocky corners and through stone archways covered in lichen; past large, strange plants and over small sparkling creeks. A few minutes in, I stumbled and leaned against the rock wall, panting and feeling sick. To say that running was not my thing would be the understatement of the century.

Gaedyen realized that I'd fallen behind and walked back to me, glancing stealthily to either side on his way. "Really, human—Enzi. You are going to have to get used to running if you are going to make this journey," he scolded me quietly. "We are almost to the Vorbiaquam."

I was about to tell him exactly what I thought about that, when he scrunched his mouth and nose together and looked down at the floor as if in concentration. His earflaps drooped toward the ground. Then he looked up abruptly, eyes wide, earflaps pointing up and out. "Someone is coming! Hurry!"

I rolled my eyes. He'd better be serious this time. Although, did I really want that? I darted off after him again, fresh adrenaline encouraging my tired legs to pump a bit faster. I did *not* want to die for accidentally touching the wrong rock when I was a little kid.

A few moments later we neared the biggest tunnel entrance we'd passed yet, and he veered toward it. "That's the Vorbiaquam. Go in there!" he pointed, panting. "There is an engraving on the ceiling—a map of the realms. Find Maisius Arborii and—"

"Gaedyen!" a huge voice boomed from behind us.

Gaedyen's face fell as if that was the one voice he did *not* want to hear from.

"What's Masius Arborii?" How was I supposed to find this—whatever it was—if I didn't even know what I was looking for?

"Bottom of the map, surrounded by etchings of trees. Find out which direction to take first after crossing the ocean. Now *go!*" He nosed me through the entrance with his giant face just as the huge voice rumbled again, "Gaedyen! Answer me!"

CHAPTER FOURTEEN

*H*eart pounding, I rushed through the dark entrance, hoping the speaker wouldn't see me and fearing that he'd smell my scent. I looked back to check if Gaedyen was still behind me, but I was alone. I guessed he waited outside the entrance to stall our company.

So I needed to find a map, and fast. I looked up at the ceiling of the tunnel and noticed that further ahead there were wispy bits of shining color dancing on it, calling to my curiosity. I hurried through the short tunnel, checking the ceiling for carvings every couple steps. A sound like rushing water grew louder.

Next thing I knew, I was in a huge, open cavern, with walls of waterfalls. They plunged into a rippling pool that filled the floor of the vast room as far as I could see. A long bridge of land stretched out from where I stood, splitting the room in half. The dirt under my shoes was soft and moist, and had shiny little flecks in it, like fool's gold or something. The cavern was so long I couldn't see the end of it.

I expected to find the stone ceiling green with slimy, algae-like growths—maybe dripping some dirty, moldy water here and there—but instead, it was smooth as glass, reflecting the water below.

a romantic person, but this would be *the place*
c rendezvous. The ceiling reflected the way the
_____ light danced across the strange pool, as if it reflected
the very soul of the water. It mirrored every liquid movement
of the little waves, every glimmer of light that floated across the
surface. These were the reflections I'd seen in the entrance. It
was breathtakingly beautiful.

I hurried across the land bridge, admiring the dancing blues
and greens on the ceiling. Underneath the shimmers, there
were deep cuts in the rock. As I slowed to peer at them, images
like trees and mountains came into focus. The whole thing was
decorated with an abundance of strange runes. Small, frequent
cuts in the stone grouped to run in different directions seemed
to indicate landmasses and bodies of water.

This was what I needed. The whole thing rang a bell in
the back of my mind, as if the map resembled shapes I'd seen
together before.

From where I stood facing the far side of the cavern, the
trees on the map seemed upside down. I jogged to the far end
to locate the bottom of the map and hopefully what I was sent
to find.

Reaching where the images on the ceiling ended, I turned
to face it from the right direction. Runes of another language
intermingled with English words on the map and around its
edges. From the orientation of things, I looked at the bottom
of it, where I was apparently supposed to find trees. There were
trees everywhere, but underneath a line of large runes, I saw
"Maisius Arborii" written with English letters.

Alright, something about directions…

After a few moments, I found it:

Take the skyway
Southwest from the northmost
Follow the river
From the ocean coast

A sharp left at the falls
You must now fly eastward
If you come with good intentions
Our greeting will be peaceful

Cross the greatest lake
Search now for the tree
You will know it when you see it
Do not doubt history

When on the horizon
That great tree appears
If your approach has been hidden
You must now yourself reveal

The guard is on the watch
So if invisible you fly
Reveal yourself at once
Or you shall surely die

Southwest from the northmost, and then east at the waterfall?
But wouldn't he need the rest of the information there, too? I
mean knowing which direction to go first was great, but what
good would it do if he didn't know *when* to change direction? I
was supposed to take his word for everything, but between this
and the surprise earlier, I couldn't say his reasoning skills had
been exceptionally impressive so far.

Would I be able to remember the whole thing? It wasn't
that long, but my memory wasn't exactly flawless. Trying to

break through that wall to use my invisibility was taxing on my brainpower. Writing it down would be a good idea.

How could I copy it without paper or a pen? I felt in my jeans pockets for anything that might be useful. A wadded-up receipt from the other day…but the laundromat had seen these jeans since then and the paper crumbed to pieces in my hands.

I looked around for a large rock or piece of wood to carve into. Nothing but water and dirt besides the stone ceiling. Absolutely nothing useful. With my hands on my hips, I glared up at the map again.

I was almost willing to prick my finger and copy the directions on my sweatshirt with my own blood, but I had nothing to even prick my finger with and I didn't think I could handle biting myself that hard. So I reread it again, doing my best to commit it to memory. We were in a hurry, so I couldn't spend all day on it. I headed back for the entrance tunnel and then tiptoed through it, listening for that voice that had kept Gaedyen outside and hoping it was gone. Not only was it still there, it was still yelling at Gaedyen.

As I eavesdropped silently, I hoped that somehow he wouldn't detect my scent.

"Why do you insist on continuing with this, Gaedyen?" the deeper voice bellowed. "You know that they are dead! *Dead!* Nothing will bring them back! No matter how much either of us may want it! And no amount of fraternizing with the other realms, or the *humans* of all things, will help fix anything. The best you can do is to *stay out of it!* If I catch you here again, you know what will happen. Do. Not. Make. Me." The slow emphasis placed on those last four words was positively menacing. "And please tell me, why do you reek of human stink?"

My heart picked up speed again. How was Gaedyen going to get us out of this?

"I was in the root tunnels when I came across the scent. I followed it here into the Vorbiaquam, but it was empty. I was hoping to pick up the trail when you barreled over to rage at me. Again."

"The root tunnels, hmm?" There was a pause, and then, "I do not know what you are up to, but I will believe you when you bring me the human and do away with it. Now leave this place!"

With a steely tone, Gaedyen said, "Of course, Padraig," and walked the opposite direction of me.

Crap! Crap! Crap! That was Padraig? The one who'd want me dead more than any of the others if he knew about me? Padraig wouldn't come in here, would he? And Gaedyen wouldn't turn me over to him, right? He needed me alive…didn't he?

Once Gaedyen's slow footfalls completely receded, Padraig grunted and walked off in another direction. I held my breath until he, too, was out of earshot.

Several minutes passed without a sign of Gaedyen. I sweated and paced. Why hadn't he returned? Was Padraig watching him to make sure he didn't come back? From their argument, it sounded like Gaedyen wasn't supposed to be here. Should I go look for him? That would be a great idea if I were able to… I don't know… like, use my ability to turn invisible or something. I gave it another try, but nothing. I didn't know what I was doing. What had I done differently before?

Despite my frustration, my curiosity got the better of me. I tiptoed toward the entrance to the tunnel and peeked outside. No Gaedyen, no Padraig—unless Padraig could turn invisible. *Hmm…that could be a real problem.* But if he wasn't Possessor anymore, then he shouldn't be able to, right? Unless he was one of those—what was it called?—Cadoumai.

I stepped back into the tunnel and took a deep breath. *I need to turn invisible.* I put all my focus on that. Closing my eyes, I pushed thoughts of Gaedyen and Shaun and Padraig from my mind. Just me and the fissure in the wall. I fought my way through it, tearing bits of rubble away, clawing deeper and deeper into it. When I opened my eyes, my hands were gone.

I looked down at my feet and legs, and they were gone, too. I'd done it! *Yes!*

Tiptoeing to the entrance again, I looked around for other life forms. I saw no one, and double-checked once more that I still couldn't see myself, either. My ability remained functional, so I took a careful step out into the light. My heart pounded. What if they still saw me? What if I became visible again without meaning to? What if my human scent was so strong that it didn't matter whether or not I'd disappeared from sight?

But I had to do something. I couldn't stay in the Vorbiaquam for the rest of my life.

So as quietly as possible, I crept under the foliage, keeping my distance from the plants themselves so as not to rustle them and give away my position—like Gaedyen taught me earlier. A few minutes into my slinking, I came to a dirt path. I considered the benefits of hiding in plain sight, walking invisibly on the path with no cover instead of sneaking through the brush that might give me away.

Soft footsteps approached. I froze, holding my breath. Something I couldn't see walked past me, making just enough noise that I could barely tell it was there.

I looked down to check that I was still invisible. Phew! No feet. But then I heard a fateful noise—a *sniff*, coming from a few feet away. The footsteps ceased. Another sniff and a step in my direction.

Oh no! I'd been discovered!

And then a whisper. "Enzi?"

Was it Gaedyen? Should I reply? Or was it a trick for some other Gwythienian to find me? But he wouldn't have told anyone my name, and only so many Gwythienians can turn invisible, right?

"Enzi? Is that you? It is me, Gaedyen."

From what I'd learned today, another Gwythienian would've flipped out over the scent of a human here in their realm. This must be him.

"Gaedyen?"

He flickered into being right in front of me, and to my horror, I became visible without meaning to. I'd lost my focus again. Why did this have to be so hard to control!

"Ah! There you are. You turned invisible! Well done!"

His praise improved my mood. "Thanks." I smiled.

"Can you do it again?" he disappeared.

I tried to relax and clear my head. But once again, nothing. "I can't get it to work."

"Alright. Then stay in the brush, touching as little as possible, and follow close to me. I have given Padraig reason to believe that I am in another section of Odan Terridor, looking for you. He will be trying to keep an eye on me there. We should not meet him on our way, but we must hurry. If he notices I am gone, he may look for me here."

"Then let's go."

I sniffed the air myself to try to get an idea of what a Gwythienian smelled like, but my nose couldn't sense a thing other than a damp, earthy tinge. They must have better scent-detecting abilities than humans.

Walking through Odan Terridor was like walking through a dream. Not quite as enchanting as the water room, but still beautiful and awe-inspiring. While it was gray and cold and wintery where I lived somewhere above this place, here it was warm and blue and felt more like a jungle than an underground cave.

A blue light with no evident source illuminated the whole place. It was a peaceful, calming sort of blue. I liked it.

As I struggled to match Gaedyen's free pace from the cramped underbrush, I noticed several other dark tunnels leading away from the rock wall on the other side of the dirt path. I looked up, expecting to find a cave-like rock ceiling above us. But instead, I saw the fantastic surface of tightly woven tree roots that I knew from earlier. The roots were of all sizes and lengths, and according to Gaedyen, they contained many tunnels of their own.

We passed strange rock formations and more greenery than was scientifically supposed to exist without a sun, increasing my curiosity about the blue light. Not only was it impossible to tell where it came from, but it must provide some sort of photosynthesis stuff for the plants, right? How could it do that?

Gaedyen's footsteps quickened and I tried in vain to follow suit.

"Enzi, you must cross the path and enter the foliage on the other side. I am visible again, blocking the view from the direction we came. Run behind me now."

I darted out of the brush and toward the other side of the road, but then something swiped my legs right out from under me and I slid painfully on my butt toward the rock wall. Leafy vines covered the place I headed for. I braced for impact, but felt nothing more than the brush of soft leaves as I sailed through them.

What? Was I in another tunnel? Did Gaedyen know that was there? Had he pushed me into it on purpose?

Then he growled, "What do you want, Padraig?"

Padraig? Again? I turned my body silently to face out of the cave, and through the screen of leaves I saw the huge hulking dragon that stared Gaedyen down. Padraig's skin was lighter than Gaedyen's—closer to beige. And his most noticeable feature was an x-shaped scar that reached across his whole face. The lines met over one eye, extending from his forehead to his mouth. He was taller than Gaedyen and looked on him with fierce displeasure. His arms and legs bulged with solid cords of muscle. I hoped the leaves were thick enough to hide my face.

"What do *I* want? I have told you and told you and told you, but you never listen! Without the rock to pass on Possessorship and Keepership, you are the most plausible candidate to keep the peace after I am dead. Your gift is so strong! And how better to regain the goodwill of your people, after what happened?

"But do you care? Do you put an ounce of effort into learning how to deal with the people of your own race or the people of the others? No! You run around like a hatchling, staring off into space and disappearing to places that you have been warned away from over and over again! And stinking of human! What have you been doing to cause that? You do not care about anything, you keep running away from your responsibilities! You are just like your father!"

Gaedyen reared up onto his back legs and let out a bellowing roar that shook my bones and literally bounced my knees off the stone floor where I knelt.

"You leave my father out of this!" he thundered as his front legs came crashing back to the ground. Uncontrollable rage rippled off his body.

I trembled.

"Do not *ever*…" Gaedyen started to threaten, and then seemed to change his mind. "If you had not run him off just as you have alienated me, maybe things would have been different."

"You dare blame me for what he did?" stormed Padraig. "I will have you know—"

"I do not care what you have to say!" roared Gaedyen with such passion my stomach dropped to my toes. "You always say the same things! We argue in circles and never reach conclusions. I have long been weary of this miserable circle, Padraig. I am finished with you. Do you hear me? I am leaving this cursed realm and if I ever see you again, you will regret it. Do you understand me? I bow to no one, now." Gaedyen's voice had gotten much quieter by the end of his threat, but the ferocity of his words and tone were still very audible.

They stared each other down, the tension causing their limbs to shake. This sounded like an argument between family members. Like all of the supports that bent under the strain of the relationship for far too long had finally snapped, tearing what sounded like a life altering rift between the two. Kind of like what lies did to me and Mom. I realized with a little pain in my stomach that I missed her, despite that.

The two angry dragons breathed heavily for several moments, glaring at each other until Padraig turned and walked steadily away. Gaedyen stayed where he was, staring after him.

Many long seconds later, warm air blew in my face as he parted the vines with his nose and breathed, "It is time to go."

CHAPTER FIFTEEN

*H*is words rang weighty with deep exhaustion, as if he'd run a marathon and hadn't yet quenched his thirst, or hadn't slept in days and couldn't find the strength to say anything more.

Emotional exhaustion—I'd recognize it anywhere. There may be nothing physical about the cause, but the physical effect could be earth-shattering.

I turned and walked further into the cave, realizing too late that I didn't want to be the trailblazer here. Why was I in front? Well, it was too late to change that. I was glad at least to be moving slower than we had earlier.

Eventually the tunnel shrank so drastically that Gaedyen had to crawl, and though I didn't have to stoop yet, I kept bumping into the uneven walls and ceiling. Since I was blinded by darkness, I walked like a mummy brought back to life with my arms straight out in front of me.

Neither of us had spoken since entering the tunnel, so I tried to piece together what I could in my mind. Padraig had some kind of problem with Gaedyen's father, who apparently wasn't around. It sounded like a family argument. Was Gaedyen related to the Keeper?

And what was Padraig's problem with humans anyway? If he wanted to be friendly with all the "other realms," why not humans too? And why had we been excluded from having a rock like all the other races? Maybe humankind was too drastically different from whatever the "other realms" were. Maybe as different as they were from the Gwythienians.

"Wait." His voice echoed all around us. "Something is not right."

I stopped in my tracks, my trail of thought interrupted. "That doesn't sound good," was my profoundly witty reply.

"Another Gwythienian has been here. It has been a long time, and it is a scent I do not recognize. It feels out of place…"

"Don't Gwythienians travel through the tunnels often?"

"Not this tunnel. It is very old, and they seldom have reason to visit the human realm."

"Could it be that Tukailaan guy you mentioned earlier? I know you said you don't recognize it, but if he left before you were born—er, hatched—then you might not know his scent, would you?" My whispers echoed all around us.

"Perhaps. But there is something familiar about it. Scents tend to run similar between family members, and this does smell a bit like Padraig, actually. But…" His voice trailed off as he sniffed. "It also smells a bit like *you*. Perhaps I am just picking up your scent because you are here. But this smell is so old. It could not possibly be a threat…but I ought to pass through first, just in case."

It smelled like *me*? How? "Well I appreciate your chivalry dude, but in case you haven't noticed, the walls are still a little tight for us to switch places. How do you suggest we accomplish that?"

He sighed with more exaggeration than was necessary. "The ceiling is taller here than the walls are wide, and I cannot risk crawling over you because I might crush you. But you must never reveal to anyone that I allowed you to pass over me. Do you understand?"

"Um, no actually I don't. Why is that such a problem?"

He huffed and bumped his head on the ceiling. He probably tried to straighten his neck to its full height to look superior to me as he responded to my idiot-human question.

"Of course, you would not know. Humans have no sense of propriety. It is the highest sign of vulnerability and surrender to bow to another person and willingly allow them to step over you or stand above you. When a battle is fought, the winner steps upon the body of the defeated one to declare his victory. When a youngling is reprimanded, he must bow to his authority before he can be excused. When a male chooses his mate, he publicly lowers himself before her to show that he has made his choice and humbly asks her to choose him as well. She will stand over him in front of all those who are present and either honor and accept him by shortly stepping back off, or humiliate and refuse him by walking right over him and leaving the place without a backward glance." He gulped a little and spoke a bit more quietly. "By asking you to walk over me, according to my peoples' culture, I practically asked you to be my mate, fully expecting you to refuse me. A severely unprecedented act."

"Well, uh, don't worry about it," I said lamely, feeling a little awkward and feeling stupid for feeling that way. "That's not how I would see it, so it doesn't have to be weird." Why couldn't I think of anything more helpful?

"As you say," he mumbled, hesitating for a moment before lowering himself completely to the ground. I couldn't see his face in the dark, but I sensed the disgusted expression in his tone.

"What, do you have a Gwythienian girlfriend waiting for you back home or something? Do you think this will bother her? I promise not to tell."

No answer.

I narrowed my eyes. Well, either way, I *was* the last person in the world another girl would be jealous of. "Or you can let me keep walking in front." The scent was old, wasn't it? He was probably overreacting about it anyway.

He sighed. "You humans. No propriety. Just do it."

I stepped toward him, blinded by the darkness in the tunnel, wondering how to go about climbing over a dragon. I started the process by tripping and getting the breath knocked out of me when I landed on his massive arm. He snorted. Rolling my eyes, I picked myself up and continued over his large head.

"Ouch! Not my eye, human!"

"Sorry!" I winced, not having meant to hurt him, though he probably deserved it after all he'd put me through.

As I crawled over his immense back, it felt more like rough skin than hard scales. When I reached the other side and found the ground again, Gaedyen immediately raised himself into a crouch and continued forward as fast as a twenty-something foot long lizard could travel through a small space.

He was being ridiculous, but whatever. He probably wouldn't understand a lot of human traditions and cultural things. What aspects of my world that would seem common place enough to a human would be as strange to him as this was to me?

So Gaedyen slunk on and I kept walking until I was sure we must have walked past the mysterious non-threatening threat. As I ran my left hand along the wall, the smooth surface gave way to a crumbling pile of debris and then abruptly formed a flat, uniform surface again a few feet further on. It was as if another passage had been sealed off with the rubble.

"I think I passed, like, a blocked hole in the wall or something."

"Yes, I felt it too. Strange, since none of the other tunnels into Odan Terridor have blocked off extra passages. I only recently discovered this one, but Padraig was nearby so I did not have the time to scout this far ahead. I do not know what that could be."

"Are all the realms reached through tunnels?"

"In a way, though the tunnels into Odan Terridor are probably the most lengthy."

"It sounds like the one that we're going to—the one that the poem was about—is in the trees. How could there be a tunnel in the trees?"

"Each of the realms is protected all the way around by something like an invisible wall that is not exactly physical. If humans or members of other realms come near that protection, they unconsciously turn slightly away from it. It is impossible to run into. You mean to go one way and keep thinking that is the way that you are going. It can even manipulate compasses.

"Members of the realm can come and go as they please through any part of the protection, but others can only come through certain openings in the wall. And each realm only has directions to one of the other realms—a sort of security measure.

"We needed the direction poem, called a 'liryk', to tell us how to get to that opening. It will of course be heavily guarded by Cadoumai, the most gifted. But they will acknowledge us and we can have our say. If we went stumbling around in the jungle looking for it, they would set a Cadoumai to keep an eye on us and just wait for us to leave.

"So then which was it? West first, or East?"

"We have to start from some northmost point, then go southwest from there, then east at the falls. I didn't have anything to write the rest on, so I'm really hoping you didn't need it."

"Take the skyway *southwest* from the *northmost*, follow the river from the ocean coast. A sharp left at the falls, you must now fly *eastward*. If you come with good intentions, our greeting will be peaceful. Cross the greatest lake—search now for the tree. You will know it when you see it, do not doubt history. When on the horizon that great tree appears, if your approach has been hidden you must now yourself reveal. The guard is on the watch, so if invisible you fly, reveal yourself at once or you shall surely die."

Wow. He has a nice voice, too. Like Shaun. Nothing like Caleb.

"Why'd I have to get the information if you already knew it all?"

"I could not remember which directions were supposed to go in which part. I have spent a lot of time in that room. I used to have every scrap of that map memorized. But it has been several years now. It seems though that I still remember portions of it, even if not the most important parts."

"Why'd you used to spend a lot of time in there? And why don't you anymore?"

He took a long breath. "For reasons I cannot discuss."

I frowned. So secretive! *Well fine then. I see how it is.* What possible reasons did he have for being in there that needed to be kept secret?

Finally, the tunnel widened once again and I heard Gaedyen move more easily, as his steps were farther apart and less cramped. We rounded a curve in the passage and light appeared in the distance. I blinked involuntarily.

"We are approaching an entrance into the above ground. We will be enjoying your human realm weather soon."

As predicted, it got colder as we neared the exit. The first chilling breeze to make it past Gaedyen's hulking form froze me to the bone. I regretted choosing a sweatshirt instead of a thick coat when I went outside to talk to Shaun. That felt like ages ago.

It snowed outside, of course, and the cold temporarily swept everything but the need to get warm from my mind. "A-Are we still in T-Tennessee?" I said through chattering teeth.

"Yes, we are." He seemed unfazed by the frigid wind.

"So can you, like, b-breathe fire or something? Not to b-be high-maintenance or anything, but we're r-really going to get frostbite out here if we don't do something to warm up."

He looked at me like I spoke Arabic.

"You know, *haahh*." I breathed out a puff of swirling white fog in a lame attempt at reenacting my idea of a fire-breathing dragon. My breath turned into little icy particles instead of an inferno.

"Oh yes, that." Gaedyen sat back on his haunches. "I am afraid the classic fire-breathing dragon is nothing more than a human myth. There are no creatures in any realm that have the ability to exhale anything more interesting than used air."

I rolled my eyes. "Great. Th-then what are we g-going to do about staying warm? I mean, going back into the t-tunnel would help a bit but the wind can still get in there. And I'm no boy scout. I don't know how to st-start a fire without matches or a lighter in good weather, much less in snowy wind. Don't you crazy dr-dragon-people ever make fires? Like, to cook food or anything?"

"Not often. We eat our food fresh and raw and rarely have the need to build a fire for anything else. But I do have a vague idea of how to build one."

"Okaaay," I said, my eyes now too cold to roll. "Can you give it a try now?"

"Of course."

"I'll meet you in the t-tunnel entrance." I turned shakily and slumped back to the gaping hole, rubbing my thin-sleeved arms vigorously to create some warming friction. *He* was the one who wanted to go on a fantastic adventure. I hadn't invited myself. If he wanted so badly for me to come along, he could provide the way to keep us from freezing to death. "Wait." I turned back to him. "Is it safe for us to be there? Won't Padraig look for us?

"We will be safe here for the night. Padraig will not want to tell anyone what happened between us. It would greatly embarrass him. Nor should we worry about him coming after us himself. After what was said, he will not. So we should be safe enough here. He may expect me to cool off and come home. He will not search for me."

"G-good enough for muh-me." I crouched against one wall trying to hold in a little warmth, wishing to no end that I had a nice thick blanket, or even my ratty old quilt. Anything to conserve some valuable heat.

His hulking form vanished from the entrance, returning minutes later with a mouth full of sticks. In no time, he had a small fire crackling on the stone floor. I reached toward the fire to warm my hands. It was a welcome improvement, but I was still cold. I curled up as close to the flames as I could and used my arm for a pillow. It was going to be a long night.

"Ahem." Gaedyen cleared his throat and I opened my eyes. "Would you care to have a wing of mine? I do not intend to be forward, but I understand that you are a good deal more uncomfortable with the weather than I am and as you have insufficient covering, and do not seem to have the same rules of etiquette that we observe, I... thought I would offer."

He seemed to be very uncomfortable with himself at suggesting this, which was kind of cute, in a way. Despite his tendency to terrify the living daylights out of me every chance he got, being as frigidly miserable as I was, I took him up on the offer.

"Yeah, I'll 'take a wing' or whatever. I'm beyond freezing and I don't want my fingers and toes to start falling off. Thanks." I didn't really want to be that close to him and his scaly wings, but I could potentially freeze to death without him. So I scooted around to the other side of the fire and laid down next to him, under the wing he'd lifted.

He gently let it fall over me and my violent shivers stopped instantly. I lay there, allowing the heat stemming from his body and trapped by his wing to wash over me, mentally unclenching the many muscles I had unconsciously tightened to stay warm. From outside his wing, my eyes took in the stone ceiling of the cave above us. Gaedyen's slow breathing pushed his back in and out of view. I pulled his wing over my face, and in no time, my exhausted mind was asleep.

CHAPTER SIXTEEN

Caleb yanked my arm hard, pulling me onto my back. My bare skin itched from the sawdust.

He was there, too close. The smell—I gagged, wishing I could puke on him. Maybe then I could escape. But the nausea stayed there in my stomach while the tears leaked out. He laid the knife on the ground…

*M*y eyes flew open. The floor underneath me was hard and cold, not like the barn.

It was another dream, just a dream.

Panting, I tried to calm the hysteria rising up in my throat. I brushed my legs together and found them still clothed. My fingers clutched the sleeved ends of my sweatshirt—still on.

Yes, definitely a dream.

Something weighed on me, but softly, like a blanket. I reached to touch it and felt the taut wing-flesh of Gaedyen. *Oh no!* Did he wake up? Had he felt me flailing around? I usually kicked and squirmed during those dreams. I always woke up with a tangled mess of quilt and sheets.

I touched my face and felt tear trails. I hoped he hadn't heard my sobs. Listening carefully, there were only steady breaths coming from him. *Whew*. The ridge of his wing was smooth and cool where it brushed against my cheek with each breath.

"Hello! Ma'am, are you alright?"

The question roused me from a deep sleep and I sluggishly raised myself up from the cold, stony ground, searching for the speaker. It didn't sound like Gaedyen. Not a deep enough voice...

It was still chilly, but the incessant wind and snow had stopped. The sun was even out. I scrubbed the sleep from my eyes and opened them on a dark-haired man.

Jumping backward in the cave, I stumbled to my feet as adrenaline coursed through my veins. Was it Caleb?

No. This guy was way too old—fifties, maybe? Then why was he here? What did he want?

I looked behind me for Gaedyen, but he wasn't there. Had he been a dream? No, of course not. I would've frozen out here without him. Was he invisible back there? No, I felt too cold for him to have still been nearby a few seconds ago. And I had leaped backward, so if he were there I would've run into him.

The man stood just outside the entrance to the tunnel, peering in at me. "Are you okay?"

"Who are you?" I demanded, my voice hoarse with sleep.

"My apologies!" He backed up a few steps with arms outstretched in a placating gesture. "I had no intention of giving you the willies, I just wanted to check that you were alright—its mighty nippy hereabouts. Name's Tony."

The willies? Hereabouts? Where was this guy from? He was average height and his shoulder-length scraggly hair caught the light and framed a smile that was a few teeth short of full. His beer belly bounced as he hopped forward another step. Dirty tennis shoes partially covered hairy feet that led up to skinny ankles. A pair of baggy beige cargo pants were too short for the legs they tried to conceal. On closer inspection, he didn't really present an intimidating figure. He was just kind of gross.

"So, does that mean you're right as rain?"

I saw concern in his eyes, despite his distracting vocabulary. "Yeah, I'm good." I stood, rigid.

"Wonderful! When I saw you laying there, all still-like, I reckoned the cold might 'a licked ya. Why, that storm last night was a sight worse than any other I ever seen."

I felt kind of silly for being so afraid of him. He hardly seemed the threatening type. But still, people could be good at hiding things. "No, I'm fine. Thanks for the concern."

"Say, you look kinda familiar-like. What's yer name? Well, I guess what I mean to say is what's yer grandmother's name? Or maybe yer great grandmother's?"

What a weird question. Was he trying to make a joke? "Why?"

"Well, never mind, never mind. But what's a gal like you doin' scrouched up in the woods all alone? We're mighty far from civilization out this ways. Must 'a took ya a long time to walk all this way. How the nation did you get this far out?"

Why did he have to point out how far from civilization we were? That was not a good sign. What was this guy all about?

"I was just..." I faked a yawn to buy myself a few more seconds to fabricate something. I'd never been a convincing liar, and I doubted the skill would randomly come to me now. "...went for a run in the woods near my apartment. I ran farther than I meant to and thought this would be a good place for a rest. About to head back now, it's not far."

I hoped he wouldn't consider my size to be an obvious strike against my running story. I mean, I *had* spent a fair amount of the previous day moving a good deal faster than usual. And dang, was I sore!

Glancing past him, I saw that the storm hadn't left enough snow to stick, but the layer of fallen leaves on the ground looked soggy.

I turned the question back around on him, half-wishing Gaedyen would show up and scare the crap out of him. "What are *you* doing out here?"

"I ain't no uppity person," he wheezed cheerfully, taking a seat inside the cave. "I reckon livin' out here beats dealing with all those razzle-dazzle people out in the world. I reckon you could say I live everywhere and nowhere. Life out here's a cinch." He gestured to the sky with both hands and then brought them down in a slow half circle as if to envelop the whole world. "This whole planet's my digs! I can go wherever I want and stay as long or as short as I please. Trust me kid, this is the way to live."

So he was sort of a hippie. Who talked like Huckleberry Finn. Okay, I could deal with that.

"That's a mighty fine gemstone ya got there." He gazed at the necklace.

"Uh, yeah, thanks." I shoved the necklace back into my shirt, not wanting to draw any attention to it. I was even more worried about people seeing it now that I knew more about it. I needed to change the subject and get this guy out of here. Where was a Gwythienian when you needed one? "So if you live out here in the woods, do you like, hunt and stuff for your food?"

If I really was going on a crazy journey with a dragon-ish-thing to the other side of the world, it would probably be useful to know how I would eat on the way. Who knew whether Gaedyen knew anything about what was safe to eat above ground? Or what was safe for a human to eat in general? It might be best not to rely on his knowledge too much.

"Why…" the old man started, then his eyes flashed away to something outside the cave. "Did you know there's a man by the river yonder?"

A man? Shouldn't there be a giant lizardy thing?

I peeked around the cave wall to look in that direction but saw only naked trees and the occasional evergreen. The river must be a little farther away—far enough away that it was really weird that this guy could tell that he was there.

"What does he look like?" I asked, wondering what he would come up with.

"He's a little short o' six feet, dark skin, long hair. Denim britches and a brown top coat-sorta-thing."

I frowned. That sounded like Shaun. But there was no way Tony could've seen him from where we stood, was there? Maybe he saw him earlier, before coming here? But then why mention it now? And if it really was Shaun, I thought I wasn't supposed to see him again? Hmm, maybe I would run into him anyway. Well, no sense admitting I was out here on my own when I could use this, whether he'd really seen anyone or not. "Yeah, I know him. That's my running buddy. He was thirsty."

"Well that's grand!" Tony exhaled dramatically. "I'm glad you know him. Now I know you'll be alright, even though you look dog-tired." He smiled warmly.

Was I supposed to buy that? Did he expect me to be all grateful for his concern or something? "Yeah, I'm all good. Thanks, see ya." I hoped he would take the hint already.

"So as I was sayin'…" he started, then spluttered. "Why, I'm quite a windbag, ain't I? I better get going for now. Bye!" With that, he rushed away with considerably more agility than I expected.

Maybe he wasn't as old and frail as he'd seemed—though, the way he talked…If his hair had any grays in it, there weren't many. I heard a whooshing sound in the distance and braced myself for another freezing gust of wind, but none ever came.

So Shaun may or may not be down by the river, but where the heck is Gaedyen? Boy, would I like to tell Shaun what I thought about him kidnapping me! After he answers my questions about him and Gaedyen, of course. Off I went toward the sound of rushing water, with precisely that intention in mind.

"Where are you going?"

I swallowed a shriek, but it was only Gaedyen. "Why? What is it with you and always scaring me to death? Every time we run into each other? And where were you?"

"Answering a question with questions?"

"What? Uh, no. I ran into a guy who said someone who looks like Shaun is down by the river. I wanted to see if it was him. To tell him what I think about him kidnapping me."

"You ran into a guy? Who?" he sniffed the air, facing all different directions. "Did you see another Gwythienian?"

"No. I would've told you if I had. Why?"

"That smell is here, like the one from the tunnel. But it is fresh, very fresh." His earflaps spun around as his stance changed from comfortable to alert. "And it smells very similar to Padraig—it is not him, but it is close. That means it is likely to be Tukailaan. And… well, you said it was a human guy you saw? Perhaps that is what is confusing my nose. Enzi, we need to go. *Now.*"

CHAPTER SEVENTEEN

Gaedyen nodded toward some trees and walked—almost trotted—away. Keeping up with that pace was about the last thing I felt like doing, but I tried anyway.

"Wait up!" Why couldn't we fly? Was it about that stupid bowing thing?

"Hurry! If that is Tukailaan, we need to get far away from here before he comes back! Turn invisible if you can!"

I tried, but I couldn't concentrate. Apparently exercise made it harder to use the ability. I gave up and focused on putting one foot in front of the other.

What felt like ages later, we finally slowed to a halt. I crumpled to the ground, panting and sweating all over. Gaedyen sat on his haunches, his gaze focused on the way we came. If he stopped, we had to be safe for the moment.

"Gaedyen, look." I tried to catch my breath. "If I'm really going on this adventure journey thing with you, I need to know more about what's going on."

"Of course. What would you like to know? But please keep your voice down."

"Why are we going to Maisius Arborii first?"

"Because that is the one that we have the liryk—directions—for. Also, Padraig has spoken of their Possessor, an Adarborian named Aven. He knew her when he was young, before he was made the Keeper. I assume she is the one who knew him best out of all the other Possessors. And as they seem to have been on good terms, I believe she will be the most willing to help us. And maybe she will have an answer for why you have Possession of the rock of the Gwythienians when its last Possessor is still alive."

"Alright then. So how do we get there? Fly? How far away is it, anyway?"

"Between three and four thousand miles. And we will have to cross part of an ocean. We will get there by walking."

"Walking? Ha! Very funny."

"You are right. Obviously not just walking. There will be a fair amount of swimming as well."

I gave him a moment to tell me he was kidding, but when that response never came, I let my jaw drop. "Walking and swimming? You can't be serious."

"Yes, I am." He drew out the last couple syllables as if to ask what my problem with that was.

"Wouldn't it be faster to fly the whole way?" For a sentient species, he seemed to struggle to comprehend this.

"Yes, of course it would. But you cannot fly, so we walk. And swim." He spoke low and slow, as if explaining that two plus two equals four.

"True, I do happen to lack the ability to fly." I rolled my eyes. "But you *can* fly. And I am much smaller than you, so the sensible thing would be for me to hitch a ride on your back and you to fly us there in a fraction of the time." *Obviously.*

His head snapped up, and he looked at me in horror.

"What the heck is wrong with you?" Was he appalled because I weighed too much?

He looked like he was about to explain something else for the trillionth time, but before speaking, he closed his eyes for a moment and took a dramatically deep breath, composing himself. "Of course, I keep forgetting that the human realm is so different from my own." Then he paused as if trying to find the simplest and least embarrassing way to explain the birds and the bees to a child. "You simply…that is to say, one cannot…it simply is not socially acceptable. A little walking will not kill you."

I gaped at him. Was he calling me fat? The nerve! Who did he think he was? Well he was lucky I didn't just leave his ungrateful butt and take his precious rock with me! If I had *Possession*, or whatever it was, I could do whatever the heck I want with it, couldn't I? I was too pissed at him to make any sort of intelligible reply, so I stood there, furious and hurt.

"Well, we have rested too long as it is. We should get moving." He stood and walked away in the direction we'd been heading.

I stared after him, willing him to stop moving so I could stay still longer. But it didn't work. I dragged myself up from the ground and followed him, legs aching.

Was it just me, or was one of his shoulders a different color? It looked like a different texture too… a giant scar? Or, was it dirty? Maybe that was a hard spot to reach when bathing, if Gwythienians bathed.

Despite the running, my hands felt chilly. I stuffed them into my sweatshirt pocket. Something was in there—the debit card! I could buy a warmer jacket! That would be expensive, but I needed it. I would find a way to pay Mom back. Though, come to think of it, I would not be making any money for an indefinite period of time. Ugh… I'd have to deal with that later.

"Hey, Gaedyen! If we're going to be roughing it out here, I'm going to need some supplies. My shoes are worn through and this sweatshirt is not warm enough. Isn't there a store we could stop by for some stuff?"

He kept moving. "There might be one on the way. But that would be risky. We do not want to be seen. How badly do you need to go?"

I frowned. Hadn't I explained that? "Really bad."

"Hmm."

Hmm? How was I supposed to take that?

We walked, and walked, and walked. We passed snow-covered trees, scaled small mountains, and trampled many a pinecone. I got more and more irritable as we went. I was so cold, despite the running and sweating. Was it true that if you walk on twice as many limbs you can walk twice as fast? I was pretty sure it must be.

I occasionally noticed his earflaps flip backward. I assumed this was a way to make sure I kept up without having to waste the effort of turning around to look at me. Well, I didn't want to see his ugly face either.

Once, when his earflaps flew to rear attention, he stopped dead in his tracks and listened hard, instead of casually taking in whatever soundwaves felt like coming his way. His earflaps twitched ever so slightly in different directions, while still aiming generally backward. It reminded me of a dog or cat trying to tell where a certain sound was coming from.

I waved a hand. "I'm still he—"

His head snapped around and he cut me off with an urgent glare. His scowl bored into me for longer than I felt was necessary. I opened my mouth to tell him what I thought of that. But his eyes opened wide and he lowered his head a little, as if silently shushing me.

I caught on then. Maybe he had a good reason for keeping both of us quiet. He'd been picking up sounds for hours, and maybe now some new sound indicated danger. I sensed that he wanted me to be quiet, and I was amused that he didn't know to put his pointer finger in front of his lips and mouth "shh" or how to mime "zip your lips," because that wasn't something his culture did. That was a human thing. I made a mental note to teach him this for future reference as soon as I could.

I was hyper aware now. What kind of danger could be following us? Tukailaan? Surely not the erratic Tony...

Gaedyen raised his head, alert and intent, and stared behind us. I sensed nothing of the danger. I remembered my earlier observation that he must have keener senses than me. That was annoying.

He looked quickly down at me again, moving nothing but his head and neck, and stared at the ground under my feet. He glanced back and forth between me and my shoes a couple times, but I didn't know what he meant. Was he looking at my feet to tell me to run? Or maybe he was telling me to get down... I went with the second one, thinking I could still run if I needed to but this way I didn't make noise while I acted on my first guess. I looked at the ground as I lowered myself into an awkward crouch, and then looked back up at him.

His face relaxed slightly, but his eyes were still intense, as if trying to communicate something else. He looked to my left and then back at me. I followed his glance and saw a big branch on the ground. I pointed to it and sent a questioning look back in his direction. He nodded dramatically, earflaps aflutter. I reached out carefully to avoid losing my balance, and retrieved the stick, returning to my crouch.

He lifted his left foreleg and presented his palm—if you could call it that—and then looked vigorously back and forth from the stick in my hand to his out-stretched one. I stood to get the best possible balance for the pitch, and then flung it sloppily toward him. He reached out and caught it before it crashed to the ground, shooting a murderous glare at me afterward.

He stuck one end of the stick into the side of his mouth, bit down on it, and pulled it steadily out through his teeth, seeming to bite more firmly as it went. The sharp, pointed tip that emerged looked just as menacing as a tribal spear.

Branches brushed against each other behind me, but there was no wind. My eyes locked on Gaedyen's as he mouthed, "Get down!" I crouched back to the ground just as he leaped up into the air above me. His body winked out of existence mid jump.

Wow, he is good.

Dry twigs crunched as he landed, speeding into the trees. There was a roar, then a crash. Trees fell. A loud, wet *thunk* and a muted yelp-growl.

Seconds passed. My heart pounded. Why wasn't he coming back?

CHAPTER EIGHTEEN

I stayed low, just in case. A ferocious wind swooshed through the trees nearby, and there was a hushed moan of pain from somewhere. Was it Gaedyen?

Another gust of wind and something hit my shoulder. I flinched away, trying to brush it off, but it was wet and melted into my sleeve. My hand came away red.

What? I've been hit!

Falling to the ground, I gingerly felt around my shoulder, searching for the wound. But there was none. And I realized I didn't feel any pain there. I tried to turn my head around to see it, but couldn't quite turn far enough.

There were heavy footfalls, and then Gaedyen appeared running toward me. "Enzi! You are hurt! What happened?" He leaned over me to inspect my shoulder from above.

"I don't know. I don't feel anything. Is that bad? Was I hit with something that numbed the area? Can you see where the blood is coming from?"

Narrowing his eyes, he put his head nearly right against mine and sniffed my shoulder, nostrils flaring. "This is not your blood. It is the strange scent of Tukailaan."

He gingerly pressed the pad of one of his long toes all over the area. It didn't hurt. A shiver spread from where he touched me.

"What? Tukailaan bled all over me? Gross! Where the heck is he now? How did he get so close?"

"I managed to hit him with a rymakri. I do not know where he went...his scent just...it is a strange combination. Confusing. But you have not been injured. That is a relief. A drop of blood must have fallen from him when he flew past. He is also Cadoumai—able to use the gifts well—so I was throwing blindly. I suppose I must have managed to wound him more thoroughly than I thought." He looked up at the sky. "We should distance ourselves from this place, in case he returns. Are you ready to move?"

Does it matter? You'll have me running a marathon whether I feel like it or not. "Sure."

My body still shook as I jogged to keep up with him. He increased the pace substantially, and I'd already been struggling. How much did our follower know? How badly wounded was he? A big drop of blood didn't necessarily mean he was in *that* bad of shape—these Gwythienians were huge.

Hours later, he finally slowed. I collapsed on the ground, all muscles turned to jelly. But I had more questions for him, so when I caught my breath I asked, "So, what's Padraig's problem with your dad? Are you two related?"

He froze and then turned to me. "I do not speak of my parents." His body seemed to vibrate.

Was that like the rage I saw when he argued with Padraig? *Okay, no thanks!* I did *not* want to piss off a dragon. Even if he wasn't technically a dragon. Seemed like a subject change was in order. "So, uh, tell me about the Adarborians. Do they have a gift thingy, too?"

He exhaled. "Yes. They look the most like you out of all the races. Humanoid bodies with elegant, bird-like wings. Their gift is to change their size. They shrink and grow to a wide range of heights. The Cadoumai can, anyway. The less gifted cannot change their size as much, some not at all.

"There is a legend that they came from a tree—the great tree referred to in the liryk. It is called 'Amolryn'. It is said to be the largest tree in the forests there, in South America. It bears flowers of a few different colors, which supposedly produced the first Adarborians."

"Weird. And Cool. Do they make those stick-knife thingies, too?"

"No, only we Gwythienians use those. Their very name—*rymakri*—refers to how we make them, which only we can do. They use a type of blow dart. I do not know exactly how it works, but there is a tube placed against the lips, and a sharp, poisoned projectile is forced out toward the victim. They do not always use killing poisons, usually something like heavy sedation so they can control an intruder until they find out why he is there. But we will still exercise the utmost caution in approaching their realm."

"Do you have, like, wonky teeth or something to make them with?"

He picked up the pace again, "Yes. No other beings have this sort of dental anomaly. We Gwythienians have uniquely shaped molars. The space between these four teeth—two on the top and two on the bottom—is always a little different, varying from one Gwythienian to the next.

"Think of it like a human finger print. Er, no, that is too specific. More like whether your little earflaps are attached to your head or hang loose. It is a small difference, but a difference none the less. Some produce sharpened ends with four corners and four sides, some are practically triangular, and some produce nearly rounded edges. But they are all meant for making rymakri."

"Hmm." *Kinda weird, but interesting.*

"We make short rymakri, like knives. But we also make longer ones, more like spears. The Arunca Rymakri, the art of knife- and spear-throwing, is a skill greatly revered among our people. It is how we fight, and we learn from a young age how to do it well. I have spent many hours in practice, many more hours than my peers."

"Why did you spend more time practicing than they did?"

"I had fewer distractions."

His shifty eyes implied there was more to it than that. "It can't really be *that* hard." I hoped to goad him into explaining further.

"Would you like to try?"

That was not what I was going for. Knives gave me the creeps. I didn't like to be around them. But this wasn't a real knife, just a wooden thing. I guessed I could give it a try. "Sure."

With what looked like a smirk on his reptilian face, he reached up and snapped off another branch from a tree behind him, never taking his eyes off mine. He broke a six-inch piece off the thicker end, dropping the rest of it. He placed one end of the small piece in the side of his mouth, then pulled it out, and a flattened, knife-like wooden blade emerged.

He handed it to me. "Good luck."

CHAPTER NINETEEN

I rolled my eyes. "What should I aim for?"

He pointed at a tree about six feet away from us, its trunk even wider than me. "Try hitting that."

I gripped the knife, focused on the middle of the trunk, stepped forward, and threw. It sped through the air, pinged off the tree, and fell into the dead leaves at its base. It lay there, lifeless.

"What? I was barely a few feet away! It must've slipped." I retrieved it.

Gaedyen snickered, but I resolutely ignored him as I lobbed the knife at my target again. It thunked against the base of the tree and flopped to the ground.

I tried again and it zoomed past the tree altogether.

"Alright, fine." I whirled to face him. "What the heck am I doing wrong?"

"You are not balancing properly, you hold the blade incorrectly, and you change the set of your wrist right before you throw… for starters."

My frown deepened. "Great. So tell me how to fix it." *You stupid lizard.*

He raised himself up to stand on his hind legs as I jumped back in surprise. And I'd thought he was tall on all fours!

"You must stand with your feet under your shoulders, so that your weight is more evenly distributed. A Gwythienian would stand a bit differently, but you will have to stand like that because of your lack of a proper tail."

Rolling my eyes again, I spread my feet shoulder-width apart, but it only made me feel more off balance.

He dropped back to all fours. "And you must stop all this business about grasping the handle like that. You need to hold the blade itself in order to aim true."

"Hold the *blade?* Well it's good that these are only wooden knives then, and not metal ones. Otherwise you Gwythienians would always have cuts on your fingers."

Gaedyen sighed. "Touch the blade's edge, Enzi. Carefully though—"

"Ouch!" I dropped the wooden weapon as a rich bead of red erupted from my pointer finger. "Shoot! How did you get it so sharp? Shouldn't it splinter, being that thin?"

"Gwythienian saliva has special chemical properties. It reacts with the fibers in the wood, making them strong as metal. Different levels of strength, depending on the type of wood of course. Some are stronger than others."

"Great. Now I have your spit in my blood stream."

"I think you will survive."

"Yeah. Okay. So how am I supposed to hold the flesh-shearing edge of this thing without losing a finger?"

"Here, like this." He retrieved it from the ground and wrapped his fingers around the sharp tip. "Hmm…" He compared the differences in our hands. His finger-toe-things had broad, flattened ends, and I wasn't sure he even had thumbs. He held the blade between his second and third fingers, while the other two contorted strangely around it. "This is how we hold it. Here, you try and get as close as you can to that." He put the rymakri back in my hand.

I took it from him, but struggled to figure out how to place my fingers as he had. Our hands were too different.

"Try putting your thumb and next finger like this—no, no, that one here. There you go. Humans have such strange fingers."

I let that one go as I raised my knife-laden hand behind my head and prepared to launch the stupid piece of wood.

"Wait! You did that thing where you change your wrist again."

"What are you talking about?" I lowered my arm to inspect the position of my wrist. "It looks perfectly fine to me."

"That is because you do not know anything about Arunca Rymakri."

Glowering, I tried to care about what else he said.

"When you aim like this, you have to keep your wrist still— exactly like that—as you raise your arm. If you allow it to rotate, it will throw your aim off course."

"Okay. Like this?"

"Yes, that is better. Give it a try."

With feet, fingers and wrist all in proper order, I launched the blade as hard as I could. There was a satisfying *clunk* as it hit the tree, but the blade still dropped to the ground.

"That was much better! Just make sure your arm is perpendicular to your target when you throw. Having it at even the slightest angle will throw off your aim as well."

I kept trying. A few minutes later, the rymakri started disintegrating. It crumbed in my hand, falling through my fingers and giving me a splinter the size of the Eiffel Tower. "Ow! What just happened?"

"As I told you, Gwythienian saliva reacts with the wood to make it as strong as metal. But that only lasts so long. The saliva keeps reacting with the wood, and eventually weakens it, turning it into slush. So we have to constantly make new rymakri as we need them."

I tried a few more times with the next one Gaedyen made, and was rewarded with one short scratch in the trunk by the end of it. But the blade never actually stuck. Eventually we left the blade and the abused tree trunk to continue on our way. Gaedyen smirked at having been right.

"Won't scratches like that lead someone to us if we're being followed?"

"If Tukailaan—or any Gwythienian—is following us, our scent will give us away long before anything like that would be noticed."

That wasn't exactly comforting, but if I could get good at that, I wouldn't have to be quite so concerned about a follower, would I? I was done for the moment, but I would give this another try. What if I could actually learn to fight with rymakri?

I'd failed those stupid self-defense lessons Mom had made me take because it was too much like the real thing. The instructors gripped me in ways I was supposed to learn to escape from, but instead of training me, it paralyzed me. I cringed at the memory of the panic attacks. It was too much like my nightmares coming alive, like it all really happened again. So, breaking out of a hold was probably not my best chance of self-defense.

But if I had something unexpected up my sleeve, like a rymakri, I might have a chance. I would definitely be trying that again.

"So what if you aren't in the woods? What do you do for weapons then, if there aren't materials for them right at your fingertips?"

He paused. "I, uh, have never been very far from the woods before. I have always had fighting materials ready to be bitten into being nearby. I am ashamed to confess that the thought has not come to me until now."

His open honesty surprised me. "We'll be going out of the woods for some of this trip, right? At least for the part where we're swimming over the entire ocean?" A fair amount of sarcasm may have colored that last sentence. I had absolutely no intention of swimming over an entire ocean.

"Yes." He sounded like his thoughts were far away. I assumed he was—unsuccessfully—trying to come up with a solution.

"Well don't you have like, claws and stuff to fight with? And obviously teeth. Don't you Gwythienians ever get into hand-to-hand combat? Surely you have ways to fight without sticks?"

"I have a wing claw on the joint of each wing, of course," he said as if he stated the obvious. "But that is not something to use in a fight. Leaping at an opponent with wing claws at the ready looks impressive, but you expose your best method of escape to easy destruction."

"What do you mean?"

"If you strike with your wing claw, your wing itself is left wide open. The membrane is tough and strong, but thin, and can be torn easily with a claw or rymakri if enough force is applied. So wing claws are rarely used. Did you see Padraig's face? Those two scars are from a pair of wing claws. He was caught by surprise, but it would have been easy for him to rip through the wings of his opponent as they executed that move. Then they would not have been able to fly anymore."

"Okay. What about teeth? Can't you bite an enemy with them?"

"Yes, it is doable of course, but it is considered a sloppy move among those of our realm. We throw knives and spears. Arunca Rymakri is our way of fighting. That is all. It is our way and it is honorable."

"Fair enough." Still though, seemed to me that if you were fighting and your opponent was too close to chuck a piece of wood at, giant dragon teeth would be a reasonable plan B. I pointed to the tips of my fingers, "So you don't use normal claws either?" It probably wasn't *noble* enough or something.

"We do have foot claws, but they are more for hunting than fighting. We have strong limbs, so kicking an enemy is more beneficial than scratching them."

"Hmm." My eyebrows were still raised as another thought occurred to me. "Well if at some point we're going to be in a place without a lot of sticks, shouldn't you have some sort of satchel for carrying premade weapons, in case we're followed or something again and aren't in a place where the materials are available?" *If I can convince him this is a good idea, we will have to go to a store for supplies, and I can grab a coat while we're there.*

"First of all, there is no such thing as premade weapons for Gwythienians. Because of how the chemical in our saliva reacts with the wood and eventually destroys it, as you saw earlier. And secondly, what is this 'satchel' you speak of?"

"A satchel is a type of bag. A thing you carry stuff in so you don't have to carry it in your hands."

He squinted at me, clearly confused. I laughed. "What part of the concept of a *bag* do you not understand?"

"How would carrying something unnecessary in addition to what I need to carry make carrying what I need to carry any easier?"

"You wouldn't carry it in your hands! It would have a strap—you know—that would wrap around your chest, or two that would go over your shoulders. That way you could have everything you need with you, while still leaving your hands free to do whatever it is that they need to do." Was I really explaining the point of a backpack to a dragon?

"It sounds odd to me," he said. "But now that I think about it, I remember you having something attached to your back whenever you arrive home from school."

I stared at him in confusion. How would he know I had a backpack? Had he been spying on me?

"That is to say," he back-pedaled, "Shaun described your appearance to me, and I remember him mentioning that particular detail." He looked askance at me, as if he didn't expect me to believe him. I did notice the strangeness of what he said and how he changed it. But what could that mean? Perhaps that he was there watching with Shaun? No, he would've been too noticeable. But he could've been invisible. Had it been Gaedyen's footprints I'd seen so many times in the snow?

"Yeah, that's the idea." I watched him suspiciously. "That little piece of advanced technology is called a backpack. School children in the human world carry their textbooks in them. They leave arms and hands free to do whatever they need to. They're very useful." Another question dawned on me. "Didn't you have to go to school?"

"Yes of course I did," he replied indignantly. "We just do not have books in Odan Terridor. Our knowledge and skills are passed on to the next generation by our elders—the old ones, those who have lived a long life and have the most experience. They are our story tellers and instructors. They provide our young with an education. We learn how to recognize hardwoods that will make better weapons, and about the histories of our realm and how we have interacted with the others. We learn about what kind of beings live in the other realms. None of that involves carrying a 'bag' as you call it. We are more efficient than that."

More efficient, huh?

I frowned, but chose to save the time and effort I would use up arguing with his last idiotic statement. "Right, so anyway, a satchel could also hold *non*-bitten sticks that you could grab and bite into a weapon later. Do you want something to carry sticks in so we can be prepared for an emergency when we don't have trees around us anymore? Or would you rather not be prepared and have to make your rymakri out of thin air? As fabulous as a verbally educated culture is, I have a feeling that physical weapons would be more useful than verbal ones for us."

He stopped and looked back at me. "What do you mean?"

"I mean I know how to sew clothes and jerry-rig things, so I can make you something to carry your stupid sticks in. As long as we can find supplies. At a store." It seemed to be against his pride to allow me to make something for him, so I pushed before he could turn me down. "Seriously man, I don't want to be caught out in the middle of some open place with no branches laying around if another mysterious something comes after us, do you? What if Tukailaan is still following us? Wouldn't you rather be prepared?"

"What materials would you need?" he inquired skeptically.

"Hmm…" The only raw materials at my ready fingertips were snow, dirt, and more wood. Did we have access to anything else?

"Some kind of fabric. And I'd need some way to secure pieces of it together and a strap or two to make it stay on you once it's made." He grimaced at that last bit. What, was it dishonorable to wear gear too, or something? *Probably.*

"How are you planning to come across fabric in the woods?" he questioned smugly, apparently glad to find a dent in my plan.

"I'm not. I'm planning to find a store where we can buy supplies and a warm coat."

He frowned. "What about a camp site? Where some people might leave things such as fabric and rope that we could take and use for this?"

I lifted an eyebrow. "Are there a lot of abandoned winter coats lying around in this place?"

"Follow me." He veered to the left. I jogged to keep up with him, annoyed at his inconsideration for the physical handicaps that being a human caused, but I sucked it up and ran. *There better be useful stuff at wherever this place is.*

The trees had steadily increased in number for the last several minutes, till now they were so thick that Gaedyen couldn't maneuver as effectively and trampled many of the smaller ones that got in his way. I appreciated the greater number of trees. They forced Gaedyen to slow down and that gave me the chance to ease my pace. Eventually, he stopped trailblazing and searched his surroundings for something.

"So what are we looking for? Do you see something?" This looked too densely treed for a camping ground.

"I smell a human scent, several days old. There is no one here now, but someone left something behind recently." He proceeded to glance around, mostly up at the trees. Maybe expecting to find something suspended to keep bears away.

I searched the ground and lower parts of the trees to balance out his higher inspection. The moment I changed my footing to turn my back toward him, something struck me hard in the back of the legs and I landed on my face in the snow.

A grunt of pain escaped me as I made heavy contact with the frozen ground. "What the heck, man?" I moaned, guessing that the culprit had been his clumsy tail.

"Oops. My apologies."

I pushed myself up into a kneeling position, and found myself eye level with a hole in the tree that had nearly busted my head open. A thin beam of sunlight struck something inside and reflected back for an instant. Animal eyes? But there was only one glowing dot...I peered closer and saw a clump of something definitely not animal-shaped.

"Maybe this is what you smell." I reached in tentatively. Cloth. I grasped it and pulled it out. A man's dark gray tee shirt, neatly folded. Ideally it would have been thicker fabric, but there was still potential. I reached in again, hoping for a pair of thick hiker-type cargo pants. I came out with a worn pair of jeans, whose shiny silver button gave off the reflection. Inspecting the pants for holes, and finding only a single small one, I nodded with approval. I reached in again, searching for anything else.

Coming up blank on that one, I stood and held the pants out so I could see how much material I had to work with. But how would I cut the material with no scissors? "Do you think you could make a wooden something sharp enough to cut this shirt?" I asked Gaedyen and held the shirt up to show him.

"Of course," he said, without even blinking.

"Alright. And something sharp enough to cut the jeans?" I held those out next.

"Yes, I can do that."

"Sweet. Now we just need to run by somewhere to buy a needle and thread." I shifted from kneeling to sitting and examined the shirt again.

"Not yet," came his annoyingly authoritative reply.

I glared up at him, waiting for an explanation and to gauge how serious he was about continuing to travel tonight. I was irritated that my coercion hadn't gone to plan and also very physically exhausted.

"We need to get farther away from here before choosing a place to spend the night." He turned and started walking again, as if I had no choice but to follow.

I stared after him, fuming. Did he think that I had super human physical powers to continue traveling now, as much as we'd already gone today and yesterday? My shoes were showing signs of extreme wear already, and it was only day two. And who knew how far we were from wherever the heck we were going? A freaking long way if it was really South America.

But what was there to do but follow? I wanted to overcome his expectations of a weak human, so I hauled myself up and jogged into pace again, bringing my materials with me.

My feet felt beaten flat, and every muscle in my legs was so sore that I didn't know how I could continue moving for much longer. But we kept up the pace for what felt like ages. I didn't really have any concept of time, though. I was too tired and the constant beat of my shoes on the ground and the monotonous surroundings had me in a bit of a daze.

When Gaedyen's steady pace finally slowed to a stop, sometime after it had grown dark outside, I crumpled into a heap on the ground right on the light dusting of snow. I was hungry enough to eat bugs, but I was too exhausted to do anything about it. With my last ounce of strength, I pulled up the arm that held the pants and shirt we'd found and laid my head on them as a makeshift pillow. I was out the moment my head hit the clothes.

CHAPTER TWENTY

The sawdust scratched my back again. Yowling came from the corner—the barn cat's kittens. I screamed with them.

No! No, please, no!

He struck me again—my cries annoyed him—but I couldn't stay silent.

An owl hooted nearby, startling me from the nightmare. I was warm, sweaty even. I could barely move, and I looked up to see a red wing with a map of veins illuminated by the bright moon on the other side. My breathing eased, and I drifted back off to sleep.

When the morning light woke me, even my eyelids were too sore to open without complaint. My fingers and toes felt like ice, and the rest of me didn't feel much better. As I gradually became aware of my body, I discovered that after using my arm to shove the clothes into a comfortable position, I'd been too tired to move it back to where it belonged. As a result, it'd been splayed out at an awkward angle all night and was now completely numb. I tried to move it without success. *Great.*

A jelly arm. Just what I need. Giving up, I focused on my legs instead.

Deep pain lashed out at me through my left leg as I tried to move it first. I winced and tried the other leg. Same story. But I couldn't lay on my stomach forever—I needed to know what was going on, and I didn't want Gaedyen to see me like this. So I gritted my teeth and told my muscles to cooperate enough to flip myself over onto my back. I finally made it, eyes squeezed shut and gasping, and had to hold completely still for a moment to recuperate.

I had experienced muscle soreness after participating—against my will—in gym, but this was an entirely new level of pain. The discomfort that came after gym class versus what I currently felt was like comparing the top floor of a two-story house to the highest level of Chicago's Sears Tower.

Our crappy apartment sounded really nice just then, with or without heat. No wind, anyway. Dry clothes. Mom used to give the best back massages. *I could use one of those right now.*

I cracked opened one eye, then the other, and inhaled sharply as I took in the giant, reptilian head staring at me from way too close inside my personal bubble.

"Uh, Gaedyen." I turned away from him. "What the heck, man? Get outta my face!" I moaned, lacking the *oomph* to make my voice more commanding. I swatted him away, ignoring the aching pain in my limp arm.

"I just wanted to make sure you were okay. You smell different than when I left to catch breakfast. Anyway, there is a fresh fish waiting for you."

I smelled different, did I? *Get some manners, moron.* Of course I smelled bad, I *ran* practically all day yesterday. Even in this weather, running equaled sweat. "If you don't want to be offended by my stench, get outta my space."

Eventually I managed to hoist my pathetic butt up off the ground. I was starving, but standing also made me realize the urgent need to pee. So off into the woods I hobbled, feeling about eighty years old.

"Where are you going, human?"

"I'll be back in a minute!"

"You should not wander off! We should stay close, just in case."

"I will be right back." Couldn't a girl pee in peace? This was definitely none of his business.

I waddled deep into the woods until I was sure not even someone with animal-like super vision could see, and prepared to squat. It was embarrassing, even though no one was around. It was just awkward, not having walls around for something like this.

And then I saw it.

No, no, no! Not now, Mother Nature! How could you do this to me?

Yep. It was that time of the month, and I was *not* prepared.

Crap. And he noticed I smelled different? Ugh. I groaned, mortified that it was noticeable.

I took care of myself as best I could, befouling the light sprinkling of snow where I'd crouched. Wobbling back to Gaedyen, I felt self-conscious and unsure how to handle this new predicament.

When I reached camp, I sought out the fish that was supposed to be my breakfast. To my disappointment, I found it raw. "Thanks for the fish, Gaedyen, but I'm going to need to cook this. Humans don't usually eat their fish raw. I mean, some people like sushi, but I got food poisoning when I tried it so I'm a big fan of thoroughly cooking things."

Eyeing me, he reached for a long branch lying on the ground near him.

I backed up a few steps. Was he going to make a weapon? Was he pissed at me for complaining about his fish, or was there a threat I couldn't see?

Before I could check, he bit the end to a point and tossed it to me. "Then cook it, human."

The flying stick evaded my flailing grasp. I bent my sore body toward the ground to retrieve it and then stabbed the fish. Thrusting it over the fire—when had he even kindled this one?—I wondered how long it would take to cook. On our stove at home, about a minute and a half per side, judging by the thickness. If it were filleted, anyway. Fish was one of those things that you had to get just right; you couldn't aim to err on overcooking it, because then it would toughen to rubber.

I had no idea how to cook something over a campfire. It couldn't be that hard, could it? How is a whole fish even supposed to be cooked? I mean, I didn't really need to cook its organs in there—I wasn't gonna eat those, but I didn't even know how to fillet a fish. I always bought fish in pre-filleted form from the grocery store.

So…fish kebab.

Placing all my focus on rotating the fish over the heat, I put off the topic of my girl problem. Instead, I imagined what I could do to make this fish delicious. Lemon-parsley sauce was my favorite. I couldn't make any of the wine sauces, since I did the grocery shopping and wasn't old enough to buy alcohol, but I would make them one day. But that lemon-parsley…*mmm!* So good.

Were there any spices in the woods? I glanced around. The ground was still covered in dead leaves and snow. Would I even recognize them? I knew about cilantro and basil and oregano, but I had little jars of them at home, or either occasionally bought them fresh. If there were any plants out here, it would probably not be smart to experiment with them.

I felt the need for a tampon reminding me of my predicament. There was nothing else I could do. I had to find a gas station or something.

"Gaedyen, how close are we to a store? I really need to buy some…things."

He eyed me again. "How badly do you really need to go? It would be most ideal not to be seen. What do you need?"

"We need a needle and thread for the satchel…" I didn't know how to explain what I needed, but I *definitely* needed it. Would it embarrass him, too, or just me? Did reptiles even have periods? He probably wouldn't even know what I was talking about. I stalled another moment by glancing down at my shoes, and they gave me an idea.

"Plus, I need new shoes. I've had these ones for years, and after yesterday, they are worn through." I pulled one off and showed it to him. I saw his displeased face through the hole in the sole. Good timing for that. "Plus, this hoodie isn't warm enough and it's not waterproof. If it snows again, or rains or anything, I'll be soaked for days. I could catch a cold from stuff like that and then running around in the woods would be even harder."

He frowned at the shoe as I put it back on. "Can you do it invisibly?"

I frowned back. Whether my flighty ability felt like working at the moment or not, I needed those items. If I left the necklace with Gaedyen, we wouldn't risk anyone seeing it. That was another option.

But I needed to master this skill, too. So I gave it a shot. I focused, pulling all thoughts away from distractions and homing in on what I needed to do. The wall was there, slick and infinite as ever. Holding the stone, I sensed a weakening in the barrier—a hairline fracture—but it wasn't expanding. I tried squeezing the stone, pressing it against my chest, everything. But I couldn't widen the crack. Thinking the words again—*I need to be invisible*—I threw them at the barrier. But they made no difference. I let my shoulders slump, exasperated.

Opening my eyes, I saw in Gaedyen's tired ones and his down-turned earflaps that he was disappointed in my failure. That hit something in the pit of my stomach. I cared what he thought of me. I really didn't want to look like an idiot in front of him. Looking like an idiot was not new to me, but for some reason it was different with him. I cast my eyes away, embarrassed under his scrutiny.

"It is risky, however, if your soft human feet are too tender to run, should danger come again, it would be even worse for us. Likewise, if you were sick and even more weak and slow as a result."

I glared at him.

"So if you must purchase more human foot coverings and rain-proof clothes, I will follow you invisibly as far as I can, but I doubt I will fit inside. I do not have the Adarborian skill of changing my size."

Victory! "Okay, great. So how far are we then?"

"We are roughly an hour's swift walk away, probably about a two-hour amble at your pace."

Ugh. That was a lot of time for my little problem to escalate. "Well then let's get going as soon as possible. I'll just finish cooking this fish—"

The fire crackled explosively, sending up a burst of sparks. I flailed back to avoid getting burned and saw my breakfast half buried in the ashes. The thin flesh of the fish had given way around the makeshift skewer and fallen into the fire.

Crap!

I dug it out of the ashes with the stick, but no luck. It was charred to worthlessness on the outside and still a raw, gushy mess on the inside. *Great. How did I manage to do that?*

"That is unfortunate. Maybe the store will have food for sale." Gaedyen stood and approached the fire. With one big forefoot he thrust dirt over the flames to extinguish them, and then smashed it into the ground. He turned and used his tail to swipe a large section of moist dirt to put out the embers. Then off he went.

"Wait, Gaedyen. Can we please travel a little slower than yesterday? I can barely move." And I had cramps. I took his silence as a "no."

As we tramped through the woods, the third day of our journey, I wondered why I'd ever allowed myself to become involved with this nightmare. *This is for Dad, who might not be crazy after all.* Still though, would I have enough money to buy the shoes I needed? And the other things? And something to carry them in? And some real food? A fresh pair of socks was definitely a tempting idea too. But how was Mom doing on money? Would this hurt her?

How was she doing on anything, anyway?

"Gaedyen?"

"What, human?"

"Does this store have a phone?"

"I do not know. Do I look like I have been inside?"

Despite the betrayal I felt from Mom, guilt gnawed at my gut. I'd barely thought of her. She was probably worried sick about me. I should try to give her a call. I certainly hadn't forgiven her, but I didn't want her to be worried about me. She could very likely be afraid that I'd been attacked again and not been able to walk away from it this time. No mother should have to fear that. That was too awful. I would call her as soon as I could.

The woods had been thick for quite a while now, since early yesterday. How did people set up tents in that supposed "camping ground," with trees as crowded as those were? They'd been especially thick where I'd found the clothes. So thick that Gaedyen had barely been able to maneuver through them and had knocked down many smaller ones to get through. Maybe some dude liked to camp without a tent, to enjoy the stars more or something? Something seemed off about that. It was too convenient for us to happen upon some clothes concealed in a tree trunk in a not-very-camp-site-ish area.

After what felt like hours of trudging through the woods, Gaedyen winked out of existence right before my eyes. I jumped, but then I realized we must be close to the store. Footprints formed in the leaves beneath him as he walked. Being invisible didn't necessarily make a person undetectable.

The footprints! Those are the same marks that were outside my window in the snow! So he had been spying on me! Maybe that was how he knew I wore a backpack to school....

"We are nearing the store. Try to turn invisible again."

He had an annoying habit of giving orders. It reminded me of how Captain von Trapp treated Maria in the beginning of *The Sound of Music.* I smiled. "Whatever you say, *Captain.*" I'd confront him about the footprints later.

But once again I tried and failed to use the ability.

A sigh came from somewhere in thin air and the footprints continued to form in the leaves.

I hung my head. I'd done it before, why couldn't I do it now?

"Well, here. You should hold on to this for safekeeping." I reached up to unfasten the necklace.

"No, it should stay with you. Just keep it concealed in your clothes. Do not let anyone see it."

"At least there will only be humans inside. None of them will know what this is. Unless there are more out there like Shaun."

Gaedyen spluttered. "There are not...should not be...in any case, keep it hidden, alright?"

A clearing came into view. A faded log cabin-like structure stretched across the grass, taking up most of the space. I was about to step out from the tree line, when Gaedyen stopped me. "Must you go?"

I rolled my eyes. "Yes, *Captain.* It will only take a few minutes. Why are you so uptight?"

"Tukailaan's scent—it keeps itching in the back of my mind. I keep thinking I am sensing it, just out of reach. I did not want to scare you, but I am quite sure he is still following us."

Oh no! Why couldn't everything just leave us alone?

"Mm." But unsavory company or not, I needed tampons. "Alright, I'll be as quick as I can. You be careful, too."

"I will walk with you to the door. No one will see me. But after this, you will need to spend every spare moment practicing invisibility. This is not an area you can afford to be weak in."

"Okay, fine." I did want to be better at it, but the idea of practicing every spare moment sounded exhausting. I'd worry about that later.

"What about your footprints? They'll be noticeable out there."

"True. I will try to step in your prints. My feet are much bigger than yours, so it might end up looking like you walked very sloppily. But your safety is the priority."

After dropping the clothes at the edge of the trees, we emerged from the woods behind the building and circled around to the front. Billy Bob's Hunting and Fishing faced a slim, gravel road that stretched out either way until the trees swallowed it up from view. It had to be the skinniest little road I'd ever seen.

Besides the big, hand-painted sign out front of the store, and the nature-park-style garbage can coated in blotchy old chewing gum on one side of the stairs, there was nothing to distinguish it from any other old-fashion log cabin-style house you'd expect to find in a backwoods place like this. Even the gravel parking lot—with two pickup trucks so muddy that their original colors were indistinguishable—could belong to a residential building. I hoped this place was capable of taking debit cards.

I gripped the splintered handrail and climbed the creaky stairs. A variety of mismatched rocking chairs crowded the porch, all appeared to have seen better days in years—or decades—past. I opened the screen door, which turned out to be missing its screen completely, and opened the second, more solid wooden one. A bell chimed, but no one seemed to be on customer alert. With a swift glance back at where Gaedyen might be, I stepped inside.

The setup reminded me of a large gas station convenience store. I immediately found the toiletries section and nabbed a pack of tampons. I raced toward the restroom sign and locked myself in. I did of course plan on paying for them, but this couldn't wait.

I immediately realized that I had stained right through my pants. "Crap!" And I thought I'd just been sweating. Of course this would happen! Why hadn't I grabbed a pair of pants before closing myself in there?

Did those trucks belong to customers? Or employees? Either way they meant there were people here, and I didn't want anyone seeing this. Did the store even carry pants?

I put my ear to the door to listen, in case someone might be in the immediate area. Hearing nothing, I risked opening it. Wincing at the squeaky hinges, I peeked out, searching for pants. I thought I saw a rack of camo gear toward the other side of the store. Of course, not within convenient stealth-snagging range. I opened the door a smidge more and stretched my head up as high as I could to make sure there were definitely clothes in the pants category on that rack.

I was pretty positive there were. Why couldn't invisibility work on demand? Pushing the door open, I took a big step in the direction of the pants… and crashed into something that hadn't been there a second ago. A moment of disorientation and then I realized it was a guy. And not just any guy.

"Shaun?"

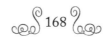

CHAPTER TWENTY-ONE

I jumped back and slammed the bathroom door in his face. How could Shaun be here? What the heck? Gaedyen said I'd never see him again. Did he know he was here? Was he following us? Had he noticed my pants?

Whether it was sensible or not, that last question was what worried me the most. If I was ever going to see this guy again, I would like to be a little more put together, to say the least.

Does he have a sense of smell as good as Gaedyen's?

Craaap!

"What are *you* doing here?" I asked through the door.

"Just happened to be in the area…"

"*Happened* to be in the one place where Gaedyen and I would be at the exact same time?"

"Yep." I heard the smile in his voice. Was he enjoying leaving me in the dark about something?

"Listen, Enzi, I saw blood in there. Are you hurt?" His gentle voice caught me off guard. It sounded…sincere. Like he really actually cared.

"Enzi?"

"No, I'm not. Forget about it, it's nothing."

"Now Enzi—"

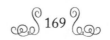

"I'm serious, Shaun. FORGET. ABOUT. IT. I'm not going to pass out from blood loss." There was no way I could get those stupid pants now without him seeing what was going on. But I had an idea. "Hey, look, could you go over there and grab a pair of those camo pants for me? I'd really appreciate it." Not that this brilliant idea would keep him from figuring it out, but it was better than him getting a better look at me.

"Okay, sure." His footsteps retreated on the creaking floor. I opened the door a little further to see if he really was doing what he said he would. He was definitely heading for the camo rack.

He wore dark jeans and a plain brown tee shirt. He was tall, much taller than me. And I noticed again his shoulder-length brown hair. He didn't seem overly muscular, but he was definitely in good shape. Better shape than me. Self-consciousness roiled in my stomach. I was *so* out of shape. Now was a bad time to be so ugly.

He reached the rack and pushed some hung up clothes out of the way, maybe looking for my size. I didn't want to tell him what size I'd probably need, but with all the trouble he'd caused me—kidnapping me and all that—I realized I was completely okay with sending him back multiple times to get a different size. I hoped he'd get the wrong one, so he'd have to make a couple more trips. It was silly, but I still indulged a smile at the thought of causing him that inconvenience.

Then he was on his way back, multiple pairs of bulky camo pants in hand. How annoying! He'd been smart enough to grab several sizes. When he caught me looking at him, he grinned as if we were friends. My face remained blank—I wasn't sure what to do with it. Guys didn't smile at me. Not nicely, anyway. But that was definitely not a menacing smile. It was a very nice one. Something flipped in my stomach.

I leaped back into the bathroom, letting the door slam shut. What was that? It wasn't... *butterflies*, was it? No way.

A knock came at the door and I jumped again. *Get a grip!*

I pushed on the door and grabbed the pants from him without looking up. "Thanks," I mumbled. My voice was also being uncooperative—I doubted even Gaedyen could have heard that if he'd been standing right there.

I pulled my old pants off and shrugged on the top most pair of new ones, wracking my brain for something not stupid to say.

"So, why are you here?" The pants didn't fit. Loose was good, but not so loose that they'd fall right down to my ankles at any second. I ripped them off and went for the next pair.

"I was just passing through. Ran into Gaedyen outside. Did not expect to see him here, that is for sure!" he laughed. "Anyway, I figured you would probably be here, so I stopped in to say hey."

He'd stopped in to say hey, to me? Why did that make me want to sing? What was wrong with me?

I tried to be witty. "So you kidnap me—in freezing weather, I might add—and then happen to run across the person you handed me off to and thought that coming in to say hi to me would be a good idea? That's kinda ridiculous on many levels." *Too harsh? Ugh.* It sounded so much better in my head.

This pair was loose enough that I could squeeze myself into them, but too tight to be comfortable. I frowned in the mirror, hating my reflection.

"Well it is what it is." I imagined him shrugging as he replied.

What to say to that? "What did Gaedyen say when he saw you?"

Two pairs down, two to go. I exchanged the ones that were too tight for some that were so tight I couldn't get them past my knees. No go there. But when I shoved my legs into the last pair of pants, it was like they'd been made for me. The perfect fit. Not too baggy, not too tight. And even better, they were cargo pants. So as dorky as it may have looked, I could carry stuff in the pockets. *Score!* I fist-pumped my victory.

"Oh, you know how he is. I was not supposed to see you again, so he was not exactly thrilled to see me."

Why weren't we supposed to see each other?

I tossed my old pants in the trash and surveyed the room for any other signs of my embarrassing incident. None remained. Then out of the bathroom I went, box of tampons and unwanted pairs of pants in hand.

"So why exactly are you not supposed to see me again?"

"Oh, you know. The realms being secret from humans and all. They do not like us knowing too much. And they do not want the two humans who do know about them to hang out and talk about it. We could be foolish and be overheard, or we could figure something out that they would rather us not know."

So, we were the only two humans that knew? "Well, no offense, but I can see why they'd make an exception for me with the whole rock thing and all that, but what made them okay with telling you about it all?"

His grin widened. "Secret."

My eyes narrowed. I was so tired of freaking *secrets!* It hurt a little to be excluded. I wanted in on it. What made him better than me so much that he got to keep secrets from me? Did it have something to do with why Gaedyen used to spend time in the Vorbiaquam and then stopped? Or why he refused to talk about his parents?

Turning, I marched up to the rack the pants came from and slung the ones that didn't fit back over it. I felt bad about that, but I had things to buy, forests to trudge through, and mysteriously impossible dudes to try to converse with. No time to hang things back up all nice and neat.

"So why do you get to have secrets?" I found a pocket sewing kit for Gaedyen's future satchel, adding that to my armload of tampons.

"That is for me to know and you to...well...*not* find out."

Alright, Smiley Face was getting on my nerves. "Fine, I don't care anyway. Why don't you go back out and talk to Gaedyen so I can buy my stuff in peace?"

Flipping through a rack of brightly-colored coats, I finally found a non-descript black one and pulled it out to check the price. *Whoa! No thank you.* I replaced it and kept looking, hoping to find something more affordable. I was too poor for warm *and* waterproof, so I had to choose between them. I went with waterproof. There was the sweatshirt I already had for *some* heat, and a lot of good a warm coat would do if it couldn't keep the rain off. I pulled down an ugly green rain jacket-ish thing, and turned to see why Shaun hadn't answered.

I frowned at the empty place where he'd been a moment ago. Surveying the rest of the room, I saw that he wasn't there. Where the heck had he gone?

Well, fine. He could go wherever he wanted.

A big backpack caught my eye and I headed toward it. It would be silly to bother with making a bag from scratch for Gaedyen if there was already a good one that would just need the straps altered.

I smiled at the image of giant, regal Gaedyen wearing a backpack. All of these were way too small for him. A quick once over on the price tags added to the hilarity of the picture. So I gave up on that and went in search of protein bars—in case I continued to fail at campfire cooking.

I grabbed as many chocolate chip and chocolate peanut butter ones as I could fit in my pockets—while still allowing plenty of room for tampons—then trooped up to the unmanned counter.

A little silver bell sat on the rustic wood. I tapped it, but it produced no sound.

"Hello?" I leaned over the counter to peer around the far wall. "Hello!"

"Ah!" A tall, light-haired man as skinny as a beanpole burst out of the back. "Find everything?" He reached over the counter to ring up my things, one eye lingering on my right shoulder. *The blood stain! Shoot! Why hadn't Shaun asked about that one?*

"Yes, thanks. Hey, is there a phone here?"

"Sorry, no. Out of order."

"Oh. Can I get cash back?" I wouldn't want to leave a charge trail...

"Sure! How much?"

"Twenty bucks?"

"Of course!" He scanned the last item. "That'll be—oh?"

A pair of woman's hiking boots landed on top of my pile of protein bars, followed by a bright white pair of socks. I stared at them, stunned. I couldn't believe that I'd forgotten *new shoes*, the main thing I'd told Gaedyen I needed and the one thing I was about to leave without.

"Forgetting something?" I heard the grin in Shaun's voice.

The cashier rang up the boots and socks. "Wait! I don't know if I can afford those, too!" But it was too late. He'd already swiped my card.

"Uh, sorry. Our machine's kinda broke and don't take returns real well. I can get you a gift certificate though, if ya wanna leave those boots here."

Yeah, since I'd totally be back in this store again next week. "No, it's fine. I'll take them." I'd just murdered the budget and danced on its grave. *Ugh!*

"Here's your cash! Have a great day!" He waved as I turned on Shaun.

"How the heck did you know I needed new shoes and socks?"

He hesitated. "Gaedyen mentioned it when I found him a few minutes ago. Plus, it is kind of obvious."

I felt stupid for asking, and self-conscious of my old shoes. But seriously, the socks were a stretch. Maybe it went without saying that ruined shoes on the feet of a traveler meant ruined socks underneath, too. But how could I have forgotten those, of all things? And then the horrible thought struck me. What if I smelled like stinky feet? Was that the giveaway?

"Yeah, well, thanks." I turned, stuffing the twenty in my back pocket, face warm.

"Any time."

"Actually," I took the debit card and plastic bags of purchases from the cashier, "probably no time ever again, huh? I mean, we're not supposed to be friends, are we?" Why was I saying that? I *wanted* to see Shaun again—that smile! Apparently, my mouth was celebrating opposite day and my brain had missed the memo.

"Well, we could always be friends anyway."

I wasn't sure what to say to that either. Sure, Gaedyen was annoying, but I did sort of trust him with the whole journey thing. I didn't want to mess that up. I needed him to help me find out what happened to my dad. But at the same time, forbidden contact—with this guy—was kind of tempting.

"I don't know…" Sometimes words were hard.

We went outside and Shaun crossed the porch and beat me to the bottom step. Still smiling that incredibly attractive smile, he offered his hand to help me down the stairs. Hiding my still-flushed face, I took it. It was warm and large; if he'd closed his fingers over mine they would have covered my whole hand. And it was such a nice color. Held against my horribly pale complexion, his rich brown skin looked much more real than mine.

As soon as I reached the bottom, I broke the connection and sat on the lowest step. I pulled off one shoe and sock and slid my right foot into a beautifully clean, dry, new sock and boot. It felt great. My fingers fumbled to untie the left one, and all my hurrying did nothing but knot the laces, embarrassing me even further.

The next thing I knew he, sat beside me. "Would you like some help?"

"No thanks, I got it." I didn't want his nose any closer to my feet than necessary. But my shoe had a conspiracy against me. I finally gave up and tugged the shoe off. Why hadn't I done that before? It wasn't like I was going to put them back on.

I shoved my left foot into the lovely new sock and boot and flexed my happy toes. *So much better.*

Placing my arms on the step behind me, I leaned back with my eyes closed. It felt so nice to have fresh socks and durable, warm boots on my tired feet. I removed the laces from the old shoes—they might be useful—and then tossed the shoes in the trash. I was surprised at the little emotional tug I felt at chucking them. We'd been through many years together. They were familiar. I distracted myself with transferring the contents of the two plastic bags to my new cargo pockets.

I snuck a peek to see if Shaun was still sitting there, and to my confusion, he was. What was his interest in me? Was he doing exactly what Gaedyen apparently feared—trying to get some information out of me that would help him connect the dots about something he wasn't supposed to know?

"So...isn't Gaedyen probably watching us right now? Shouldn't you be worried that he'll be upset with you?" I continued packing my pockets with my purchases, discarding the plastic bag and the cardboard boxes into the can as I went.

"Yes, he is around here somewhere..." he shielded his eyes from the sun and peered at the tree line. "Oh! Right there! Can you see him frowning from the trees?"

I scanned the tree line where he pointed but I couldn't see anything.

"Well, you are right, I should probably get going. Glad I could help you remember some of the things on your list." He winked at me.

That stomach flip thing happened again. What was going on? I'd never felt like that before. Guys like him didn't wink at girls like me. "Yeah, thanks."

He laughed softly, shoving his hands into his jeans pockets. He had a very nice laugh. "Well, I guess I will see you around."

"Okay, see you."

With one last wave at where Gaedyen supposedly was, he turned and jogged toward the parking lot. Maybe one of those trucks was his?

I didn't wait to find out. I wasn't going to stare wistfully after someone who I knew was beyond the level of too-attractive-to-look-at-me-twice. Who was I kidding? Of course he had something up his sleeve.

But what?

CHAPTER TWENTY-TWO

*B*efore reaching the edge of the forest, I saw Gaedyen's frowning face watching my approach.

"Hey, don't get pissed with me. I didn't go looking for the guy I'm not supposed to talk to. He found me."

"Hm."

"So, *are* you pissed that we talked to each other?"

"That is not important. The itch—Tukailaan's scent—it's growing stronger. We need to move."

Over the next several days, Gaedyen took on the habits of a frightened rabbit. As we covered ground during the day, he froze out of nowhere, eyes wide and earflaps twitching. At night, he'd jump up over nothing more than a gust of wind, knocking me over and scaring me to death.

I never sensed any of the sounds or smells he did, but the way he stood when he was hyper aware—eyes focused, brow serious, arms and legs poised for a fight—was kind of impressive. I'd heard about dragons when I was a kid and seen tons of drawings of them, but nothing compared to how regal Gaedyen looked in the moonlight, alert and intense.

The exercise was another matter entirely. Each morning I woke up miserable and had to stretch for several minutes. In the evenings, Gaedyen made me rymakri and I practiced throwing at various things while he caught fish or the occasional rabbit for our dinner. I tried to help with the hunting, but my skill with the rymakri improved at a sluggish rate, if at all.

My campfire cooking did improve. I no longer dropped the meat into the fire, but I rarely got anything thoroughly done. I would eat whatever was cooked enough and Gaedyen finished the rest. If there were anything green growing, I would've risked experimenting with it. That meat seriously needed some flavor! And some veggies or rice or something to go with it! *Gah!* But I was better at dissecting the fish—cutting them open with the debit card and cooking the fillets flat on two sticks instead of skewered on one.

The Captain was also constantly on my case about turning invisible on demand. I struggled every time, but I steadily improved. As soon as I got up in the morning I nearly always got through the wall and held onto it for probably a couple of minutes, but as the day progressed and I got more physically and mentally tired, my meager ability decreased.

Even so, the gift was thoroughly unpredictable. There were some mornings when I had absolutely no luck, and some afternoons where it was easier. I tried to find a pattern in it, but if there was one, it was lost on me.

Most of the time I felt useless. I slowed Gaedyen down, I was no good at catching food, and I asked annoying questions. I felt guilty for being a nuisance, but this whole expedition *had* been his idea. He'd wanted me along.

But why me, instead of a group of Gwythienians? They could all fly, catch their own food, and handle themselves in a fight. Even though he supposedly needed me because I was a

Possessor, why not bring more Gwythienians with us? Would they be afraid to go behind Padraig's back the way Gaedyen had? Or was he as low in the friends department as I was?

He'd said that he practiced throwing the knives more than his friends because he'd "had fewer distractions." Did that mean he didn't have many friends? As much trouble as I'd caused him so far, he still seemed just as inclined to keep me alive as he'd been in the beginning. Did that make us friends?

I did make him that satchel, though at first he refused to wear it. I used one leg of the jeans to make something like a giant fabric quiver, and I used all of the waistband material to reinforce the top so it was stiff enough to hold its shape decently. With some of the tee shirt and some of the other pant leg I crafted a strap to go over one shoulder and under the other—like one of those side backpack things—and fixed it so that the two pieces could be tied or untied at his chest. Then I made something like a drawstring to tie around the opening so the sticks wouldn't fall out. It wasn't ideal, but it was better than being caught in the ocean by some enemy and having no weapon.

I didn't care that he hated it or that it looked like crap. At least, that's what I told myself. I made him wear it and he tried pulling sticks from it once. It didn't go very well, but still, better than nothing. He was also picky about which shoulder it went around. He didn't want the strap touching his left one—the one with the discolored scar. I'd tried putting it there the first time and he shook me off, throwing me to the ground. Maybe the scar hurt?

My curiosity about life as a Gwythienian only increased. I wanted to know about their culture. What was all that business about not having any books? History being passed down from generation to generation through verbal means? They must have amazing memories. Could a Gwythienian get dementia? What would happen then?

Sometimes I practiced restraint and didn't bug him, but other times, I asked him a lot of questions.

Once, when I sang one of my favorite pop songs in my head, I wondered whether Gwythienians could sing and whether their culture included songs or music of any kind. When I asked Gaedyen, he said, "Of course we can sing. What would a people be without their music?"

A fair point. Props to Gwythienians for that. "Well then, what do you sing about?"

"We sing legends mostly. Stories that are part history and part fiction. Most important things happened so long ago that no one knows the difference anymore, despite our long memories."

"What are some of the legends?"

"How each realm came to be, for one thing, and the Great War between the realms. How we were all united by the rocks. There are tales of the ancient Sky Realm, whose people are like great cats. Cathawyr, they are called. They supposedly had a strange pattern of markings on their coats, unlike any other species.

"Many of our legends have members of this mysterious race dancing here and there throughout them, especially the one White Cat. The story goes that she made a grave mistake and nearly died, and lost all the color from her skin and coat as a result. She comes up in most of the stories, and some say that it was she who made the rock of life, a fifth rock that can heal wounds and even bring back life to a dead body—but no one has ever actually seen this rock.

"No one knows whether she or her people ever existed. Every Gwythienian has an opinion though, and some love to argue theirs. Of such things as that and other old stories are the epics that have been around since before Padraig's grandfather's grandfather hatched. Those are the songs we sing."

"Will you sing one for me now?" I longed to hear his voice in song, just to hear music again. It'd been too long since I'd taken in any music, and with all this time to think in silence, I really missed my distraction.

"No!" he exclaimed, aghast. "A Gwythienian never sings alone! We only sing in the midst of others singing. It is our way."

I frowned. "*Why* is that your way? Are you sure you're not making this up, just because I want to hear a song?"

"It is our way."

And that was the end of that.

Another time when I was very hungry and had food on the brain, I asked, "Gaedyen, what do Gwythienians eat? I mean, you obviously eat fish, but is that only while we're traveling? Do your people usually come out of Odan Terridor to catch fish? Or are there places to get fish in Odan Terridor? Or do you all eat something else?"

"Yes, I eat fish now because we are traveling. No, we Gwythienians do not leave our home just to catch fish from the human realm. Yes, there are fish farmers in Odan Terridor. But also yes, we do usually eat something else entirely whenever we can."

I waited expectantly for what that something was. "So… what is it that Gwythienians usually eat?"

"Malwoden. That is to say, snails."

I wrinkled my nose. "Gross."

"Actually, they are much tastier than fish. There are many more malwoden farmers than fish farmers in Odan Terridor for that reason. Mostly the fish farmers only breed fish for the feeding of the snails."

"You must have to eat a lot of them to equal the size of the fish you catch out here."

"Oh no. They are much bigger than the fish here. One reasonably-sized malwoden would satisfy me for a good two days."

I gawked, revolted. Eating snails was bad enough, but *giant* snails? *Ugh!* "Oh, man, that is *so* disgusting! How the heck big are they?"

"The top of the shell of an average-sized snail would reach," he glanced back and gave me a once over, "about halfway between your hip and shoulder."

I shivered at the thought of such hideous, slimy creatures coming in such ginormous sizes. I hoped I would never meet one. "Do you just… suck the meat out or something?"

"Oh, we eat the shells as well. Plenty of nutrition in those. And the crunch is a nice contrast to the squishiness of the snail meat itself."

"That is nasty, man. Seriously…nasty."

"No stranger than you insisting on cooking all of your fish dry, not even willing to try it raw."

"That's because it would make me puke all over the place, and neither of us want that."

It was evening. Gaedyen had made me a rymakri and then gone down to the river to fish. I chose a tree about twenty feet away, the farthest I'd ever tried. I positioned my legs and shoulders in the proper stance, made sure to hold my wrist consistently, aimed, and threw. The knife missed the tree entirely and I wasted several minutes looking for it in dead leaves.

Each subsequent attempt was met with a similar level of success. At last I got so frustrated that I chucked the knife as hard as I could in no particular direction. I knew it was long gone and probably about to disintegrate anyway, so I sulked off toward the river, hoping Gaedyen would make me another one.

I found him standing over the water, staring intently into it—probably at a fish. I stood still for several seconds, waiting for him to strike. I didn't want to interrupt him and cause him to lose it. But after a while, when he still hadn't moved, I wondered if he was okay.

"Hey, Gaedyen! Are you okay?"

He turned to me. "Come, look at this."

I jogged to him. "What is it?"

"So we know that the rock allows you to turn invisible, and we know that it almost allowed you to see through water the night before you met Shaun. But you have not seen through water again since then, have you?"

"No, I haven't. And I have no idea how I did that. Do you think I could learn? Is it as mentally challenging as learning to turn invisible?" It would be a pretty cool thing to be able to do, but I didn't know how I could ever learn how to do that on top of getting better at invisibility and knife throwing.

"Come, look into the water and concentrate. Think of a place that you could see if you were looking out of a body of water near it."

"Do I have to have seen it from that angle before?"

Gaedyen cocked his head to one side. "No, I don't think so."

I thought of the bridge—the one near home that mom hated—with the churning white water underneath. It would be cool to look out at the world from under that water.

Focusing on what I knew of the bridge from where I'd seen it, and then shifting my thoughts to imagine what I would see from beneath the water, I searched for some kind of mental blockade. Something like what I ran into when I tried to turn invisible. But I felt nothing.

Was this going to be easier? I looked hard into the water, hoping to see an image of the bridge ripple into being, but nothing happened except for the return of that tired feeling I'd had by the mountain. It was a kind of tired that I only felt in my mind, not like the soreness of physical exercise... something else. It was pretty uncomfortable.

"You got any other tips? I'm getting nothing"

"Perhaps this is harder for you. But I think you will be able to get it eventually, if you did it once by accident."

"Hmm..." I didn't want to give up so easily. If I could look into the water, there might be some way I could check on Mom. Not that she was frequently near any large bodies of water if she could help it. But maybe I could see her walk into work from a puddle in the parking lot or something like that. I hadn't forgotten what she'd done, but I still wanted to know if she was okay.

Again, nothing.

"Were you looking into somewhere when I walked up a minute ago?"

"Yes, into the Vorbiaquam."

"Why?"

"To see if anyone was looking for us."

"Were they?"

"No."

"Oh. Good. Well, I lost the knife you made me. Would you mind making me another one?"

"Of course." He took a few steps back toward the trees and selected a limb. A few moments later it was a sleek, sharp blade ready to hit its mark.

"Thanks, Gaedyen." I took it from him, careful not to touch the blade itself. "I'll be working on this. See you in a bit."

CHAPTER TWENTY-THREE

A few long days later, I was running low on breakfast bars, and the guilt over leaving Mom in the dark really nagged at me. "Gaedyen, we need to make another stop. I need to stock up on some human food, and…stuff."

He frowned. "I do not even know where we are now. This is not like before when I knew of a place that was relatively secluded. I have no idea what the nearest human habitation is like, how densely populated it is. It is not safe. A silly dislike of fish is no reason to risk your life."

"Come on, *Captain*."

His earflaps turned down slightly as his frown deepened.

"I never said I disliked them. I just also like to have another option on hand in case I need it. And look, I really need to call my mom. I haven't talked to her in ages. She's probably afraid I'm dead."

His eyes widened. "You want to call home and tell your *mom* what is going on?"

I rolled my eyes. "Yes, Gaedyen. I'm going to call home and tell my mom that I'm *hiking* through the woods with a *dragon* to take my dad's rock to South America because of its *magical powers*. I'm sure telling her all that would relieve any fears she has for my safety and mental welfare." Did he think I was an idiot? "No, Stupid! I wanna let her know I'm okay."

"I do not think that is a good idea—"

"Please, Gaedyen. This is important to me."

To my surprise, the lines around his eyes softened a little. "Alright. If you insist," he sighed. "I will go take a look at what is in the area. Can you try to disappear? I would hate to leave you visible. That would be too dangerous."

Gripping the stone in one hand, I closed my eyes. The fissure was there, in the slippery wall. I dug into it, hurled the need for it to work at it. In a few seconds, I was through.

I opened my eyes to a smiling Gaedyen.

"Whoa, Gwythienians actually know how to smile?"

"Yes, we do." It was his turn to roll his eyes. "Stop making a big deal out of it or I will never smile in front of you again."

I couldn't have that. It changed his face so much…from serious to almost content-looking. *Wow.* He had a really nice smile. I laughed. "Okay, fine. Well I guess it must have worked this time." *Yes!*

"Well done. Stay there. Stay invisible. I will be back in a few minutes."

"Okay." *This would be a lot more fun if you would let me ride on your back while you fly around. But, whatever.*

He let me have my way for the most part, so I guessed I shouldn't complain too much about how he went about it.

A strong wind erupted from the sky a few minutes later. I turned to watch his approach. He was invisible at first, but his mighty wings winked back into existence before he landed. Then there was all of him, standing completely visible. He folded his wings, walking the rest of the way toward me.

There was something about seeing him come out of the sky like that. His hugeness was much more noticeable. He looked almost...*glorious.* Was that too big of a word? Anyway, he was something mighty and foreign and really beautiful. And he was coming to talk to me. I actually knew this guy, this dragon. How cool was that?

"What'd you find?" I shielded my eyes from the sun shining behind him.

"This place is too busy, in my opinion. And there are not any outside phones here like there are in some human cities."

"Okay, well I can use an inside phone. Did you scout out a place where I can stock up a little on food?"

"Yes, but if you use an inside phone I will not be able to keep an eye on you."

Should I be annoyed or should I think that's nice of him? I lifted one eyebrow. "Gaedyen, I think I'll be fine for a few minutes. I'm not planning on talking to her for hours or anything like that. So where am I heading?"

He heaved an exaggerated sigh. "There is a gas station on the outskirts, about a mile from here. Shall we get this over with?"

"Sounds good to me. Lead the way."

He walked into the forest, shimmering into invisibility.

Was I still invisible? I glanced at my new hiking boots. Nope, I forgot to concentrate on it when he came back. I hadn't even felt it slip away. Why was it so easy to lose without noticing? That was not good.

I filed the knowledge away for future reference, striding after Gaedyen to keep up.

"You might as well stay visible for this. I'm leading you to the road a few hundred yards from the station, so when you get there you will look like a hitchhiker or some other similar person who would be expected to look like you."

I wrinkled my nose. "What do you mean by that?"

"Well, you have not exactly bathed yourself much recently."

Heat rose into my cheeks. "Do I stink?"

"Not *stink*, per se, but you do smell and look a bit rougher than the typical human girl."

Great. So I'm disgusting, am I? Fabulous. And he had such a good sense of smell. How bad did I smell to him? That was really embarrassing.

I took my rain jacket off. Wherever we were now was warm enough in the afternoon to do without it, though nights and mornings were still chilly.

Should I really go into a public place like this? People might recognize me. But, no... the only being hunting us wouldn't go around with a picture asking humans if they saw me. If there was a Gwythienian following us, a stinky me would be much easier to track than a me that smelled more average.

Crap. It was too cold to bathe in the river, and I didn't like being naked without four walls around me. "So, suddenly you're okay with me staying visible?"

"You might be able to get away with using an outside phone invisibly, but you cannot walk into a store, buy things, and use the phone inside without being visible. People would really have a problem with a ghost. Do you disagree?"

"Fair point."

Semi-trucks rolled down the interstate from the other side of the trees. Cars whizzed by even louder. Before long, the busy interstate came into view.

"Alright, walk along the road, but stay a safe distance away from it, and stay outside the tree line. It needs to look like you are coming from the road, not the woods. Go in and buy what you need, and then use the phone if they have it. If you are not out in fifteen minutes, I will come in and get you, and that would best be avoided. Do you understand?"

Alright, now I was annoyed. He was going to "come in and get me?" Kind of unnecessary, wasn't it? "Fine."

"I will be walking in the woods next to you or flying above, invisible. If you need me, you have only to call. I will always come."

Perhaps it was how he worded it, but that kind of touched me. I'd never had someone to call if I was in danger before. It was so reassuring to know that there was someone nearby who'd rush to my aid. It would've been nice to have that in the past, and I realized I was glad to have it now, even if he was getting a little ridiculous about it.

I couldn't help smiling. "Thanks, Gaedyen."

"Of course. I will see you soon."

I stepped beyond the trees and headed along the road. A rundown gas station came into view a few minutes later. The ugly red roof over its two gas pumps was faded and the sign missed light bulbs in a few of the letters. Once I was closer, I saw that one of the pumps was out of order. There was only one car in the parking lot.

This is his idea of over-crowded?

A buzzer sounded when I opened the door. Its obnoxious alarm stretched out for several seconds at an uncanny pitch. It was as if the nails-on-a-chalkboard-sound screamed in pain.

I found the breakfast bars quickly and gathered a wider variety than last time. Throwing a snack bag of chips on top of the pile, I passed the feminine products and was relieved not to need them today.

Slowly approaching the counter, I glanced around for a phone, but didn't see one.

Well, it's not like I really want to call her. I wasn't exactly looking forward to it. But still, I should. It's not fair to let her wonder whether or not I'm alive.

"Will this be all for you today?" the cashier—whose beat-up, red baseball cap had seen better days—spared half a glance at me before returning to his cellphone. With one hand, he typed madly at it and with the other he scanned my purchases. Quite the multitasker.

"Yes, thanks."

"That'll be…" poor thing had to look away from his phone for an *entire* second to check the register, "…fifteen sixty-seven."

At least I wouldn't have to worry about him noticing or remembering my nasty, bloodstained clothes.

I handed him the twenty. "Is there a phone here I can use?"

"Uh, sorry, no public phone." He opened the cash drawer and dealt out my change without looking up. Skills.

"Okay well it is kind of an emergency. Can I use your phone? It'll just be for a couple minutes."

"Sorry, can't lose this game."

I stared at him, determined. "Come on, please? It's an emergency."

He handed me the handles of a plastic bag full of my things. "Uh, sorry—"

"No, you don't seem to understand the situation. Someone thinks I'm *dead*."

He looked at my face for the first time. "Uh, okay. Just a sec."

I crossed my arms. He stretched his torso over the whole counter, holding the phone with both hands right in front of his nose.

A whole minute passed. Was he trying to wait me out?

"Oh, please!" I snatched the phone from him and closed the game.

"No!" He collapsed onto his elbows with hands outstretched. "How could you do that? I was almost to level seventy!"

Ignoring him, I tapped the phone button and entered the number for Mom's work.

It rang once… twice… someone picked up on the third ring. "Tennessee's best logistics company, Jer'my speakin'." *Not this guy again.* "How can I help you on this fine—"

"Hi, I need to talk to Lisa Montgomery. It's an emergency."

"Sure thing." How was it possible to make four syllables out of that?

There was a click before the classical composition buzzed statically in my ear. I tapped one foot, impatient. Red Hat continued to stare at me with indignant shock.

"Hello? Enzi? Is that you?" Her voice was hoarse and too high-pitched.

"Yeah, hi, Mom—"

"Oh my gosh! Enzi, are you okay? What happened? Where are you?"

"I'm totally fine, Mom. I'm in...well I'm not exactly sure. I needed to get away for a bit. But I'm very sorry I didn't tell you about it. I'm—"

"You needed to get away? You weren't kidnapped, or taken against your will or anything? You just...*left?*"

"Yes I—"

"How could you do that to me?" she shrieked. "Here I've been thinking you were taken by men or who knows what...you could have been *dead!* I had no idea...you left me to imagine the worst! I've been sleeping at the police station, waiting for news, bugging the officers... and you left because you just *felt* like taking a trip? What were you thinking, Enzi? How could you do that? I get that you're pissed at me for not telling you about your father sooner, but did you have to do *this* to make me pay for it?"

Sobs mixed with her words now.

"Well I've paid for it, okay? I looked for you everywhere! I checked around that mountainside by the highway that you think is *so* beautiful. I slid down to the river under the bridge that you always want to take to work in the morning to look for *your body.* You'd been so upset, how was I supposed to know you hadn't committed suicide? I searched all over every icicle-covered mountain I could find! I thought I saw your reflection in the icicles, staring up at the sky, as if I was supposed to look for you up there!" Her voice broke. "I was so afraid you were dead! I'm losing my *mind*, Enzi!"

She burst into tears.

I guess I partly deserved that. But I hadn't up and left. I *had* been abducted. But clueing her in on that would hardly help the situation. "Mom, I am *really* sorry. But I had to—"

"You better be on your way home right now, young lady! How far away are you?"

"I'm not on my way home, Mom. I'm going to be gone for a while longer, okay? I'm sorry but there's something I need to—"

"No! That is not okay! Enzi, you need to come home now!"

"Mom, listen to me. I can't come home yet. I'm fine and safe. You don't need to worry. But I can't come home yet."

Silence.

"Stop sleeping at the police station, okay? Go home and tell Dad 'hi' for me, next time you see him, okay? I love you."

I hung up before she could answer. My hands shook. I took a deep breath, nearly to tears myself. That was enough for one day.

Tell Dad hi for me? What was I thinking? I still didn't even know if *he* knew I existed.

"Here, I'm sorry I ruined your game. Thanks for letting me borrow your phone."

He snatched it from me with a glare and then flipped back to the game—all thumbs again.

The door buzzer pierced my eardrums as I left, stuffing my groceries into my many pockets. Wincing, I wadded up the empty bag and stuffed that in another pocket, just in case.

I headed back the way I came, shielding my eyes and looking into the sky for Gaedyen. If he was there, I couldn't see him.

Something twisted in my gut. It hadn't been my fault that I'd left. Maybe I should've tried harder to let her know I was okay sooner, but she'd lied to me for who knew how many years. I didn't owe her an explanation for everything I did. This was kind of a big deal, though. But still, she didn't need to yell at me like that.

Gosh, sleeping at the police station? She must've been really worried. That was probably more comfortable than sleeping in the woods though. I missed my stupid mattress. And the *Tin Can*. My legs would appreciate a break from all this foot travel. Would I even remember how to drive after not using a car for so long?

Gah!

I needed to think about something else. I could sift through these emotions later. It was too much right now.

As I crossed the tree line, Gaedyen materialized several paces in front of me. "How did it go?"

I stared at him, unsure how to respond. "Let's just get out of here."

"With pleasure."

CHAPTER TWENTY-FOUR

I took my frustrations out on a thick oak that night. Gaedyen gave me a rymakri even before I asked for one. I severely scarred the poor trunk within a few minutes, but I still couldn't hit the spot I aimed for. If I ever needed to use this skill to defend myself, I would undoubtedly be weaker than whoever my enemy was. So I needed to be a heck of a lot better.

I took aim again, standing erect and holding my wrist like Gaedyen taught me. I let out a slow breath, then stepped forward and threw my blade at the tree. It hit the bark to the left of the bullseye and bounced off.

"Ugh! I'm never going to get this!" I marched to where the knife lay on the ground, picked it up, and stabbed it point blank into the bullseye. My hand slipped with the impact and sharp pain burst across my palm. Blood seeped from the thin slice. "Ugh! Why?"

The knife fell to the ground, one edge bright red. I picked it up with my other hand, planning to hurl it into the woods, but it splintered at my touch—*ouch!*—and then crumbled away.

Of course.

I left the remains of the rymakri there and stomped to the river to wash the cut, trying to pick out the splinters with my fingernails.

When I reached the edge, I plunged both hands in. The water was frigid. I dried them off on my clothes the moment they were clean, wondering again which was the lesser of the evils: freezing to death or dying of embarrassment from what I looked and smelled like.

My reflection appeared in the surface as the disturbed water calmed, that one scar still peeking out from my shirt collar. Why had Mom thought she'd seen my reflection on the icicles and in the river? That was weird. It even sounded a little Gwythienian-ish…but, no. There was no way this could have anything to do with her. Dad was the one who'd found the stone.

Something was different about my reflected face. I leaned further out to get a closer look. It was—better?—than it used to be. Not really pretty, but there was less pudginess in my cheeks and chin. And my neck was slimmer too! I was still nowhere near Carlie's slenderness, but wow!

It was nice to see myself like that. I'd always wondered what I'd look like in better shape, but I'd had a reason to stay overweight. Being pretty was too risky, and it wasn't like I could go through life being invisible all the time, even if I did reach that level of mastery someday.

I couldn't keep losing weight like this…but with all this exercise and the amount and type of food I ate, I was on track to keep this up. Part of me was anxious to see what the real me would look like, but the other side of me was afraid.

This adventure wouldn't last forever. Someday I'd go back to our apartment in our little town. Caleb would still be around sometimes. He might do worse than say nasty things to me if he saw me looking like, well, how I might be able to look.

But I would've gotten in a lot of practice with the knives by then. I could fight him!

Ha! Who was I kidding? There was no way I'd get *that* good. Not at the rate I was going. And besides, the fear would paralyze me like it always did when he was near me. It wouldn't matter if I were a whiz with a blade by then.

I refocused on the mirror image of my face. I'd never realized my eyes were shaped quite like that—was that what they called almond-shaped? I looked a lot like Mom. I wondered if anyone would confuse us if I ever got perfectly down to her size? That reminded me of Tony—that slimy old man I'd met in the woods outside Odan Terridor. He'd thought I looked like someone. He'd asked for my grandmother's name. That was odd, why her name? Why not Mom's? Did I resemble her closely as well?

My face really was dirty though. Like, *wow*. Good thing Mom wouldn't have seen me like this when she imagined she could see my reflection in the icicles. How mental. That wasn't like her. But she'd always been adamant about cleanliness. We were dirt poor, but not dirty. Showers every night before bed. Always showers though, never baths.

What had she said it looked like I was doing? Staring up at the sky or something? Why in the world would she imagine me doing that?

Dried leaves crackled behind me. I whirled. "Gaedyen! You scared the crap out of me!"

"Are you alright? I smell blood." His eyes were wide, his head held erect, earflaps twitching for signs of danger.

"I'm fine," I sighed. "Just cut myself on the rymakri like an idiot. Came down here to wash it off." My heart kept pounding even when I recognized that I was not in danger… I was too busy wondering if he smelled unbathed-human stinkiness over there.

"Oh." His eyes relaxed as his earflaps stilled. "I am glad you are not badly hurt."

"Thanks." It was nice of him to be concerned, but I was still distracted.

"What are you thinking about?"

I considered whether to share my thoughts with him, then decided, *why not?*

"My mom said something weird on the phone. She said she searched for me at the places that I liked—the icy mountainside, the river—and she kept thinking she saw my reflection. She said one time it looked like I was staring up at the sky. Something about it doesn't seem right. Maybe she was seeing things because she was panicking? I mean, I couldn't have accidentally shared Possession with her... like, she couldn't have somehow gotten the ability to see through water because of being around me with the stone for all those years, could she?"

He shook his head. "Absolutely not. Only one person at a time."

"But I, being a human, shouldn't have been able to gain Possession of the rock. What if other weird things could be going on with it?"

"As unexpected as your Possession of the rock is, there is still no way that could have happened. It is simply not how it works. Whatever it is that gives the rocks their power, they can only affect one person at a time."

"Hmm...." It was a dumb idea anyway. "Well your stupid rymakri lodged a giant splinter in my finger. Any advice for how to get it out?"

On the ninth morning of our travels, ten days after I was drugged and dumped on Gaedyen, I awoke feeling adequately refreshed for the first time since taking on this venture. I sat up and stretched, and it actually felt good. It wasn't the same miserable, achy feeling I'd experienced the past several days that made me long for my mattress and old patchy quilt. It made me feel energized instead of beaten down. On this particular morning, I was surprised to find that I wasn't dreading the workout I knew was coming. I didn't look forward to it, but I didn't dread it either. Satisfied, I stood up without the usual winces and groans. My legs were barely stiff at all.

Turning toward Gaedyen, I hiked up my stretched-out pants. He had a fire going. His back was to me and his skin glistened in the sunlight, as if he'd been in the river, maybe to snag some fish. He always brought one for me, and I always cooked it on a stick over the fire until I was sure I'd charred it thoroughly.

I stuck fiercely by my motto that burnt was better than raw, and even though fish didn't need more than a couple of minutes on each side, I still didn't have skill with an open fire and a stick like I did with a stove and skillet. But since acquiring the breakfast bars, I'd always cooked my fish from his evening feeding, to avoid wasting the daylight in the morning like I had in the beginning. I'd eat half a bar—the number was dwindling—to start the day, eat the other half for lunch, and then end the day with a cooked fish. Gaedyen absolutely never cooked his and was as steadfastly against cooking as I was for it, which was why the roasting meat smell confused me.

"Gaedyen? What's going on?" I asked his back as I approached.

His weird scar-thing looked like it was covered in mud, again—at least that's what I thought it was. It never ceased to amaze me how he always came back *dirty* from a swim, as if he rolled in the mud after capturing our meal. And it was always his neck, the one part that submerged for fish, even if the rest of his body stayed on land. It was a mystery to me.

I walked around the fire to get a better look.

He sat on his haunches, bent in concentration, clumsily grasping one of his sharpened sticks with a skewered fish on the end of it. It dangled over the fire, much too high up for the heat to affect it.

"I thought you said cooking dried it out and ruined the flavor." I gave him the eyebrow. This had been another frequent discussion of ours during our long tramp through the woods.

He glared at the roasting fish. "It does. But *apparently* you like it dry and flavorless, so I am preparing it that way for you."

"You're making me food?" My question ended on an incredulously high note. Had I missed something?

"I told you that I was. What does it look like I am doing? Making *myself* food?" He stared comically at the still raw fish.

"Well, thank you?" Was there some reason behind this?

"You can thank me when it is done."

I frowned. "Sure. And just so you know, that moment would probably come sooner if you held the fish closer to the fire. How do you expect the meat to cook if it's dangling three feet above the heat? You *do* know how cooking works, don't you?"

The ridges above his eyes, where he would've had eyebrows if he had hair, furrowed even more deeply. He looked undecided for a few moments, as if he didn't want to admit he'd done something wrong, but then he slowly brought the stick lower, close enough that the flames licked the scales of the fish that hovered sideways above them. I thought I saw him sneak a glance back to see if I watched, but I wasn't sure.

I smiled. He had to listen to *me* for a change. But why would Gaedyen do something so kind for me? It felt nice—him doing something for me that wasn't for the sake of saving resources or getting us there faster. I realized that I felt strangely girlish about it, as if some boy I had a crush on had held the door open for me, or something.

Whoa, this makes me feel like that?

Was he trying to butter me up for some reason? Was bad news coming? And me, having a crush on someone…where had that notion come from? It had been a really long time since

I'd felt feelings anything like that. Sure the occasional cute guy caught my notice—especially like Shaun—but I was usually too scared to actually feel anything.

But I felt a jumping feeling in my stomach last time I saw Shaun, and I felt something today, too. Though it wasn't a jumping-stomach feeling like that. It was more… warm, I guess. Subtler. Quieter. But equally as nice and as unexpected.

I spent the remaining several minutes of Gaedyen's fish-cooking time coming up with wild and outlandish reasons for why he would do something nice for me that didn't benefit him in any way, especially something he disapproved of. But I couldn't come up with anything legitimate by the time he proclaimed the fish "probably dry and flavorless enough for silly human preferences."

He pointed the sharp end of the stick at me, indicating that I should now remove the cooked fish from it. I did so slowly, doubting that it was really cooked through enough. Hesitantly, I used the debit card to cut out a minuscule bite, testing the doneness. My eyebrows raised. "It's completely cooked, and delicious. Thanks, Gaedyen."

He smiled a small smile, once again brightening his usually glowering face. "You are welcome."

When he said it quiet and calm, I remembered the first time I heard his beautiful voice in the darkness of his home in Odan Terridor. I hadn't thought of it that way since then—he'd always spit out orders or was irritated by my ceaseless questions. But now, I heard the smile in his voice, and it actually *warmed my heart*, for lack of a better expression. It redoubled my desire to hear him sing, though I knew that was a lost cause.

Smiling back, I took another bite, a bigger one this time, and chewed appreciatively, closing my eyes to enjoy the taste. The thoughtfulness and surprise of the meal made it taste really good, despite the lack of herbs and spices. I finished it quickly, my sense of hunger awakened by the satisfying flavor, and threw the remains on the ground behind me. "That was very good. Thanks again."

"You are welcome, again," he answered once more with that melodic voice and a smile.

That heart-warming feeling bubbled up once more, and suddenly, all I wanted to do was keep him talking. I wanted to hear his voice more—this happy, contented version of it—and I wanted to make him smile again. It was so...*nice*. I wanted to keep it going. "Gaedyen, tell me something about Odan Terridor."

CHAPTER TWENTY-FIVE

*H*e met my gaze steadily, but his smile was gone. "What do you want to know?" The sweet, harmonic voice was still there, but this time it sounded subtly mournful.

"Tell me more about your, uh, style of education. You said you don't have books, right?"

"That is true, we do not pass on our history or our skills through literature, as you humans and some of the other realms do. We pass it on verbally, from one generation to the next." He rose and kicked dirt over the fire, stamping it out.

I stood to follow, hungry for more information about him and how he grew up, and eager to hear that voice while it remained calm and pleasant.

"We have not always been so fastidious a people, however. Our histories only go back so far. We do not know how we came into being, or whether we have always lived on this continent or came from another place. There are legends that our ancestors did not have the same form that we have now. And there are rumors that we were once a people of great magic-wielding. We know that some part of that must be true, if even to the vaguest degree, because we are bound to the rocks, and it is our race that has been charged with the keeping of them since as long as anyone from any realm can remember. But as I said, those ages back are very dim in the minds of our old ones, and no one knows for sure."

"Tell me more about the rocks," I said eagerly, sidetracked from my original question.

"Ours is purple, as you know." He glanced at my neck. It gave me chills. But the nice kind? "Another is red, another blue, and one green. Each one was bound to one Possessor and kept hidden somewhere in our realm. Only the Keeper knew the location of the hiding place, and they were never removed from that secret location, except for Possessorship Ceremonies. It was during these, when all four rocks and each of their Possessors were together, that Possession could be passed on without the deaths of the previous Possessors. When each changed at once, they all remained alive. These events were always the cause of great celebration and feasting. I wish I could have seen one. I would love to have seen all the different realms coming together in such peace." He sounded so wistful, and his descriptions were so captivating.

I wanted to witness one of these events at least as much as he did.

He heaved a deep sigh. "Unfortunately, I can only tell from what I have heard and imagined, I cannot tell from real experience. There is a painfully slim chance that such a thing will ever take place again. The other realms do not trust us now, and I cannot blame them. The whole system of existing peacefully together as friends and allies is thrown off, and it was our realm that had the greatest responsibility of keeping them safe.

"Now all of the Possessors are old and weak. They should be able to pass on the stress and burden of responsibility to a pair of younger shoulders. They should be free to enjoy some of the things in life that they had to deny themselves for years and years while they put all others before themselves to keep things going smoothly in their own realms and between all of the realms collectively." He stared wistfully into the distance. "But they cannot. Nor can the younger generation have their turn, as is their right, to elect a new leader. Lacking the rocks throws things horribly off balance."

"But if Possessorship can only be changed when they're all together, and if they haven't all been together since Padraig became the Possessor of the rock of the Gwythienians, and if Padraig is—obviously—still alive, how is it possible that *I'm* the Possessor of your realm's rock?"

"I have no idea. It has been bothering me since I first began suspecting that you had Possession of it, before I was even sure that it was the actual rock. I have been puzzling over it every minute, but I cannot come up with any sort of plausible reason. It is most frustrating."

He spoke with his usual, business-like tone. I regretted interrupting him and losing the nice voice. But really, how could I be the Possessor? Would Padraig be horribly angry when he found out? Or maybe just as puzzled as we were? Did he know something we didn't that could explain it?

I needed to keep Gaedyen talking, so I asked the first question that came to mind. "Tell me about your family. Do you have any brothers or sisters?"

His whole body stiffened and his face hardened into that angry-brows look. I mentally slapped myself. He'd made it clear only a few days ago that the topic of his parents was off-limits. No more of that smile, no more nice voice. *Shoot.*

"I have no family."

Maybe none that you recognize…but you have to be related to someone.

I didn't dare push him further. Something about that question really upset him. From what I could piece together about that, Padraig didn't get along with Gaedyen's father. Why? Maybe that was what made Gaedyen too uncomfortable to talk.

We continued on in silence for hours. I eased into the tuned-out state brought on by the monotonous beat of my constant footfalls. It was getting late, probably almost time to call it a day. I was so deep in my own thoughts that I ran several paces past Gaedyen's halted form before realizing he was no longer in front of me. I whirled around, searching for him. Had I lost him?

No, there he was behind me. I hurried back, just as the sky started drizzling. "What's up, Gaedyen?" I held out my hand and watched the raindrops splatter on it.

"Shh!"

I raised my eyes to his and his expression worried me. That furrowed-brow look, plus the stance of his earflaps. Did he smell that Tukailaan-ish scent again?

Oh no. "What's happening?" I barely heard my own whisper, but I knew he could hear me.

He stared past me, earflaps flicking this way and that at top speed, and an instant later, his intense gaze was leveled at me—at my soul. I stared back, wide eyed and wondering what the heck he was doing.

Then he parted his lips almost imperceptibly and breathed, "Get on."

CHAPTER TWENTY-SIX

What? Hadn't he drilled into me the improperness of that? How he'd rather take months on a journey than have me riding on his back?

J stared, unsure what to do. Had I misunderstood what he'd said? How would I even get all the way up there?

The next thing I knew I was being flung through the air by the hood of my sweatshirt and thrown backward over his head. I stifled a scream and landed painfully on his back, one leg hanging over his side, the other draped sloppily around one wing shoulder. As the sticks in his satchel bruised my back, my hands flopped around, grasping for a hand hold. Finding none, I reached up, flexing my non-existent abs, and grabbed at the wing shoulder under my left leg.

"It's Tukailaan! Shut up and hang on to something! And get invisible *now!*"

Then he bolted. I tried to get a firm grip on something but it was too bouncy. I nearly fell off, holding on for dear life with one leg. He ducked his head and shoulders, pitching my body forward for an instant. I threw my arms around the thick muscles of his neck and held on as tight as I could while he pushed off into the sky and pumped his wings with enough force to carry us into the blackness above.

My stomach dropped and a scream stuck in my throat. I opened my eyes to see nothingness beneath me—he'd turned invisible, which did *not* help the stomach situation. I squeezed as hard as I could with my arms and legs, afraid of falling off and plummeting through the air to certain death as I tried to turn invisible myself, but I was too distracted to focus the way I needed to. My stomach pitched again. I gave up on invisibility and instead placed my focus on not puking.

A roar came from behind us.

Was that a second set of wingbeats?

Gaedyen's wings attacked the air harder, the muscles of his neck and shoulders ever-changing beneath me as I held on. But he didn't roar back. He didn't want a fight. He wanted to stay hidden.

Was Tukailaan after us? How big was he?

I glanced back just as lighting struck the sky. There was no visible Gwythienian there, but the rain pooled and bounced off an invisible form—one much bigger than Gaedyen.

As Gaedyen pumped harder, fighting gravity, I tried to attain invisibility again. There was the crack, now just to reach it...

We swerved in the same moment that I heard a chomp of teeth where Gaedyen's tail would be.

Must focus...the crack...reach for it...

A heavy slapping noise—had Gaedyen whipped our enemy with his tail?—and a huge roar from right behind us. Did I dare turn and face whatever it was?

The crack in the wall...almost there...

Up and up we soared, through wind and rain. I was completely drenched, blinded by the now heavy drops streaming down my face. I was so glad I'd chosen the rain jacket!

Focus...focus...almost there...

I had it!

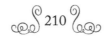

At that moment, Gaedyen dove toward the ground and I nearly lost it again with the nausea. A few moments later, just as my stomach had almost caught up with us, he twisted and soared upward again.

This must be an elusive maneuver...well it worked on my stomach! I'll never find that again!

Reaching behind me, I fumbled for the satchel. If I could just get a grip on one of the sticks, I could pass it to Gaedyen. I finally got ahold of one and pulled it out, but it was too heavy. Another quick change in direction, and I dropped it. Gaedyen spiraled down after it. It went horizontal as soon as his invisible hand wrapped around it. He bit it and launched it behind us.

I waited to hear the rymakri find its mark, or wingbeats getting closer, but the only sound was the pouring rain. A minute went by, then two—maybe more. Had the rymakri done its job? Were we safe? The invisibility was getting harder to hold. It would soon slip.

As he raced through the sky at incredible speeds, I risked lifting my head to search for distant shapes. The biting wind and icy drops flew at my face, making it even harder to see anything that might be hiding itself. I leaned closer to his neck and tried to shield my face with an arm. There was nothing I could do to help with the escape now.

The rainwater seeped through my pants and accumulated around the rim of my boots, dripping frigid water down into them. It chilled me all the way down to my toes. I shivered violently, holding even tighter to him, scrunching my eyes closed. I thought I felt him shiver too. Maybe he wasn't quite so impervious to the cold.

Then he changed directions again, flying both up and forward at the same time. I felt the tension in the movements of his back muscles. One moment I plunged into the cold, and then the wind was suddenly calm. I waited for it to get loud again, and when it didn't, I opened my eyes.

There was the moon. We were above the clouds.

As he leveled out, my stomach finally eased its threat to return my last meal. I gazed at the glowing silver orb, shocked by how magnificent and enormous it was from this high up. It was so beautiful. And, wow. I was really sitting on the back of a flying dragon. We soared through midair...no, *higher* than midair.

When we slowed, I looked back for signs of a follower. Another flash of lightning revealed that our trail was clear. Would it be harder for him to find us above the clouds? Why were we up here?

I tentatively held my arms out to feel the breeze, not yet brave enough to sit up straight in my seat. Flying was the most unbelievable, incredible feeling, but also *really* high up. I closed my eyes, enjoying the exhilaration and holding on tight as ever.

My mind went back to my life in the real world and how this was exactly what I'd wished for. I wanted to fly away from it all, and now I was. Although, who knew what exactly I flew to. But for the moment—at least for this moment—I was free. Despite the cold, despite whatever flew after us, or whatever disasters we may be flying toward. It was like the good music that made my soul feel fresh and whole as I reveled in the melodies around me, flying away on them. With a joyful smile, I realized I had been right about that. Music really was like flying. It was beautiful. It was peaceful. It was freedom.

He flickered back into visibility. We must be safe now. I looked down at his shoulder and saw something other than mud or a scar. The rain washed the mud away, revealing a black mark of some kind. A tattoo? *Whatever it is, it must be important if he wants to keep it hidden. Which means I should definitely check it out.*

I placed my hand over it and then slid forward with my whole body as if I slipped, conveniently smearing away more of the grainy covering. Thin, dark lines sprouted from a central point like an eggshell about to crack open.

Weird.

My fingers lightly traced the lines of the mark, trying to see it all to figure out what it was. And the skin over his neck was softer—made of smaller scales—than the rest of him.

My stomach was left somewhere up on the north side of the clouds when Gaedyen and I practically free fell into a nosedive. My arms and legs burned with the pain of how tight I gripped to stay on board. The drop was as terrifying as the flight had been exciting. Another scream stuck in my throat.

His wings expanded to slow him for a moment. He landed hard. I lurched off over his head and hit the ground with a teeth-jarring crash. I stayed still for a few seconds, waiting to see if anything was broken, but no body parts screamed out in pain at me. I rose slowly to my feet.

"I think we lost him." Panting, Gaedyen shook off excess water almost like a dog. He stepped toward a group of trees, probably for some cover from the downpour. "I have not sensed his presence for several minutes."

I hurried into the trees with him. "Well that's a relief. And look, you carried me on your back and didn't die. And I'm not over here expecting a proposal or anything, so..." I let my implication hang, confident he was capable of interpreting it.

He cleared his throat. "Yes, well...get some sleep. I will stand guard. And no fire tonight. We do not want to risk attracting attention."

I felt a little guilty. I didn't want to be like a spoiled child, sleeping while my superior stayed awake to watch for danger, especially after he'd already done all the work in the first place, but I didn't have the finely-tuned senses that he did. If I stood guard, we'd probably get attacked before I knew anyone had even gotten close.

He ignored my point about the whole flying instead of walking the rest of the way thing. But since he was going to stand guard, and the two of us flying would mean a continuation of him doing all the work, I cut him some slack. I'd wait until morning for that conversation.

My clothes were drenched through. I quietly pulled off my coat and boots. I would just have to live with the soaked pants—I wasn't taking those off in company. Fortunately, the raincoat had kept my sweatshirt mostly protected. Draping the coat over a low branch to drip dry, I turned the boots upside down and dumped out the accumulated water.

I found a dryer place near Gaedyen and lay down on one side, resting my head in the crook of my arm. Gaedyen scooted close enough to me that his side was against my back, and then laid a wing lightly over me.

I was touched. Even after doing all the work for the day, he was still there, considerately keeping me warm. That was more than I deserved.

CHAPTER TWENTY-SEVEN

The sawdust scratched my back. Caleb was there, already too close again.
 "I said, shut up!"
 But I couldn't hold in the sobs—the whimpers of pain.
 I was not brave.
 But he'd meant what he said. He brought the knife down....

*T*he smell of cooking meat woke me in the morning. I rubbed my temples, trying to shake off the memories storming through my head. My stomach growled and I sat up, looking for the source. Slowly, the events of last night came back to me. My arms and legs were incredibly sore—again.

Must've been that *smooth* landing. I wanted to tell him that he was going to have to work on those landings, because the two I'd experienced so far had *sucked*, but he'd been so considerate to shelter me and stay up to keep watch that I couldn't bring myself to complain.

I guessed the muscles used while running extensively are not the same ones used when gripping a dragon for dear life.

The way I held my arms while jogging—it always made them tired—must not have been much of a work out, because my arms were worse off than my legs today.

"So, Tukailaan?"

"Yes—what a strange scent. I do not understand it. I had to get him off our trail. Of course he must know we have the rock, but I do not think there is any way he could know you are the Possessor. If that were the case and you were found, you would, as you know, be in grave danger for your Possession. There is a cooked fish on the fire for you."

My heart skipped a beat. It was the nice voice. So musical and…seductive.

Whoa, whoa, whoa! Seductive? How could I think that at all, especially about the voice of a *different species?*

Rein it in there, Enzi. There is no one you will ever be good enough for. You are too broken. Plus, that isn't even a physical possibility.

Actually though, that limitation was more of a plus for me anyway.

Contemplative, I strode over to the fire and picked up the stick with the sloppily skewered fish. There were other sticks over the fire too. To my surprise, I found my rain coat and boots suspended there. Holding the skewer in one hand, I pulled the boots down and slipped into them—so warm and toasty!—and then shrugged on the rain jacket. Dry as a bone. And my pants had mostly dried out overnight thanks to Gaedyen's body heat. It felt wonderful to be so warm and dry.

Sometimes, you can be the most considerate dragon in the world. The words stuck in my throat. For some reason, my tongue became shackled to the roof of my mouth at the thought of saying them out loud.

I took one hesitant bite of the fish. It was delicious. Perfectly cooked. I gobbled down the rest, ready to be on our way.

Since we'd broken the ice over the whole flying thing, I was pretty confident that we would be taking the sky for the remainder of the journey. But I was anxious to find out for sure. If it took being followed and chased to change his mind, better that it happened before we started swimming. I really hoped that possibility would be off the table now.

"Thank you for the fish, Gaedyen. It's delicious."

"You are welcome."

Though he was turned away from me when he replied, I thought I glimpsed a small smile on the side of his face. Alright, it *was* attractive. That was a fair enough word, right? Not weird. Just…well, I didn't really know. I liked hearing his voice and I looked forward to hearing it again. I'd be very sad if I never got to hear it again. Shaun had an attractive voice too, if a bit deeper than would be expected. Gaedyen's fit him exactly.

My eyes wandered over his back as he stared up at the sky. He'd already covered the mark with mud again. What was that all about? "Hey, what's that mark on your shoulder?"

He froze. "What mark?"

I rolled my eyes. "You know what I'm talking about. The one on your left shoulder—that you're always trying to cover up? I've already seen it so there's no point in pretending it's not there."

He slowly turned toward me. "That is something no one else can see."

"I saw it and the world didn't implode. What's the big deal? What does it mean?"

"It means trouble for both of us if anyone else learns of it, alright? If you ever notice it showing again, you need to tell me immediately so I can hide it. It is getting more and more difficult. The farther we get from Odan Terridor, the more the surface earth changes and the harder it is to get mud to stay where I want it and be the right color. Please inform me if it is ever noticeable in the future, okay?"

"Only if you tell me what it means."

He pierced my eyes with his own. "This is not a light matter, Enzi. Please do not ask again."

Maybe another subject change was in order. "So, since we broke the ice over the whole flying together thing, and since I obviously don't expect you to marry me for it," I almost choked on that last bit, hoping he couldn't read on my face how that sounded to me after I said it out loud, "are we going to fly the rest of the way?"

His brow pinched together. "As much as it is not ideal, walking has taken much longer than I thought, and we may not have that kind of time for the rest of the journey. At this rate, we will be traveling for months before arriving at our first destination. The whole endeavor could take years longer than necessary. So, in light of the time constraint, I believe I will have to make an exception. But I would appreciate it if you did not mention this to anyone. Ever. And you must give up on the mark as well."

I rolled my eyes. I would give it a break for the time being. "Agreed."

To get to fly again! The feeling of being wrapped in music and of soaring through the serenity that is a beautiful sound… Yeah, I'd felt a little sick during takeoff, and yeah, the really fast ups and downs had done it, too. But that was probably because we were under such stress from being chased.

"No worries, man. Your secret's safe with me. *Both* of them."

"One other difficulty with that plan. You will have to turn invisible and remain invisible for long periods of time. Especially during takeoff and landing. I will be invisible as well. We cannot risk being seen by humans in planes above us or on the ground below. And we cannot risk showing ourselves so obviously to any followers. Do you think you can do that?"

Well, I *had* been practicing, and I had improved—at least some. Even though I was never able to do it without touching the stone, I could probably manage it, at least enough to give my legs a break from walking. Not for a whole day of travel though.

Before replying, I felt in the back of my mind for the crack in the wall. With the cold rock against my chest, I tore through the crack and disappeared. "I think I can do it. I'm not sure how long though. Maybe only like ten minutes, if that."

"It is a start. And once we reach a high enough altitude, no one on the ground will be able to make you out from a bird. It is the planes we will have to keep an eye on."

"Alright. Let's go." Standing, I took the few steps toward him. How could I get up to his wing shoulders again without being picked up and tossed like I had been last night? Glancing back at me, he must've guessed my predicament. He leaned the shoulder facing me far enough down toward the ground that I could hook one leg over his thick neck and pull myself the rest of the way up.

I squirmed around until I felt situated, then gazed around us to enjoy the view from this vantage point. I took a deep breath, smiling hugely, and turned invisible.

"Ready?" he asked.

"Very."

He burst forward with powerful strides, then pushed off hard with his huge back legs as he pumped his wings. In the excitement of the actual flying last night, I'd forgotten how scary the taking off part was. My stomach jerked and I felt breakfast rise. I held on for all I was worth, to both the invisibility and this morning's fish.

We burst upward, his wings pumping at an incredible speed. His powerful muscles moved and flexed under me. Once we leveled out, my arms slowly released their death grip on his neck and I gradually raised myself up a little, not quite into a sitting position. I was glad to have only wind instead of rain pelting my face.

When I opened my eyes, I saw the forest directly beneath me. Gaedyen turned invisible at some point while taking off. That did not help the sick feeling in my stomach. Would it be a problem if some poor innocent soul got puked on from no discernible source in the sky? We'd be long gone by the time it hit. Still though, I'd rather not. So I distracted myself with the view.

We passed the river Gaedyen had caught fish in that morning. It snaked along beneath us, shimmering in the sun. The view wasn't as nice with the snow exchanged for grey slush, but I was glad it was getting warmer.

We flew much longer that day. It was still chilly, but no longer wet—a major improvement. Due to the noise of the wind, Gaedyen couldn't hear any of my questions, so as we whizzed past trees, ponds, buildings, fields and neighborhoods, I sang my heart out. It was so nice to be alone in that way. I could sing, and he couldn't hear me. Nobody could. I could barely hear my own voice, which was definitely a plus. I didn't like to hear my voice, but I loved the *feeling* of singing. I hadn't sung in…how long? Like almost two weeks! The days all blurred together a bit now.

I'd had countless songs playing over and over again in my head as we walked and jogged, but I'd never even considered singing around Gaedyen. That was way too personal a thing to do with an audience. But now, I sang and sang until my throat hurt and I knew my voice would be hoarse and raspy next time I was actually able to hear it.

When we landed, talking hurt and I sounded like a dying frog whenever I tried it, but I didn't mind. It'd been a very enjoyable day.

Gaedyen caught us some more fish again, but I cooked my own this time, enjoying the new taste of this different-looking type. Most of the fish we'd eaten so far were white on the bottom with green, gray, and yellow speckles on the top, and a bit more stocky and round. These were smooth gray on the back, though their bellies where white as well. They were longer, skinnier, and tasted saltier. Must've been a different species. Was that a sign that we were nearing the ocean? A new kind of fish, possibly due to that whole thing about salt and fresh water mixing? But we probably weren't that far south yet. It did taste saltier though, and that felt good to my irritated throat.

Gaedyen and I ate in silence, and when I laid down, he came to curl up next to me and shelter me with his wing. That gesture was always so warm and comforting that I fell asleep with a smile on my face.

There was the sawdust. The knife. Caleb.

Something real jostled me, pulling me out of the dream into consciousness. Delirious, I strained to open my eyes, realizing after a few confused moments that they were already open, it was just that dark out. Was I still dreaming? I thought the nightmare had ended. This wasn't part of it anyway. It was never dark, always light enough for me to see more than I wanted to. I shifted, reaching out for Gaedyen, but I felt nothing but cold, empty ground next me.

"Gaedyen?" I croaked, vocal chords still in recovery.

Only silence answered me.

CHAPTER TWENTY-EIGHT

"*G*aedyen?" I whispered sharply this time.

Still, nothing. I stood and shuffled around, arms extended like a mummy rose from the dead, hoping to run into my traveling companion.

A deafening crash pounded through my ears and shook the ground beneath me. I fell to my knees and shoved myself back up, fully alert, adrenaline coursing through my veins. What was happening?

Whirling, I caught a glimpse of trees colliding with each other and dominoing to the ground as an invisible force ruthlessly assaulted them, forging a path through their midst. Moonlight shone bright through the gaps where the trees no longer stood.

There was a threatening bellow. It sounded like Gaedyen, but I wasn't sure. A moment later that same voice roared in pain as more trees crashed to the ground under the invisible whirlwind.

Was Gaedyen fighting Tukailaan? Had he found us at last? Or was it Padraig? Had he found out that I had Possession of his rock?

They came toward me, roaring and crashing. I leaped back to avoid them. I wanted to help Gaedyen, but I had to protect the stone. What if I went after Gaedyen to try to help and got killed, and then Gaedyen wasn't the first to touch the stone? He was a Cadoumai, but the abilities of a Gwythienian in Possession of the rock would be unbeatable, no matter how good he was.

They rolled past me so quickly I couldn't keep up with them.

"You are supposed to be dead!" an incredibly deep, gravelly voice boomed. "And you are still causing me trouble! But you will never take her away from me! Never again!"

That didn't sound like Padraig's voice. It had to be Tukailaan! There was a dull thud and a pained grunt from one of them. Gaedyen?

"She was always meant to be mine!" There was a loud *chomp*, and one of them roared again as a pool of red appeared under the invisible fighters. I stifled a scream.

Was that Gaedyen? There was too much blood!

I must not have stifled the scream as well as I thought, because the noise of their fight ceased after I let it out. There was more struggling from the bleeding one, another blow and one of the fighters was still. Heavy, somber footfalls increased in volume as they approached me.

I had to turn invisible. Now was so not the time to be distracted! Grabbing the stone in one hand, I held still and focused. The crack in the wall was wider now. I held it more easily, but the difficulty was breaking through it. I thought hard at it, struggling to concentrate over the frantic beating of my heart.

Just when I was almost through, a pair of large nostrils exhaled right behind me. Two jets of warm air rushed against my neck. I was frozen to the spot. *Did I turn invisible? It won't matter if he can smell me! Why hasn't he eaten me yet? Can Gwythienians get colds? Maybe his nose doesn't work! That would be too easy.*

He turned around my tree and kept walking, sniffing the air as his huge feet trudged through the damp leaves on the forest floor. I dared a look down at myself. I *had* vanished. *Success!*

He turned back and started coming my way again. I considered moving to the other side of the tree, but the ground was covered in noisy leaf litter. Movement would make noise and maybe footprints, too.

Oh no! The footprints! I glanced down again in horror and saw my trail lead right to where I stood. *Shoot!*

His breath was in the air only feet away. He had to be on to me. Was he just playing with me? The cruelest of predators did play with their prey.

He circled back. The puffs of breath grew closer. I searched for anything that could help me. There were two trees a couple steps away—one still standing and the other stretched out on the ground. In a rush, I bent down, scooped up as big a pile of dead leaves as I could manage and threw it at where I thought his face was. Then I took one straining leap to my left and reached for the tree.

It felt for a moment as if I flew. I almost soared over my mark and landed in an awkward crouch, freezing in place. I desperately hoped that any noise I made was covered up by his angry splutters.

Crouching against the fallen log, I listened for footsteps and breaths. Eventually clouds parted from over the moon, and I saw the forest floor even more clearly. In the new light, I saw the shadow of a crumpled and contorted form, blood streaming around it. He hadn't moved. Was he dead? He couldn't be dead! *No!*

My heartbeat was the only sound, pumping so loudly I was afraid it would give my position away, if my boots hadn't already. I forced myself to take several more controlled breaths, trying to calm the frantic beating. I had to stay focused on keeping the wall down so I could stay invisible.

I glanced back toward the crumpled heap of Gaedyen, worrying about his blood loss. The moon shone with its betraying silver light, illuminating the sickening pool of red that had left his body forever. I was gripped by the utter wrongness of it, of blood being *outside* of where it belonged. I shivered with paralyzing memories and tried to shove the images of my own blood away by focusing on the present horror of Gaedyen's.

But then, it was only his blood that lay there on ground. The shadow of his invisible body was gone. I leaned away from the tree trunk, looking for his shadow. Where had he gone?

A throbbing blow struck the back of my head and my face slammed against the tree trunk. There was no time to scream. I was blinded by roaring pain, but I still felt myself being hefted in one large hand and chucked across the forest into another tree. I didn't have time to brace for the impact. When it came, it knocked the breath out of me. I gasped and heaved, trying and failing to inhale precious oxygen.

"How dare you try to sneak a Shimbator past me!" the enemy roared.

"She is no Shimbator!" Gaedyen bellowed. *He's okay!*
"Shimbators are nothing but a legend!"

"Do not speak such lies to me, you *filth!* You know they are real! *He* was supposed to kill you, but I see I will have to finish the job myself!"

There was shuffling in the snow nearby. Maybe I was somehow still invisible? The rock could be touching my chest…I wasn't sure.

And then there was the hand, lifting me up by the middle and reaching back again. It chucked me through the air. Time went by in slow motion, my thoughts whizzing at the speed of a sonic boom. What was he talking about? Gaedyen was supposed to be killed by what?

I still hadn't managed to breathe yet, and I was afraid I never would if I hit another tree with the same impact as the first, but when I hit this one it felt different. It was as if the tree curled around me to cushion my fall. I knew I must be losing consciousness if hurtling through the air into an immovable object felt like nothing more than landing on a rough leather sofa.

I wasn't sure if I'd managed to breathe yet, I couldn't remember the last few seconds. I lifted my head up and opened my eyes as wide as I could, searching for someone—I couldn't remember who.

Were my eyes even open? Why was I trying to open them? I stopped trying to remember.

CHAPTER TWENTY-NINE

"*E*nzi?"

My name pierced the deep sleep and brought with it a splitting headache.

"Enzi, can you hear me?"

Where was the voice coming from? I wished it would shut up and leave me alone—it made the headache pulse. I tried to open my eyes, but scrunched them tightly when the sharp sunlight struck them—also not helping the headache.

Had Gaedyen crashed when we were flying? No, I vaguely remembered hearing Gaedyen getting his butt handed to him by another invisible creature, and then having my butt thrown into a tree.

I bolted upright, squinting into the blinding light and searching for Gaedyen. The motion cut into my chest and I cried out.

"It is okay, it is just me. You do not need to get up yet. Lay back down."

Gentle pressure met my shoulder, encouraging me to heed his words. But I wasn't at ease enough to consider obeying. "What happened?" I groaned.

"When you screamed, you announced your presence and revealed your location. Until then, he must have thought that whoever had been with me had left. Thinking that he had dealt a greater blow than he had to me, he dropped me and went in pursuit of you. I remained on the ground pretending to be weaker than I was.

"When he was at his most intent focusing on you, I rose to attack him from behind. Unfortunately, at that same moment, you stuck your head out from behind the tree and he took the opportunity to strike. He threw you across the forest before I could stop him, but I caught you before he could do it a second time, and then ended him."

"But I was invisible! How did he know where my head was?" Was I ever going to get this stupid thing right?

"Your shadow. If the light is right and there is mass there to cast it, no matter how invisible the mass may be, there will still be a shadow. Invisibility does not make you not there, it just keeps your physical body from being visible. That does not mean you are impossible to see."

I groaned again. *Ugh. Stupid shadow.* How could I have been such an idiot?

"What about the other Gwythienian? Where's he?" Then I remembered the chomping and thumping. "Are you okay?"

"Calm down!" he ordered. I kept trying to look at him, but it was too bright. "I am fine. Our attacker is dead, Enzi. He cannot hurt either of us anymore."

I gave in to the increasing pressure of his giant palm then and lay down, sighing in relief. "Was it Tukailaan?"

"I think so. There was always something off about the scent...it smelled different. But it also smelled like him."

Hmm...well I really hope it was! I don't want any more surprise visits!

"How are you feeling?" he whispered.

"Headache." I brought both of my hands up to my face and began massaging my temples, hoping to alleviate some of the pain. I took a slow, deep breath, and moaned as something stabbed my chest. "Did the satchel help at all?"

"Unfortunately I had taken it off to sleep, so I was not wearing it when we were ambushed. There were plenty of branches available still, but it may have turned out better if I would have had some available right there. I do not think I will take it off for the rest of the trip."

I smiled, proud to hear him admit that something I made was useful. I breathed again, and the sharp pain shot through me again. "Oh, crap." Was it a broken rib? Or maybe more than one? My head fell back to the ground and tears welled in my wimpy, burning eyes as I took in the full extent of the damage.

Lots of pain around my ribs. Were they broken or just bruised? Something wrong with my left ankle—like it was made of rocks and they scraped against each other. A dull ache concentrated around my nose and right eye. Not to mention the overall raw tenderness of my entire body.

I pulled my hands away from my pulsing temples and felt gingerly along my sides. I winced as my right hand discovered the location of impact with the first tree. Starting below my armpit, down all the way past my hip. I had a feeling my right side took black and blue to a whole new level. "I must look like serious crap."

Gaedyen chuckled. "You do have a black eye, and your clothes are a bit more ragged than they were before the fight."

Eyes adjusted now, I turned to look more closely at my companion. One eye swollen completely shut, the other only slightly less so. Face asymmetrical. Mouth hanging a little off center and slightly open on one side. Multiple unsightly patches of thickened skin covering his neck and what I could see of his limbs. One of his back legs was thrust out at a wrong angle, and a wide, jagged gash at least two feet long stretched down it from the inside of his upper hind leg toward his foot. It gaped, like a sneering maw, and a line of blood still trickled from it.

"Oh Gaedyen!" I tried to raise myself up again.

"Stay down, Enzi! I cannot have you passing out on me again. You do not need to get up yet. Right now, we need to stay calm and strategize. Alright?"

"But, your leg!" I sputtered, ignoring the threat of tears that my movement induced. "We need to stop the bleeding—"

"My leg is fine. You are the one who got pitched into a tree by a monster ten times your size. How are you?"

"Not bleeding out." I swallowed the pain and rolled to face the ground, then carefully tucked my knees under me, preparing to stand.

"Enzi, stop. Are you getting light-headed? Stay still already!"

But I was not letting him win this one. Blood was meant to stay *inside*, and I intended to make it stay where it belonged as much as it was in my power to do so.

Facing him, I took the first step with my left leg. I managed that fine, but when I removed my right leg from the ground to make another step, blinding pain swirled up from my left ankle, collapsing me back down to the ground.

The unruly tears stampeded down my face as I muttered several nasty words under my breath, trying not to choke on the sobs. My ankle throbbed and my chest screamed out in agony at me for jostling it so inconsiderately. I took several breaths through my teeth, trying to get control of myself again.

"Enzi! Good grief stay down! You will not be doing either of us any good if you pass out from the pain again! Calm down! I am fine!"

The desperation in his voice was touching. He was obviously not fine, but he didn't want me attempting to make him better at the expense of my own discomfort. I appreciated his consideration, and it only fueled my resolve to do what I could for him anyway.

But I didn't get up yet. I sat where he asked me to, gingerly situating my legs into the least painful positions possible. I searched my pockets for leftover crafty supplies after making his satchel: most of the tee shirt, part of one denim pant leg, and the sewing kit.

I went through various versions of a bandage quickly, trying not to think too much about the needle in the sewing kit. The tee shirt was softer, so wrapping it over the wound and then placing the denim over it for some stiffer protection…that was the best option, but I had nothing to tie it in place with. The shoestrings were already in use. I'd have to put the denim straight on the wound, though that wouldn't be as comfortable, and then tie it in place with scraps from the tee shirt.

"What are you doing?"

"I'm going to wrap your leg. And uh…stitch it up, too, to try to hold it together. Okay? How far away are we from Maisius Arborii?"

He reexamined his leg, perhaps to assess whether he agreed with me about the need for stitches. "By air, probably two more days."

"Okay, well that's not as bad as I thought, although you really need to rest and not exert yourself like that. If you don't get to someone who can clean and repair it properly, it's going to give you a nasty infection. It might be life-threatening, Gaedyen. And I'm no doctor. We've got to get there as fast as we can."

"I know what happens with a wound as severe as this. But besides the fact that flying would be extremely painful for *you*, consider the location of the wound."

I glanced toward his folded wings. "It's on your back leg, so what? Nothing's wrong with your wings, is there?"

He sighed. "No my wings are in good working order. Flying would be more painful for you than me. The problem is getting into the air in the first place. I need both hind legs for takeoff. I think I could manage with the wound, though it would probably increase the bleeding again. But the bone is out of joint. Even if I could get past the pain, I could not actually use the leg at all."

My eyes returned to his ruined leg to stare in horror. So that was why the angle was so wrong. "Oh, Gaedyen..."

"I hate to ask this of you—I know you are in a lot of pain yourself—but the only chance we have is if you can pop it back into place."

"What? I've never popped a *human* bone back into place! I have no idea how to do that! I'll hurt you worse."

"I have tried leaning and rolling on it every possible way and I cannot do it myself. I need you. Do you have a better idea?"

I desperately searched my brain for any other option, something that Gaedyen hadn't thought of yet, but I came up empty. Broken as my body was, I had to try to fix Gaedyen's. He was right. It was our only chance. "How do you propose I do this?"

"The only plan I can come up with is far from ideal, so if you have a better one please speak up."

"Oh no. What is it?"

"The leg bone is on the outside of the joint, pointing away from my body. It needs to be shoved back in toward me. But even in perfect health I do not think most humans would be strong enough to move something that heavy with that amount of resistance. You will have to jump on it. Unless you can come up with something else?"

I stared at his bad leg in horror.

"Judging from your expression," he sighed, "you are going to have to jump and land just right on it to knock it back into place. That is our only option."

Dragging the bandaging materials with me, I crawled over to his ruined leg, favoring mine and trying to ignore the stabbing pains in my chest. The bone stuck out grotesquely from his hip, still covered with muscle and skin, but obviously not where it was meant to be. The sight of it made me wonder whether it was really blood, or just any part of the body, that appalled me so strikingly when it was where it shouldn't be.

I winced, terrified of how much this would hurt both of us. I hadn't ever had a joint out of socket before, but I'd seen it in movies and I knew it had to hurt an awful lot.

"What if you pass out on me?"

"I will not," he replied with such grave confidence that I couldn't help but believe him. "But we must splint your ankle before you try it."

Reaching out, he yanked a large branch from a nearby tree. He broke it with his hands. I knew that if he used his teeth instead, the wood wouldn't last as long. Once he had three of the right length, he rubbed off the bark, leaving a smooth surface of naked wood to rest against my skin. I smiled at his thoughtfulness.

A moment later he handed me the three pieces and I fixed one to either side of my ankle and one behind it, sparing two small strips of tee shirt to tie it in place. I was ready.

"Alright then." I rose shakily to my feet, bearing most of my weight with my right leg. I took my first step toward him, testing the results of our labor. It couldn't bear my whole weight, but I was better off with it than without if for sure.

Gaedyen reached out with one foreleg, offering to steady me. I took hold of his arm with both hands, leaning on it every other step. I limped toward his injured hip, preparing to jump.

CHAPTER THIRTY

*I*t took three miserable, agonizing tries before the stubborn bone finally popped back where it belonged. To keep dirt from my boots out of his wound, I first sewed up and wrapped his leg by pulling the strips of tee shirt as tight as I could over the denim and triple-knotting them. I knew it would hurt him to tie them tightly, but the wrap wouldn't do him any good if it slipped during the rest of our journey to Maisius Arborii. I wanted it to stay right where I left it. By the time I finished with that, we were both so exhausted that we lay on the ground for a few minutes.

Every bit of me ached to varying degrees, especially the freshly butchered ankle—I landed on it as I fell off his leg each time I jumped—and the new assortment of bruises I'd acquired in the process of repositioning the stubborn joint.

"It is time to go." Gaedyen stood on his three good legs.

I groaned, carefully rolling onto my stomach. My legs shook as I got to my feet, bearing all of my weight on my right leg, I tried to leave the left alone as much as possible.

Now that his stupid leg bone was properly where it should be, that gash was my biggest concern. There was already a dark, wet spot forming in the center of the bandage. How much blood had he lost? I didn't know how long it would take for it to heal enough to stop actively bleeding, but I knew taking off and flying around would *not* help with that.

Part of me was almost willing to lie back down and never get up again. It all hurt too much, and moving made it impossibly worse. But if Gaedyen was going to push us off into the air with that leg and then fly us around for hours after the beating he took, I could get myself onto his back and sit there while he did it.

There was just the matter of getting all the way up there in the first place.

His shoulders loomed dreadfully high above me. I hobbled over and he was kind enough to lean his shoulder down extra low. Cautiously, I lifted my bad leg and slid it over his broad neck, catching my foot on his wing. I yelped and repositioned, glad the splint was there to keep it from bending too much. Once my left leg was as far over as I could get it, I held my breath and pushed off hard with my right, thrusting myself into place above his wing shoulders.

The sudden jolt caused my ribs to scream in protest, but thankfully I hadn't knocked my ankle into anything else. Even so, it was several moments before I trusted myself to speak. "Okay." I whispered, holding back the scream that wanted to erupt from my lips. "I'm ready."

Gritting my teeth, I braced for more pain as Gaedyen shifted to stand upright. I dreaded takeoff most, as I guessed he probably did, too. Could he do it? Even if he pushed himself through all the pain, bodies tend to have that self-protection mechanism of shutting down when there is too much. Mine had done it after I slammed into a couple of trees. His could probably do it at any moment.

He took the first trembling step, then the second. I felt the limp in that one. Again, and again, he forced himself forward, gaining speed until he was running. I was glad I couldn't see his face—there was probably a frightening grimace there. I felt the limp less and less. Pity for what it cost him welled in my eyes.

At last he pushed off, roaring and flapping violently. We teetered to one side, his bad leg unable to push enough. He dug it into the ground and pushed off again, grunting this time.

We were airborne.

The sharp discomfort numbed to a dull ache after half an hour or so. I was still conscious of it, but a bit less than before. I hoped it was the same for Gaedyen.

It was more comfortable to sit up straight than to lean over him, death-gripping with my arms. I looked down at my hand on his neck, ready to grab a hold if it needed to, but resting comfortably now.

My fingers brushed the thick neck muscles there and I found myself staring down at him. The dark reddish-purple skin rippled over large, corded muscles, flexing and extending in time with his wingbeats. I watched the shadows come and go as the muscles moved, and was struck again by how powerful he was, and yet how smooth and soft his skin was here.

I reached out to feel them again without thinking. He seemed not to notice or care, so I tried again, and nothing. I let both hands loose to trace his skin and feel the constantly changing shape of the muscles, avoiding the place where the skin was thickened—those were probably bruises.

Realizing how creepy that was, I yanked my hands away, setting them on my legs instead. I forced my eyes to focus on our surroundings. They were a fair distraction. The scenery was more glorious than I could ever describe. I took it all in—the sky, the trees, the tiny cities.

But still, my hands tingled and my mind stayed on Gaedyen.

Landing that evening was rough, but I didn't fall. He came toward the ground at a much nicer angle and slowed significantly before putting his feet on the ground. It would still be a drastic understatement to say that it was uncomfortable, but it was better than it could've been.

I was terrified of dismounting and having to mount again in the morning. So when Gaedyen said, "Would you like to sleep on my back tonight? It would save you the pain of getting down and back up," I agreed.

Neither of us was hungry or had any interest in moving. Once he was situated, I leaned back between his wings, weakly shoved the satchel out of the way, and left my legs dangling over either side of his neck.

I let out the breath I held while I repositioned myself, slowly releasing pent up muscles. "Gaedyen, do you know who Tukailaan thought you were? I mean, I assume whoever he was thinking of isn't you."

"No, I do not know who he could have mistaken me for. That was very strange."

"Hey, what was that word that he called me? A 'shem-batur' or something?"

"Shimbator," he replied. "They are nothing but legend."

"What do they do in the legends?"

He started to shift his position, but then must have remembered that wouldn't be a good idea. "Shimbator means 'one who can change form.' Some, like our attacker, believe that there used to be Gwythienians who could take on the form of another creature. I suppose he may have thought I was trying to sneak another Gwythienian into his territory in the form of a human. Though for what purpose, I cannot guess. But Shimbators do not exist."

"He also said that he thought you had been killed by one of those things," I reminded him.

"Yes. That is troubling. I would also love to know who he thinks I am. And since I am not who he thought, should we also be concerned about running into whoever that is?"

"Mm."

He had a point.

The stench assaulted my nose as he waved the knife again. My blood mixed with the dirt on the blade. I couldn't stop the tears, the sobbing. He cut me again, a third time....

Gaedyen woke me in the morning with gentle words before moving. Sore as I was from sleeping in such an odd position, not to mention everything else, I was grateful that I didn't have to do anything more than sit up to be ready to face the day's agenda. That was difficult enough.

He warned me when he was about to get up, and I held on as best I could, bracing for another jostle. He rose on his good back leg first, balancing on it as he stood on his forelegs. I hung at a precarious angle until he pulled his other leg up and prepared to move. When he stepped forward to place weight on his bum leg, he almost collapsed, nearly flinging me off.

"Gaedyen, wait a minute. Maybe we don't need to leave just yet." I winced more at his pain than mine.

He commanded through gritted teeth, "Hang on!" as he started forward.

I felt the difference in his gait as he ran on three legs, unable to use the other one at all. I dreaded takeoff.

He made one frail jump, using only his good leg, but it wasn't enough. He kicked off with both legs, roaring in pain and flapping wildly.

It was another long day.

Eventually we stopped for the night, and this time I was eager to dismount. My back muscles were scrunched tight after holding me up straight for so many hours. I flopped down from him, stiff and miserable, jarring my ribs again but thankfully not bumping my ankle. I slowly gathered myself up from the heap of exhaustion that I was and walked rigidly to the place where Gaedyen seemed to want to start a fire.

"It's not fair for you to have to catch dinner," I informed him. "Since you just flew with an injured leg, while carrying the weight of another person, you deserve a rest. All I did was sit for hours. It's more fair for me to catch something for you."

I hoped he couldn't sense how glum I felt about offering to hunt for us. I sucked at throwing the short rymakri and I'd barely tried throwing the long ones. I wasn't in such great physical shape either, but in our present circumstances, I felt responsible to do whatever I could to be useful.

"Make me a rymakri, please, Gaedyen. Let me bring you food tonight. Let me at least try."

He gave me the eyebrow—hardly encouraging. "Sure." He smiled a little with his crooked face—the swelling had gone down some—and reached up with one foreleg to secure a suitable branch.

His skepticism fueled my resolve to prove that I could do it. He broke the branch into one long section and one short piece and bit each one in turn, making me a knife as well as a spear.

"Thanks, Gaedyen. I'll be back in a bit." I hefted the spear in my right hand, shoving the wooden blade into my left most belt loop, so I could grab it with my right hand once I'd thrown the spear. *I mean, there's a chance I'll be able to catch something, right?*

Several yards into the woods I paused, checking my surroundings for signs of game. I saw no tracks in the dirt, no droppings, and no signs of nests of any kind. But I didn't know anything more than that about tracking or hunting. Probably part of not growing up with a dad.

I searched above me, hoping to see a giant bird stuck by some horrible soul's littered string or something, but there were no birds of any size or in any state of capture that I could see.

I stared around at the ground again, thinking hard. I had to come up with something for him. Then it dawned on me that he would need a lot more food than I would. If I could eat an entire fish, he could probably put away at least, like, fifteen of the same size. How many did he usually eat before bringing me one? If I could eat a rabbit, he could eat at least a deer, maybe two. How was I ever going to get enough for *me* to eat? Much less *him?* I remembered the last protein bar in my pants pocket. I could always fall back on that. So, just one deer to capture. *Fat. Chance.*

There were none. No deer, no rabbits, no squirrels, no birds to be seen. I hated to go back empty handed, but I didn't want to go too far either. Limping angrily toward the river, I hoped I'd have better luck with fish.

I caught the sound of rushing water and headed toward it, hiking my pants up several times as I went. Reaching the water's edge, I leaned out over it, hoping I'd be able to see past the bright moon's glare into the shallows and spot some fish. A ripple spread across the surface. The tip of a fish's tail? I peered harder, piercing the water with my gaze. Slowly, shapes took form, gliding lazily here and there, oblivious to the clueless hunter staring them down.

Raising the spear, I ignored the pain in my chest, and focused on one fish. Of course, it darted away for no reason before I decided to throw. I frowned harder and chose another. Closer and closer it slowly came. Then *wham!* I pitched the spear at it. I threw it so hard it stuck straight out of the water, vibrating. The action hurt terribly but was hopefully worth it.

I leaned over the water again, waiting for the surface to calm enough for me to see if I had a victory to celebrate. To my surprise, I did. The poor thing was quite impaled, and equally dead, to my relief. I felt sad, knowing I took its life, but Gaedyen needed it, and it was well past my turn to provide some food for us.

One down, fourteen to go. Oh boy.

CHAPTER THIRTY-ONE

several minutes later, I had yet to add to my bounty. The pain grew more intense and I became more frustrated and sloppy. I changed locations twice since they were smart enough to avoid me after I disturbed the water enough times, but now they seemed to avoid this whole side of the river. I resolved to give it one more shot before I returned to Gaedyen a practically empty-handed failure. I'd offer him the one measly fish and eat my last breakfast bar without worrying about what we'd do for food in the morning.

As I mentally grumbled at my inability to catch a freaking animal whose brain was probably smaller than my big toe, I gazed into the water yet again, intent on catching just one more stupid fish. As I was about to give up, two large ones drifted lazily into view, tailfins swishing slowly back and forth. I selected the bigger of the two, which was fortunately also the closest. Once again, I hefted the frigid spear, took aim, and launched it with every last speck of my energy, falling dramatically into the water after it.

Seriously? I waited impatiently for the water to clear, but there was no fish.

Great.

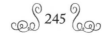

I'd drenched myself for absolutely nothing. *Screw it all.*

Scowling, I tramped back to Gaedyen, single fish in hand. My heavy, sodden pants tried very hard to fall off. What was with life today?

"How did it go?"

I closed the distance between us, faced him, dropped the lone fish at his feet, and sulked off toward the pile of wood he'd scraped up.

I hadn't once made the fire either. That was something else he miraculously knew how to do that I didn't. With the kind of luck I had, I should have skipped it and gone to sleep, but tonight I was soaking wet and cold. Plus, the only way to warm up was next to him—the living oven—and I was too ashamed and pissed at myself to be close to him right now.

I knelt down next to the pile and grabbed two sticks. I laid one down on the ground and put one end of the other perpendicular to it and rubbed my hands in opposite directions to drill the vertical stick into the horizontal one, like they did in movies.

The horizontal one kept slipping out from under the other, no matter how carefully or forcefully I drove the other one into it. Every time I replaced the vertical one, it was in a slightly different place, resulting in a very scarred but unignited horizontal stick—and a very pissed off me. The motion murdered my ribs, but I barely felt it now, I was so irritable.

After a few minutes, I slammed the sticks into the ground, giving up. None of the things that I tried to do worked out like they were supposed to. All I wanted was to do something right for a change. Was it so much to ask for it to just once work out like it was supposed to?

I heard Gaedyen limp toward me with a less graceful approach than usual, thanks to the gimp leg.

Great. He was gonna come and do it for me and make me look like a totally incompetent failure at life. He was gonna do it all in a matter of two seconds. Why had I even tried? I'd be way better off asleep by a warm fire that he would build right now than cold and even more exhausted than usual from trying and failing to do useful things myself.

Embarrassed and defensive, I angled my body away from him as he approached, vainly attempting to hide my miserable expression.

I felt one stick appear in my right hand, and then another, larger hand wrapping around mine. Gaedyen placed my hands at a different angle over the other stick, and then removed his fingers from mine to lay them over the escape-prone twig below, whispering, "Do not be so aggressive. You have to rotate the driving stick slowly at first, until it makes a firm indentation in the other one. Then you can impose more pressure on it. There, just like that. Start slow."

He leaned over me, with one arm practically around me to steady the horizontal stick while I used both hands to drive the vertical one down into it. My hands grew numb to the discomfort of constantly turning the stick back and forth, probably because I was so distracted by his closeness. It reminded me of the first moment in a movie or show when the couple start falling for each other. He has his arms around her, she leans back against his chest....

I was more concerned about him collapsing over me, considering that one of his legs was out of commission. I felt more like leaning away from him so I could try to somersault out of the way if it seemed that he was about to crash. What kind of abs would someone have to have to hold himself at that angle for so long?

As I leaned out, I noticed a sizeable divot in the stick resting on the ground. I eagerly increased the speed of the one in my hands, proud of how much I'd done without losing the other one, and anxious to be warmer. My arms burned, but my back and legs were ice cold. I saw the first spark come to life, but a gust of angry wind blew it away into nonexistence before it could spread its life around. I found myself crouching more toward Gaedyen as the wind picked up.

Then my stick shifted a little, and I darted a look at Gaedyen's hand. Was he abandoning my attempt as useless? Probably leaving to start his own fire, or skip the process altogether, since it was really me who needed it. But no, he just shifted the position of his hand so that he could use the outside edge of it to secure the stick and have the great width of it propped up to protect my fledgling sparks from the hungry wind.

The sudden gut feeling of heartfelt appreciation startled me into slipping my hold on my stick. I corrected my mistake, putting my gratitude aside for the moment so I could concentrate on the task at hand.

I drove that stick down with the greatest measure of violence I could muster, and then finally, three sparks burst out and landed. Two of them still glowed on Gaedyen's stick. I hastily apprehended several small twigs from the pile Gaedyen had swept together and built a little teepee around my sparks. Then, at Gaedyen's instruction, I cupped my hands around them and blew gentle breaths of encouragement into them. With a small *whoosh*, the two sparks kicked up a small flame, dancing and writhing in the night. I quickly supplied more wood for it to grow on, and grow it finally did.

Despite the wild wind, it flared up into a bonfire taller than me in a few minutes. By then, Gaedyen had moved from my back and gone to lay between the fire and the direction of the oncoming wind, protecting it with his massive frame. Again, immense appreciation. I also saw that he'd positioned himself so that the wing I was to sleep under was the one facing the fire, even though it was on the side of his injured leg.

Surely it would be his natural instinct to offer me the wing on the side with the leg I couldn't hurt?

248

I walked around the fire to point out to him that he could turn around, so that his good leg would be on the warm side and his bad leg would be safe from me.

"It is safest to sleep with your good side out, so that you do not need time to switch sides if you wake to a fight. It saves time and could save our lives. So, I will risk my bad leg on you tonight."

I detected a small smile as he said that, but then his head was turned away from me again and I couldn't be sure. I stared at him. What was he thinking? And why had he taken the trouble to help me? Why was he still offering to let me sleep by the fire at the risk of further troubling his bad leg when he could just tell me to sleep on the cold side?

Once again, he was nicer than I deserved.

I gave up contemplating for the night. The day had been long enough. I lifted his wing gingerly to avoid bumping it on his leg and crawled carefully underneath. His muscles tightened as if I'd hurt him and I froze, trying not to make it worse. After a few moments, I very slowly sunk into my place and tried not to move too much. I gave up on being comfortable though after I felt him stiffen at my movements again. I lay where I was and tried to fall asleep.

He pulled the blade against my skin again, but no matter how much it hurt, I couldn't control myself—I couldn't help screaming. He raised the knife again, brought it down...

Gaedyen was there, leaping over me to knock him off.

I stood to see what was happening—was Gaedyen fighting him?

The barn was gone and I was by the unlit fire again, leaning awkwardly toward the sticks I vainly rubbed together. Before I could coax any sparks from the lifeless wood, Gaedyen was there, his arms around me and his chest right up against my back. I felt the warmth seep through from him to me, and it calmed me and somehow drained the fear from my mind. It felt so nice to be held by him.

I smiled, so content, and then looked down to see how his giant hands and long arms could possibly fit around me so perfectly.

But there were no reddish-brown reptilian forelegs around me. There were only human arms and hands.

I stiffened, paralyzed.

Was it Caleb?

The arms loosened and the hands gripped my shoulders gently to turn me toward him. I scrunched my eyes closed, too horrified to see his jeering face again.

"Quit worrying about the fish, Enzi, really. One is plenty. I am totally stuffed. I would not be able to eat anymore if you had caught them. This way nothing is being wasted. You did a great job."

It was the liquid silver, soothing, irresistible voice of Gaedyen that spoke. I opened my eyes to see him and to thank him for being so kind about the measly fish.

But it wasn't him. It wasn't Caleb, either.

It was Shaun.

My eyebrows knit together. "How do you know about the fish?" But no words would come out of my mouth. I tried to cough—to clear my throat—but couldn't make any sounds.

"Come on Enzi," he said in Gaedyen's voice again. "Come on, it is time to go."

"Go where?" I mouthed, still mute.

"Come on, Enzi." He backed up, only his feet stood still. He got further and further away... smaller and smaller.

I tried moving my heavy legs to run after him, because I needed to know how he could possibly have known about the fish, but they did me no good. He left faster than I could catch up.

"Come on, Enzi. Wake up, already!"

I shot upright from the cold ground. Gaedyen was still Gaedyen, with his usual voice, and the coast was clear of other humans. They were far away and I was in no danger from them. I was still with Gaedyen, and I was still safe.

"What's the matter?" I yawned. I stretched my arms up and out flexing my fingers, rotating my wrists to relieve some of yesterday's stiffness. My right arm was especially rigid. I guessed all that failing at fishing and failing at building a fire on my own took a toll on that arm in particular.

"We have slept long enough. It is time to go."

Carefully I got up and moved far enough away from him that he could rise without knocking me over. Balancing on one leg, I waited until he was up and then hopped to his side and clumsily pulled myself onto his back.

I felt horrible for him, knowing he must hurt so much worse than I did. I regretted the extra poundage that I was, especially since I was more extra weight than the average human. Even after slimming down the little bit that I had.

With another bumpy start, we were off again, soaring over the trees and eventually over the clouds. Once again, I left my stomach somewhere behind us. It was exhilarating and terrifying. My heart raced with the thrill of it and my eyes watered as they were met by chilly gusts of wind.

It was colder up here, but it was so worth it. The elation once again reminded me of music. Safety, though I could fall to my death if I leaned wrong. Peace, though my heart beat faster than ever. It was pure serenity as I took in the sun and the sky above us, and the earth beneath.

Breathtaking.

I inhaled, eyes closed, relishing the fresh air. Yeah, I'd breathed nothing but fresh air for several days now, but this was different. This air up here hadn't been breathed even by trees in a long time, or maybe even ever before. It was mine—mine and Gaedyen's.

The sun intensified as the day passed. I even removed my sweatshirt, tying it around my waist with the rain jacket. As we flew, I sorted through some of my questions, trying to decide which to ask next time I got the chance. Why was he so touchy about his parents? Had he ever even known them at all? How old did Gwythienians have to be to learn how to fly? That was probably the only safe one. I resolved to ask that one next.

After a few hours, we landed in a small clearing surrounded by thick trees. The foliage was different here—palm trees and other exotic-looking plants. No more evergreens or oaks. We were definitely getting farther south. The ground was still dirt—not sand—but it was warmer and the sun scorched my skin.

I dismounted cautiously, dreading having to get up there again but really needing to go to the bathroom. When I came back to him after hobbling off into the woods, I asked my question.

"Gaedyen, tell me about when you first learned how to fly."

CHAPTER THIRTY-TWO

"The first flight is usually accidental. But the day a young one first experiences it is a proud one. However, I was terrified of being suspended on nothing more substantial than air in a place with nothing to grab hold of if I started to fall. And as I had always been distanced from my peers, I did not have the same competitive streak encouraging me to try anyway. My grandfather had been working with me before my first solo flight, as is very untraditional. He was concerned I would never find the first flight myself.

"Of course, knowing how it should be—that a young one would find the first flight themselves and then begin to work with their parents to improve the skill—and that he was making an... *exception* in my case, I began to doubt I had the ability. I thought that if he was trying to make my first flight happen, there must be something wrong with me that meant I could not fly at all. Knowing that mentally paralyzed me, in a way. I was afraid I would die if I tried to fly, knowing that I could not do it myself. But the Keeper could not very well allow his only heir to choose *not* to fly."

"So you are related to Padraig! I'd wondered."

"Yes. Which makes Tukailaan my great uncle. Some fantastic genes I have."

Yeah, it does mean that. Wow. Related to Tukailaan, too...

"One day, I...I overheard some very grave information that contradicted an important part of my identity. What I heard could not be true, but I was still shaken by it. I had to confront Padraig immediately. He was the only person I could trust to tell me the truth, the one who had been telling me what I believed to be the truth ever since I was a hatchling."

He trusted Padraig to tell him the truth about something important? What made their relationship change so drastically?

"I needed to know that what I heard was false immediately, but he was in another part of Odan Terridor, many miles from where I was. I ran in his direction, taking great leaps and bounds on the way. Sometimes, I caught air as I strained as much speed as I could from my young muscles. When I realized that I covered more space less painfully and more speedily when I flew, I tried to fly more. By the time I reached my destination, I was full on flying for a minute and a half at a time, more than the usual young one could manage after weeks of practice. That is how I learned to fly."

I stared at him attentively, waiting to hear the rest of the story. "Well you can't just stop there!" I threw my arms up.

He cocked his head and raised a brow. "You asked how I learned to fly. That is how."

"But what about the rest of the story?" I demanded. "What did Padraig say? Did the information turn out to be true? What even *was* the information you needed to confirm?"

His expression darkened. Then he sighed with an air of defeat. "I suppose you might as well know. You will be there when I tell this story to the Possessor of the rock of the Adarborians. There is no way to keep it to myself."

An expression of deep grief overshadowed his face, and I sat expectant.

"The day of my first flight…No, I must go farther back. Up until the first day I flew, I knew only that my parents were away, but was allowed to believe that they loved me and would come back to me as soon as they could. I believed them to be honorable Gwythienians, parents that a young one could be proud of. As I grew up, I learned that it was unusual for a Gwythienian—or even a pair of Gwythienians—to live away from Odan Terridor. And I gradually became aware that everyone was in a constant state of discomfort because some rocks had gone missing. But I did not understand the significance of those things, since I had grown up with them.

"That day, when I was in a more populated section of Odan Terridor, and one that I did not frequent, I overheard some older Gwythienians cursing my parents' names for stealing the rocks and forcing everyone to live in constant fear. I knew it must be wrong, but I needed to be reassured. So I went to Padraig."

"And what did he say?"

"As I told you, it was decided long ago by the collective realms that Odan Terridor would be the safe place where all of the rocks would be kept. Only one person, the Keeper, was supposed to know the location of the hiding place. But somehow, my father, Ferrox, discovered it. He was greedy for power and wanted the rocks for himself, to rule all the realms. He wanted to be the king of everything, to have ultimate power.

"So, working with my mother, Geneva, he stole the rocks and flew away with them. But they had a quarrel on their way, and the fight got physical. They both died that day."

"Oh, Gaedyen. I'm so sorry." How awful! His parents had killed each other?

"In a matter of seconds I was informed that not only were my parents dead and never returning to me, but they were also not honorable citizens. Instead, infamous criminals, and they had been the ones to cause the state of distress that everyone was stuck in. They were not a loving couple, but a hateful pair.

Maybe only committed to each other in order to steal the rocks. My existence was nothing more than an unwanted accident."

I'd wondered before if that was all I was, too.

"That was the day that I stopped visiting the Vorbiaquam. I had gone there nearly every day when I was a young one, hoping to see my parents in it and to tell them to come home. But then I learned that they could not return to me. Nor would they have wanted to if they could have."

"Oh, Gaedyen! Surely it's not as bad as that! I'm sure they would've wanted to come back for you, to know you. Even if they didn't mean to have a kid yet, I'm sure they loved you anyway."

"How could you know?"

I didn't have a response. I just wanted him to feel better.

"Sometime later, once the initial shock wore off, I realized that others had always known this, even those as young as I. And that it was because of my parents' history that I was left out and made to feel different and lacking. My people feared that I had my parents' bad tendencies, so they kept their young ones away.

"I wanted to do something to prove to my people that I am not like my parents, that my blood is not bad. But for years there was nothing I could do. Until I discovered you, with one of the very rocks that my parents had stolen and died for, draped around your neck like jewelry. Then I knew that my chance was in front of me, so I took it.

"And so we are on this journey, in the middle of the woods somewhere between my realm and Maisius Arborii. And we have been sitting and talking for longer than we should have. If you are ready, we should be off."

He stood and offered his shoulder to me to mount.

"So there's a lot more to it than restoring the reputation of your realm and uniting the realms together again. It's much more personal than that for you. You need to prove yourself not only to an entire race, but to all the other races as well. That's why you brought me instead of a bunch of other Gwythienians who'd be able to fight with you and take care of themselves without you having to catch fish for them or carry them in flight."

"Yes."

What a burden! "That's a lot to take on, Gaedyen."

His eyes bored into mine, and they were full of such sadness that I felt a tear emerge from my own for his pain.

"Has your future never depended on proving your worth?"

I was barely aware of the rocky takeoff or the beauty before me on this flight. I was too busy imagining Gaedyen as a young Gwythienian, left out of the activities of his peers for some reason unknown to him, thinking that something was wrong with him, waiting and hoping for his parents to return and make him feel loved. Then to have his poor hopes dashed and to find that they were dead criminals who hadn't wanted him. And everyone in every realm had known it, except for him.

I could relate to that. A family member that I trusted had lied to me about a parent, and I'd grown up without a father and very nearly without a mother, in some ways. I'd been ostracized by my peers for something that wasn't my fault, and then been left out of everything like the freak that they all decided I must be, based on a lie.

And his burning question, "Has your future never depended on proving your worth?" Whether or not I could become a professional chef depended on proving my worth to colleges and scholarships. I used to want to make Mom proud of me, but now all that was confusing and I wasn't sure. Did I have anything to prove to my dad? Did he even have the mental capacities to understand who I was to him, much less be proud of me for anything?

Eventually the ocean stretched out before us on the horizon. I thought Gaedyen would want to stop and rest for a bit before continuing, since who knew how long it would be till we reached land again, but he didn't stop. Maybe it was because we'd been flying over civilization for a while and he didn't see any safe stopping places. Or maybe he was afraid I'd ask more questions. Had I been too nosy?

We soared over the ocean for hours. It was a relief not to have to try to be invisible for a while. We were high enough that boats would not distinguish me from a speck in the sky. Before long, we were so far out that even Gaedyen felt comfortable becoming visible again.

We flew much deeper into the night than usual. I half expected Gaedyen to land in the water and try floating for a bit to give his wings a rest, but he plowed on without complaint. At last, I saw a patch of land in the distance by the light of the moon. Gaedyen descended and we landed on a sandy bank a few minutes later. As soon as I was off his back, Gaedyen curled up in the sand and fell asleep.

Poor guy. He deserved a week off. How would he be able to continue flying like that tomorrow? He'd be so sore when he woke up. And that leg…ugh! It had to be awful.

He needed sleep so desperately that I couldn't bring myself to risk waking him up. It was much warmer here on land in the middle of the sea, so I decided I could do just fine without his wing for cover that night. I laid down a few feet away from him, determined to let him sleep in peace.

The mosquitos were bad though. I was afraid I'd wake him from swatting so frequently at myself to stop them biting me. I contemplated burying myself in the sand for protection, but would that mean I'd get the same concentration of mosquito bites except all on my face? Maybe better to let them be spread out, if they were going to come after me anyway.... Eventually I fell into a fitful sleep.

Caleb was too close. The sawdust and dirt scraped against my skin. He cut me once, twice...again. I lost count. What a strange way to try to make someone stop screaming...

When he was done with that, it would be worse for me.

Tears ran from my eyes as I dreaded what came next. But then a huge arm came out of nowhere and scooped me up.

Gaedyen pulled me closer to him across the sand and draped a protective wing over me. Sand built up between us when he slid me to him, and I scooped it away quietly so I could touch him. I needed to be close to him, someone who would never do something like that to me, who could probably eat anyone who tried. It was my only comfort, and it was a good comfort.

When I fell asleep this time, it was a peaceful and dreamless one. And there were no more mosquitos.

CHAPTER THIRTY-THREE

J woke the next morning to sunlight streaming through palm trees above me. Throwing a hand over my eyes for shade, I sat up and squinted around for Gaedyen. He wasn't anywhere I could see. Maybe in the exotic trees behind me or the ocean several yards away.

Yawning, I stretched my arms. They were bright blotchy red and tender—sunburned. *Ouch.* But even though my ribs were still sore, they felt a bit better.

A huge splash erupted from the water. I jumped up, heart racing, but my pulse calmed as Gaedyen emerged from the millions of droplets. He soared up for a few seconds and then leveled out, facing me. I waved at him, and a moment later he glided toward me. He landed a few feet away, favoring his bad leg. How did he have the strength to use his wings at all after yesterday?

I got up and limped to meet him halfway. As we got closer I noticed a strange yellowish something sticking out of his mouth. It flopped with each step he took.

"What is *that?*"

He reached back as if to scratch the back of his neck with one hand. Probably smearing sand over that tattoo that I wasn't supposed to see. Then he shook that hand out, flinging sand into the air, and placed it under his mouth to catch the thing. "It is some strange kind of fish—very delicious. I thought you might like to cook one for yourself."

Trying to hide my grimace in light of his consideration, I closed the distance between us with a limp of my own and poked the thing. "Oh. That's an octopus."

Gaedyen frowned and cocked his head a little to one side. "What a strange name." He shrugged. "I am telling you, it is worth a try. And I kept it from getting sandy for you. Sand does *not* taste good."

I laughed, grabbing the slimy octopus by a suction cup-covered tentacle. "Thanks, Gaedyen." Our gazes lingered on each other a beat longer than usual, and we both quickly looked away.

"Um, could you help me with the fire?" I hobbled up the beach to collect sticks.

From the sound of it, he didn't immediately follow. He was still for several seconds, then slowly ambled after me. Was he in pain? What caused the delay? What was going on in that dragon brain of his?

He had a fire going in no time. Then while he bit a branch into a rymakri for me, I peeled the bark off a fallen log for a place to cut up the octopus. I thought with a smile how probably only rich people got to eat fancy stuff like octopus for breakfast. They didn't cook it themselves on an uninhabited beach, but then only the really, *really* rich people got to be on an uninhabited beach at all.

There was this song by Ladide Nothing, an alternative rock band, that was really catchy and it was about being rich without being rich. I hummed along to the tune, trying to remember all the words.

Gaedyen handed me the short rymakri.

I smiled as I took it from him. "Thanks."

"You… are welcome."

"Is everything okay?"

"Yes of course. Let me make you a skewer for the meat as well."

"Okay, thanks." What was up with him?

I didn't know enough about where we were or what poisonous things might grow in the shapes of herbs in this place, so I elected against seasoning it. But it was actually pretty decent without seasoning.

When I'd eaten as much as I could, I offered the rest to Gaedyen. "Here, do you want to finish this?"

He looked sideways at it. "But you have cooked all of the flavor out of it."

I sighed. "Come on, it's really good. Just give it a try." He seemed unconvinced. "Would you rather waste it all?"

He glared at me for a moment before reaching out and picking up a piece of cooked tentacle. After eyeing it suspiciously and giving it a long sniff, he hesitantly popped it into his mouth.

A couple moments in and he wasn't complaining yet. A good sign? Maybe he would find that it was actually better than he thought…but then he grimaced and made a noise like coughing and choking at the same time. His throat had a muscle spasm as if he were about to throw up.

"If it's that horrible, spit it out!"

He hurled it right into the fire, covering the rest of the roasted meat in Gwythienian saliva.

"Ugh! Gross!"

He looked both squeamish and mortified—a combination of expressions that were hysterical. I couldn't help but giggle. His expression became further horrified when he realized I was laughing at him, and that was even funnier.

I burst out in uncontrollable laughter. Gasping, I tried to apologize. "Gaedyen…I'm…I'm sorry I made you…" But I couldn't get the words out. I didn't even know why it was so funny to me but there was no stopping now.

Moments later, a soft rumble came from his direction. I looked up at him through tears of laughter and saw blurrily that he was laughing too.

"If you think *I* look ridiculous, you should see yourself, Enzi."

I got control of myself for long enough to say, "I really doubt it, Captain."

"But I am not the one with octopus stuck between my teeth."

Laughter erupted again before I could feel to see if he told the truth. The idea was so incredibly silly! He really laughed now, too, and the sheer joy of us laughing together about nothing overwhelmed me.

By the time I finally got control of myself again, he'd calmed down as well, but still smiled. I blushed, and then felt stupid, but I was in too good of a mood to remind myself how ridiculous the idea of "us" was. The truth was, I liked him, dragon or no, and he looked at me as if he felt the same.

In a burst of confidence, I got up and hobbled the few steps to him. Throwing my arms around his neck I held him as tight as I could. The smooth scales of his neck felt soft beneath my fingers and I couldn't help stroking it. And then one large, wide hand was at my back, pressing me even closer to him. It was so big that it covered my entire back, one finger even reached the side of my neck, which felt nice. Before I knew what I was doing, I kissed his cheek.

He stiffened.

CHAPTER THIRTY-FOUR

*T*hat woke me from my happy trance. What had I done?

I yanked myself away. "I'm sorry, Gaedyen...I didn't mean..." I tried and failed to meet his eyes. "I'll be back in a minute."

I limped away from him toward the trees. What was I thinking? *Kissing* him? Of course, he would stiffen! A wimpy human had no business kissing a majestic Gwythienian.

I threw myself behind a thick palm tree and leaned back against it. I moved instantly when the pokey bark dug into my back. So different from his warm hand that had been there only a moment ago. What an idiot I was! I'd screwed everything up. What did he think of me now? He probably pitied me, having a crush on someone out of my league on so many levels. Was he disgusted?

But this wasn't a television show where the idiot could avoid the person that she had embarrassed herself in front of. Nope. I had to woman up and face him. We had to get to Masius Arborii no matter how foggy my brain had become.

I touched the stone hanging at my neck. An idea struck me. Even if I had to face him, I didn't have to let him see my face—

my embarrassed, red, teary face. I could go out there invisible. I might have to turn invisible when we left anyway.

There was something under my lip. I ran my finger by it and sure enough, it was a piece of breakfast. I flicked it to the ground. Regret jerked at my insides again. Why hadn't I left it at a good laugh? It had been a perfect moment. Why did I have to ruin it?

With a deep breath, I held tightly to my rock and fought with my mind to rip the wall apart. It took only a few moments. Perhaps my best time yet. But I couldn't enjoy the victory. I couldn't tell Gaedyen about it. I had to just go out there and pretend nothing had happened. Maybe he would forget that I'd kissed him. Maybe he would think he must've imagined it.

Knowing that was ridiculous, I limped back to the beach.

Gaedyen glanced up at my approach, probably hearing my footsteps and thrown off by not being able to see me. "Enzi?"

"Yeah." I hated how thick my voice sounded. "It's me. Ready to go?" I tried to stuff some cheerfulness into my tone but I couldn't tell if it worked.

"Sure. Are you—"

"Yeah, I'm good. Let's go."

He looked askance in my general direction, but then stood on his three good legs and offered me his shoulder.

By the time we found a place to land and built a fire, neither of us had looked the other in the eye or spoken a word beyond what was absolutely necessary. Gaedyen called over his shoulder that he was off to hunt and I stayed behind to tend the fire. I wracked my brain for a way to get rid of the awkwardness, but I was too distracted by it to find a way out of it.

While he hunted, I used the rymakri he'd left for me for a little more practice.

I assumed the stance, gripped the blade, and flung the knife at a tree. There was a *thunk*, and I looked to the ground for the blade. But it wasn't there. I looked back up and there it was, lodged in the trunk.

Whoa. I did that. I did that!

Thrilled with my success, I wrenched the blade from the trunk and tried again. I missed that time, but I got the next two. I was improving!

I kept at it for a while, hitting as many as I missed instead of less. I still had a ways to go, but I finally made progress.

Once I was completely winded, I sat on a log to watch the fire, thoughts of Gaedyen returning.

How had it been for Mom and Dad when they met? Of course, they were the same species, so that probably helped. But if he was a perfectly normal human being then, what had he been like? Romantic? Had they ever had awkwardness like this between them?

How was my dad doing now? Were they trying any new drugs or treatments on him? Was it making a difference? How was Mom holding up?

"What are you thinking about?"

I jumped and fell backward over the fallen log.

"Sorry, I did not mean to scare you. I was just curious about why your face looked like that."

"I was thinking about my parents, I guess." I blew hair out of my face as I climbed back over the log.

"Oh?"

"Yeah, you know. Wondering how they're doing and stuff."

"Do you miss them?"

"I think so—somewhat, anyway. I just met my dad right before leaving with you, so I've hardly known him long enough to miss him like I probably should."

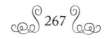

"You just met your father?" His eyes grew wide. "But I thought you had told me that your father passed away before you hatched—that is—were born."

"Well yeah, it's a long story."

He made a show of sitting down without taking his eyes from my face, asking for more.

I sighed. Well, he'd told me the ugly truth about his parents. I guessed it was only fair that I share mine. "Mom always told me that my father died while serving in the military. I always wished I could have known him for just a few minutes, if only to meet him. But I accepted the fact that he was dead and that I would never know him. But before starting this trip, on my birthday, I found out that he is actually alive. And she'd known it all along. He lives less than an hour away from our apartment. But he's not exactly right in the head."

I went on to explain all about how I found him in the hospital that was actually a psych ward, and how he thought he was being chased by flying monsters and all he could talk about was how he needed to return the stone to them so that they would leave him alone.

"And that is why I decided to come with you in the first place—a total stranger and previously unknown species—to who knows where. I want to find out what happened to him and how it may have involved this stone and your people. And even if I can't find out anything about what happened to him, I need to keep the rock. I want to take it back to him in the hospital and see if maybe there's a way to make him think that he has returned it to whoever he thinks is after him and see if that could somehow cure him of his fears.

"I know it's a long shot, but I've got to try. I want my dad back to the way he is supposed to be."

"That is why you told Shaun that the rock was your father's only chance at recovery?"

Shaun had shared that with him? "Yeah. That's right."

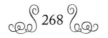

"I am sorry, Enzi. I do not know how, but I will do what I can to help you discover what happened. And if at all possible, I will help you with your theory for curing him. I swear, as soon as this journey is over, we will go straight to him and do everything we can."

I was speechless. I'd never expected his help, or even thought of asking for it. And I never would've asked after how I screwed things up today. But if there was an actual "flying monster" present, there might be a way to make it work!

"Wow. Thank you, Gaedyen. That would really mean a lot to me. Thank you very much."

"Think nothing of it."

Silence pressed on us again, but it wasn't awkward this time. I felt less self-conscious. If he was offering to continue being around me after this whole journey thing was over, he couldn't be too disgusted with me. I schemed how to break my father out of the ward and get him to some woods somewhere, some place where Gaedyen would be safe visible and we could have some kind of interaction between them involving my father returning the stone. Would that do it? Would he be back to the wonderful person he supposedly was before something crazy happened to him?

Odd that my father, of all people, would think he'd been attacked by a dragon, and then his daughter, of all people, would end up meeting one. Interesting that the stone would turn up right after his supposed death—or encounter with flying monsters, according to him—and that it would also be the reason for me meeting Gaedyen.

And the stone only left Odan Terridor because of his parents. He must have been somewhat close to them if he'd found the stone—they would've had to have just dropped it. Maybe he really did see two dragons fighting! Maybe he saw them fighting right after he picked up the rock! Maybe he wasn't crazy!

But he couldn't have been involved in their fight, could he? I mean, he *was* missing a couple of limbs. But they were horrible Gwythienians. They probably would've killed him as soon as look at him. Like Padraig would me. So then how would he have gotten those injuries?

Could our parents' demises be intertwined? And if they left Gaedyen when he was so young that he never knew them, and my dad lost his mind before I was born, and he and Gaedyen's parents were at the same place at the same time, then Gaedyen and I must be almost the exact same age! But he seemed so much older.

"Gaedyen? How old are you?"

"Why?" He didn't seem offended, just at a loss to imagine how that could be interesting.

"I'm just curious. I'm wondering how much older you are than me."

"How do you know I am older? I believe that is an offensive suggestion in human culture, is it not? To assume someone is older?"

"Oh, well, I uh…I didn't think of that." I felt a little embarrassed, and then caught a glimpse of the tiny smile forming on his face. Was he *messing* with me? I didn't want to embarrass myself like I had earlier, but we were separated by the fire, so I decided to take a risk and mess back. "What I mean is, that's something that usually 'in human culture' is only offensive to middle-aged women. I was operating under the assumption that you are not a middle-aged woman, but I suppose I could be wrong. Is there something you need to tell me about?"

To my surprise, he let out a rumbling burst of laughter at my stupid attempt at witty banter. I was aiming to be funny, but it sounded way better in my head than it did when I said it out loud, so I hadn't been expecting a favorable response.

Then he asked, in that liquid silver voice, and sounding as if he could barely contain another laugh, "How old is middle-aged?"

I had a dim awareness that I wasn't sure of the exact parameters of middle-aged, but I was mostly taken aback by his smile. He was really smiling, not just with his lips, but with his eyes, and it was beautiful. It was a truly sincere smile on a majestic face, even if it was kind of reptilian. Somehow that added to the dignity of it.

"Uh...like forty to sixty, maybe, I guess." I shrugged half-heartedly, still focused on his unusual face.

Smugly he replied, "Well then I am nowhere near being middle-aged, so I guess I *should* be offended at your assumption."

I chuckled. "I guess you should be! Really though, I didn't say I thought you were middle aged, just that I thought you were probably older than me. So how old are you anyway?" If my logic were right, he'd have to be within a few months of me. But sometimes he seemed like he could be hundreds of years old.

"What makes you think I am older?"

"Answering a question with a question?"

He smiled, nodding acknowledgement of my using his phrase, but remained silent.

"Well, the fact that you're like ten times my size does make you seem older than me. Now that I think about it though, I'm sure even young Gwythienians would likely be much bigger than me. Still though, your knowledge of where we're going and what we need to do makes you more knowledgeable than me, to some extent, which makes you seem older. So, am I right?"

He nodded as if everything I'd said made sense. "Since I do not know how old you are, I do not know whether or not I am older than you, but for what it is worth, I am seventeen. So, who is older?"

"That is a very good question, considering that I am also seventeen."

"Really?"

I gave him the eyebrow. "Odd coincidence, isn't it?"

"Yes it is, but you know," he began, "If we are the same age in years, one of us must be slightly older by a more precise measure. I doubt we are the exact same age."

"Point." I nodded in his direction. *Which is why I'm still guessing you might be older.*

When he didn't offer his birthdate, or ask me for mine, I inquired, "So when is your birthday?"

"I do not know the exact date."

How did someone not know his own birthday? "Well I was born in January, when it's cold outside. Was it cold outside when you were born—er, hatched?"

"That I also do not know. I lived in Odan Terridor for years before I ever went into the human realm. I do not know what the weather was like at the time of my hatching."

"How about important events?" I suggested. "Was anything important going on when you hatched? Maybe we could use that to pinpoint the difference."

He frowned. "As with the weather, I am ignorant of the happenings of the human realm at the time of my hatching. All I know is that the night that I hatched was the night that my parents flew away from me with their wealth of power in hand. Naturally, it is an important event in my life, but I doubt it could have affected the human realm in any way."

"Actually, it may have." I thought of my dad, and of his insane ravings about the flying dragon-monsters that tore him apart because they were after a stone.

"How so?"

"Oh, I don't really know. I was just thinking out loud."

His face was grave, and a little suspicious. I didn't like lying to him, but I didn't want to accuse his parents of being the cause of everything wrong with my life. He was already ashamed enough of them. It wouldn't be good for him to have more reasons to weigh him down. Besides, I had no idea if anything like that had happened. If I needed to tell him, it could wait until I found out that it was really true.

"Well I guess that makes you older then. I mean, if you were born—or hatched—the day that they left with the rocks, and my father found one of them before being thought dead, and I wasn't born until after he was supposedly killed…yeah, you are a little older."

"And does that matter to you?"

His question, and overly-casual tone, surprised me. "No. Why would it matter to me? You obviously know more about all of this rock and realm craziness than I do, no matter how old or young you could be. And really, a few months hardly count for being older."

"I see."

He searched my eyes. As I stared back, I glimpsed something new there. To my immense confusion, it looked like *vulnerability*, but I couldn't be sure. Why vulnerability, of all emotions to be on the face of such a majestic and powerful creature as he looked into the eyes of a chubby and travel-worn human girl in desperate need of a shower and a haircut?

I was imagining it, wasn't I? Yes, I had *feelings* for him, like the insane freakazoid that I was. I wasn't sure if it was what people called "love," and I was really terrified of the idea of ever becoming in love with someone. But that voice, that smile…

He was so strong. He could hurt me if he wanted to, but somehow I knew he never would. Something about how huge he was happened to be attractive to me. He was warm and protective, despite being introverted and sometimes surly.

There were two other problems, besides the species variation. One, he would never think of me that way. It would surely never dawn on him in his wildest dreams. And two, even if he did, even if we were equally in love and confessed our undying devotion to one another from the top of the most public mountain in the face of billions of witnesses, it could never last. I was too afraid. I couldn't handle reliving that nightmare, and no one could ever truly want me if I couldn't give him that. And there was no way that I ever could. Not that it was even physically possible!

I sensed him watching me and looked up, glad that mind reading wasn't one of his gifts. His piercing gaze grew more worried. Fearing that he could somehow interpret my thoughts from my face, I turned away once again.

He looked down at me with such sweet concern. He was worried about me, like he wanted to make sure I was okay. No one had ever looked at me like that, with such caring. Except maybe Mom, but she flat out lied to me about my father for all those years, so that didn't really count anymore. How could I be sure that anything she did or said had ever been sincere?

But this look on the face of this mythical creature from another world, who was ten times my size and a totally separate species, this look felt true. I saw the sincerity of it in his eyes. It was as if he saw that something hurt me, and that hurt him. Like he wanted to make me feel better.

Could I really comprehend all that from his eyes? I could have imagined all of it, couldn't I? How could one being communicate so much in one look? What if I could? Friends care about each other when they are sad. It didn't mean what my insane side wished it did.

He asked in that silvery voice, "Enzi, what is wrong?"

Hearing him say my name that way melted me. It was so perfect. I wanted to hear that voice saying my name for the rest of eternity. But I shook myself mentally and focused on his words alone, trying to ignore the voice he used to say them.

"Oh, um, no. Nothing's wrong. I felt a bit sick to my stomach there for a second. I'm sure it will go away soon."

I couldn't risk glancing up to guess whether or not he believed me. The unrequited feelings had brimmed over when he said my name and I needed time to compose myself before I let him see my face.

It took a few moments until I was all good. I glanced up at him then and my resolve almost broke at the tenderness waiting for me there. I should've appreciated that he wanted me to be happy. But instead I couldn't help but focus on the fact that the care he had wasn't what I wished it were.

Heck, he might even have a female Gwythienian waiting for him back in Odan Terridor! Oh crap. I'd asked him that back in the tunnel, when he thought he sensed Tukailaan for the first time, and he never answered me. My heart plummeted into my toes—which was stupid, but still... ouch.

"You know, shouldn't we get some sleep now? If we are going to be meeting the Adarborians tomorrow, we should probably both be rested up a bit." I tried to fake a convincing yawn. Judging from the eyebrow he gave me, I hadn't fooled him.

"Alright. You win. Keep it to yourself. But whenever you are ready to talk about it, I am here."

The irony.

"Thanks, Gaedyen." I didn't quite meet his eyes as I lay down on the other side of the fire. It felt wrong to go sleep next to him, now with the idea that he might have someone else waiting for his return. But when he ambled over and laid down next to me—not quite against me but still draping a wing over me—I didn't argue. Despite my weird, confusing feelings, being close to him did make me feel stronger. He was the one person in the world I could trust with my life.

Strange noises kept me awake for a while. Noises like monkeys calling to each other up high in the trees, frogs croaking their songs, and other sounds whose origins I couldn't imagine.

CHAPTER THIRTY-FIVE

I was in the barn again, bare skin between the sawdust and Caleb. He brought out the knife, waving it at me, sneering, threatening. Out of nowhere, I slashed at him with a rymakri, surprising even myself.

His eyes widened. I missed, but it was enough to make him tumble off me.

And then I was on my feet, fully dressed in my traveling clothes, running at him.

I swung again. He ducked, but I nicked him. He let out a gasp and covered the cut with his hand.

A cold smile spread over my lips. "Let's see how you like this game."

Leaping into the air, I aimed the blade at his abdomen—I would cut him where he had cut me.

*C*rash!
I sat up, blinking away the nightmare out of habit. But it hadn't been the way it usually was. Something had drastically changed. *What woke me?*

Cool morning air surrounded me, along with the many noises of jungle creatures.

"Gaedyen, what was that?"

"A large, curious monkey was getting too close to you. It did not want to leave, so I threw it into the trees. It caught on a vine that was not secure and crashed. The idiot."

"What?" He threw a monkey through the forest because it was getting too close to me? Random, but sweet of him. No, not sweet. Kind, and friendly.

Not sweet.

I rubbed the sleep from my eyes. *Dang it. That was the first dream I've ever wanted to see the end of. Will it be like that again the next time I fall asleep?* I wasn't sure I wanted to know. If the nightmares would stop altogether, that would be fantastic.

I inhaled my last fraction of breakfast bar and Gaedyen skipped food. He pawed a hole in the ground, scooped up a little dirt, and smeared it all over his tattoo.

"Why don't you want the Adarborians to see your mark?"

"Your silence on the subject was one of the conditions for changing our travel methods."

I frowned. "Well, if I'm supposed to keep an eye on it to make sure it stays hidden, maybe I should know why it is so important. You know, 'cause then I'll be more motivated to make sure it stays hidden."

"It could cause us grave trouble. That ought to be enough motivation for you."

I limped around to get a better look at it, rolling my eyes. "It's kind of obvious that you are trying to cover something up. The dirt isn't anywhere near the same color as your skin."

"It will lighten when it dries."

"If you say so."

We were back in the sky within fifteen minutes of waking. After a few minutes more we were past the island and soaring over ocean again. I saw lots of shadows in the water, but we were too high up for me to tell what they were. Shallow places? Giant schools of fish or groups of whales or stingrays?

The sun beat down on us. I actually started to miss the overcast skies of home. Would invisibility stop the rays from burning my skin? We were both visible. There was nothing around to be concerned about, but I tried out invisibility just in case.

It felt just as hot. Beads of invisible sweat became visible when they fell from me onto Gaedyen. That was gross. I hoped he didn't notice that. I gave up on hiding from the sun after several minutes of continued sweltering.

It was a long day.

Hours later, a tiny dot came into view on the horizon. Was that land? Slowly it spread out into a long line.

Yes! Trees! Shade! Not that we'd be flying under the trees or anything, but still.

The line gained depth and lengthened until it stretched as far as I could see either way.

"Southwest from the northmost…" I was glad Gaedyen had a good sense of direction.

Half an hour later, I saw a break in the trees—the river. We were on the right track!

But as we got closer to the beach I realized the structures that I thought were trees were something else. They were buildings. Civilization. People. We had to avoid being seen by them, but if we approached invisibly, the Adarborians would take that as a threat.

"The guard is on the watch, so if invisible you fly, reveal yourself at once, or you shall surely die!"

What were we supposed to do? We'd need to turn invisible soon, but he couldn't hear me when we were flying. *Should I, like, slap him or something to get his attention?*

Just then, Gaedyen slowed his wingbeats and we descended toward the ocean.

Oh good. He must be wondering the same thing.

He carefully controlled our descent until we splashed into the surface of the water, far enough from land that Gaedyen seemed comfortable with being visible.

"So what are we supposed to do about not being spotted by the people here but also not showing up as an invisible threat to the Adarborians?"

"I do not know how far out their guard will be posted, but I would rather be seen by the people and the Adarborians and not surprise the Adarborians, than not be seen by either and having the Adarborians shoot at us. So if in doubt, show yourself. But I think we should be safe invisible at least up until we reach the falls. Whether we should show ourselves at that point or once we cross the greatest lake, I do not know."

"Well, I think you know better than me about this one, so I'll follow your lead here. I'm better at invisibility now, so I think I'll be able to keep it up for longer. When you go invisible and stay invisible, so will I. And when you show yourself, I'll follow suit."

His deep, steady breaths pulsed beneath me. Then he turned his head halfway toward me. "Thank you for placing your trust in me, Enzi. I will not let you down."

I only saw the side of his face, so I couldn't read his expression, but there was something about his tone… a fresh energy, almost. Maybe he'd taken my words as a bit of a pep talk?

"We will approach the land invisibly, and I will decide when we reach the falls whether we should continue so. Should you have any reason to think otherwise, tap twice on my neck and I will change whatever state I am in. Agreed?"

He trusted *me* to make a call like that? "Uh, yeah. Sounds good."

"Enzi?"

"Yes?"

"You do realize the risk we are taking, right? They really will kill us if they see us as a threat."

"Yeah, I know."

"I do not want you to die."

I let out a short laugh. "Yeah, I don't want me to die either. I don't want either of us to die."

"Should anything happen to me—"

"Nothing will happen to either of us, Gaedyen. We'll become visible as soon as we can and they'll have no need to feel threatened by us."

I couldn't imagine Gaedyen dying. It was impossible. He was too mighty, too huge. Yeah, these people could change their size and all that, but none of them could be as giant and majestic as this dragon. If he died, our goals for this whole journey would die. I wouldn't have a way back home—and I wouldn't want to go back anyway. I wasn't ready to leave this world, and I wanted Gaedyen to stay in it with me.

"You're not allowed to die, Captain. Understand?"

"Understood."

I might have caught the edge of a smile in his voice.

He paddled, shooting us forward in the water. He threw his wings up and brought them crashing back down toward the waves.

Taking off from water would have to be really hard...

Before long we were back in the air, both invisible, probably both worrying about the encounter that we'd been heading toward for two weeks now. It felt bizarre, knowing that distant event was now so close.

Am I going to die today?

CHAPTER THIRTY-SIX

Sometimes smoky cities with tall towers stretched out beneath us, and sometimes crowded towns with tiny houses were smashed together and built on top of each other, sprawling over every surface. After a while the dwellings thinned out and gave way to rich, green trees.

Before long we soared over strange mountains. Their tops were flat instead of gradually tapered to a point, as if they'd been smooshed or had their points chopped off. Their flat surfaces were covered in rich greenery, and their sides were so sheer that nothing but moss grew on them. They were also less crowded than most of the ones I was used to seeing, and much larger, too. If we weren't in such a hurry—and you know, rushing into probable death—I would've enjoyed landing on one to check it out. But not today.

It was getting harder to stay invisible. I slipped once, but got a hold again quickly. I was fairly confident that we were over an unpopulated area when it happened. I hoped I'd be able to keep it up. Reaching behind me, I considered pulling a branch from the satchel to pass to Gaedyen in an emergency. But how would that action be interpreted by the Adarborians? Better not.

I heard the waterfall before I saw it. We soared over the widest flattop mountain yet, when a rushing, rumbling noise overcame the sound of the powerful wind. I looked around for the falls, but didn't see them on either side. Then we passed the edge of the mountain, and there it was. Right underneath us.

The line of white expanded as we got farther away. It poured into a river and rushed into the distance—a distance we would not follow. Gaedyen adjusted his wings to change our direction.

"A sharp left at the falls, you must now fly eastward…"

Now was the time. There were probably several jungle villages down there, hidden under the trees. Should we take the chance that they might see us, or take the chance that the Adarborians might not?

We should risk the locals seeing us. It looks pretty darn secluded out here. What will it matter? No one would believe that they saw a dragon if they tried to tell anyone, unless there were enough people backing up the claim, and I don't think there are enough out here.

Gaedyen was still invisible, and I did trust him, but I had a gut feeling. I lifted my hand to tap his neck twice and indicate that we should change states. Just before my hand met his skin, he turned visible. The tap turned into an awkward stroke across the back of his neck as I tried to take it back.

Ah! No! Did he feel that? Would he read it as a tap? I didn't want him to think I was caressing his neck!

My face felt hot with more than sunburn. But he was still visible, and his wings hadn't missed a beat. Of course, I was visible too. I'd already been having a hard time and my embarrassing mistake had totally taken all my focus.

At last we came to a place where two rivers crossed.

"Cross the greatest lake…"

Gaedyen adjusted his wings again to take us perpendicularly across the larger of the two.

"Search now for the tree, you will know it when you see it, do not doubt history."

And now the moment of truth. Was Gaedyen's guess right? Was the legend about the Amolryn tree the "history" the liryk referred to?

I searched for brightly colored flowers in the treetops rushing under us. I saw yellows and oranges, a few pinks, and one with only red flowers, but none with blue, purple, or any combination.

I felt Gaedyen slow the pace a bit and looked up to see why. This tree popped out slightly above the rest and was by far the most colorful. Bright bursts of blue, red, and purple sprouted everywhere. Gaedyen descended and started to circle. Were there guards waiting for us?

As we got closer, I saw the green flowers, too. They were hard to distinguish from the leaves at a glance, but they were distinct now. Each of the four colors of blossoms reminded me of stargazer flowers. From their middles grew a thick stalk, surrounded by little stalks with white pollen on the tips. Three petals reached out from there, and one secondary petal peaked out from between each of the others for a total of six. The flowers attached to their branches by very short stems, some in clusters and some alone.

Could these blossoms have sprouted tiny humanoid beings once... decades or centuries ago?

We circled several times, but there was nothing more alive than the blossoms. I thought about the directions again.

"When on the horizon, the great tree appears...."

Was "horizon" the keyword here? This tree barely poked out only a few feet higher from the ones surrounding it. We saw it when we went over it, not looming up on the horizon in front of us like the liryk described.

Maybe we should keep going? Maybe there's a bigger one?

"Gaedyen, I don't think this is the one." He half turned his head to me. "What did you say?"

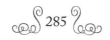

I was surprised he could hear me, I didn't really expect it to work. "The tree is supposed to be on the horizon—from the liryk. We should keep going and look for a bigger one!"

"A good plan!" He straightened out to get us back on course.

I sat back down in my spot in front of his wing shoulders.

He thinks my plan is good. I couldn't help smiling a little. But he wasn't supposed to be able to hear me. Had he heard me singing before? I winced, a wave of embarrassment washing over me.

A few minutes later I spotted something in the distance. The sun was setting, so this something stood out like a black shadow against an orange sky. We flew closer. It was definitely a tree—not another tall building in a city. We were still in the jungle.

Before I could tell whether there were flowers on this tree, I sensed Gaedyen's nervousness. Tension was evident in the slight increase in frequency of wingbeats and the barely-noticeable upward tilt of his head, so that he was focused more ahead than below. But most evident were the flailing earflaps—always a sure sign that something was about to happen.

Oh my gosh! This must be it. What kind of a mess were we heading into? It'd been so many years since there'd been communication between Odan Terridor and any of the other realms, how would they accept us? It didn't matter to them that losing the rocks wasn't Gaedyen's fault. Gaedyen—and me, by association—were coming in from the enemy's side.

Will they give us a chance to explain ourselves?

I caught a flicker of light from somewhere ahead. Shielding my eyes from the sun, I saw that the one flicker had multiplied. There were many little trembling points of light, at least twenty. Maybe more.

Gaedyen's earflaps were all over the place.

I squinted ahead, trying to focus on the growing shapes. The little points of light were now small splotches of vibrant pigments: greens, reds, purples and blues.

A row of winged, fairy-sized humanoids stopped right in front of us.

My head lurched forward and slammed into Gaedyen's solid neck as he halted mid-flight to avoid hitting them. His wings flapped awkwardly as he struggled to maintain height without running smack dab into them. It killed my chest, but I held it in. I immediately righted myself and looked at the Adarborians, relieved that they hadn't darted us yet.

One woman stood out from all the rest—probably their leader. She had attractive, yet unusually angular features. Her hair was cropped short, almost like a pixie cut. She was chocolate-skinned, slim, and wore a glimmering green dress that hugged her figure. It came down to different lengths in front, stopping just above her left knee and then curving down to cover her entire right leg. It looked like it was made from the same kind of hummingbird-green feathers that covered her wings, and there was a curvy, purple line down the front of her dress, also featherish-looking.

"You are not wanted here, human." Her words were sharply accented and she spat them with vehemence. I'd expected her voice to sound as small as she looked, but it sounded big and strong. "Members of our guard spotted your approach hours ago, and it was our hope that you would veer off and find another place to blight with your presence. But as you are here now, I will deliver a message to you from the leader of Maisius Arborii, the Possessor of the rock of the Adarborians.

"'We do not welcome you here, Gwythienian.'" She said the name as with a sour taste in her mouth, looking at Gaedyen for the first time and with disgust. "'Our realm has not forgotten what the people of Odan Terridor did to us, nor have we forgiven. Turn now and leave us in peace, or accept your death sentences.'"

Half of her company reached over their shoulders and pulled slender, wooden tubes out from behind them, placing them in front of their mouths.

Ah, the blow darts. Oh no. We didn't come all this way for nothing! Hurry up and talk, Gaedyen! You've got a few seconds to make it count! Otherwise we'll have to leave now or die!

"I understand your feelings toward me and my people," Gaedyen spoke above the wind of his wingbeats. "Indeed, it is what I expected. But there is a new development of which I am confident your Possessor would like to be informed."

The leader's eyebrows arched ever so slightly higher. "And that is?"

"One of the rocks has been found."

A collective murmur rumbled through the delegation as the armed ones let their weapons drop to their sides. They stared at us.

Yeah, take that!

"This human is called Enzi. And around her neck, she bears one of the missing rocks. Please show them, Enzi."

It was that voice again, saying my name. I couldn't have resisted, even if I'd wanted to. This was my moment. This was the one thing Gaedyen had needed me for, the one reason I'd been taken to Odan Terridor and started this whole journey. Would he be done needing me once I completed this one act?

I gripped the chain and pulled the gem out from my shirt. It glimmered brilliantly in the sun and, as always, looked like it had just been drawn from the purest brook.

Every pair of eyes in the captivated crowd was glued to me and the rock. Was Gaedyen going to share that I was the Possessor of it? I wouldn't offer up the information myself. As little as he knew about these other people, he knew more than me, and I was not going to do or say anything more than absolutely necessary. I wasn't going to risk messing this up.

 288

"Very well then." The leader blinked, and I saw the shock cross her face before she masked it. "We will take you into Maisius Arborii if you will agree to being guarded at all times and to not so much as sneeze without permission on penalty of the darts. I will explain the change in circumstances to our Possessor, and you may be allowed into her presence. We will see. But you must give up your weapons."

Gaedyen half turned to look at me.

I nodded.

"We agree." He inclined his head slightly to the leader.

"I will hear it from the human herself."

I nodded. "I agree to the terms."

"Surrender your weapons."

Gaedyen fumbled with the knot at his chest. Could he untie it? I'd always done it for him—his fingers might be too big to manage it…but then he got it and the satchel fell to one side. He gathered it in one hand and reached out to offer it to our welcoming committee. Two of the little guards fluttered forward to receive it. I expected them to plummet to the ground under its weight, but they didn't struggle.

The leader's eyes bored into mine for a moment, then she turned, beckoning us to follow after her and her tiny party. Some of the feathers on the backs of her wings were the same shade of purple as the shape on the front of her dress.

Our escorts picked up speed, so we followed suit. I saw no sign that we were in an inhabited place as we flew. There were a few other colorful trees, and the giant one that we approached—that one looming above the horizon—it was definitely the great tree, Amolryn. So huge… so many flowers of each color.

Once we were close enough to see how high the great tree loomed above us, we took a sudden downward turn toward the ordinary treetops. We plummeted straight toward them for a few moments—they knew that we couldn't shrink, right?—and then out of nowhere, a hole appeared amongst the branches.

We dove through it—Gaedyen barely fit—and then turned abruptly to the right, still zooming after our escorts. The foliage was so thick that I only saw straight ahead, as if we were in a tunnel with walls of leaves and branches.

The way into Maisius Arborii—like the tunnel into Odan Terridor.

There were a couple sharper turns. We nearly slammed into the leafy branches of the walls before we emerged into a less dense space.

The group slowed abruptly as their leader faced us. She gave some quick instructions to a woman with pursed lips and then took off so fast, it looked like she became significantly smaller in less than a second.

Was speed a gift of theirs in addition to changing size? There was no way that they could alter their height *that* drastically. We could've gotten here from Tennessee in a couple of hours and saved ourselves a lot of time if Gaedyen could've flown that fast. Then again, I would probably have had a very hard time hanging on against the wind at that rate.

Those remaining of our escort continued on with us a few more minutes, until a wooden structure came into view. By the time we arrived it looked big enough for Gaedyen and me to fit very comfortably and still have room to spare. It was almost like a type of log cabin, except that the wooden beams ran vertically instead of horizontal, and were lashed together with bright green, living vines. There were three walls, low enough that you could see into the structure from outside. The fourth side was open, as if designed for Gaedyen to land in. He did so, and I ducked to avoid hitting my head on the roof.

As I dismounted, painfully once again, he spun to face our company. Favoring his bad leg, he said, "Thank you for allowing us in."

"Mm," replied the woman with pursed lips. Judging by her expression, she doubted that my gemstone was really *the* rock. "I am to tell you to wait here for Annwyl to bring news of whether the Possessor wants to meet with you to discuss the...*rock*." She looked only at me while she spoke with the same accent as Annwyl.

I felt like I was expected to respond, with how she kept looking at just me. "Ok, we will wait for her return."

Then she also was gone, leaving the rest of our escort behind. They had their backs turned to us, standing guard. Not one of them was over six inches tall.

The men wore similar dress-like clothing, but theirs were loose and long, covering their feet. Their wings were a duller green than the women's, and instead of one thick, curvy line on the front of their clothes, they had two thin, straight lines, one going down either side.

The men had remained speechless while the females spoke to us and gave orders. Did they have some type of matriarchal system going on? Wasn't their Possessor also a woman?

I wanted to see what Gaedyen thought, but I was unsure of whether it would be wise to reveal how little we knew of their way of life. What if they had enhanced hearing in addition to their other gifts? So I filed my thoughts neatly away to discuss with Gaedyen at the first opportunity.

While we waited, I took in the beauty of the landscape from this altitude. I leaned my arms on the railing, drinking in the beauty of the nature in front of me.

Green-gray tree trunks sprawled in unbalanced, twisted spirals covered blotchily in dark green moss. From scattered branches hung skinny, creeping vines that drooped in various places with the weight of large clusters of pink and orange hibiscus-like flowers. Giant leaves of many different kinds and colors sprouted everywhere. Some reaching for the descending sun, and some drooping lazily toward the far away ground.

Birds of all different sizes and colors perched on vines or flew among the greenery. The largest ones were like reddish peacocks, with longer, skinnier necks and taller, wispier tails. The smallest ones were like hummingbirds, and of a vibrant, shining green. There were some like the black-bodied and large-billed toucans with a variety of colors painting their bills.

The variety of colors and shapes was fascinating. A light breeze rustled the leaves and flower petals. I caught the scent of jungle flowers in the air and inhaled deeply again, eagerly absorbing the delicious scent.

I turned to see what the opposite window had to offer, and saw Gaedyen's eyes dart away from me. He must have looked at the same scenery that had captured my attention. If I was honest with myself, I secretly wished he looked at me and thought that I was as nice to look at as the scenery in this magical place.

Will I ever get over this ridiculousness?

I stepped to the other side of the hut. The same variety of plants and animals arrayed the space before me. As I enjoyed the view, the perfumed air, and the warm breeze on my skin, I wondered what took the woman, Annwyl, so long. And, now that we were so deep in their territory, I grew more nervous about our safety, should this not go according to plan.

Would their leader see fit to give us the time of day? Even if she did, would she believe us? And if she believed us, would she kill me to transfer my Possession to one of her people for some kind of vengeance against the Gwythienians and leverage against everyone else?

By the time they came for us, the sun had long since set. The world was darker, but in a strange way. Everything had a silvery sheen—from the moonlight maybe—unlike anything I'd ever seen at home. It was like a summery silver, not a wintry one. Beautiful.

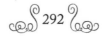

Annwyl was in the lead, carrying a lantern as big as she was. Several yellow points of light danced within it, like fireflies in a Mason jar. "Our Possessor has agreed to see you. Come now. And mind your tail, Lizard. We will pass several villages and I won't have a single *leaf* of them damaged by your bumbling." She spoke tersely, and then took off over the treetops again, barely allowing time for me to mount and for Gaedyen to follow, especially with our injuries.

It annoyed me that she called him "Lizard." Sure, I'd called him the same thing a couple of times, but it was different with me. She was just being rude. I called him names because *he* was being stupid and deserved to be taken down a notch. So it was with narrowed eyes and a poorly concealed scowl in her general direction that I gritted my teeth as the wind whipped my hair.

It wasn't long before we flew over an actual village. As soon as I saw it, I scoffed. The tiny tree houses were so far away, it would take Gaedyen several moments of freefalling before he or his tail could reach one to destroy it.

It took us a few minutes to reach a large wooden platform with no railing—like an oversized fishing dock suspended in midair. More Adarborians waited on it.

As we got closer, I realized they were all as big as giants.

CHAPTER THIRTY-SEVEN

*A*nnwyl reached the structure first, and promptly erupted into a giant like the others. She took a few steps to stand near them, next to an ornately carved wooden throne. The Adarborian seated there was also abnormally tall, but the lighting was too dim now for me to see her features.

Okay, so they can *alter their heights that dramatically? Wow.*

Annwyl spoke to me, once again ignoring Gaedyen.

"Human girl, our leader and the Possessor of our rock for many decades, the revered Aven of Masius Arborii, is ready to hear your story and judge your proof for herself. You have permission to speak."

Aven beat me to it.

"What is your name, child?" Her voice was as richly accented as Annwyl's, but sounded more hollow and raspy, carrying an even greater, more ancient, air of command.

"My name is Enzi." My voice shook, and I tried to straighten it out. "And this is Gaedyen. We have come a long way to speak with you because one of the missing rocks has been found. The rock of the Gift of the Gwythienians."

I drew the chain from beneath my shirt to reveal the hidden gem. Gasps came again from all around.

I shoved it back into my shirt.

"Tell us your story. And how you acquired your injuries." She sat up straighter.

I swallowed the nervous lump in my throat. "The rock was found many years ago in my father's belongings. We think he must have found it somewhere on the ground while serving in the military. My mom had it made into a necklace. Somehow, even though both of my parents touched it, neither of them was affected. But even though I am human, I gained Possession of the rock."

A shocked murmur rippled through the crowd surrounding us as many pairs of eyebrows raised in astonishment.

"How could you have arrived at that conclusion?" Annwyl barked.

"By how we came to meet." Their eyes flashed to Gaedyen as he answered. "I saw her through the water, as is another gift among my kind, and to my astonishment, she saw me as well. Eventually we were able to meet in person, and I explained about her new, accidental abilities. Strange things had happened to her already, things that my story clarified. That was how I was able to convince her to believe me, when, as you can imagine, the truth sounded very outlandish to a member of the human realm.

"She agreed to join me and help in my search for the other rocks in exchange for my teaching her how to use her new talents. Your realm is the one for which we have a liryk, so we came to you first to tell you the news and to seek your counsel, if you would be so kind as to offer it. Is there anything you know about the missing rocks, anything that could be of use in our quest? And, though I know it is forward to ask, is there any way you will share your liryk for another realm with us? We must visit all of them to find out what we can and share the news that a rock has been found."

Her narrowed eyes flitted between us. "Prove to me that you are the Possessor of this rock, human girl."

The cold stone rested against my chest, directly on my skin. I felt for the crack in the mental barrier, ready to rip it open. I dug into it and was through in only a few seconds. I sighed, relieved that I had been able to make it work. Gasps came around again, and I saw how the guards all moved in front of Aven, protecting her from an unseen and potentially hostile force. Releasing my concentration, I became visible again. I didn't want to make them too nervous.

The guards stood resolute in their new posts, so I peered between them toward Aven, awaiting a response.

She looked down for a moment, seeming to consider something. Then she demanded, "How long has Padraig been dead?"

Gaedyen relaxed slightly. He must think she accepted our story. She must believe that I was the Possessor if she concluded that Padraig was dead.

"He lives, still," he told her. "That is one of the most perplexing oddities about the situation. His rock is here, and Enzi is clearly the Possessor, but Padraig is very much alive. I saw him just days ago, after I had already met Enzi and discovered that she had Possession of the rock."

"So did he send you to us then? What does he think about the girl having Possession of his rock?"

"He did not send us. And he does not know of the girl or her Possession of his rock. You may not be aware of his deeply-seated hatred for humans. There was too much risk that he would kill her before hearing me out. So I could not ask him for advice on the matter. For that reason as well as because I knew that he would not allow this journey, with or without Enzi being involved. So I left without discussing any of it with him."

"You are a bold one, young Gwythienian. But is not Padraig in favor of treating the humans well? I remember vividly when he once was. It was his strong beliefs on the subject that eventually led to his becoming Possessor, though he did not want the post. I was very young then, and my memory of those days is still sharp, despite the years."

A look of surprise passed over his face for an instant, but he was quick to erase it. "Whatever positive feelings he may have had toward humans at one time, he no longer bears such opinions. He distrusts them passionately."

Her next statement came out cold. "You speak as though you know Padraig better than I would have expected. Why is that?"

Gaedyen took a deep breath. Now was the time to reveal his identity. If there was anything worse than being a Gwythienian in Maisius Arborii, it was being the son of the specific Gwythienians who lost the rocks.

"Because I am the grandson of Padraig, the son of the infamous Ferrox and Geneva."

Dozens of soft gasps filled the air around us, more intensely than with any of our previous revelations, building the tension further. This was the moment they would discover the whole truth about him.

Aven seemed to have trouble controlling her voice. "Do you mean to tell me, that you are the son of the Betrayers of the Realms? Of Ferrox and Geneva, the cursed Gwythienians who stole the rocks for themselves and died in the process of losing them, destroying the foundation on which all of the realms were once balanced?"

"I am."

CHAPTER THIRTY-EIGHT

"*I* am exactly that," Gaedyen confirmed softly, his shame showing in the hang of his head. "And it is because of that," he added, raising fierce eyes to her face, "that I have made this journey. I intend to find the rocks and restore the honor of my people and my family. I have grown weary of living in the shame of my parents' shadows, and I aim to change that. For my entire life, I have been treated as an outcast for something that, though more terrible than words can express in its ramifications, was *not* my doing. Nor was it the fault of my people. And though all the realms have suffered extensively for their actions, Odan Terridor has suffered the most, for something that was caused by a mere *two* of its members, not the realm as a whole.

"I set out to prove my worth and honor to my people, and to prove my people's worth and honor to you and to the other realms. If you support me in this, I will never rest until I have restored to you your rock, or died trying. You have my word. And once they have all been returned to their Possessors, the Possessors can pass them on to the next generation and be relieved of their burden as they should have been many years ago.

"Because of my parents' actions, every member of every realm has suffered. I want all of their lives to be made a little better because of me, by completing the mission I lay before you now, whatever the cost may be to myself. Will you help us? Or will you cast me out for a crime that I did not commit?"

By the time he finished, every eye in the place stared at him in reverence. *And he'd been afraid he wouldn't be a convincing speaker!* I was beyond impressed, totally moved. If I wouldn't have already been on his side, I would've switched in a heartbeat. How could they *not* believe him? There was no way he hadn't convinced Aven to help us. A speech like that could've swayed the hearts of an army.

Silence.

"You have not yet informed us about your wounds. What happened to you?"

"We were attacked on our way by another Gwythienian, one who I did not recognize, but who I believe to have been Tukailaan. I am sure I have never seen him in Odan Terridor. I could not say that I know every Gwythienian by name, but I remember their faces and his was new to me, as well as his scent. He was a Cadoumai, so we fought invisibly, but he returned to visibility after I killed him.

"He said nothing of the rocks, but he repeatedly accused me of trying to take something from him and claimed that I was supposed to be dead. Perhaps he was deranged. In any case, he is dead now."

"Hm. This is not the first report we have had of a rogue Gwythienian." She glanced at Annwyl who hastily turned to another standing near her and whispered speedy instructions. The other one leaped lightly from the floor and flew off in the direction we had come from.

"One more question, Gwythienian." The suspicion on Aven's face lessened, but remained visible. "I am shocked by what you say of Padraig's new views on humans. When I knew him many years ago, he was a peaceful soul who did not wish harm on anyone, especially humans. I remember very clearly when he even imprisoned his own brother, Tukailaan, whom he deeply loved, for mistreating humans."

He imprisoned Tukailaan for mistreating humans? I thought he locked him up for something more important to the realm than that—for something he did to a Gwythienian, maybe.

"Even though it meant he would have to take his brother's place as the future Keeper, which he would rather have died than do, I remember well. What happened to change his views so drastically as to make you fear so for the life of the girl?"

For a moment Gaedyen appeared dumbstruck. Had he not known the reason for the imprisonment as well as he'd thought? He took a moment to collect himself. "I suppose the event that rendered the change was the death of his beloved mate—the grandmother I was not fortunate enough to meet—at the hands of humans. He has always been of this frame of mind as long as I have known him."

"Hm." Aven had leaned out into the light again, and she now pursed her wrinkled lips.

I thought I heard a hand's worth of fingers drumming lightly on a wooden surface. It was barely noticeable over the nighttime jungle sounds. She was thinking. At least that meant she would consider our request, rather than booting us out without a second thought.

"I am sure the two of you are hungry. It must have been hours since you last ate. My guards will escort you back to your lodgings and provide you with food. I will send our best healer to see to your wounds while I discuss your request with my people. We will meet with the two of you again in the morning. You are dismissed."

I hadn't realized how hungry I was until she mentioned it. I was on pins and needles about her decision. I could tell Gaedyen, too, was disappointed at not having an answer tonight. But he also seemed a little distracted as he said, "Thank you for your generosity" a moment too late.

Half of the guards shrunk down to fairy-size again and flew off in the direction we came from. I clumsily mounted Gaedyen and he prepared to take off.

I glanced back at Aven. She stared intently at Gaedyen, it looked like at his shoulder.

Oh no! His tattoo! But it was still covered pretty well. I could see only bits of it—you wouldn't notice if you didn't know it was there. She must have been staring at him in general.

We reached our little tree hut after a short flight. There was a fresh delegation of fairy-like guards stationed out front. I supposed they were probably the relief for our current babysitters.

My stomach growled embarrassingly again as one of the women from the group said, "Food is being prepared as we speak. It should arrive shortly."

I smiled, pleased at the prospect of food. "Thank you."

Then that group flew away, leaving us with the new set of tiny locals. They each inclined their heads to us as we entered the hut, and I replied in kind, though Gaedyen failed to notice. I was afraid that they would be offended, but it seemed like they were only paying attention to me anyway.

Their strange deference to me over Gaedyen struck me once again as odd. He was this beautiful, exotic being with the ability to fly and the strength of at least a dozen men, while I was nothing but a human, who looked rather like them, except for being less beautiful and way less interesting.

Was that because I was female? Did they consider me above him, because I was a girl? And why did our guards stay small? Seemed to me if I was guarding something big and could alter my size, I would go as big as I could to look the part.

While we waited for food, another Adarborian flew toward us from the distance.

She grew to a height slightly taller than me just before entering the open side of the tree hut. Her green feather dress had a red design on the front of it, but she also wore her hair cropped, like Annwyl.

"Hello, I am Parva, the healer sent to see to your wounds." She barely met my eye. Her tone wasn't exactly rude, but very businesslike.

She unslung a bag—also made of feathers—from her shoulder, and took from it many tiny brown things that looked like acorns, a crude knife, and a coil of fabric that looked like it was made of some kind of woven plant material.

"Show me your wound, Gwythienian."

He resituated himself so that his bad leg was accessible. She looked down at it with disdain, then back to her small stash of supplies. Heaving a huge sigh, she turned back to me.

"I do not have nearly enough materials. Please excuse me, I will be back in a few minutes."

She buzzed away and returned several minutes later, her bag bulging. Walking straight to Gaedyen, she knelt next to him and once again opened the bag.

"Here." She produced several little black seeds and tipped her hand over Gaedyen's, dropping the pile into his humongous palm. "Take these for the pain."

He eyed the stuff suspiciously, then poured it in his mouth and swallowed.

She cut away my makeshift stitches, then scraped off debris and scab material. It was really gross. One by one she broke open each of the little nuts and poured a dark green fluid into the cleaned wound. Once the green stuff had a minute to seep in, she took the woven fabric and wrapped it in a few layers around the wound.

"It is most unfortunate that you cannot shrink, Gwythienian. You have nearly emptied me of all my supplies."

"Can't you just pick more nuts?" I caught myself too late. I shouldn't be asking questions and giving away my lack of knowledge of their culture.

She turned a dark look on me. "No, I cannot. I have to make the salve myself, and store it in the nutshells. It is a time-consuming process."

She didn't need to be so snippy. "Couldn't you store the salve in something bigger?"

"You seem to be quite ignorant of our customs. Now... what is wrong with you?"

I pointed to my ankle, still in the makeshift brace. "A sprain, I think. And my chest hurts."

Reaching into her bag, she brought up a pinch of the seeds— much less than what she'd given Gaedyen—and dropped them into my hand. "Eat those." She left the hut again, then returned a few minutes later with more odd things. In no time, she'd reinforced my splint.

"You need to stay off this as much as possible or it will not heal properly. And I have nothing for your chest, I am sorry. Will there be anything else?"

"No, thanks." *Where's the food? I'm getting hungry over here!*

She fluttered away quickly, shrinking as she went. Her red and green wings were pretty, but the purple looked better to me

Gaedyen was very quiet while we waited for the food. What was he thinking? I didn't question him yet. He looked a bit too thoughtful to be interrupted just then.

What type of food exactly would be arriving? I hoped it wouldn't be anything bug-related. I pondered how hungry I really was, and whether or not it would be considered offensive for me to not eat something they brought if it looked gross.

A horrendous scenario played through my mind where I tried to politely get out of eating the bugs, but was then forced to, and right before eating one I realized that they weren't completely dead yet, but were still trying to escape the plate with their nasty little wriggling legs. I was gagging at the thought when a tantalizing aroma wafted past.

I followed my nose out of the unpleasant daydream and toward the delicious scent. A young boy, about ten years old or so and normal human-boy-size, landed with less grace than the adults of his kind at the edge of our hut and carried a small wooden tray.

"I have brought meats and fruits for you, our honored guests." He glanced askance at Gaedyen, though he addressed only me.

"Thank you." I smiled, looking around for the rest of it. There was one roasted carcass of some kind of bird about the size of a starved young pigeon, one golf-ball sized purple fruit with odd tendril-like leaves sprouting from its top, and one small cluster of reddish berries.

It looked like a nice snack, but Gaedyen would need twenty or thirty times this for it to count as a snack for him, and he probably wouldn't like any of the fruit. Surely their rules about gender didn't dictate starving him because he was male?

Plus, he'd done all of the flying, while I just held on. He deserved some good food, and he would need it to replenish his strength for the journey. I was sure we'd be heading out again in the morning.

"Is this for both of us?" I expected him to say that Gaedyen's was on the way, or maybe, to my horror, that I had to eat before he would be allowed to.

"Yes, it is." He trembled, seemingly afraid of inciting my wrath. "They told me you would eat that much, because you are foreign and do not shrink at all." He winced, as if expecting to be reprimanded for saying something he shouldn't have. "I told them that it was too much, but they insisted. I am so sorry to offend you, honored lady. Please, allow me to return it and come back with a more suitable amount."

He thought that this was too *much* food?

"No, no! I'll keep it, thank you." I reached for the tray before he could take off and bring back *less* than this meager mouthful. Was he pranking me? It seemed like an inappropriate time for that, and Aven didn't seem the type of person someone would want to displease.

He handed it to me hesitantly. "If you say so... that is, as you wish, honored lady."

He turned and shrank, flapping his now tiny wings with vigor and vanishing in seconds.

I looked after him, wondering again at their strange ability to shrink and grow, and then turned to Gaedyen. "Well, Captain, looks like this is all we get for the night... to share." And I held out the piddling rations for his inspection.

He glanced at them without focusing. "Eat as much as you can. I am too tired to eat. I need to sleep now." Without once meeting my eyes, he turned and lay down with his head in the corner like a dog that had been scolded for pottying on the carpet.

"What's wrong? Shouldn't you be excited that we are still alive, and that their Possessor listened to us? And that we didn't get thrown in prison? They even treated our wounds! Could be worse."

"Padraig never told me that he did not want to be Keeper. I thought it was what he wanted, and I was annoyed with him for changing his mind. But now I hear he never wanted that? Why did he never tell me the truth? And he never directly told me what he had imprisoned Tukailaan for, but he implied it was something else. First, he may be less of a hypocrite than I thought, but then I discover more hypocrisy."

Trouble trusting a parent figure? I could relate.

"Why did he keep something so important from me? Does the rest of my realm know? It is just another reason for everyone to distrust *me*."

"It's not your fault you have crazy relatives."

That didn't seem to help. "By the way, that was a pretty kick-butt speech you gave earlier. Really inspiring. You're a good speaker, you know?"

"Thank you, Enzi. At least Tukailaan is dead now. One less thing to worry about." He continued staring at nothing. Well, if he needed time to think, then he could have it. I was going to dig into this delicious-smelling—though sparse—food.

CHAPTER THIRTY-NINE

Again, I fought back, and again, I gained the upper hand. Caleb jeered, trying to belittle me. But I was not so easily distracted now.

My blade had grown somehow—it was longer this time. But I could still use it with the same level of skill. It was long enough that I could plunge it all the way through him.

He sneered. "You don't have the guts, little girl. What do you think you could ever do to me?"

Nostrils flared and eyes aflame, I wanted to kill my shame, the thing that had ruthlessly destroyed my life without facing any consequences himself.

I raised the knife. His mocking face went blank.

Then I hesitated, and his smile returned at my weakness.

*I*t was still dark when I awoke from the new dream. I heard something in the distance… maybe just a strange echo off the landscape. But there it was again—like a distant roar. Like a *Gwythienian* roar. Was I still dreaming?

Pulling my arms from where they were folded behind my head, I pushed myself up into a sitting position. It wasn't pitch black—more like a thick dark blue. The silvery sheen from earlier was barely visible.

But Gaedyen killed whoever followed us.

There it was again. Gaedyen looked up from right beside me. I didn't remember falling asleep next to him. But I was glad he was close.

I turned to him. "Did you hear that?"

"Yes. It sounded Gwythienian."

"But how?"

"I do not know." He pushed himself up on all fours, staring into the jungle. "If we leave to investigate, they may suspect us of being in league with whatever Gwythienians are out there. But if my people see me here, like this, they will think I am a traitor. They already despise me."

"Do you think there's more than one out there?"

"I cannot tell from the roars, but if I killed Tukailaan, why else would any Gwythienian be here on the other side of the world? What could it be other than a group sent by Padraig to force me to return? I was so sure he would not try anything like that…"

So we were in potentially hostile territory with dangerous homelanders flying in to further complicate things. *Great.*

"Even if they had the liryk from the Vorbiaquam, they couldn't get into the realm without being escorted, right? They have to be taken to the portal. They can't just get in from anywhere."

"Then why do we hear them?"

"What?"

"Gwythienians do not roar without reason. There is a fight going on between Gwythienians and Adarborians. This is exactly what I hoped to prevent. I have already failed. Worse than that, I caused this fight." His earflaps drooped.

I put a hand on his shoulder. "Gaedyen, we haven't failed yet. We're not giving up."

"Human! Gwythienian!" A harsh female voice sliced through the air. "What do you know about this?"

It wasn't Annwyl, though it sounded like her. Maybe she was out there, causing those roars.

"We know nothing of this." Gaedyen stared her down. "I came seeking peace, I have no desire to start a war. What could you possibly think I have to gain from such a thing?"

Her face was screwed up in a snarl. Her eyes blazed beneath slanted brows. "Aven wishes to speak with you both. *Immediately.* You will come with me."

She leaped off the platform and promptly sped away, shrinking immediately as if she didn't want us to be able to follow. I was on Gaedyen's back in a second and we caught up quickly.

We reached the wooden platform and found Aven there with twice as many guards as she'd had last night. We approached, but the guards stopped us several feet away from her.

She didn't immediately meet our eyes. "Tukailaan lives."

I heard nothing but the pounding of my heart in my ears. *No, no...*

"Have you brought him to us?"

"I swear, on my honor, we have not. I honestly believed I had killed him."

She looked up at us, chin jutting out defiantly. "On your honor, is it? I thought the inspiration for your journey was your lack of honor."

His body tensed ever so slightly.

Ouch! Knock it off! I glared at her. She had no business speaking like that to Gaedyen.

Aven stood. "I have lost three of my most valuable Cadoumai guards tonight."

"How many did he bring with him?"

"He is alone, but he is a skilled fighter. I wonder at how you could have defeated him on your own."

What? There was no delegation? It was only Tukailaan? How could three of her greatest guards have lost to him when Gaedyen fought him alone? But he hadn't died...or had he come back to life?

"Then he is a mightier foe than I originally thought. Perhaps he faked his death. Did he find the way into Maisius Arborii?"

"No, he did not. We stopped him before he came too close."

"Where is he now? It has been many minutes since the sounds of battle reached my ears."

"He also is Cadoumai. He fought invisibly, and when he ceased fighting shortly before I called you here, my guards could not track him far. He seems to think that we are offering refuge to a Gwythienian criminal and a human offender of Odan Terridor, and he informed us that if we do not surrender the two of you to him, there will be a war within the month between our realms."

"He has no such authority! Surely, you cannot believe him! You said yourself that he is a deplorable criminal!"

"And you are the son of the greatest criminals yet to walk the earth! How can you expect me to trust your word blindly over his when the two of you could so easily be the same?"

My heart ached for Gaedyen. I knew those words cut him deeply. But I knew who he was. He wasn't like Tukailaan or Geneva or Ferrox. But how to show Aven? How to make her understand that we were telling the truth?

"Did we not come peacefully into your realm? Bearing evidence to support our claims? And what has he done? Stormed in and murdered three of your people, demanding things from you yet offering nothing in return!"

Aven smiled. "Ah, now you are thinking." She placed her withered hands on her hips and strode toward us, the size of a regular human woman. "There is something different about you, is there not, Gwythienian? And something different about you as well, human. You each…*reflect* the other, in a way. I cannot tell what it is, but there is something. Am I right?"

What was she talking about? Did she know I had a crush on him? What did she mean by *reflect?* I didn't have an answer, and apparently neither did Gaedyen.

"In any case, you do have one of the missing rocks, and the Possessor of it. He has no proof, but his threats are too great to be brushed aside. But think harder, young ones. If Padraig is still alive, while you clearly have Possession of his rock, then something has happened to strip away his Possessorship, possibly without him noticing. He was already a Cadoumai before becoming the Possessor, so if his gifts have not been under great stress the past several years, perhaps he would not have noticed."

She slid past Gaedyen, running a hand over his neck and down his shoulder. I blushed, annoyed. She had no business doing that, either.

"But what if this happened to all of the other Possessors? We were all given Possessorship at the same time, and we are all now many decades past the age of a proper leader."

Rubbing her fingers together, she looked down at her hand, examining them. They were sandy.

Oh no! The tattoo!

Sure enough, a dark spot showed through the dirt and sand coating. Was she onto us? What did it even mean? Why did we have to keep it a secret? I tried to subtly lean forward a bit and cross my arms over the spot, as if to rest on them. It really hurt my ribs.

"What if, then, all of the rocks are now free to be possessed by whoever touches them first? I know that the Gwythienians searched high and low and across a much greater radius than many thought necessary for the rocks, yet none were found. Until now. Therefore, someone else must have found the others first. If this human girl's father could have found one of them, how much more likely is it that another of the realms could have found the others?

"Perhaps Tukailaan has them hidden somewhere and has been waiting for a chance to kill off the other Possessors so he can gain Possession of all of the rocks at once? Or perhaps he somehow learned that Possessorship expires with age, and he chose to let us live long lives so that we could see it when he took our Possession away. I do not know. But if he has them and has Possession of any or all of them, we are all in grave danger."

Could she be right? Could he already be collecting the rocks? How many could he have?

"You seemed surprised by some of what I told you about Padraig and Tukailaan last night. Perhaps Padraig never shared the whole story. You should know that Tukailaan was the chosen future Possessor, but right before the ceremony, his secret affinity for torturing humans to death was discovered. If those evil ways are still in his heart, it is a very serious matter that he may have Possession of any or all of the remaining rocks."

We already knew that it would be bad if he got Possession of a rock, but torturing humans, too? *Eek!*

"And if that is so, he will be coming for you, Enzi. He will want to take Possession from you. While it would be possible to surrender your Possession without dying, by passing it on at a Possessorship Ceremony, he will not take the time and trouble to simulate one to spare you when it would be so much easier just to kill you. And as you may be the only Possessor on the side against Tukailaan, which places you on the same side as us, I intend to do whatever I can to protect you."

Wow, that seemed like a pretty big deal.

"That is why I will leave Maisius Arborii for the first time in decades to escort you on your way to Ofwen Dwir. I cannot take you all the way there, however, as my daughter was injured in the fight and I must return to her soon."

My eyes widened. She was going with us? "But how will we leave when Tukailaan could be lurking outside the entrance?"

"We will take a guard, and I have already positioned many all over the surrounding area to protect us as we fly. But more than one entrance exists into our realm. I place my expectations upon your eternal discretion. We will leave immediately."

Another entrance?

She crossed back to the wooden throne, grew to its giant size, and reached behind it. When she stepped away, she pulled with her an ornately carved bow and matching quiver, though it was empty of arrows. Returning to normal human size, she slung the bow and the strap of the quiver over her head and one shoulder.

Wait. Adarborians fight with poisoned blow darts, don't they? Why does she have a bow?

Another guard drifted in, holding Gaedyen's satchel. He handed it to him and I dismounted to tie it for him.

"Why do you choose Ofwen Dwir for the next destination? Why not Sequoia Cadryl? Is Ofwen Dwir the realm that you have the liryk for?" Gaedyen questioned.

"Yes. But there is more to it than that. Gwaltmar, the Possessor of the rock of the Rubandors, was a close friend of Padraig's once. They spent much time together during the time leading up to the Possessorship Ceremony. Gwaltmar was your best bet for a sympathetic soul all along, though apparently Padraig did not share much of his young years with you, or you may have known that he was a better bet than me."

Following Aven and her guards into the air as they shrunk, Gaedyen pumped his wings to keep up.

I never heard another roar. Eventually there was a rumbling sound in the distance, and the air became misty. As the sun rose, it illuminated a mountain just ahead.

We reached it, and followed Aven and her people straight into the stone wall, which morphed into another stone tunnel like the ones at Odan Terridor. Then the tunnel became water, freezing, falling. Soaking wet and spluttering, we emerged through a waterfall a few moments later.

It was many hours later, when the sun was well over its halfway mark, that Aven finally motioned to us that it was time to land.

I was amazed that Gaedyen managed to land with grace. All that flying and carrying my weight had to catch up with him. How did he still manage it—and on an empty stomach, too?

"Here we part ways. I must warn you though, the entrance into Ofwen Dwir is much trickier than ours. The entire realm is shielded by an impenetrable dome—a physical one, not like the ones that protect our realms—with only small openings placed strategically to allow for fresh water exchange. They are small enough for one of us to enter, but if there are any secret openings large enough for anything the size of Rubandors or Gwythienians to pass through, they are only known to them. I cannot guarantee that you will be able to fit as a Gwythienian, but you must try. I think you will be able to find a way, do you not?"

What did she mean? And why did Gaedyen stiffen when she said that?

"If you can get through, they will take you to an atmosphere chamber where you will be able to discuss with them everything that you have told me. You may tell them that your quest has my blessing. Perhaps that may help.

"This is their liryk.

Three days' flight
From Maisius Arborii
Past water and land
To the Pacific Ocean-sea

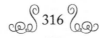

Where the cliffs meet the waves
At the westernmost place
Against water and time
You air-breathers must race

Swim so far out
That you cannot see the land
Then dive into the depths
If you think you can

If you find the entrance
Then lucky you are
But be warned—
Our minds are sonars

You cannot hide from us
So if threatening you be
Do not come near Ofwen Dwir
Or fire-water will be the last thing you see

Repeat it back to me."

Gaedyen and I both tried and failed to get it right a couple of times, but eventually between the two of us we had it pretty well memorized.

"Well done. Now I must return to my daughter and my people. We have a mighty foe to face."

She approached me. "Enzi." My name hung in the air between us. "Please accept this bow as a gift from me. May it bring you what you need."

I reached out with shaky hands, unsure whether I should accept. I mean, I didn't even know if I had the right not to or if it would be rude to actually take it. What was the right thing to do for their culture?

She placed it in my hands before I decided how to react. "Thank you." Was my voice trembling? I mean, the Possessor giving me her personal weapon was kind of a big deal.

"And the quiver, of course." Up close, I saw that it was covered in carvings. She handed that to me as well, gently as if it were a newborn baby. As I drew slightly away from her, accepting the gift, she let her fingers trail down over the etchings on it, like a caress. A single tear rolled down her cheek. Why was she so affected?

She fluttered to Gaedyen's earflap and whispered something. He stiffened again.

What did she say?

Then she moved to stand in front of us, jutting out her chin. "I do not know what lies in store for you, but the fate of the realms hangs in the balance. And right now, it looks like that balance can only be swayed by the two of you. Gaedyen, may your rymakri stay sharp, and your aim ever true."

Gaedyen straightened at her words, his earflaps rising ever so slightly.

And then she was gone, speeding away into the sunlight. She met her guards in the air and they zoomed away like a swarm of hummingbirds.

"Gaedyen, what did she whisper? And what did that last phrase mean?"

"That is the phrase that a father speaks to his son when he reaches maturity. It means that the speaker has the utmost respect for you and trust in your judgement. No one has ever said such a thing to me."

I slung the quiver over my shoulder and did the same with the bow. "And what did she whisper about?" She better not have been hitting on him.

"Nothing."

He ran for takeoff before I could press the issue.

We flew for hours and hours—way past the point of me getting hungry again and needing to pee. When we finally landed, it felt like we'd flown for days straight, which we basically had. It was already dark and Gaedyen passed out almost the moment we landed.

Removing the bow and quiver, I laid down next to him and tried not to think about how sore I was from clinging to his back all day, or how annoyed I was that he wouldn't tell me what Aven had said, or how much responsibility she seemed to think we had in this situation. That was all too much for me. Her belief in us made it all seem more real.

Eventually sleep took over my troubled mind, and I slept deeply.

Sawdust. A rymakri in my hand. Once again, I fought back....

When I woke, it was early. The sky was still dark blue, the stars were beginning to fade. I heard rushing water nearby and got up to look for the source.

I stepped quietly, trying to avoid the many twigs and sticks strewn all over the ground. I didn't want to wake Gaedyen. He needed to get as much rest as he could.

When I reached the edge of the stream, I knelt and cupped my hands to bring the refreshing coolness to my parched lips. It tasted good—fresh—but it was warmer than I expected. Not icy, but rather lukewarm. I glanced around. What heated the water?

A little ways upstream the water fed into a cluster of three round pools, not quite all the same size. Each one was filled to the brim and steam floated from them.

A nice, quiet, steaming hot bath alone in the still-dark morning with the world to myself sounded awesome.

I stood swiftly and crossed the distance between me and the little, natural hot tubs. How hot were they exactly? Squatting next to the largest of the three, I first let my hands hover above the water, to make sure it wouldn't be too hot. When I felt nothing but soothing warmth, I lightly dipped my hands in. My eyes closed involuntarily—the temperature was perfect.

Silently, I stripped, letting my clothes drop into a small heap at my feet. I felt awkward doing that, but Gaedyen was asleep and no one else was around.

I stepped one foot into the water to test how deep the pool was. My foot found the bottom when the water level was mid-thigh. Plenty deep enough to sink my whole body under the deliciously toasty water and get totally clean, even wash my hair. Granted, I had no soap. But any bath was better than no bath, and a hot bath was the best possible thing in the world at this moment, soap or no soap.

Easing the rest of my body down into the blissful warmth, I closed my eyes and waved my arms slowly through the water to keep my balance. It felt so peaceful and relaxing. The pool was just barely large enough for me to stretch out all the way and float peacefully on the surface.

I continued to sway my arms lazily back and forth, enjoying the warmth and silence, the pure aloneness I had been so long without. Not that I really craved being alone all the time, it had just been so long since I had a moment to myself.

My mind started dozing, and I tried to think only of nice things as the dreams came closer. I wanted to take all measures against nightmares.

A slight noise from behind roused my calming heartbeat a little. But I didn't need to worry. Gaedyen had crazy-good senses even in his sleep and I was barely twenty feet from him. If anything dangerous approached, he would sense it and I would know about it before I was in any actual danger.

I smiled at this very logical excuse to drift right back off into a deeper sleep.

A whisper tickled my ear.

"Enzi."

CHAPTER FORTY

*T*he black-haired, white-faced, sickening grin of Caleb flashed in front of my closed eyes, and before I had a chance to wonder how he got past Gaedyen, I leaped up from my vulnerable position in the water, arms flailing and eyes wide open.

A scream formed deep in my throat. I faced the place my head had rested as I peacefully slept, searching for the horrible face of my nightmares. The dark, menacing smile that still made my insides cower wasn't staring down at me. Instead, there were two huge, bright eyes in the giant lizard-like face of Gaedyen.

As the initial fear rushed out of my stomach and a smidge of relief filled its place, a host of other unpleasant emotions beat the relief and twisted my face into a rage filled glare.

"You!" My voice jumped several octaves on that single syllable. "You unbelievable idiot!" I half-whispered, half hissed. "You sneaking…little freak!" As I railed at Gaedyen, my arms made angry, exasperated gestures of their own.

Gaedyen looked at me, confused.

The stupid idiot. Then I realized the ramifications of him looking at me. I still stood in the shallow pool, stark naked from head to toe with only the lower bit of my legs concealed by the water. I immediately wrapped my arms around myself and dropped back down into the water to hide my body, glaring menacingly the whole time. Crashing back into the water like I did splashed Gaedyen hard in the face, which resulted in a satisfying reverse snort from him.

I hoped it burned his nose.

Once my northern lady parts were safely concealed, I shooed him away with one hand. "Get the heck out of here, you perverted lizard-freak!"

He had the nerve to look as if I'd offended him as he turned and stalked away.

I stared until he was too deep into the trees for me to see him anymore, and then relaxed a little. This time I lay so my head faced toward his direction instead of away from it, not that I could really relax again after that. My heart pounded so loud I heard it in my ears.

Heavy waves of embarrassment washed over me and lapped at my stomach. Right where the disbelieving terror, then red-hot anger, and now face-palming mortification yanked at my insides.

No one had seen my body since Caleb. *Ugh.* No one had any business seeing it. I didn't even look at it myself. At home, I showered in the dark with just the little strip of light from the hall gleaming in a line under the door. After brutally abusing the long mirror in my bedroom, I had refused Mom's offer to replace it.

I did everything I could to pretend they weren't there. I didn't want to think about them—didn't want to remember them. The dreams were one thing, and they were horrible, but the scars were physical evidence.

And now Gaedyen had seen me. He saw all of them. Now he knew my shame.

It was wrong. Wasn't I entitled to a little privacy where my own body was concerned?

I closed my eyes, and Caleb's revolting face appeared in my head yet again. I cringed and tried to think of something else, something to calm me and slow my racing pulse.

Seriously? He was the first thing I thought of? When I heard my name whispered in a part of the world he could never be? What did I have to do to get away from him?

What was Gaedyen thinking? Was he imagining the feminine traits of my body? Those details weren't meant to be seen. They'd been spoiled for me before I even really owned them, and it wasn't like they were attractive, anyway.

Or was he thinking about all the scars? The jagged white lines that covered my torso and branched out asymmetrically all over the rest of me? Was he pitying me, seeing me now as a victim? Or, instead of thinking dirty thoughts about my feminine features, as a human guy might—if I were attractive— was he thinking about how ugly I was, covered in uneven, hideous lines?

Which was worse?

What was I thinking? Of course it would be more embarrassing if he thought of me only as a victim now and pitied me, instead of seeing me as someone who was a necessity for saving his world and reputation, and all that jazz. Of course I'd rather him be disgusted with my hideous body and then never give it another thought.

Or would I?

Well it didn't really matter either way. He was a Gwythienian, and I was a human. What did it matter how he thought about my body or whether he viewed me as a pitiable victim? We would finish out this crazy journey thing and then I would go back to my home and he would go back to his. He wouldn't need me anymore, and that would be great. I would finally get time to myself again. I would finally get to sleep in a bed again. I would have a refrigerator with food in it, a real stove to cook on, even if only one burner worked.

What a load of crap. My life has changed too much to ever go back to normal, now.

I was not able to distract myself enough to calm down, so I checked that the coast was clear. I hurriedly tugged on my clothes, not taking time to dry off. Not only did I not have a towel and not feel inclined toward air-drying, I had also soaked my clothes with the stupid sneeze-splash from earlier. On top of that, I would be way high up in the sky where the air was colder, flying at racecar speeds for the next several hours.

So much for a nice, peaceful, toasty start to a nice, peaceful, toasty day. Freaking Gaedyen. What the heck did he have to sneak up on me for? And how the heck did he manage to be so quiet? He weighed as much as a couple of prize-winning horses, at least.

Fully dressed again, I walked back to where we'd slept the night before. I sat down by a thick tree trunk and pulled my legs up against my chest, wrapping my arms around them tightly.

"Hey Enzi!" He sounded as if he could barely contain his excitement about something. That didn't seem to be the appropriate sentiment in this situation, to say the least.

He galloped over to me, presuming incorrectly that I could possibly give a crap about anything he could have to say to me just then. He caught a glimpse of my face. My murderous expression sobered up his exhilarated one pretty quickly. His legs froze mid stride. Gravity took over and he flopped awkwardly to the ground.

What was his problem? Now he was clumsy all of the sudden?

He looked at me from the dirt, head cocked slightly to one side, brows raised. I smirked at his fall and then tightened my grip around myself, protecting my shame. He shot a nervous glance at me as he righted himself.

"Enzi?" he asked yet again, much less boisterous.

"What?" I snapped, avoiding his eyes.

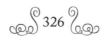

"What is wrong with you?" His eyes narrowed as his tone challenged mine for most snappish.

"What's wrong? What's wrong?!" I glared at him incredulously. How could he be so slow on the uptake? "Well how about how you barged in on me when I was trying to relax, when I was *naked*, no less! Couldn't you at least have turned away or something, instead of staring at me with no clothes on? I can't believe you!"

He must not have listened very well. "But I have a mark too! Don't you remember?" he turned his shoulder to me, scrubbing the dirt away. "Your mark is like mine! This must have something to do with how you are able to have Possession of our rock! Don't you see? We are alike! How did you get yours? Were you born with it? Or did something... happen?"

"What? What are you talking about?" Did he think I *wanted* those hideous lines? That there was something *cool* about them?

"I am saying that my tattoo is not really a tattoo! I did not have ink imbedded into my skin. I did not ask for it, either. It just happened to me!" Why did he sound so excited about having a permanent mark put on his skin without his permission where people could see it?

"Gaedyen, I don't know what you're talking about. If you got your mark the same way I got all mine, you would not be excited to talk about it."

"Then tell me how you got them!"

"No!" I shot up from the ground. "I'm done talking about this! Forget about what you saw, Gaedyen. They aren't cool. I'm *not* proud of them, and I'm not going to relive the whole thing to satisfy your curiosity. Give it up!"

Glowering at him, I crossed my arms, waiting to see whether he would finally listen. I wanted to run, to hide in the woods until I had a chance to cool off, but we didn't have time for that. Instead I picked up my new bow and quiver and slung them over my shoulder.

"Enzi, I—"

"We should probably get going." I swung myself up, ignoring the pain in my chest and ankle.

Sighing, he turned to face a clearer route for takeoff.

So there was something up with his tattoo-mark thingy. I knew it. What was he hiding? How could he think that our marks could somehow mean something similar? What was he thinking now?

As we soared back over the jungle, the ocean came into view. Had he figured out now, based on my reactions, where I got my scars? Would that change how he thought of me? We already had a zero percent chance of any kind of relationship, and now there would be even less than the zilch that there was before. *Ugh.*

"So what is it that's so cool about your stupid tattoo thing that isn't a tattoo?" I dismounted, careful to land on my right leg.

"I will tell you if you tell me what your problem is."

I bristled and opened my mouth to tell him he'd heard a good darn plenty and wasn't about to get a peep more out of me about my personal past, but he held up one toe of a forefoot in my face.

"And if you stop being so childish and go back to being yourself."

I pursed my lips, about to explode. "How dare you call me a child! You don't know what I went through getting those scars... how it still haunts me."

"Then *tell* me so I *can* understand," he said softly and desperately in the silvery voice that melted me. He sounded so sincere, as if he really cared.

How could I trust my feelings? They'd been wrong before, and I wasn't about to embarrass myself any further today. "No." My voice shuddered with the feelings I failed to suppress.

He took one step closer to me, then another. "Enzi."

The way he breathed my name made it sound like the name of a fairytale princess. I couldn't help looking up at him.

"I am sorry I surprised you at the hot springs. The only reason I was there was because I thought you were in danger. When I woke and saw that you were gone, I was afraid Tukailaan may have caught up to us and kidnapped you. I followed your scent, and I went silently, to avoid alerting an enemy if one was nearby. When I found you, I wanted to get your attention without causing a scene, in case someone had taken you and then left you as a trap in an ideal place for an enemy to incapacitate me. I had no intention of startling you. I just wanted to be sure that you were safe. That is all."

Oh yeah? And where's your apology for prying into my past? But I swallowed my dissatisfaction and focused instead on his explanation and how sincere he sounded. It wasn't what I expected, but I had to admit, it made sense. And if it was true, it was sort of sweet. Maybe I had overreacted. And it wasn't like I hadn't been curious about his life, too. How could I stay mad at him?

But *I* wasn't ready to apologize yet. I needed more time to cool off.

"Thank you for telling me that, Gaedyen. I appreciate it." I was too worked up to say anything more than that, anything as good as he deserved after I railed at him. That was all I could come up with in my riled mood, but I hoped it sounded as sincere as I meant it.

"You are welcome. Now we need to make a plan for when we near Ofwen Dwir."

CHAPTER FORTY-ONE

I was lying in the sawdust again. Bloody and tired. He was there, too close to me, his stench overpowering.

Somehow, I mustered up the strength to pull the rymakri from nowhere and slash at him. But he was faster this time. He knocked it out of my hands and gave me another cut with his blade for my trouble.

There were the tears again. Hopelessness. Frustration. Why me?

As he bellowed with sick laughter, I managed to kick up a knee and hit him between the legs. In that moment of distraction I crawled away from him.

But I had no blade—my rymakri was gone. And my traveling clothes hadn't appeared. I was naked, bloody, and weaponless. But I couldn't take it again. I had to do something. But there was nothing I could do…

I woke up sweating, crying. I hoped Gaedyen hadn't heard me.

When I was about to mount for takeoff, I paused. "Look, um, I wanted to say thank you for making sure I was safe yesterday, and I'm sorry I took it wrong. I hope you'll forgive me."

Then I climbed onto his back before he could look me in the eye. I wasn't used to saying things like that. It was uncomfortable. I didn't want to see his eyes just then.

"Thank you," he replied in the silvery voice. "And of course, I forgive you."

I tensed then, expecting a return to the subject of my incident and his "mark," but thankfully he bounded and wobbled into takeoff immediately, without even a hint of bringing it up.

As we flew, I took in the sights. So much beauty...so much openness. I wished I felt as peaceful in the air right now as I had when I first started flying, but I worried about our next step.

Since there was no way I could hold my breath long enough, and we didn't have time to come up with scuba equipment, Gaedyen would have to go alone and I would stay on land. Would he be able to hold his breath long enough? It sounded like it would be really far down there. How long would it take? How would I know he was okay? What if anything happened to him? He could be held captive, or die. And I could wait around for days, not knowing anything.

I resolved that if it took him longer than a few hours, I would find a beach town and break into a scuba gear store and then go in after him. But I would not tell him that. I had a feeling he wouldn't like it. Well, that was just too bad.

I couldn't get a song to stick in my head. Too many horrifying scenarios of how this could play out warred for top priority in my mind.

At last we came to a place where the water and land met. There was a drop off, like a small cliff, and then the beach several yards down. It looked deserted, but there was mist all over so we turned on the invisibility.

Gaedyen landed on the cliff. "This is the westernmost point, I am sure of that."

I dismounted, dreading the impending separation.

Gaedyen flickered back into sight, and I followed suit. He gazed out to sea, then surveyed the surroundings, earflaps twitching. There were a few small clumps of trees, but otherwise it was open—*too* open.

"I need to go now. The sooner I go, the sooner I can come back. I am sorry I have to leave you here, Enzi. I wish there was another way." He removed his satchel and handed it to me. "I wish I could take this, but I am afraid it will slow my swimming too much. Hold onto it for me, will you?"

I nodded, accepting it.

He pulled one stick out and broke it in half, then bit each of them into a short rymakri. Handing those to me, he said, "These will only last so long. I am sorry I cannot leave you with something better. Do you know how to use the bow?"

"No, not really. I mean, I've seen people use them, but I haven't ever touched one."

"Hmm." He covered his face with one hand. "This is such a ridiculously terrible plan. I should not be leaving you like this."

I didn't want him to, but what choice did we have? "Gaedyen, I'll be fine." I pointed to one of the groups of trees. "See those? I'll go over there and hide. There's no one around anyway. I'll be fine. It's you that you need to be worried about. How are you going to be able to hold your breath that long?"

"It should not be too long. I just have to find the entrance, and that leads immediately to the atmosphere chamber where I will be able to breathe again. I will swim down, tell them our story and find out if they know anything and are willing to help. Then I will be right back up for you, I promise."

"How long do you think it will take?"

"You saw how careful the Adarborians were about letting us into their realm and near their Possessor. I do not know how long it will take to talk to the Rubandors and convince them to let me speak to their leader, especially if I cannot take you down with me to prove my story. I have no way of knowing. It could take days, or it could take just long enough for them to kick me out and then we will have to find some way to get them to see you without endangering you to get them to believe our story. I hope it does not come to that."

"Well you have to take the rock, Gaedyen. You'll have to show them proof." I reached up to pull it over my head.

"No! You must keep it. I will not leave you alone *and* take away your best chance of safety! What do you think I am?"

"But then how will you get them to listen to you?"

"I will find the entrance to their realm. I could only do that if I had the liryk. And only the Adarborians have access to that. Why would the Adarborians give me their directions if they did not believe my story?"

"But Gaedyen, they will suspect you are in league with the Adarborians, that you have some kind of agreement with them to team up against the Rubandors."

"I will reason with them. Their Possessor may have noticed a decline in his abilities, and they will listen to what I have to say if I can explain that. And I will tell them about Tukailaan. If we and the Adarborians all feared a person gaining Possession of multiple rocks, then it had to have dawned on these people, too. The risk of not heeding my words if they are true is greater than the risk of listening if they are false. They will have to help."

"I hope you're right." I still thought he should take it, but it looked like there would be no convincing him. "Please be careful, Gaedyen."

I was more afraid of letting him go without me—as physically powerful and built for defense as he was—than I was of staying behind. I desperately hoped he would be safe and that it wouldn't take days. I couldn't handle waiting that long with no news.

"Of course. You do the same. And if someone should find you and want the rock, and you cannot hide, do not fight. Throw it at them and run for your life. That would catch them by surprise enough for you to have a chance. Remember, they will want to kill you so that they can possess the rock. You *must not* give them that chance."

He looked intently into my eyes, as if he tried to impart some secret message deeper than the words on the surface. I longed to understand, if there really was something there. Then he lifted one great red forefoot and laid it lightly on my shoulder. It reminded me of when we were on the beach and he put his arm around me. My heart raced.

"Promise me you will do everything possible to remain safe, Enzi," he whispered urgently.

"I promise."

And then he was gone, remaining visible as he took off into the sky. Gliding toward the surface of the sea, he disappeared into the mist.

I stood in my shaded place staring at the sky, full of anxiety and dreading the long wait ahead. My stomach rumbled, but I ignored it. My throat begged for a drink, but I was too afraid of missing his return to risk leaving my spot here to find food or water.

Hours passed. I looked at the ornately carved quiver, trying to see what was there. But I was too worried to focus.

What was Mom doing? How many days had it been since I called her? She'd probably be worried sick, still. She might've even found a way to call that guy's phone from the gas station. I hoped she pestered him.

Why had she imagined me looking up at the sky? Did it mean this adventure was going to be the death of me? Would I ever see her again? It wasn't like I'd spent a whole lot of time contemplating the sun or the stars. It wasn't something she saw me do frequently, so it shouldn't have been something her subconscious mind would dream up.

She must've been really worried to go look by the mountain and under the bridge, those two places she avoided at all costs because of her fear of heights. Still though, she was always at the bottom of the mountain. Why would that mess with her fear of heights?

Wait. There was one other thing that those two places had in common: water. The river and the icicles. And didn't she always avoid puddles? When I was younger, she never took me to the aquarium or the pool…what if her fear of heights was a lie? What if it was really water? What if she saw things in the water, like a Gwythienian somehow, and that made her think she was crazy? What if she actually saw me through the ice on the mountain?

But no, that was impossible! Only Gwythienians did that, and I was the most likely human to be able to, and I couldn't even come close. Plus, Gaedyen had said it was impossible that we had some kind of accidental shared Possession of the rock. Besides, the only time I ever looked at the sky was to watch Gaedyen land, which only took a few moments. She wouldn't have kept seeing me looking up, like she had said.

Was I missing some detail? It felt like I was on the edge of something…I had a vague memory of my neck being sore from holding it up unusually at some point on this trip.

The Vorbiaquam!

Holy crap!

I'd stared up at that map of the realms for ages when I looked for the way into Maisius Arborii! Could she have *seen* that? She'd said that was the first place she'd looked. The timelines might match up!

Whoa. Could my mom do that? There was no way…but what if Gaedyen was wrong?

It kind of made sense! She avoided everything water—no dolphin show at the zoo, no splashing in puddles with rain boots, no fish aquarium, no driving over the bridge or looking at the mountain icicles…

Wow!

My ears caught the sound of approaching footsteps. I whipped around.

There was someone there—a man.

Tony?

CHAPTER FORTY-TWO

*I*t was too late to hide—he'd already seen me. How could he be here? He'd been back in Tennessee.

"Oh, hello!" He waved and limped determinedly in my direction. "Enzi! Imagine, meeting you here, of all places! Gosh, you really do look like…well, never mind that. What in the nation brings you here, to the same place as me, so far from where we last met?" He seemed far less surprised to run into me again than I would've expected.

I stared back in shock. Who did he think I looked like? Why'd he keep mentioning it?

He came closer and I backed up. "Tell me, Enzi, do you happen to still have the necklace I saw you with last? I would really like to buy it off you, for my granddaughter, you see. She loves purple. She would think it was ever so fine."

The necklace again. This was too much. Him, showing up here, and asking about the necklace? Both my rymakri had diminished to dust already. "Sorry. I'm afraid I don't have it anymore. Lost it on the way here." Was that even remotely convincing?

His countenance darkened. "Well then, as I can see that you are lying, it seems we're at an impasse."

My heart stopped. His voice was different now, younger and stronger, no longer wheezy.

He stood straighter, losing the hunch and limp. Taking an authoritative step toward me, he said, "You see, I'm gonna leave with that necklace and I won't let a human stand in my way. Hand it over and cough up the location of the backdoor into Maisius Arborii—yes, I know it exists! How else could you have escaped me?—and I might not hurt ya."

He'd called me "human." But wasn't he also a human? Of course he was… *How else could you have escaped me?* But I didn't escape him outside Odan Terridor. He just left.

When I didn't submit, Tony flashed a menacing smile, and then his body curled in on itself at lightning speed. The back of one shoulder split open and from it the body of a large, reddish-brown dragon appeared—first the wings, then the snarling head. As the rest of the body followed, Tony's human form turned inside out and disappeared beneath the huge Gwythienian.

A Shimbator. So the legends are *true.*

"Tukailaan?" My voice shook as horror spread through me.

"Very good, human. I'm impressed. What else do ya know?"

I had to stall. But I wouldn't be able to come up with a convincing lie on the spot. What was safe to tell him? "I…I think you're a Shimbator."

His brows rose. "Indeed? He told you about us, did he? He's nuttier than I thought."

"'Us?' There are more of you?"

He chuckled. "Ah, so he didn't tell you everything. No, I'm not the only Shimbator."

"What didn't Gaedyen tell me?"

"Well, mayhap he don't know it all himself. I wondered whether he did, when I found you left all by your lonesome outside the entrance into Odan Terridor. I should've taken the chance when I had it. You've caused me a great deal of nuisance since then."

"How did you know I was outside the tunnel?"

"Ya think Maisius Arborii is the only realm with a back door? Odan Terridor has several. That one had been forgot about for many years. I used to be the only one who knew about it. That was the tunnel I left through when I made my escape. I left a trigger there, a thing that would alert me if anyone ever found the tunnel and came through it. I wasn't popular among my fellow Gwythienians, see. I hadn't thought about that trigger in years, and I wouldn't have expected it to still work, but when it was triggered, I came to check it out."

That was what Gaedyen sensed! The thing that he thought wasn't exactly dangerous, but he wasn't sure. That was why we switched places in the tunnel!

"Imagine my surprise, after searching for the rocks for years and only ever finding one of them, to see one hangin' 'round your human neck like a common gemstone."

He has another one! Which one? I've got to keep him talking...
"Why didn't you try harder to attack us? If you're this much bigger than Gaedyen, you probably could've beaten us. Why didn't you do that?"

"Because I needed to know the way to Maisius Arborii, and I couldn't risk venturing back into Odan Terridor to find the liryk, and I wasn't sure I'd be able to get the two of you to tell me by force. Though, I am confident I could now, if I needed to. But I followed you, hoping to overhear your full plans."

"Then why attack us at all? Why not let us feel safe so we'd be more likely to talk about stuff like that?"

"Because I was herding you toward the rogue Gwythienian, the one that your friend thought he killed. Now tell me where the hidden way into Maisius Arborii is, or I'll take the stone by force, and your head along with it."

So it wasn't him that Gaedyen fought. And the Adarborians fought him off before he got in...that was good! But I couldn't tell him what he wanted to know. And he'd seen that I still had the rock. He must not know I had Possession of it. If he did, he would've killed me already. The stone would be more important to him than the backdoor, and he could always force it out of Gaedyen when he returned.

But what if he *did* know? He would wait to kill me until I revealed the way in. And then he would possess two of them! I couldn't let that happen.

I placed my hand over it, ready to turn invisible and run. But what if he didn't know? If I turned invisible right in front of him, that would confirm it and he would definitely kill me. What should I do?

"Don't fret, little human. I'll let you say goodbye to your friend before I kill him and take Possession for myself. That will make this all the more as it should be."

So he didn't know! He thought it was Gaedyen! *If I turn invisible, he'll know it's me. And even then, he could probably smell me. But if I don't show him that I am the Possessor, he will kill Gaedyen as soon as he surfaces! But if he kills me before Gaedyen comes up, he will have Possession of two rocks and Gaedyen will have to fight someone that much more dangerous.*

I hesitated, unable to decide. I needed to keep distracting him. "I thought it was you that Gaedyen fought two days ago. If not you, then who?

"A Gwythienian named Bricriu. I'd been herding you toward him for days. But neither of those lunkheads was any good in a fight either. So here we are. Now cough up the information, and give me the rock."

Neither? Had there been another enemy there? Or did he mean Gaedyen?

He reached out a huge reddish foot—bigger than Gaedyen's—to accept the stone. Gaedyen had warned me to give it to anyone who came for it, but I couldn't just hand it over!

"Fine then. I'll use one of you to torture it out of the other when the young one returns. If he does. That may be unlikely, though, after what I told the Rubandors he is on his way to see."

Oh no. My heart plummeted into my toes. "What? What did you tell them?"

He grinned at me, evil eyes blazing.

That did it. I ran.

He roared and bounded after me.

I dug into the crack in the wall with all my strength and had a hold of the other side in a moment. I disappeared.

"So it's *you?*" He stumbled.

He really hadn't known. I'd surprised him. And sentenced myself to death.

I fought to outrun him, but instead I found myself engulfed by enormous, Gwythienian hands, like Gaedyen's, only bigger and more menacing. He was larger than Gaedyen, larger even than Padraig.

The rough beating of his wings pounded in my ears as he charged forward, leaping into flight. He leveled off over the ocean. "You're going to show me how to get in to Masius Arborii. Do you understand?"

I couldn't answer. *He wants to murder Aven! What if it's her rock that he has? I can't tell.* "But, Gaedyen—" I gasped as he tightened his grip.

"Oh, he'll follow us. As soon as he catches my scent and finds you missing. He'll know where to find us. I have no doubt. Then it'll be his life in the soup if you don't do what I ask."

"In the soup?" Where did this guy get his wonky expressions? But I knew what he meant.

We soared over the ocean, where Gaedyen still mysteriously existed. *No! I can't leave without knowing Gaedyen is okay!* I struggled to wedge my knee between two of Tukailaan's huge fingers, longing for a blade. *A sharp stab might make him drop me.*

A crashing splash erupted beneath us, and then a deafening roar permeated the air as my assailant tightened his hold. My already bruised chest gave way to the pressure, sending a dozen or more white-hot daggers of pain through me. I screamed, blinded by the impossible pain.

"Enzi!"

Gaedyen?

My eyes pierced the mist. I fought for consciousness, hoping I hadn't already lost it. Was I only dreaming that he was still alive? My captor squeezed again, driving the daggers of pain deeper, my own bones betraying me.

"Ah!" I pushed against his grip. I had to fight, had to try.

Another roar. This one had that strange, silvery tone, except it wasn't silvery with gentle friendliness or amusement so much as it was bronze with determination and ferocity. But I felt the flecks of silver in it, and I knew that voice! It was *his!* Gaedyen had made it out of Ofwen Dwir!

He's alive!

There was a *chomp,* and Tukailaan bellowed in my ears.

I searched the hazy sky for Gaedyen, my vision blurry. Relief flooded through me as I glimpsed my dragon in hot pursuit of us, dripping salty water and red with my captor's blood fresh on his face. In a flash our eyes met, and his were unfathomable. His mouth formed my name again, though I couldn't hear his voice now. The last bellowing roar still echoed in my ears.

The pain was too much. I looked down to my chest, to the source, and though it was dark, in the dim light of the moon I saw the redness blossoming there. I was probably bleeding on the inside, too. Numbness washed over me and I couldn't think clearly. I felt myself sinking... for a long time. Was I falling into the ocean? Or still falling through the air? Would Gaedyen catch me? I felt sure that he would, and with that reassurance, I gave in to the numbness, unable to fight it anymore.

CHAPTER FORTY-THREE

Through Gaedyen's Eyes

I COULD NOT BEAR TO KNOW THAT SHE WAS IN HIS ARMS. THE one who would murder her in a second to secure Possession of the rock for himself. I dug my wings harder and harder into air, never having felt slower or heavier in my life. Gasping, I reached farther and farther, taking the longest wing strokes possible. That was Enzi, and I had to get to her before he could hurt her. She was too precious for that. She would be even if she were not the Possessor of my realm's rock.

On and on I struggled, slowly gaining on him. He angled back toward land. Then he stopped, cradling Enzi in one arm, squeezing the necklace to constrict around her throat with the other hand.

"Tell me how to find the backdoor into Masius Arborii, or watch her turn as purple as this stone!" he hissed.

Why did he want to get in there? Murdering Aven would accomplish nothing if all the Possessors had lost their Possession. It could not have only been Padraig, could it?

I answered him truthfully, not even considering the fate of those whose lives I traded for the life of the human in front of me. "There is a mountain with a waterfall behind their realm. The entrance is through the waterfall—there is a tunnel through the mountain there. Fly through it and you will be inside." Guilt gnawed somewhere in the back of my mind. I had betrayed Aven, a good person and an excellent ally.

But Enzi was more important.

"How will I know where the end of their realm is if I can't even get near the beginning? Stop stalling, youngling, or she dies!"

"You know the tree you are looking for. It is the mountain a few miles south of that! Now let her go!"

He stared into my eyes for a moment, perhaps to determine whether I told the truth. Then he ripped the necklace off of her, spinning more quickly than a flash of lightning, and pitched her through the air.

I dove for her.

She had to live.

He threw to kill, so that he could become Possessor—a possibility I could have kept from him if I had protected her and her secret better. That guilt made my heart heavy, but it did not help me plunge any faster toward the ground.

Time slowed.

As she plummeted toward death, I strained every muscle past its limit to reach her. Finally my forefoot wrapped around her arm, and pulling her into me, I wove myself around her body in a wild tangle of legs, wings, and tail.

An instant of joy and relief—I reached her in time!

And then pain. Deafening, searing, withering pain. My shoulder met the ground with incredible force, the joint shattering on contact at the same instant as my miserable skull. I felt the burn of rent skin meant to conceal the flesh now exposed. Then my wing shoulder hit something and I no longer felt it wrapping around my treasure.

Aven's last words to me flashed through my head. Was it too late now to find out if she was right?

With a cracking thump, the rest of me crashed to the forest floor.

Oblivion.

THE
CRIVABANIAN

Odan Terridor Trilogy: Book Two

COMING NOVEMBER 12, 2019

ACKNOWLEDGEMENTS

Thank you so much to everyone who helped me bring this story to life!

Thanks to my husband, Ben, for believing in me in the beginning when the story was at its smallest and for letting me bounce endless ideas off him. Thanks to my Mom for all the encouragement and to Missy for helping me make things happen and always believing in me.

Many thanks to my beta readers, Caity Nemer, Brie Worrell, Beth Quillian, Naija Fields, Bree Owens, Jessica Rodgers, Lauren Wyatt, Brenda Glass, Vel Smith, Linda Williams, John Walker, Kathy, and Missy.

A huge thanks to everyone in the Heartland Christian Writer's Group, especially Michele and John, for your endless support and insightful suggestions. To my editors, Nadine and Elizabeth, for believing in this project and giving it your all. To my cover designer, Dave, for working through several revisions and meeting my every desire to craft this perfect cover. To my book map artist, Trent, for finding a way to map a journey instead of a single place. To Rob Costacorta for creating the beautiful illustration of the portal into Odan Terridor. And to Jeff Collyer, who rescued this book with his incredible formatting skills when everything tried to go wrong at the last minute.

Special thanks to Caity for the constant support of a fellow fantasy book nerd and the many book hunting trips, and to Brie for the knife throwing lesson.

You have all been such an encouragement and inspiration to me! I could not have done this without you!

VOCABULARY

Adarborian (Ah-dar-bore-E-an)—a humanoid creature with hummingbird-like wings capable of dramatically growing and shrinking.

Amolryn (Am-ole-wren)—a great South American tree that produces a variety of colored flowers, and according to legend birthed the first Adarborians from its blossoms.

Annwyl (Ann-will)—an Adarborian leader, daughter of the great Possessor, Aven.

Arunca Rymakri (Are-un-kah Rim-ak-ree)—the art of knife- and spear-throwing, according to the Gwythienians' traditions.

Aven (A-vin)—an Adarborian, Possessor of their rock, mother of Annwyl.

Bricriu (Brick-ree-oo)—a rogue Gwythienian, whose identity and intentions are currently unknown.

Cadoumai (Cad-oo-my)—any member of one of the four realms whose gift is very strong.

Cathawyr (Cath-ah-we're)—the fabled race of great cats about whom the realms have many legends.

Crivabanian (Cree-va-bane-E-an)—a creature like a large flying squirrel with hidden depths of physical strength.

Ferrox (Fare-ox)—a Gwythienian, father of Gaedyen and son of the great Padraig, husband of Geneva. One of the Betrayers of the Realms.

Gaedyen (Gay-dee-yen)—a Gwythienian, son of the Betrayers of the Realms, Ferrox and Geneva, and grandson of the Keeper, Padraig.

Geneva (Gin-E-va)—a Gwythienian, mother of Gaedyen, wife of Ferrox. One of the Betrayers of the Realms.

Gwaltmar (G-walt-mar)—a Rubandor, the Possessor of their rock, friend of Padraig.

Gwythienian (G-why-thin-E-an)—a dragon-like creature with the ability to see through water into other places and to turn invisible.

Liryk (Lie-rick)—the directions to one other realm given in the form of a poem from one realm to another many years ago.

Malwoden (Mal-woe-den)—giant snails, found only in Odan Terridor. The favorite food of the Gwythienians.

Masius Arborii (Maze-E-us Are-bore-E)—one of the four realms, home of the Adarborians, located in the jungles of South America.

Ofwen Dwir (Oaf-when D-we're)—one of the four realms, home of the Rubandors, located under water off the coast of California.

Rubandor (Roo-band-or)—a creature like a giant axolotl who can sense their surroundings with sonar-like abilities.

Odan Terridor (O-dan Tare-i-door)—one of the four realms, home of the Gwythienians, located under Tennessee and the surrounding states.

Padraig (Pah-j-rig)—a Gwythienian, the Possessor of their rock and the Keeper of all the rocks, father of Ferrox and grandfather of Gaedyen.

Parva (Par-vah)—an Adarborian healer.

Sequoia Cadryl (Sec-oi-ya Ca-drill)—one of the four realms, home of the Crivabanians, located within the redwoods of California.

Tukailaan (Too-ky-lahn)—a Gwythienian, brother of Padraig and one who wishes to steal his place as Possessor and Keeper and to gain Possession of all four rocks.

Rymakri (Rim-ak-ree)—the wooden knives and spears made by the Gwythienians. They do not last long and must be used immediately.

Shimbator (Shim-bah-tore)—a legendary type of Gwythienian, one who is able to transform into a human and back into a Gwythienian at will.

Vorbiaquam (Vore-bee-ak-wam)—a cavern in Odan Terridor with walls of waterfalls and pools of water on either side of the strip of land within, a place for Gwythienians to look into the water for other places.

Connect with Savannah!
@savannahjgoins

Instagram | Goodreads | YouTube | Twitter | Facebook

Visit Savannah's website for writing tips and story updates!
savannahjgoins.com

Did you enjoy this book?
If you have a minute, a review would be greatly appreciated!

CPSIA information can be obtained
at www.ICGtesting.com
Printed in the USA
LVHW111412030620
656997LV00001BA/57